WAR OF HEARTS

⌐⌐ A TRUE IMMORTALITY NOVEL ⌐⌐

S. YOUNG

ACKNOWLEDGMENTS

It has been an absolute joy to delve into the world of adult paranormal romance. For months, Thea and Conall have lived inside my head, running across Europe, kicking ass and falling in love. There were days, however, I needed guidance, especially with the translations. As Scottish as I am, Scottish Gaelic is not my forte so thank you so much to Laura Chapperton and Lisa Moyes for helping me with Pack MacLennan's clan motto and pronunciation. It is so appreciated! My Scottish wolves sound pretty badass before they shift thanks to you guys.

There are many reasons to thank my Facebook Group *Sam's Clan McBookish*, number one being their never-ending support and encouragement. I'm grateful to have members from all over the world in my group, and I have to thank a few of those ladies by name for helping me with translations for this book. For the Hungarian translations, a huge thank you to Zsanett Varga, Kati Kipilla, Biró Andrea, and Durkóné Simándi Rita. You are wonderful! And for the Polish translations Katarzyna Poliksza, Justyna Krzema, Magdalena Szabelska,

Marta Walentynowicz, Sandra Witowska, Anna Zadrożna and Kasia Smyk. Thank you for not only translating full sentences, but for helping me with that confusing "what is the plural of zloty for English language speakers?" question, ha!

How lucky am I to have such amazing readers to turn to with research questions? You're all phenomenal!

For the most part writing is a solitary endeavor, but publishing is not. a massive thank you to my editor Jennifer Sommersby Young for taking a process than can sometimes be excruciating for a writer and making it pretty painless. I love working with you!

And thank you to my bestie and PA extraordinaire, Ashleen Walker, for handling all the little things and supporting me through everything. Congrats on a very special year, my friend.

The life of a writer doesn't stop with the book. Our job expands beyond the written word to marketing, advertising, graphic design, social media management and more. Help from those in the know goes a long way. Thank you to every single blogger, instagrammer and book lover who has helped spread the word about my books. You all are appreciated so much! On that note, a massive thank you to Nina Grinstead at Social Butterfly PR, for agreeing to jump into this new venture with me. You're fantastic!

To my family and friends, for always encouraging me to follow my gut.

Moreover, to Hang Le, thank you, thank you for creating yet another stunning cover and for bringing Thea and Conall to life in image. You're so talented!

To my formatter Jeff Senter at Indie Formatting Services, thank you again for making my stories look great in digital and print.

As always, thank you to my agent Lauren Abramo for making it possible for readers all over the world to find my words, and for always having my back. I'm so grateful for you.

And finally, the biggest thank you of all, to you my reader. Thank you for coming on this new adventure with me. I couldn't do it without you.

PRONUNCIATIONS

SCOTTISH SLANG

'nae' on the end of a word is the equivalent of ''nt', the contraction of 'not'.

Didnae – Didn't

Dinnae – Don't

SCOTTISH GAELIC

Ceannsaichidh an Fhìrinn – Cyown-seech-ee in yeer-in

Mhairi – Var-ee

IRISH GAELIC (CONNACHT DIALECT)

Aine – Awn-ya

Samhradh – Sow-ruh

Solas – Sol-as

Geimhreadh – Geev-ru

Réalta – Rail-tuh

Earrach – Err-ack

Fómhar – Foe-var

Éireann – Air-un

I

The city held no danger for Thea as she strolled down the nearly deserted street on the outskirts of the eighth district. In the dark, the seedy neighborhood in an otherwise beautiful Budapest, could almost pass for a nicer area of the metropolis. Graffiti tags covered the walls, marring its beauty. The only reason she'd chosen the street, almost an hour's walk from the Danube and the stunning historical buildings in the clean tourist districts, was because she could afford the flea-ridden room her creepy landlady had the audacity to call an apartment.

During daylight the tree-lined street was almost pretty, if you ignored the stench of dog waste and the sight of homeless people pressed up against the graffitied buildings and sprawled on the sidewalk. In the dark, the tall, slender oaks seemed to bow over Thea, a shadowy protection as she walked to the twenty-four-hour convenience store. She'd always felt a strange affinity with nature, her soul yearning for a quiet place in the woods somewhere. Would they find her in some far-off forest?

But let's be real, she thought, *I'd die within the month.*

Her survival skills were strictly urban, and she couldn't afford to stop anywhere for too long. She'd been in Hungary for almost three months, liked it more than most places she'd been, but already she felt that itch to run. However, waitressing did not pay a lot and half the tourists who came through the café she worked at in the Palace District didn't seem to realize you could tip above 8 percent. She *would* get a job working for the last café in Budapest to add a mandatory service charge.

Grumbling to herself, Thea strode a little faster past the young homeless guy who looked prepared to grab her around the ankle to stop her. She hardened her heart against the visual of him, scrawny, filthy, and cold in the chilly April night. She was saving every penny she had for train fare. Thea had to run at a moment's notice and right now her savings wouldn't get her very far.

The young man yelled something down the street to her and although Thea only understood a little Hungarian, she'd heard her boss use a certain word enough to know the homeless guy had just told her to do something pretty nasty to herself. Thea curled her lip in a mixture of guilt and irritation.

Shrugging it off, she pushed open the door to the late-night convenience store and ignored the look of rebuke the owner gave her. He was an older Hungarian man. Thea put him in his late sixties and again she couldn't understand the actual words, but every time she came into his shop in the middle of the night, he forced her to endure a lecture she technically didn't understand.

But she understood him all right.

He did not like a young woman wandering the streets alone at night.

Thea appreciated his concern. However, he had nothing to worry about. Still, she liked the old guy. Few strangers gave a shit what other strangers got up to, especially beyond spending money in their establishment. She gave him a nod, trying to hide her small smile at the fatherly glower he sent her way, and wandered deeper into the store. Thea liked the occasional glass of wine on nights she couldn't sleep, and the shop sold a red she could kind of just about afford. Plus, there were these European potato chips that were addictive. She couldn't get enough of them. Paprika flavor.

Thea's belly rumbled.

Just as she was reaching for the large family-size pack, the hairs all over her body stood on end and her heart raced.

Her head whipped to the left up the aisle and the bell above the shop door tinkled as someone else walked in. Pulse thrumming hard, Thea pulled her hand back from the chips. All her life, she'd experienced a feeling akin to walking through an electrically charged space when something *not good* was about to happen.

Had they found her?

Looking up in the far-right corner of the shop where the owner had an old TV mounted to the wall, Thea watched the live footage of the front of the store. There was a man standing at the main counter talking to the owner.

Thea heard the old guy's voice rise just as the new arrival pulled a handgun out of his pocket.

Oh shit.

She knew what she should do, and that was everything it took to not draw attention to herself. Thea was good at being quiet. She could creep up the aisle and make a quick dash for the door and be out of there before the guy with the gun could even blink.

Do it, Thea, the survivor in her urged.

Masking her steps with the otherworldly ability she'd had for as long as she could remember, Thea was almost at the end of the aisle. Ready to make a run for it. Get out of there. Save her own skin.

Not get involved.

Yet, Thea knew that the electrical charge she'd felt earlier didn't happen just because a guy came into a store to rob it. That feeling was like a sixth sense. Something bad was going to happen here.

It wasn't her business.

It wasn't!

But the shopkeeper's concerned expressions of admonishment filled Thea's head.

Oh shit.

She couldn't leave him here to get hurt.

Taking a deep breath, Thea listened as the argument between the shop owner and robber grew more heated. It sounded like her stubborn shopkeeper didn't want to hand over his money. *Really? Is it worth your life?*

With a heavy exhalation, her stomach churning, Thea stepped out from behind the aisle and the shopkeeper's eyes widened in concerned horror. The gunman had his back to her.

"I think maybe we should all—"

A crack ripped through the air, followed by a sharp sting of pain in her shoulder. She didn't even get to finish her sentence because the gunman had whirled around in fright and shot her!

Thea glowered down at her shoulder and then up at the gunman whose eyes had widened. His hand trembled.

"Was that necessary?" Thea took an angry step toward him.

He fired again; the bullet ripped through her just inches from the last. She flinched at the burn.

Okay, now she was pissed.

The air crackled around her as she touched the bloody holes in the only jacket she owned. Feeling a little murderous, it must have shown on her face as she looked up because the gunman wasn't the only one freaking out.

The shopkeeper was no longer looking at her like a concerned father. His face was pale with terror. He yelled something and if Thea had to guess, it was probably along the lines of "What are you?" or "Demon!" or "Monster!"

And then he scrambled out from behind the counter, slipping on the tiled floor, before throwing open the shop door to tear out of there, crying out at the top of his lungs.

Disappointment flooded Thea. "Nice," she mumbled. She stepped into help, got shot *twice*, and that's how he thanked her. When would she learn?

She cut a look at the gunman. His tawny skin was pale, his hand shaking hard as he backed into the counter, muttering what sounded like a plea under his breath.

Thea knew how she appeared. When someone pissed her off, her eyes transformed from brown to a gold so bright, no one could ever mistake her as human. Plus, she'd been shot, and she'd barely flinched. They knew she wasn't *just* a woman. She was something else entirely.

And it looked like this guy would shoot her again for it.

Just because the bullets couldn't kill her didn't mean they didn't pinch like a bitch. Thea didn't much like the idea of another one. Plus, she could feel that while the first shot was through and through, the second wasn't. There was a bullet inside her shoulder; she'd have to dig it out, and that would only slow her down. She didn't fancy digging out two.

Just as the robber's finger trembled on the trigger, Thea bridged the distance between them in less time than it took a human to blink. She grabbed the wrist of his gun hand and twisted it with such force, his high-pitched scream of agony followed the sound of it breaking. The gun clattered to the floor and Thea kicked it out of range.

Tears streamed down the robber's face and he begged in a language that wasn't Hungarian as he cradled his wrist and tried to get up. He scrambled to his feet and backed away from her as if she *were* the devil.

Shaking her head, Thea watched the guy run out of the store. Dread immediately weighed in her gut.

That little stunt was like sending up a flare to any supernatural after her. Or worse … *him*. Now she had to get out of Hungary, and she hadn't saved enough money to get a train out of the country. She automatically zoomed in on the cash register. Guilt niggled her at the mere thought.

But he did run out of here, leaving you to possibly die.

That was true.

Thea rounded the counter. People always disappointed in the end. Why should she be any better? Before committing the crime, Thea opened the cupboard behind the counter and found the old-fashioned VHS security. She pulled the tape, wincing at the flare of pain that spiked up her neck from her wound. She could feel hot blood sliding down her chest and back, soaking into her shirt and jacket. She needed to move fast.

The register was locked so Thea tore it open with a brute strength that belied her five foot eight, for-the-most-part-slender build. Remorse pressed down on her shoulders as she took what she needed plus a little extra from the register. However, she reminded herself she had to do what she needed to do to survive. And she'd just saved this guy's life. It wasn't unreasonable to ask for monetary compensation for the two goddamn bullet wounds in her shoulder.

Sirens wailed in the distance, shooting a jolt of renewed adrenaline through her. Walking calmly out of the shop, Thea strolled down the street, toward her apartment, with her head held high.

Then she felt blood trickle off the fingertips of her right hand and cursed. She'd leave a trail that led right to her apartment. Curling her hand into a fist and lifting the arm to rest against her chest, Thea winced against the pain. Then she saw the young homeless man from earlier staring intently at her.

He'd probably seen the gunman and the shopkeeper run out of the shop.

But she'd counted on that.

Digging into her pocket with her good hand, she found the "extra" she'd taken from the cash register and stopped by the homeless man. She held it out to him.

He smirked as he took the money from her. "Ha kérdezik, sosem láttalak."

Deducing he understood the payment was for his silence, Thea nodded and took off. She moved faster, the shadows of the trees seeming to envelop her, turning her into shade as she returned to her apartment. The sirens had gotten louder, giving her less time to get the hell out of there. But first things first.

The old building smelled of urine and mustiness. The plaster had fallen away from the walls not only in the stairwell but in Thea's apartment too. The space was just big enough for a bed, a small counter with a sink, burner, and microwave, and a tiny room off the side where they'd squeezed in a toilet and shower. The apartment was dark because the only window in it looked down into a courtyard typical of the architecture in Budapest. Drawing her threadbare curtains closed in case any of her neighbors got nosy, Thea tore off her ruined jacket and shirt, growling in pain. It wasn't agony, like it would be for the average person, but it still wasn't fun.

It also, unfortunately, wasn't the first time someone had shot her.

Moving around the small space like a gale, Thea pulled out the backpack she kept packed so she could run at a moment's notice. She rummaged through it to find the first aid kit. Stumbling into the bath-room, she stared into the cracked mirror above the sink and saw her olive skin was pale with blood loss. Her eyes zeroed in on the bullet holes. The through-and-through was almost healed over completely. The other was fighting the foreign object inside her.

Picking up her tweezers, Thea gritted her teeth and plunged them into the hole. A wave of nausea swept over her, but she fought through it and moved the tweezers deeper toward where she felt the bullet residing in all its foreignness.

Widening the tweezers to catch hold of it caused a flare of hot, sharp pain down her arm. Grunting, clenching her teeth, Thea yanked with all her might and out came the bloody squashed bullet. When it hit the sink, it tinkled, almost merrily.

"I hate guns," Thea sneered at the blood-spattered sink.

There was something so dishonorable about using a gun in a fight.

Then again, it was easy for her to say that. She could handle herself.

The skin around the bullet hole tingled and Thea watched as it began to close over, good as new.

Cleaning off the blood, she watched her skin return to its natural golden tan. Good. The last thing she needed to look like was a girl recovering from two bullet wounds. Thea layered up with a T-shirt and sweater since her jacket was ruined, bundled all her bloody stuff into a trash bag, and swept the apartment for any remnants of herself.

Pissed to be leaving somewhere new so soon, she took it out on her landlord by not leaving what she owed in rent. The hag charged a small fortune for the shithole and there had been more than once she'd used her key to come into the apartment unannounced. Just last week Thea had watched the landlady evict a single mother and her two young kids for missing rent by a week. Thea had listened to the woman beg, asking for more time, while the landlady beat at her with a broom, shoving her down the stairs while her kids tripped at her feet.

It had taken a lot not to intervene.

Thea had given the woman money afterward, which she'd tearfully accepted. Hence why Thea hadn't saved nearly enough to get out of Budapest.

She needed the money more than the landlady. Maybe it was

smarter to leave the money so if the police did somehow come knocking, she'd cover for Thea. But Thea knew no amount of money would buy that woman's loyalty.

Screw her.

Hurrying out of the apartment, Thea swiftly departed the building. The train station was in the north of the eighth district where the streets were busier with bar-goers at this time of night. She took a detour into the southwest, using the shadows to obscure her journey. Finally, she found an apartment block with a broken front door and dumped the trash bag in their communal garbage. Hopefully, the police wouldn't find it. But if they did, it didn't matter. Her DNA wasn't human. She did, however, worry *he* might find her through the bloody clothes. He had the means. He'd definitely recognize her DNA. Which was exactly why she had to get as far away from Budapest as possible.

As she made the normally forty-minute walk to the train station in just under twenty-five, Thea didn't bother covering her hair. The station was an international depot, so it was busy, even in the early hours. There were police patrolling it, yet if they stopped her upon description, there were no bullet wounds to be found. Thea wasn't worried.

Nah, she looked like a perfectly normal human woman.

Instead of what she was.

As for what that "what" was ... that was something not even Thea knew.

2

THE BLUE SKIES REFLECTED IN UPPER LOCH TORRIDON WAS A STUNNING sight from the rocky beach Conall stood upon. The Torridon Hills surrounded the glen, *beinns* with peaks that reached over three thousand feet high. They stood over the small villages along the coastline of Loch Torridon with such exaggerated summits and valleys, they gave the appearance of a vast, rugged castle. Forestry sprouted across some parts of the mountainous landscape, a wolf's dream playground.

Conall took a deep breath, smelling the light scent of the loch, the fresh, crisp air of the Scottish Highlands. There was no place more beautiful in Scotland than Loch Torridon, with its serene lochs and awe-inspiring glens created by the magnificent *beinns*—hills—that cloistered them in this haven and kept them safe from human intrusion.

His werewolf pack lived in every village that surrounded the banks of the loch. Torridon had the occasional human visitor as not even the narrow, single-track roads into this part of the northwest could keep every human away. But wolves en masse emitted an energy that deterred the average human from venturing too far into their vicinity.

He'd been told it was akin to dread. As if they sensed they would no longer be top of the food chain if they drove into Torridon.

Not that any of his pack members would dare harm a human.

"Are you going to stand there all day procrastinating?"

Conall sighed and turned from the glorious landscape that reminded him not only of his fortune but of the massive responsibility weighing on him. Everything here was his. The land, the people. His to command and his to protect.

James, his beta and closest friend, stood in the garden of Conall's large lochside home.

"It's time, then?"

James nodded, his expression grim. "They're waiting for us."

As Conall took long strides up the beach to the garden, James commented, "You would think on a day like today, it would at least piss it down raining to reflect the situation."

He shot him a look. "It's not that bad."

"Aye, she's quite attractive."

"It wouldnae matter if she had the face of a badger's arse." Conall yanked open the driver's door to his Range Rover Defender and got in.

James chuckled as he jumped into the passenger seat. "Thankfully, she doesnae. Well, from the photos we've seen. Those could be a lie."

"Looks dinnae matter in a betrothal agreement. If they did, I'd be fucked."

His beta snorted. "Such modesty."

However, Conall wasn't being modest. As an alpha it was no surprise he was one of the largest men in his pack. He stood at six foot six, built of natural muscle human men had to work hours in a gym to maintain, and he was born with more supernatural strength than most werewolves. It drew female wolves to him. But that was despite the deep scar that scored down the left side of his face, from the tip of his eyebrow to the corner of his mouth. When his parents (the alpha couple) had died, Conall had to fight many wolves, male and female, who wanted to be alpha of the last werewolf pack in Scotland. If he'd lost to any one of them, Conall would always be Chief of Clan MacLennan, but another alpha would undermine his command.

One of the wolves was a Cornishman, and he was a tough, sleekit son of a bitch. Before they'd even shifted to wolf form, he'd slashed Conall's face with a silver blade. He hadn't worn gloves to hold the weapon, burning his own palm in the process to show just how tough he was. Silver meant Conall's scar was permanent. When they'd finally shed their human skin and fought their battle the *honorable* way, Conall had made sure the Cornishman's defeat was permanent. After he'd won that fight and become alpha, more had come over the years, hoping they could best him.

As his sister, Callie, proudly said loudly and often, Conall MacLennan was more alpha than most. But he didn't think that was the reason he won fights against wolves who came to claim what was his. He won because he cared more. The wolves of Clan MacLennan, of Loch Torridon, were his family. His to protect.

Which was exactly why he was about to agree to marry a female he didn't know to secure the pack's safety.

"Remember, Canid might be alpha of one of the largest North American packs, but you have the upper hand here," James offered.

Conall shook his head as he drove the single-track lochside road from his home in Inveralligin to the Torridon Coach House, a fifteen-minute drive along the coast to the other side of the upper loch. The roads were winding, sometimes dark with silver birch and fir trees arching over from either side. The firs were lush and green while the birch trees were still in transition from winter to spring, their sparse leaves plum. Just as suddenly, the road would change, the trees disappearing from the rugged hills, opening to views of the loch glistening in the spring sun. Even after all these years, the view could distract Conall.

An older hunter couple, Grace and Angus MacLennan, ran the Coach House for the wayward humans who found their way here and for visiting werewolves. They had been a part of Conall's life for as long as he could remember. Angus was his father's cousin and he and his wife were pseudograndparents to Conall and his sister. "I'd say we're on equal footing."

"Not according to Smithie," James disagreed. "Canid's finances took a sharp hit when his shares in Opaque Pharmaceuticals became worthless. Opaque," he snorted. "Ironic."

Peter Canid was Alpha of Pack Silverton in southern Colorado. He'd heavily invested much of the pack's wealth in several business ventures, including shares in a pharmaceuticals company that went under when a newspaper did an exposé on their illegal practices.

"Canid still runs the largest pack in America."

"And you run the only pack in Scotland."

Conall smirked. "We are mighty, but we are small."

"Conall, Clan MacLennan is five times as wealthy as Pack Silverton. We have the upper hand here."

Wealthier than even that, Conall thought. Although his grandfather had died before he'd met him, Conall knew much of him. His legacy was respected in Clan MacLennan. It had brought them their wealth, meaning seclusion, if that was what a wolf wished for. His father took the whisky distillery his grandfather had started and turned it into one of the biggest whisky exports in Scotland. They situated GlenTorr distillery twelve miles north of Torridon near Loch Maree. There was no visitor center, for fear it would bring too many humans to their small paradise. A few years after Conall became alpha, GlenTorr became the third-biggest-selling whisky out of Scotland. The pack could live happily off its proceeds. Moreover, Conall's dad bought shares in the largest oil company in the North Sea. Conall had sold the shares and that, along with the successful fishing company his delta, Mhairi Ferguson, managed, meant Pack MacLennan lived a comfortable life.

Most of the pack worked at various jobs in the surrounding areas, especially Inverness, the nearest city, while a few others lived and worked farther afield. Conall supplemented all their incomes with a share of the pack's fortune.

Now Peter Canid was offering his second-youngest daughter, Sienna, in a betrothal agreement that would suit both packs. Conall would pay a substantial dowry for Sienna, and Canid and his large pack—made up of an impressive percentage of warrior-ranked wolves—would become a powerful ally to Conall's small pack.

"You dinnae have to do this, you know," James said as Conall parked the Defender in the car park of the Coach House.

Ignoring that comment, Conall got out and didn't bother locking the car. No one would dare steal it.

"Callie doesnae want you to do it."

That stopped Conall in his tracks. He turned to face James. "Callie's a romantic."

He could still see her pretty face red with frustration when he told her about Sienna Canid. Dowries and betrothal agreements weren't unusual in the lives of werewolves. They were a primal race, and that meant most of them still based their idea of power on physical strength. There were a few alpha females in the world, but males outnumbered them and few could outmatch an alpha male when she faced one. That meant, unfortunately, males ruled the werewolf world.

It wasn't the way with Pack MacLennan. Conall's inner circle wasn't male-centric, like most packs. His beta was male, but his delta was female, and before she got sick, Callie was his lead warrior. As for his warriors, they were a mix of male and female, his two healers one of each.

Bowing to tradition chafed at Conall, but in this case, for the pack, he would do it. Even if it meant upsetting the one person he hated distressing.

Anguish crossed James's face. "This is hurting her, Conall. Could you not at least wait until …"

Inwardly, he flinched. Outwardly, he took a menacing step toward his friend. "Until what? Until she dies?"

"You know I didnae mean that." James shrugged helplessly. "I just want her to be happy."

"You care too much for my sister's happiness." Conall strode from his friend, bristling with frustration. He was well aware his beta was in love with his sister. Under normal circumstances he would give his blessing, grateful that Callie would be with someone who equaled her in strength of body and spirit. But Callie was no longer the alpha she'd once been.

And encouraging a relationship between her and James would only lead to heartbreak.

Irritated that James had upset him seconds before he was to meet with Canid, Conall attempted to shrug off the feeling as he entered the Coach House.

Grace greeted him. She was a petite woman in her late seventies and yet, with her dark brown hair, bright blue eyes, and fairly wrinkle-free, pale skin, she didn't look a day over fifty. Another reason the pack sought seclusion. They could live to a good thirty years beyond the normal human life span and aged at a slower rate.

Grace patted Conall on the arm and muttered, "They're in the pub."

Nodding, he strolled down the narrow corridor that led into the pub, feeling James fall into step behind him. He was so tall he had to bend to avoid the low ceiling, which thankfully opened up as soon as he stepped into the cozy public house.

A fireplace that took up much of the far wall hosted a lit wood burner. Despite the bright sun outside, the days were still cold this far up the coast, and although wolves did not feel the chill as humans did, the fire was still welcome. On the opposite wall was the bar, a tradi-tional chestnut counter that gleamed under candle bulbs set into black iron fittings. Angus, Grace's husband, stood behind the bar. They shared a nod in greeting.

As it was a Monday morning, the pub was quiet. Even if it had been busy, Conall would have known where the Canids were before he saw them. He'd met Peter Canid before. He had his scent, and it was more than just a wolf's heightened senses. Conall had a gift for finding people. In another life, he would have made an excellent private inves-tigator.

James followed him as he crossed the room.

He didn't ask Conall if he was ready. The Canids would hear anything they said now, even at a whisper. But Conall could practically feel the question from his friend.

Wishing his sister and James would stop worrying about him, Conall couldn't think of what he could say to convince them. They should know him by now. It absolutely did not make a difference who he married. He wasn't a romantic like Callie. Or James. He'd never loved a female other than the familial love he'd had for his mother, and for Callie and female pack members.

Human women, the ones not terrified by him, were good for sex when Conall wanted fragile and feminine under his hands. Female wolves were excellent for fucking, wild and free. There were several single wolves in the pack happy to indulge in casual sex with the alpha, though he never spent a night with a female who lived on Loch Torridon. That was just asking for trouble.

So no—marrying Sienna Canid made no difference to Conall. As long as the female was willing and not under pressure from her father, and that she understood their arrangement was more about business than anything else, it would satisfy Conall. It would be nice, yes, if they developed mutual affection through the years, but Conall would make do either way.

Peter Canid and his daughter rose from the table by a Tudor window. Like most alphas, Canid was tall, but a few inches shy of Conall's height. His light hazel eyes were hard with determination. He was an ambitious bastard to be sure, but Conall felt he was also an honest one.

As for Sienna, she was almost as tall as her father, athletic, strong. At twenty-six she was five years younger than Conall. However, she had the bearing of someone older. Confident, not easily intimidated. Her green eyes met Conall's, assessing, neutral. Usually females stared at his scar for a few seconds, before a blatant exploration of his body. Female wolves were mostly very up front about sex. But Sienna was guarded. She wore her blond hair swept back in a high ponytail and there was little makeup on her face. She didn't need it. Dressed in a T-shirt, plaid shirt, and jeans, she also hadn't bothered to dress to impress him.

Conall liked her immediately.

Aye, she'll do.

"My daughter, Sienna," Peter introduced her without preamble.

She held out her hand to Conall. "Nice to meet you."

He shook it, even more impressed to find her palm dry. She wasn't nervous then. "Nice to meet you too." He gestured to James. "My beta, James Cairn."

"Sir! Can I help you?"

Conall spun around at the sound of Grace's raised voice, just as

Angus moved with the speed of a much younger wolf from out behind the bar. A tall man dressed in a well-fitted suit strode into the pub with Grace on his heels. He drew to a sharp halt as he came face to face with Conall.

The man was human.

A stranger.

Of course that wasn't unusual.

What was, however, was the way he was looking at Conall like he knew him.

"Conall MacLennan?" the man asked, taking a step toward him.

Something about the man caused the hair on the back of Conall's neck to rise. He looked beyond the man at Grace, sensing she'd felt something from the stranger too.

"He's not alone, Conall," Grace informed him. "There are three SUVs outside with armed men."

This knowledge pissed Conall off. Humans daring to enter his land, armed and loaded. For what?

"Who is asking?" he demanded of the man.

"Conall MacLennan of Clan MacLennan?" He was American, like the Canids.

Conall shot a questioning look at Canid but he shook his head. He didn't know the stranger. This human.

"What is your business here?"

Sincere, dark eyes stared into Conall's. There was an air of gentle culture to the man, the kind a werewolf could never hope to replicate. "I am Jasper Ashforth. I've come all the way from New York to meet with you."

"Is that so?" Conall crossed his arms over his chest. "Well, Mr. Jasper Ashforth, although it may not look this way to you, I'm in a business meeting. Perhaps you and I can talk later."

Ashforth shook his head. A grim sadness marred the sincerity in his eyes. "We have little time to waste, Alpha MacLennan."

Every wolf in the room tensed at the title.

History had taught werewolves that, in general, humans aware of their existence were a dangerous thing.

"You've got some balls to walk into pack territory and declare your knowledge of us, Mr. Ashforth," Conall replied, his voice low with menace.

Ashforth didn't even blink. In fact, he took a step closer to Conall. "I need your help, Chief MacLennan."

"And why would I help a stranger? A human one at that?"

"Because your sister Caledonia is dying from a rare lycanthropic disease that no drug on earth can cure … and I can save her."

James sucked in a breath beside Conall.

Conall's blood began to turn molten hot, his claws itching to protract. Nothing tapped into his temper like the disease eating away at his sister. Or people who wanted to use it against him as a weakness.

The growl of his wolf entered his words. "I'd advise you to run, Mr. Ashforth."

The man had the good sense to feel fear, the musky scent of it tickling the air. "I can prove it. Please."

James clamped a hand on Conall's left shoulder. He turned to look at his beta. James's expression was bordering on pleading. "Conall."

He looked to Peter and Sienna and said, "It appears something has come up. Can we reschedule for later this afternoon?"

"Of course." Peter scowled at Ashforth before addressing Conall. "If you need my assistance, let me know."

Conall nodded and the father and daughter departed the pub. Sienna threw him a curious look over her shoulder before she left, and Conall cursed the interruption. He wanted the betrothal agreement signed and done.

There were only three other wolves in the pub, sitting at a table across the room. They were three of Mhairi's fishermen but also warrior ranked. They were alert, waiting on Conall's orders.

"Some privacy, folks," he said.

They nodded and left.

Grace and Angus were still in the room. Conall didn't ask them to leave. They loved Callie like a granddaughter.

"Prove it," he demanded of Ashforth.

A knife, hidden up his sleeve, appeared in the man's hand, and James made to push in front of Conall. Although appreciative of the protection, he stubbornly refused to move. If the man tried to attack, Conall would kill him. End of story.

Then to Conall's stupefaction, Ashforth opened his suit jacket, tugged his shirt out of his waistband, and lifted it to show a hard stomach—that he then plunged the knife into.

"What the fuck!" James barked, backing off at the bizarre act.

Ashforth fell to his knees as he removed the blade, thick blood slipping out of the wound. Pale and trembling, he dropped the knife and reached a shaking hand into his suit jacket. He grimaced at Conall as he pulled out a vial of what looked and smelled like blood. "This ... this is the last ... the last of the cure." He threw back the blood, drinking it like a fucking vampire. Whereas a vampire wore a look of bliss upon drinking blood, Ashforth appeared nauseated.

"Watch." He gestured to his gut.

And just like that the wound healed.

Not only that, the color returned to Ashforth's face, and he stood, seeming stronger, appearing to vibrate with an energy he hadn't walked in with.

Conall had never seen anything like it.

Supernaturals healed faster than humans and could survive injuries humans couldn't but he'd never seen a supernatural heal as fast as that. Like the injury had never happened. Moreover, it wasn't vampire or werewolf blood. Despite what television and movies would have humans believe, vampire and werewolf blood did not heal a human of injury (although vampire blood was a key ingredient in turning a human into one of them).

"What the hell was that?" James asked.

With those sincere eyes of his, Ashforth turned to Conall instead. "It was the last of the blood cure. It cures any injury, ailment, or disease, fatal or otherwise. It will cure your sister."

The air around James changed with his fury. "Then why not give it to us?"

Conall cut him a look. *Calm down*, it said.

His beta glowered but nodded.

"Why do you need my help?" he asked Ashforth.

"This blood"—Ashforth shook the empty vial—"it comes from a

woman. A very dangerous woman of unknown origins. I discovered her abilities when I adopted her. I …" He gestured to a seat. "May I?"

Conall nodded, taking the seat opposite the man.

"Chief MacLennan—"

"Call me Conall."

Ashforth appeared pleasantly surprised by the offer. He nodded. "Conall, I was an ordinary man. I had no awareness of the world of the supernatural. I ran a successful telecommunications company and considered myself a blessed man. When I adopted this girl, my wife and I thought we were doing a good thing. We tried to protect her when we realized she was … different. When we discovered she had these healing abilities … well … we asked too much of her.

"My son was diagnosed with stage IV cancer. We wondered …" He looked genuinely ashamed as he stared out the window, lost in memories. "We were desperate, and we asked the girl if she would let us try her blood on our son." He looked back at Conall, eyes wild with awe. "It worked. Her blood healed my boy. Made him stronger even. Instead of rejoicing, the girl seemed to fear us. We would never have hurt her." Ashforth shook his head, apparently horrified by the thought. "We did, however, ask her if we could keep the vials of blood we'd taken from her, for emergencies. She agreed but I fear she misconstrued our actions.

"As she got older, she turned from a lost girl into a very angry young woman." Tears brightened his dark eyes. "I researched the world of the paranormal, trying to find answers for her, but we couldn't find anything definitive about what she was. She grew more distant, out of control and aggressive. Finally … she killed my wife and two of her security detail."

"I'm sorry to hear that, Mr. Ashforth. But I still dinnae know why you would seek me out."

"Yes, you do, Conall." He leaned forward. "That was six years ago. She's been on the run ever since, leaving bodies and a trail of destruction across Europe. It's my responsibility to find her and make sure she can't hurt anyone again."

Conall wasn't sure he bought that. "You mean you want revenge?"

His nostrils flared. "Perhaps. But had you seen what she did to my wife and those men, I doubt you'd deny me that."

Nodding in thought, Conall released a slow sigh. "How did you hear of my ability, Ashforth?"

"I've continued my research of the paranormal, trying to find those answers I couldn't before. And money can buy a lot of information. I met a wolf who fought you. He told me that once you have a scent, you can track it anywhere in the world. It's extraordinary."

It also wasn't quite how it sounded. It wasn't as if Conall went around sniffing the air until he found his prey. It was more that he had an internal GPS and a scent was the postal code. It sounded like an odd ability, but matched with his reputation, it meant no supernatural on the planet would fuck with Conall MacLennan, knowing there was nowhere on earth they could hide from him if they did.

"So," James interrupted, "let me get this straight. You want Conall to find this woman and bring her back, and in exchange you'll give us her blood to cure Callie? What's stopping Conall from finding the woman and taking her blood for himself?"

Ashforth nodded. "Because I won't tell you where to begin, where you'll find her scent, until you agree to release Caledonia into my custody."

"Never." Conall's voice was deep with his inner wolf.

The thought of handing Callie over to a stranger made him murderous.

"I would never hurt your sister," Ashforth assured. "And you could send one of your men to stay with her. But I'm sure you'll agree that as a prudent businessman, I will need Caledonia as insurance."

"Where would you keep her?" James asked.

Conall cut him a filthy look for even considering the notion.

"I've rented a castle on Loch Isla."

"Castle Cara?"

Ashforth nodded and Conall narrowed his gaze. The castle he spoke of was situated about ninety minutes down the coast. Lord Mackenzie, who had renovated the centuries-old castle, owned it. Conall had never heard of him renting it out before so obviously Ashforth had offered a hefty incentive to do so. And Conall knew why he would. The castle could only be reached by boat and it had once been considered one of the most defensible castles in Scotland.

But that was then. This was now. Even so, he didn't like that Ashforth would choose somewhere like Castle Cara to hole up in.

"No."

"Conall." James scowled. "Perhaps Callie should be the one to decide."

Ignoring him, Conall addressed Ashforth. "Let me ask this. If I dinnae retrieve the girl, what happens to my sister?"

"If you can't retrieve her, or if she kills you, I will release your sister. But if you betray me"—Ashforth's expression slackened with weariness—"I will keep your sister and she will die of her disease before you ever get the chance to say goodbye."

James lunged at Ashforth but Conall was faster, yanking his beta back by the scruff of his neck. James's claws were out.

"Calm yourself."

"I'm sorry to be so harsh," Ashforth apologized. "But a desperate man does what he must."

"Conall," Grace's voice cut through the room.

He looked at the woman he considered a grandparent. "Grace?"

She stepped forward, her expression one of heartbreaking sadness and hope. "If it would save her … shouldnae we try?"

"What of the girl?" Angus frowned. "Can we really barter a girl's life for Callie's?"

"She's a murderer," Conall answered. "I have no qualms about handing her over to save Callie. I do not, however, intend to offer Callie up as collateral."

"It should be up to your sister," Grace disagreed. "Dinnae take this choice away from her, Conall. Not when it could change everything."

Worry needled him. But the hope in Grace's eyes tugged at Conall's heart. Callie could live. Like a true wolf again. Not trapped in her human half until it withered to nothing.

He looked at James.

The hope had buried its way into him too.

Callie and James.

They would be free to be with each other.

Sighing, Conall nodded. "If Callie agrees … then so must I." He turned to Ashforth whose entire countenance was transformed with his own kind of hope. "The woman. Who is she? Where is she?"

"Her name is Thea Quinn. She's twenty-five years old, of unknown species, and she was last spotted in mainland Europe where she murdered a shopkeeper."

Well, didn't she sound like a charming wee thing. "If Callie agrees, I'll need Thea's scent and a list of her known abilities."

Anticipation tingled in Conall's blood. It was instinctual, primal. Deep down he knew Callie would do anything to live.

Meaning it was time for Conall to go hunting.

3

THE BAR AND RESTAURANT ON STOLARSKA HAD A RELAXED, HAPPY VIBE. IT smelled of Guinness and good food, and its vibrant energy appealed to Thea. Stolarska was a clean, brick-paved street just off the thirteenth-century square in Kraków's Old Town. It was teeming with tourists. Not great for anonymity but she'd make up the terrible waitress salary in tips.

That was if she got the job.

The bar was owned by an Irishman named Anthony Kerry and his Polish wife, Maja. When Thea had first inquired at the bar about the waitressing position advertised on the board outside, Anthony had appraised her with a gleam in his eyes.

Then as he conducted a casual interview in his office, he grew visibly unsure. She wasn't the bubbliest person on earth. In fact, she was taciturn and no matter how desperate for cash she was, she just couldn't force herself to play the part of super enthusiastic All-American girl. What she had to say next wouldn't help matters.

"I lost my work visa, so I had to ask for new papers," she lied. "I don't have a bank account either. I need to be paid in cash."

He looked incredulous. "You lost your visa? You mean that electronic document they send these days?"

Thea kept her expression carefully blank. "Yeah, that one."

The Irishman considered this a moment. "Well, if you don't have papers or any formal ID, I'd have to pay you less than the advertised salary."

Of course, he would. They all did. Thea understood. She was a risk. They needed to get something out of it. She nodded.

"Do you know any Polish?" Anthony asked.

Several years ago, Thea had lived in Warsaw for nine months, which meant she knew some Polish. Ashforth had caught up with her and run her out of Poland, but she was hoping a U-turn would throw the bastard off her scent. "Znam troszkę. Wystarczająco, aby zrozumieć."

I know a little. Enough to get by.

He nodded, satisfied. But then he frowned as he stared at her mouth. "Do you ever smile?"

She forced her mouth to curl at the corners.

Anthony smirked. "Not really what I was after."

"I can smile and flirt with the best of them if it means bigger tips."

Sensing her sincerity, he nodded. "Fine. We'll give you a trial run. You start tomorrow. You can shadow Maja on the lunch shift and then you're on your own for the dinner shift."

Nodding, Thea asked, "What *is* the salary?"

He answered, and he lowballed her beyond what was even fair for her circumstances. Bastard. Still, she needed to make rent on the crappy apartment she'd just secured and hopefully her tips would more than make up for her new boss being an asshole.

He stood and Thea followed suit. Watching him rummage through a cupboard behind his desk, Thea dreaded the waitress work that awaited her. This urban life she led was so far from what she wanted deep inside, but she'd given up on the dream of having anything more a long time ago. All that mattered was surviving.

"Be here tomorrow at eleven thirty." He turned and held out four items covered in thin plastic. "Your uniform. Two tank tops, two T-shirts. You can wear a skirt, jeans, or pants with it, just as long as it's black. Skirts are preferred."

Surprise, surprise. "I'll wear jeans." And she had no intention of wearing the tank tops, but he didn't need to know that.

He sighed. "Maja will kill me for hiring the angry girl. Your only saving grace is you're bloody gorgeous."

Thea frowned. She didn't consider herself angry. More like resolute, resigned, and older than her years. "I'm not angry."

"Well, you're something. Now out. I have things to do."

Nice. "See you tomorrow."

He didn't answer and Thea made her way out into the busy restaurant. As she passed a waitress with long, dark blond hair, the young woman turned to her. "Did you get the job?" she asked with a Polish accent. It was easy to get by speaking English in Poland because most Polish people who worked in the tourist area had a a good grasp of the language.

Thea nodded.

The woman balanced her tray on one hand and held out the other. She smiled brightly. "I'm Zuzanna."

Thea accepted the hand with a smile of her own. "Kate." She used a different false name every time she moved country.

"When do you start?"

"Tomorrow. Lunch shift."

Zuzanna smiled brighter. "I will see you tomorrow."

Thea nodded and waved goodbye, reassured there would be at least one friendly face at her new job.

The train journey north to Kraków from Budapest had been a little over ten hours. Upon her arrival, she'd stayed in cheap hostels while she tried to find a landlord who would let her stay with none of the normal legalities. It put her in a shit position because it meant her landlord could turn her out anytime he pleased, but it was the only way. She couldn't leave a paper trail. Although Thea had a talent for making people see what they wanted to see, she hated using that ability. It reminded her too much of what it felt like to be at the mercy of someone else. To feel invaded. To be stripped of what made you who you were.

The ability only worked on humans, unless they knew her weakness, and there were only a few humans in the world who did. She'd learned when coming up against a female werewolf Ashforth had forced her to engage with that the mind warp was useless against the wolf. Thea guessed it might be useless against other supernaturals too. That was fine by her.

She rarely used the ability as she stuck to countries within the Schengen visa agreement. These were the European countries who had mostly abolished internal border control so that tourists and visitors could move freely between them. It still required you to carry a passport, which Thea didn't have, but there had been fewer than a handful of moments when she'd had to use the gift to trick border control into thinking she had the passport and Schengen visa.

Shrugging off memories she'd rather forget, Thea strolled along the narrow street and out onto the main square. The medieval Old Town was stunning, a feast of architectural delight, the most impressive of which was the towering red brick St. Mary's Basilica and the blond and red sandstone market hall that stood center stage. Everywhere there was something to look at on the market hall, from the pillared archways with their hanging lanterns to the pillars themselves. If you looked closely, you could see faces with bulbous noses carved out of the stone.

Stalls selling artwork sprawled across the square while restaurants had set up outside eating areas along the perimeter. Inside the market hall, known as the Cloth Hall, Thea wandered past stall after stall, many selling the same items of Polish nesting dolls, amber jewelry, and tourist crap.

She had no money to buy any of those things and really no inclination to as she clutched her new uniform shirts to her chest. She was merely passing time, putting off the inevitable: that she had to return to the one-room apartment she was renting on the edge of the Nowa Huta district. Her belly grumbled, signaling it was time to leave. She didn't have cash to eat out and had already bought food that was waiting for her at the apartment.

Reluctantly leaving the market, Thea jumped on a tram and less than forty minutes later, she got off at her apartment complex. It was one of many gray, industrial-looking apartment blocks in this part of Kraków. Despite the square of grass and trees in the middle, nothing could pretty-up her new neighborhood. The windows on the ground floor had decorative iron bars. Thea glowered, steering clear. Not even their floral motifs could detract from the prison-like appearance.

Someone had broken the lock on the door of her apartment block, probably ages ago, and Thea felt her mood plummet as she stepped inside the dank entry hall, the smell of cannabis trickling out from one of the apartments. The building reminded her of the one she'd stayed at in Budapest, but it was nothing new to her. For the last six years, this was all she'd been able to afford. It was all many people could afford, which meant like everywhere she'd stayed, Thea's neighbors would be a mix of the good and not-so-good kind.

On the third floor, inside her dark apartment, she ignored the smell of damp and set about heating the can of soup she'd bought yesterday. Just as she was settling down to watch a television show on the crappy television that came with the apartment, the hairs all over Thea's body rose.

She froze, turning away from the American comedy she was watching. As a shiver skated down her spine, Thea reached for the remote and switched off the television. This feeling, this awareness, differed from the one she'd experienced back in Budapest with the gunman. There was no thudding heart or feeling of dread.

But it was still her body's way of warning her.

There was another supernatural near.

Putting down the bowl on the old scuffed coffee table in front of her, Thea's footsteps on bare feet were barely audible to a human ear. But a supernatural would hear them, so she masked the sounds of her movements as she used a talent she'd labeled her cloaking gift. Pressing against the door of the apartment, she peered out through the spyglass. A man and a woman who seemed farther away than they were in real life stumbled down the hall kissing. They fell against the wall in their passion, the young woman giggling as the tall man broke away from her and walked toward Thea's end of the hall.

"Come back," the girl whined in accented English.

The man looked over his shoulder at her and then turned toward Thea, grinning. As his head turned, the light from the bare bulb overhead caught in his eyes and they flashed silver, like liquid mercury, before returning to normal.

Vampire.

Well, that explained all the hair on her body rising in warning.

The vampire stopped at the door next to hers and stuck a key into the keyhole.

She'd moved in next to a freaking vampire!

Of course, she had.

Thea groaned to herself and rested her forehead against the door. She'd have to move. Find somewhere else to stay. It was too dangerous living in proximity to another supernatural.

"What are you doing?" The girl's voice brought Thea's head up and a cry caught in her throat when her eye looked into a blue one.

She froze, cloaking herself in silence.

"Abram?"

Finally, the eye began to retreat until Thea could see the vampire's whole face, and then finally his body. His eyes narrowed on Thea's door.

"Abram." The girl snuggled into his side. "You're being strange."

"More so than normal?" he asked in a British accent.

Thea watched him focus his attention on the girl's neck and forced herself to remain still, silent. The girl's fate was no business of hers. The last time she'd stepped in to help a human, she'd had to go on the run again.

She couldn't take on a vampire for a stranger.

She just couldn't.

An emotion Thea would not label as guilt swept through her.

"Take me inside," the girl whispered, but Thea could hear every word. "Take me inside and bite me again. I love when you sink your teeth into me."

Oh.

Well then.

No need to feel guilty about a lack of a rescue effort.

The vampire and his … whatever … disappeared into the apartment but not before he threw Thea's door one last curious look.

She sagged with relief when he was finally out of sight.

And then Thea immediately threw everything into her backpack and got the hell out of there before the vampire decided to satisfy his own curiosity.

4

CONALL SURVEYED THE MAP ON HIS COMPUTER. IT WAS PART OF A FILE
Ashforth had collated over the years, tracking Thea Quinn's movements across Europe from information he'd gathered from different
witnesses and even the authorities.

"Why have the police not arrested her?" Conall asked, frowning as
he flicked through document after document that Ashforth had loaded
onto his computer. Many of them were photographs of her victims.
The only victims missing from the images were Ashforth's wife and
security guards, but Conall understood those were perhaps too
distressing to have on file.

Ashforth sat on the edge of Conall's desk, looking out at the view
of the serene loch and its surrounding mountains. "Her DNA isn't
human. Which means some authorities have grown a little too curious
about it, so I've made sure it's not in the system. And anytime a police
officer seemed especially dogged in his or her pursuit of the truth," he
said, turning to Conall, "I silenced them with money. Most of these are
city police officers already overworked and underpaid. They're happy
to take the money and let the mystery go unsolved."

"Not all of them, surely?"

The older man shrugged. "There are other ways to silence someone."

Unease settled over him. "I dinnae work with murderers, Ashforth."

His eyes widened. "I would never. I merely meant that ... I've done things I'm not proud of in my pursuit of Thea. Blackmail, as you know, has been useful in that pursuit."

Blackmail was dishonorable and against the code of his pack. Conall bristled, not entirely happy to be joining forces with a man who used it like a weapon. But Callie had agreed to go with Ashforth when Conall departed on the hunt for Thea Quinn, and James would stay by her side at Castle Cara.

Pulling up the next document, he frowned at the image of a newspaper clipping. The headline read "MIRACLE CHILD SURVIVES PLANE CRASH."

"What's this?"

Ashforth glanced down at the computer. Sadness darkened his expression. "It's how Thea came to live with us. This is information important to your hunt, Conall. Thea's parents were British. William and Laura Quinn. They moved to the States before Thea was born and not long after Thea's birth, Laura worked for my company. She was extraordinarily intelligent and worked her way up to CFO. It meant there wasn't a lot of time for vacations. During the summer the family always drove up from the city to our estate in the Hamptons and stayed with us for a few weeks.

"Thea had never been on a plane before ... so they didn't know." He got a faraway look in his eyes. "Anyway, when she was twelve years old, Laura and William took a family vacation to Hawaii." He looked directly into Conall's eyes. "Thea knew something terrible would happen. One of her gifts. A preternatural awareness of danger. She told me she'd begged her parents to get off the plane, that she felt *funny*, but they didn't listen. Later the investigation unearthed that the plane suffered mechanical failure. It crashed, killing everyone on board ... everyone but Thea. Someone found her outside the wreckage with barely a scratch on her."

Jesus fuck, Conall mused, staring at the newspaper article. *No wonder the lass is fucked up. She watched hundreds of people plummet in terror to their deaths, including her parents.*

"You can't bring her back by plane."

That brought his head up. "What?"

Ashforth shook his head. "I tried a few times to get her on an aircraft and she blew the windshield out of one and fried the engine in another. Obviously before we took off. Thankfully."

"How did she manage that? What *is* she?"

"I have no idea. I wish I knew." Ashforth scowled at the computer. "But when her emotions are heightened … things … happen. Things I'm not sure she can control."

"So how the hell am I supposed to bring her back?"

The businessman gave him a clipped nod and pushed away from the table. He walked over to the briefcase he'd placed on Conall's armchair.

Ashforth pulled a syringe out of the briefcase. It was filled with a dark liquid. "A full dose will knock Thea out, long enough for you to get her into your vehicle. I'm afraid the safest way to travel will be by car."

"I thought you said nothing could harm her?"

"This drug merely weakens her."

"What is it?"

Looking regretful, the older man shook his head. "I can't divulge that information."

Growing increasingly suspicious, Conall relaxed in his chair and eyed the man with lazy perusal that belied his tension. "If you dinnae know what Thea is, how on earth did you concoct a drug that affects her?"

"Trial and error through the years."

Wait a second … "You experimented on her?"

"When she started to become volatile, we had to find a way to calm her."

Conall stared at the computer. Question upon question buzzed around in his mind and tightened in his gut.

"Callie's a vibrant young person," Ashforth said. The man was studying a photograph that sat on the sideboard in Conall's office. It was of Conall and Caledonia with their parents.

"Aye."

"If it weren't for the chair, you wouldn't even know she was sick."

"I know what you're doing." He let the man hear his displeasure.

"I'm not very subtle, am I?" Ashforth shrugged wearily.

Callie.

Callie, whose whole being had brightened like a full moon when she heard there was a cure. She'd had reservations when she learned the trade-off was the capture of another young woman, but Conall had assured her that Thea was a murderer who deserved to be brought to justice.

And there was proof she was.

She'd killed people. Innocent people.

What did it matter if Ashforth was lying about the past?

The woman was dangerous, and Callie needed her blood to live.

"I havenae forgotten why I'm doing this. I will bring Thea to you. However, I dinnae fully understand how I'm supposed to pass through border control at Calais with an unconscious woman in my car?"

Ashforth waved the syringe. "A full dose will knock her out. A slight dose won't but it will weaken her. She'll be too weak to make a fuss. And she wouldn't. One of Thea's fears is being captured by the authorities."

Somewhat satisfied by that answer but irritated by the news that their journey back to Scotland would be longer than he'd presumed, Conall exhaled. "So … her last known whereabouts was Budapest?"

"Yes. She won't have a passport." Ashforth reached for his briefcase again. "Thea has a gift for making people see what they want to see so she could travel to Europe by making border security *think* they could see her passport."

The more Conall discovered about the girl, the more uneasy he became. A gift that invaded people's minds was no gift at all. It was despicable. What the hell was she? "And what if she uses that particular talent on me?"

Ashforth shook his head as he brought a blue passport over to Conall. "It doesn't work on supernaturals, much to her frustration."

"How do you know that?"

"I've witnessed it." He put the US passport on Conall's desk. "I'll arrange a car for you to be there in Budapest when you arrive. Her last known address is in that information." Ashforth gestured to the computer. "Her scent will still be in that apartment."

Scents faded over time and Ashforth had nothing of Thea's that was recent enough to use. Conall would have to collect that himself. "If I pick up the wrong scent?"

"You won't. I've worked with other supernaturals who've met Thea. They tell me she has a distinct scent. Something that marks her as different from human, vampire, witch, or wolf."

Understanding, Conall nodded. At least that was something. He didn't want to go on a fucking wild-goose chase.

Turning back to the screen, casually clicking through the documents, he came to a photograph of a young woman. Everything in the room faded out but the image.

It was a candid shot of a brunette looking over her shoulder as she stood in an outdoor restaurant. She wore an apron around her hips and held a notepad, clearly a waitress.

Heart beating fast, Conall clicked on the mouse and zoomed in on her face.

She didn't wear makeup. Everything about her was extraordinary enough without it and Conall couldn't even pinpoint why. Long, dark hair pulled back in a ponytail. Eyes big and dark, thickly lashed. Her nose cute. Her lips small but lush. Round, high cheekbones. Skin smooth and tan. If it weren't for the golden freckles that lightly covered her nose and cheeks, she would have the appearance of an exotic Latin beauty.

As it was, she was a cross between that and the girl next door.

"Thea," Ashforth murmured.

Conall let go of his breath, unease and trepidation moving through him. Thea was technically no more beautiful than any good-looking woman … and yet, she left a man feeling as though he'd never looked upon anything so lovely.

"Don't be fooled by her beauty, Conall," Ashforth implored. "It's one of her gifts. A weapon. Part of whatever makes her the dangerous creature she is."

Conall tore his eyes from her photograph. "She looks young."

"She's twenty-five. Old enough to know better."

Nodding, Conall clicked off the page, disturbed by his reaction to the image, and transferred the file Ashforth provided to his laptop for his own records. "Arrange the flight and a car for three days from now."

"But—"

"The full moon is in phase, Ashforth. I'm not flying anywhere for three days. Understood?"

The man frowned but nodded. "Of course."

"Callie and James will be given over to your custody on the morning I leave." He stood up, towering over the businessman. "And if anything happens to my sister or my beta, or it turns out this girl's blood cannot cure Callie, by the time I'm finished with you, there'll be nothing left to bury."

"Thank you for allowing us to join you tonight," Peter Canid said as they walked through the Coach House, heading toward the kitchen and back door.

Conall glanced over his shoulder at Canid, his daughter Sienna, and her brother Richard, whom Conall had met a few days ago. The betrothal agreement still wasn't signed. They had decided to wait until Conall returned unscathed from his hunt. Upon his return, they would sign the agreement and hopefully marry within the next few months, joining their two packs in a powerful alliance.

Between preparation for the hunt and his responsibilities to his businesses, Conall had no time to spend with Sienna. They'd spoken little. Not that it mattered. Once they married, they'd have plenty of time for that.

As for tonight, he felt it only right to ask the Canids to join the pack run. They were to be family after all. His gaze brushed over Richard

Canid before turning his attention forward. Not that it particularly pleased him to add Sienna's brother to his list of familial responsibilities. The wolf was arrogant and spoiled.

"Yeah, it'll be cute to see such a small pack running together," Richard sneered.

Case in point.

The little fucker thought he was better than them.

"Small pack they may be," Peter said, a warning in his words, "but Pack MacLennan are one of the oldest packs in the world. You're about to experience something extraordinary, son."

There was a genuine appreciation in Canid's voice that pleased Conall. The man's respect for him was honest and true. Conall couldn't ask for more than that from a father-in-law and ally.

Leading them outside, they faced a good percentage of Pack MacLennan—all of those who lived on Loch Torridon and even a few who had returned home from the city for this special event on the last night of the full moon.

Torridon Coach House sat on the water, surrounded by towering trees. Those trees acted like a trail from the land to the rear of the house, up the hill, interrupted by the single-track road, and then up and up again. Eventually the trees dispersed, baring the rugged moss- and grass-covered rock of the vast mountain peaks.

Conall stood, watching his clan who had crowded in to run with him.

"You may join the pack." Conall gestured to his people.

Peter and Sienna bowed their heads respectfully and strode toward the others, while Richard walked away without looking at him. He felt tension emanate from his pack members and knew he was not alone in his dislike for the wolf. Perhaps he'd teach him who was alpha here once the shift began.

The tiny villages along the coast of their loch, and the mountains beyond, were scoured for any sign of human activity. Thankfully, they found a climber in trouble and had him airlifted to the hospital in Inverness.

Otherwise they detected no other humans.

Which meant they could run in their true forms.

A werewolf needed to unleash their wolf and the moon seemed to agree. The legends were true. They had no choice but to turn under the full moon. Conall imagined that inconvenient for some, but here the pack had the privacy they needed to turn. Staying in human form all the time was a kind of imprisonment, anyway. When they turned on a full moon, they usually ran and hunted the mountains separately or in small groups. Mostly they did this unscathed as Conall owned not just the land around the loch but the entire estate beyond.

However, it took a lot of coordinated effort to make sure their small drop of earth was safe to run as a pack, and so pack runs were few and far between. It was one thing for a human here and there to witness the presence of a wolf—an animal extinct from Britain for centuries—but it was quite another for a human to witness over a hundred running together.

However, their alpha, their chief, was leaving for dangers unknown and the pack had requested a run of solidarity, hoping their combined energies would imbue him with their strength and support.

Conall would not say no to that.

He sighed and strolled over to where Callie sat in her wheelchair. After Ashforth dropped his bomb, Conall and James had gone to Callie to break the news. The hope that bloomed in her eyes was hard to see. That hope meant he could not fail.

"What are you doing here?" he asked, hands on his hips.

Callie gazed up at him with the same pale gray eyes his mother had also given to him. James stood by her side. As always. "I can witness this now, knowing I'll get to run soon."

No, he *would* not fail.

A few months ago, his little sister complained about fatigue and pain in her lower spine. Conall had asked her to go to Inverness to see their pack doctor, Dr. Brianna MacRae, but she'd refused.

Until the first time she couldn't shift.

Her body just refused to give in to her wolf, even on a full moon. That's when she finally allowed him to drive her to the city where after several tests, Brianna announced Callie had what wolves commonly referred to as apogee. Brianna knew of it but hadn't ever seen a case before because it was so rare in wolves. Just like the human disease cancer, it was an uncontrolled division of abnormal cells in the body. In Callie's case, it was a malignant tumor on her spine.

Unlike cancer, there was no way to beat apogee, and the cases were so few, little funding had gone into developing treatment. Conall had given money to Brianna to share her research with a wolf in Sweden who was already studying the disease, but Callie would be long gone before they made any breakthroughs.

There was not a lot of time left to save her, and Conall couldn't lose another member of his family.

He wouldn't.

Chucking Callie under the chin, he grinned as she rolled her eyes and turned back around to face his waiting pack and the Canids. A man of few words, he merely watched them as the sun began to dip below the horizon, turning the leaves of the trees from green and plum to black. A burning, tingling sensation skated down his spine, signaling the call of the full moon.

A growl burrowed up from deep in his gut and he felt the sting of his teeth elongating. He yanked his shirt over his head and threw it aside. "Ceannsaichidh an Fhìrinn!" He bellowed their clan motto in Scottish Gaelic, the words warped by the guttural rumble of his wolf.

His pack lowered to their knees; everyone but Peter and Richard Canid followed suit. A pack alpha did not bow to another pack alpha, that was understood. Richard, however, should have been on his knees beside Sienna. His father clamped a hand on his shoulder and forced him to them.

While Conall's packs' expressions strained from the forced beginnings of the shift, Richard's strained with distaste. Conall concentrated every inch of his powerful energy toward the recalcitrant pup and watched the blood leach from Richard's face as he felt the power of the alpha overwhelm him. He fell to his knees, trembling.

Conall's pack felt his power too, their own growls, purrs, and howls filling the air. And then as one they all cried, "Ceannsaichidh an Fhìrinn!"

Truth Conquers.

Their truth conquered them every full moon, and they reveled in it.

5

THE STUDIO APARTMENT THEA RENTED WAS FARTHER INTO THE NOWA Huta district than the last, which meant an even farther and more expensive commute to the pub restaurant on Stolarska. But there didn't appear to be any vampires nearby, so Thea was calling it a win.

Not that the shitty apartment with its stained mattress could normally be considered a win.

However, the apartment was not what was on Thea's mind. For the last few days, she'd felt like someone was watching her and she was constantly on guard. Suspicious that the vampire called Abram might have followed her scent, she'd been looking over her shoulder everywhere she went. Today that feeling of being watched was heightened but since there was no internal warning of danger, she didn't let herself get too worked up about it.

Still, it was annoying. Every time she swept the busy bar for a possible source, she couldn't find anyone paying any particular attention to her.

Well, that wasn't strictly true. The middle-aged American couple she was serving were watching her with a gleam in their eyes she recognized and did not like. She nicknamed them The Oranges as soon as they walked in because they were both wearing fake tan. They weren't exactly orange, but it was obvious their current skin color had been purchased. The Oranges signaled to her as she was passing. "I'll be right there," she promised.

Once she'd given an order to the kitchen, she reluctantly returned to the couple's table. "Would you like to see the dessert menu?"

Mr. Orange curled his finger at her. An unpleasant feeling roiled in Thea's stomach as she bent toward him.

"My wife and I," he said in her ear, his lips almost touching her skin, "were wondering …" Thea felt his hand smooth over her ass. "If you'd like to join us at our hotel after your shift? We'll generously compensate you."

If Thea hadn't been exposed to the worst of humanity at such a young age, perhaps she would have scoffed to hear such a story. It was so cliché. A western couple with more money than sense trying to pick up a poor fellow countrywoman in a foreign country working a menial job, to prostitute her for their shared pleasure.

Well, clichés were clichés for a reason.

They were often goddamn true.

And it wasn't the first time Thea had to brush off that kind of offer.

She pushed his hand from her ass and straightened. "I'll bring you and your wife the check and then you should probably leave."

Mr. Orange's face reddened to blood orange with indignation while Mrs. Orange's lips pinched together. Not long later Thea gave them the check and returned to get the cash they'd left while they were over at the alcove by the door to the kitchen, shrugging into their coats.

They hadn't left a tip.

At all.

The guy felt her up and then attempted to prostitute her and he hadn't even had the decency to tip her.

The bitter ugliness that Thea tried so hard to fight down bloomed in her chest. Pasting a serene expression on her face, she strolled toward the kitchen and just as she reached Mr. Orange, she pretended to trip on a chair leg. Colliding with him, she expertly slipped her hand inside his coat to the inner pocket where he kept his wallet and withdrew it. As they fumbled against each other, she slipped the wallet into her apron pocket.

It all happened in a matter of seconds. No one was the wiser.

"I am so sorry." She gave an embarrassed, innocent smile as she stepped away from him.

"Clumsy girl," Mr. Orange huffed, tugging on the lapels of his coat.

"Really, I'm so sorry. You have a wonderful day." Thea turned away as Mrs. Orange muttered something insulting about Thea to her husband, thinking she couldn't hear.

Smirking to herself, Thea wandered through the kitchen, grabbed a filled trash bag, and stepped out into the alley behind the restaurant. The feeling of being watched lessened, and she dumped the trash before opening the wallet. She grinned seeing the wad of *zlotys* and promptly hid the wallet beneath the wheel arch of the left back tire of Anthony's car. Zuzanna said the car had sat untouched in the alley for months because he hated driving in the city.

If the Oranges returned before her shift was over, looking for the wallet, they wouldn't find it on her or in her locker. After her shift, she'd grab the wallet and dump everything but the cash.

That Thea didn't even feel guilty about it probably made her a terrible person, but there was no one in her life to judge her, to care about her actions, so why should she?

As Thea stood from her haunches, the hair on her arms and neck rose like she'd walked through static. Reflexive instinct made her whip around, and she choked out a gasp at the appearance of the tall man towering before her.

Where the hell had he come from?

The surrounding air shifted and an earthy scent like damp soil passed over her.

She knew that base scent.

He wasn't a man.

He was a werewolf.

Hence all her hair standing on end.

But the back of her neck wasn't tingling, and her heart wasn't beating fast, so apparently, he didn't present a danger.

Still, she glanced around, freaked out he'd gotten this close before her instincts kicked in.

How?

Looking at him, Thea wanted to take a step back, but she worried he'd misconstrue it as a sign of fear. Not that it mattered. Thea knew wolves could smell fear.

Staring up at the powerfully built supernatural that stood at least six and a half feet tall, Thea should've probably felt fear and would have if her danger signals had been blaring. A deep scar cut through the werewolf's left cheek. He looked battle-hardened. Cold determination blazed out of his startling pale gray eyes.

Despite the simplicity of his clothing—T-shirt, jeans, and hiking boots—everything about him screamed warrior. It was the scar, the scary ruggedness of his countenance, and the aura of power that emanated from him, caressing her skin like a hum of energy. She would bet her life he was an alpha.

What the hell did an alpha werewolf want with Thea?

His gaze flickered to the wallet under the wheel and his upper lip curled into a sneer. "A thief too." He looked back at her in icy regard. A shudder rippled down Thea's spine. "I shouldnae be surprised."

He sounded Scottish.

"Who are you? What do you want?"

And then something happened Thea never expected. The hulking werewolf moved faster than she knew werewolves could. As fast as she'd seen a vampire move. It was too late to react, to respond.

Something pricked her neck.

Fury blasted through her as she glared up into his cold eyes.

Determined to teach the wolf a lesson, Thea readied herself for battle ... and then she finally noted the almost-empty syringe in his hand just as the burn began. A familiar substance clung to the base of the syringe.

No!

He'd found her.

Ashforth had found her.

The burn spread and Thea's knees buckled as a familiar agony rushed through her. She could almost visualize the concoction merging with her blood, heating her cells to the boiling point. Refusing to scream, she fell to her knees and curled in on herself, choking back the misery.

And then like always, the pain became too much, and her body did what it needed to do to protect her. It shut down.

Everything went black.

UPON ARRIVING AT THE SHABBY, DANK FLAT IN BUDAPEST, CONALL HAD detected Thea's scent immediately. It was floral and fresh, like summer back home, but there was also a touch of something heady and sweet. Similar to toffee or molasses but not quite either. In fact, it was a scent he had never come across before and it marked Thea as different.

As soon as he inhaled the remnants of her presence in the shithole flat, Conall closed his eyes and let his mind take him to her, tapping into that internal GPS of his. Like a magnet, he felt his mind, his body, tugged northward.

He needed to travel north.

Following the otherworldly pull of his gift, Conall followed Thea's scent through Slovakia and into Poland.

Sensing her nearby, Conall opted to sleep first and paid for a room at a hotel in Kraków's Old Town. Refreshed and more than ready to grab his murderess and get the hell back to his sister and pack, Conall felt Thea's presence grow nearer to him as he ate breakfast in the hotel.

His nose led him to the restaurant on the street just off the main square, and peering into the bottle-green windows, Conall spotted his prey.

At first, the look of her struck him, the impact far greater in reality. Watching her move through the increasingly busy restaurant, the male in him was sorry that her outside did not reflect her inside.

Thea wore her long dark hair pulled high into a ponytail that swished in rhythm to the sway of her sweetly curved arse. She had the kind of body he loved. Slender in the waist and legs, but fuller in the hips, arse, and breasts. Her body moved with so much grace, it gave away her supernatural status. At least to those in the know.

Ashforth was right. Conall scowled as Thea turned to flash a barely there smile at a patron. Everything about Thea Quinn was a weapon, even her beauty. Despite her dark coloring, she reminded him of summer, just as her scent did. Light, almost ethereal.

The darkness within her was well hidden.

As if she sensed his study, Thea had turned to look out the window and Conall had moved out of sight just in time. He cursed himself for staring at her like a prepubescent pup glimpsing his first naked woman.

A cold determination coiled around Conall. That woman in there was the key to saving Callie. Nothing about her, nothing she said or did, would stop him from dragging her back to Scotland.

He waited.

Trying to watch as inconspicuously as possible as people walked by or into the restaurant wasn't easy when he was built like a brick shithouse. Thankfully, just as he thought he might need to move along, he watched the scene with the American couple unfold. When the arsehole crooked his finger at Thea, Conall had focused, using his heightened hearing to cut through the chatter of the other diners. Although muffled, he made out the proposition and watched with distaste as the man slid his hand over Thea's jeans-clad arse.

For a moment, he forgot whose side he was on, cheering his prey on when she shoved the man's hand off her and suggested he leave.

But then she stole his wallet and as much as the guy was a prick, thievery was dishonorable. Murdering innocent people made you scum. Thievery just made you scummier.

Watching her disappear into the kitchen, Conall followed her scent and soon detected her in the alley behind the restaurant.

When he'd come upon her hiding the wallet, he felt a moment of disgust before he shut his emotions off completely. When Thea turned to him, Conall had smelled no fear, which surprised him considering most people were afraid of him before they even knew him.

He hadn't enjoyed watching the supernatural fall to the ground in agony from whatever fucking drug he'd injected into her neck.

Ashforth hadn't mentioned that part. Conall had just expected her to pass out.

Instead, whatever pain she was feeling strained her features as she crumpled to her knees. Her eyes had turned from their natural warm cognac to a supernatural bright gold, as a hoarse sound rattled in the back of her throat. And Conall saw it. First the recognition, followed by intense fear.

She knew who'd sent him.

And he'd smelled the musky odor of fear, like fresh sweat, sharpen to an intense coppery, blood-like tang. So strong, Conall could taste it on his tongue.

Terror.

Not fear.

Terror.

Conall refused to overanalyze it. It would terrify anyone to face a man whose wife you'd murdered, knowing what awaited you.

However, he couldn't ignore the determination and grit he saw in her eyes. She wouldn't scream. She wouldn't give him the satisfaction. And as much as he tried, Conall couldn't help but admire that just a little.

When she slumped to her side, eyes closed, body limp with unconsciousness, Conall bent toward her. Lifting Thea into his arms, he refused to think of how fragile and feminine and helpless she felt. Instead, he focused on getting her back to the car. People stared at him in suspicion as he strode through Old Town with an unconscious woman in his arms. A few people even stopped to ask what he was doing, some of them tourists. Others were natives asking in broken English. He explained his girlfriend had passed out and he was returning her to the hotel for care.

One man tried to stop him from continuing on.

Conall growled, the wolf rising. The human sensed it and backed off in confused horror.

The minutes-walk seemed to last forever, but finally Conall reached the hotel where he'd parked the rental car. For a second, he tightened his hold on the feminine, powerless form in his arms, ready to gently settle her into the back seat. Then he remembered the photographs of her victims and he practically threw her in with a snarl.

His prey was caught.

It was time to get the hell back to Scotland, hand the murdering little wench over, retrieve his cure, and except for rejoicing in his sister's recovery, forget the whole bloody thing had ever occurred.

The first thing Thea became cognizant of was the whooshing sound she'd soon realize was the noise of the road passing beneath her. Then the smell of leather. The feel of leather beneath her cheek. Followed closely by a slight rocking motion.

Instinct held her frozen, and she automatically cloaked her body in silence. Just until she got her bearings. Eyes still closed, she let awareness move through her, and with it came the memories.

The wolf.

She tensed and then forced herself to relax. Using her preternatural senses, she pushed beyond herself and the scent of earth and something darker, spicier, filled her nose. The wolf was here, driving her somewhere.

And Ashforth had sent him.

Rage and terror fought for supremacy and she was thankful for her cloaking gift that kept her shuddering from being detectable to the wolf. The bastard had injected her with Ashforth's concoction, one of the few things on this planet that caused her agonizing pain.

If she thought she could get past Ashforth's hired muscle and no doubt a supply of the drug, Thea would be tempted to stick around to teach the wolf a lesson about manners. Unfortunately, or fortunately, she was all about survival and escaping the wolf was her priority. Thea didn't know how long she'd been knocked out or where the werewolf was taking her. Needing some idea of her surroundings, she risked opening one eye.

She was lying in the back of a small car with old black leather seats. The car smelled damp. Why did everywhere she went smell old and damp? For once she'd love to wake up somewhere literally smelling of roses. Or anywhere that didn't smell like one huge, wet, dirty sponge.

Viewing the masculine profile in the front seat, Thea opened both eyes. Like the US, Poland drove on the right side of the road, and the werewolf was sitting in the driver's seat on her left. He was mammoth in the small car, his dark hair brushing the top of the roof.

She couldn't see his scar from this angle and yet he still looked formidable. It was the hard line of his jaw and the knifelike hilt of his cheekbones. She couldn't see anything beyond his profile and the intimidating breadth of his shoulders because her own head pressed up against the right back passenger door.

The window framed gray skies, but that was all Thea could see from her position. She could sit up without making a noise; however, he'd see her out of his peripheral without the aid of hearing her move.

The car was so small it forced her knees to bend, her feet touching the door. If she hadn't been dosed, Thea could've blasted the door off with one almighty shove. But she could still feel the drug. It was like a poison her healing abilities fought to overcome, slower than they combatted most things, but still, she'd win. Eventually.

For now, she was weak and unable to free herself from the car.

Thea would have to wait for the wolf to stop. She needed an opportunity where he turned his back, just long enough for her to run. Yes, she could run, escape. She was just in no shape to fight.

A shrill ringing made Thea jump. She slammed her eyes closed and forced her body to relax.

"Aye?" the deep timbre of the wolf's voice caused her heart to race.

"I got your message."

Ice slithered through Thea's veins as Ashforth's voice filled the car.

For one frantic second, she thought he was here, in the passenger seat, until she fought through the panic. The phone was connected to the car. Ashforth was on speaker.

"Aye," the werewolf repeated.

"You have her, then? She's unconscious?"

A creak of leather sounded, and Thea swore she could feel the heat of the wolf's eyes on her face. "Aye." The creak sounded again. "You didnae tell me the drug would hurt the lass."

The wolf sounded pissed.

Interesting.

"Don't make the mistake of thinking she's just a girl, Conall," Ashforth said, his anger evident. He was angry? What the hell did he have to be angry about? "She can handle a little pain."

The vile, acrid taste of loathing filled her mouth. Ashforth was a murderous megalomaniac. One she should have put down years ago. Unfortunately, the bastard had the ability to reduce her to a terrified, traumatized teenager.

"It seemed more than a little," the wolf called Conall replied. "How's Callie?"

"Comfortable. Happy. James is with her. Where are you now?"

"Still in Poland. We're not far from the border."

"How many days will it take you?"

"I calculate we'll be back in Scotland in three days."

Scotland.

Ashforth was in Scotland?

Thea visualized the map of Europe, familiar with it after six years of traveling across it. If Conall was taking her to Scotland, then he was driving to Calais. They'd drive through Germany and France, take the boat from Calais to Dover, and then presumably drive up to Scotland.

No planes.

Ashforth must have warned the wolf that planes were a terrible idea around Thea.

"You've succeeded where others have not. You certainly live up to your reputation." How smug and pleased Ashforth sounded. One day she'd kill him. But Thea would have to delay the inevitable a little longer.

"I'll call you when we reach Calais, and I expect to talk to Caledonia."

"Done."

The conversation ended abruptly, and Thea sensed a thick tension from Conall. A feeling of resentment or anger—some negative feeling that had heightened the longer he spoke with Ashforth.

It pricked her curiosity but not enough to convince her she could trust Conall the werewolf. Ashforth was right. Conall had gotten the better of her. She'd been unbeatable for six years. Until the Scot.

Consternated and irritated by his defeat of her, Thea scowled.

Not defeat.

Defeat meant the battle was over.

This battle was definitely not over.

NOT TOO LONG LATER (THANKFULLY, BECAUSE THE GUY DROVE IN TOTAL mind-numbing silence), Thea sensed the car slow, turning off what she assumed was a freeway heading toward Germany.

Her pulse raced as she readied herself to put an escape into motion. Anticipation thrummed in her blood, but she had to stay relaxed, lolling in the back like a drugged-out woman.

Finally, the car came to a complete halt and the gentle vibration of the engine stopped.

The familiar burning sensation on her cheek followed a creak of leather; she knew he was looking at her.

After what felt like an interminably long time, Thea heard the driver's door open. The car rose beneath her with relief from the wolf's impressive weight, and then the door shut. She held her breath, waiting as she heard his footsteps move around the car. Something rattled, hissed, and then glugged.

They were at a gas station, she realized.

Pulse increasing by the second, it took everything within Thea to hold still, not to just push open the door and run. But she still wasn't at full strength and he'd catch her.

So she waited. Heard the glugging stop, the hissing and the gentle rattle of the gas cap closing.

Then the sweet sound she'd been waiting for.

Conall's heavy footsteps moving farther and farther away.

Without a second to lose, Thea sat up, head low, and spied the tall, imposing figure of the Scot striding toward the gas station to pay. She gently opened the car door facing toward the freeway, and slipped out, keeping her body hidden behind the car.

Thea looked around, taking in the fast-moving traffic beyond, her eyes searching the signs. She couldn't figure out from here where she was, and she had no time. To the left of the gas station was a shopping center. Beyond that, IKEA. Behind the gas station was a KFC and a furniture store and on the other side of the freeway, another shopping center.

All of that told Thea she was near a town. Possibly one large enough to hide in.

Decision made, Thea took off. She wasn't as fast as she would be at full strength, but she was still faster than a human. Fast enough to run across a freeway without getting hit.

If a human-shaped blur streaking across the road astonished the humans, Thea couldn't give a shit. Her priority was to get out of sight. Pronto.

Safely across, she jumped off the freeway, running across a field of grass toward the huge parking lot of the shopping arcade. Her limbs burned with exhaustion, her body still weak from fighting off the drug, but she persevered forward. Diving behind the first car she saw, Thea peered over the hood. The gas station was no longer visible and there was no sign of the werewolf.

Not yet anyway.

The car she was hiding behind was too nice, too new. Not inconspicuous enough. It was broad daylight, midday on a workday, and the parking lot wasn't very busy. In the far corner, however, there was an old Ford, a little rusty, more than a little uncared for.

After checking to make sure there were no witnesses, Thea yanked on the door handle, breaking the lock. Her limbs trembled as she scrambled to get in the driver's seat. When she was younger, Thea tended to fry things like engines when her emotions were high.

But that was years ago.

She'd learned a lot of control since then.

Placing her hand over the empty ignition, she sent what was left of her depleted energy into the car. It started abruptly.

Satisfied, Thea tore out of the parking lot, searching the roads for signs of where she was.

Wrocław. They were near Wrocław. Thea hadn't visited the city, but it should be big enough to hide in until she got her strength back. If Conall was determined to hunt her, she needed to be strong enough to either fight or throw him off her scent entirely.

Following the signs into the city, Thea reached into the glove box and searched. A cheap pair of sunglasses, a map, and some old mints. Sighing in frustration, she flipped up the armrest and relief moved through her.

There was two fifty *zloty* banknotes and a handful of coins. That was nothing. About twenty-five dollars. But in Poland, it was enough to get you a room somewhere for the night.

She needed to find a cheap hotel. Somewhere she could rest up and get her strength back.

Although it was a risk, Thea dumped the car on the outskirts of the city center and began to walk. Paranoia caused sweat to soak under her arms and bead across her top lip. She tried her best to look calm, to not draw attention, as she stayed to back streets, following signs where she could.

Thea wandered into the heart of Wrocław, wishing she had time to fully appreciate the colorfully painted facades on some of the buildings. There was a Gothic structure in a square like the market square in Kraków's Old Town, but she didn't have time to find out what the building was. She gathered from the paved roads and lack of vehicles in this part of the city, however, that this was Wrocław's Old Town. Her curiosity over a new city niggled but she had no time for it. Instead, she worried about being somewhere so visible.

On the outskirts, she found a hostel. The streets there weren't nearly as pretty and graffiti covered much of the buildings, but the sign outside said she could get a room for the night for fifteen dollars.

Sold.

7

FRUSTRATION TORE THROUGH CONALL AS HE DROVE THROUGH THE STREETS of Wrocław in search of Thea. He'd become aware as he stood in line to pay for petrol he couldn't feel her. This hadn't occurred to him since injecting her only a few hours ago because they'd shared a small car together. However, as he waited, testing his grasp on her scent, Conall realized it wasn't working.

It must have been the drug. There was no other explanation.

Yet, under the assurance from Ashforth that the drug would incapacitate Thea for hours, Conall hadn't expected to return to an empty fucking car!

Now, having guessed the little murderess would have taken off for the nearest town to hide in, Conall had driven into Wrocław. For the last hour he'd circled the town, searching the faces of pedestrians as he waited for his ability to kick in. His stomach growled with hunger, only intensifying his irritation. Seeing a stall selling what looked like bratwurst, he pulled over, ignoring a Polish man who seemed to berate him for parking his car in a no-park zone.

Fuck that.

Conall paid for the oversized hot dog and wolfed it down in two bites. Wiping his mouth with a napkin, he gazed around the streets, hoping Thea would miraculously appear. He didn't have time to chase her.

A warning tingle made the hair at the nape of his neck stand on end. Turning slowly, Conall searched the passing faces, looking for one that was watching him.

"You can't park there," the man behind the food cart said.

Narrowing his eyes, giving the street one last sweep for a threat, Conall nodded at him. "I'm just leaving."

His whole body felt even more wired as he crossed the street to his car, and his senses screamed at him he was being watched. Was it Thea?

However, as he climbed into the car, he felt a familiar tug on his mind and just as suddenly as he'd lost her, Conall could smell and feel Thea again. The drug was wearing off.

Satisfaction and anger mingled as he drove, following her scent.

Conall did not forget, however, the warning sensation he'd felt on the street, realizing it couldn't have been Thea watching him. She was somewhere in the opposite direction. Which meant there was a possibility he was being followed.

But by who?

"One bloody problem at a time," he said to himself as he pulled up outside the building he felt her in. After searching for an English language sign, Conall realized Thea was on the top floor of the building in a cheap hostel.

Where the hell did she get the money for that?

Then he remembered her so-called "gift" that invaded people's fucking minds, and he sneered with disgust. God, he couldn't wait to be rid of her. Whatever the hell she was.

Agitated beyond belief, Conall drove down the next street, searching for an alley into the back of the building. He couldn't park on the main street where anyone could see him dragging an unwilling female to his car.

Thankfully, he found what he was looking for and pulled into the car park behind the hostel.

He hesitated.

Conall could wait for nightfall, hope that Thea fell asleep, and then drag her out, or he could bet on the chances she wasn't at full strength from Ashforth's mysterious concoction and apprehend her now.

He was already throwing open the car door before his mind had come to a conclusion. Conall was considered patient for a werewolf but today his patience was nonexistent. He didn't want to be around Thea Quinn any longer than he had to be.

After striding upstairs to the hostel, it dismayed Conall to see a common room near the reception busy with a group of young people chatting and laughing. Too many witnesses. He felt curious eyes follow him as he passed.

The receptionist took in Conall with a frown as he towered over the desk, and he could smell his slightly musky scent of fear.

"I need a room."

The young man nodded and stammered in broken English, "Do you have identification?"

To leave no trace of his presence, Conall reached into his wallet and pulled out a bundle of *zlotys*. He slapped them into the receptionist's open palm. "That's my ID."

The musky smell thickened, but the boy nodded. "Name …"

"John Smith."

He typed into the computer behind his desk and then turned to a locked cabinet of keys. Not meeting Conall's eyes, he handed over a key and told him his room number and directions.

He could give a fuck which room he was staying in. He only cared about finding Thea's room.

Marching away from the reception and prying eyes, Conall bounded up the stairs to the next floor, feeling Thea's presence grow stronger. Anticipation flooded him, making his heart pound and his hands flex. Glancing down through the drop between the railings, Conall realized he could take this back staircase to the exit without having to go through reception.

Perfect.

The hallway on the next floor was empty. Conall tried to move his hulking figure as quietly as possible. He stopped outside the door of the room at the farthest end of the corridor and rested his palm against it.

Thea was behind the door.

Brat.

Grabbing the door handle he gave it a jarring tug and heard the lock break. Conall strode inside, coming to an abrupt halt at the sight of Thea in fighting stance, facing him.

She held her fists up to her face like a practiced boxer, her knees bent.

Exasperated at the thought of delaying their journey with a fight, Conall swung the door shut behind him and crossed his arms over his chest.

Her olive skin was a little pale, her features strained from the obvious painful toll the mysterious drug had taken on her body. Dark circles were still visible beneath her wide, tip-tilted eyes. She was still weak.

Good.

"I have no wish to fight you."

Thea grunted. "You're trying to kidnap me, and you don't expect me to fight back?"

"Are you capable of fighting in this state?"

She narrowed her eyes. "I could kick your ass any day of the week, Wolf Boy."

A growl erupted from him before he could stop it. "Call me that again and see where it gets you."

"I'm not afraid of you."

Conall tested the air and realized he couldn't smell any hint of fear from her. Huh. Maybe that should give him pause.

It didn't.

"Listen and listen carefully." He took a step toward her and her lush lips pressed tightly together. "I'm no ordinary werewolf. You can run from me, Thea, but I'll always be able to find you. So let's give into the inevitable and not make a big deal out of this."

Thea let out an incredulous laugh and Conall tensed at the musical sound. "You're delusional, *Wolf Boy*, if you think I'm going anywhere without a fight."

If she called him that one more time, Conall was afraid he'd shift right in front of her. He tried not to curl his hands into fists, giving away his mounting anger. "I'm not kidding. How do you think I found you when others have failed? How do you think I found you here? I hear you have talents, abilities … well, you're not the only one. I have your scent, Thea Quinn. You'll never be able to run from me again."

She studied him a moment, perhaps trying to deduce if he was lying. She wrinkled her nose. "Well, that's not creepy."

Ignoring her sarcasm, he gestured to the door. "Let's go."

Conall waited, studying her impatiently as she considered him in return. As her soulful eyes wandered over his body, an electric awareness shivered through him, reminding him of the call of the full moon.

Ashforth was right. She was a dangerous creature in more ways than one.

She relaxed her fighting stance, exhaling wearily. "Fine."

Relieved but still alert, Conall nodded. He'd barely turned a millimeter toward the door when he felt the blast of a forceful wind against his back. A dark blur shot past him but his reflexes were fast and he reached out for what he hoped was the scruff of her neck.

Making purchase, he shoved her against the door and slammed his body into hers.

She gasped, her cheek pressed hard to the door along with the front of her body. With a grunt she pushed against him but Conall leaned his entire weight into her. "How?" she panted, looking up at him in shock.

Conall tightened his grip on her neck and bent his head to her ear. "You may be fast, lass, but I'm faster."

Her upper lip curled. "I'm not at full strength."

"Aye, well, I suppose we'll see how we get on when you are." He took hold of her wrists and brought them down behind her back.

Thea squirmed, and he tightened his hold, knowing it must be painful, but she never showed it. "Let's go."

"You really think I'll believe you're the world's best bloodhound without testing that theory?"

He heard the warning in her voice.

In the name of expedience, he transferred his hold on her to one hand and quickly pulled the syringe out of his back pocket. Just like that, the coppery, blood-like tang of her terror filled his nostrils and Conall forced down a prickle of guilt. He couldn't imagine she felt guilty about all the people she'd murdered. He didn't want to use the drug now that he knew it messed with his ability to track her, but she didn't know that. "Easy way … or hard way?"

"I … I can pay you more than Ashforth."

"By stealing from people. No thanks." Conall kept the syringe in one hand while he yanked open the door and quickly grabbed her arm with the other. His huge hand wrapped easily around her small biceps. For a tall woman with generous *assets*, she felt fragile and small beneath his touch. Most human females did.

But she wasn't human, he reminded himself, as he yanked her out into the hallway.

"I would think someone who is mercenary enough to hunt a woman he knows nothing about for money wouldn't care where the money comes from."

Conall stopped and hauled her close, bending to enunciate the words in her face so she could make no mistake about his determination to finish this job. "Ashforth isn't paying me. Someone important to me is dying and I hear you're the cure. I bring you to Ashforth to answer for murdering his wife, and he'll give me some of your blood."

If she felt anything about this information, she did a wonderful job of not showing it. Instead, she tilted her chin in defiance. "I'll give you some of my blood, if you'll just let me go."

"No can do." He shook his head and continued to pull her down the hall with him. "I struck a bargain with this man and my word is my honor."

"You've got to be kidding me, right?" she sneered, trying, and failing, to yank free of his hold.

Conall gritted his teeth and held on tighter. If she kept fighting him, he'd inadvertently hurt her. Stupid lass. "Keep moving."

She stopped as they entered the stairwell. "Seriously. My life is more important than your goddamn honor."

"There's a trail of bodies from the East Coast of the US through mainland Europe that makes the latter questionable."

"You have no idea what you're talking about."

Exasperated, wishing he could drug her without causing her pain or him to lose his connection to her, Conall let the growl show in his voice. "Let's cease talking entirely."

To his surprise and relief, she did.

THEA HAD SPENT A GOOD FEW HOURS RECUPERATING IN THE TINY ROOM OF the hostel, feeling her strength slowly come back.

Do you know what she didn't feel?

That internal goddamn warning system that alerted her to danger! Conall was standing right outside her door when she heard him. Not felt him. Heard him!

Her internal warning system was broken.

Or so she thought.

As the bastard hauled her none-too-gently down the rear stairwell of the building, it took Thea a moment to feel the warning because her heart rate was already speeding. But the prickle of heat down her neck and spine, the overwhelming feeling of dread, alerted her.

Conall abruptly stopped, his hold tightening as he scowled down at her. "What is it?"

Thea scowled back. "What?"

"Your scent changed. Not fear ... but something like it."

He could smell her emotions? Well, that was invasive. "There's nothing wrong with me. Stay out of my ... scent."

His growl was intimidating. The guy was huge. But thankfully he kept moving. However, that feeling didn't wane and Thea began to realize it wasn't about the Scot. There was danger waiting for them outside.

Great. Her instincts *were* working. They'd merely decided the werewolf hunting her wasn't a threat. She gave an internal huff and prepared herself for whatever was coming. She could warn Conall there was something dangerous outside but why would she do that when she could use whatever it was as a distraction to escape?

The big bad wolf had just pushed open the fire door that led out into the parking lot when he went rigid. His grip on her became painful as he stared out into the shadowed lot.

"Someone's here. A threat." He glared down at her. "You felt them."

She shrugged.

"You could have warned me."

"I could have."

"Brat," he muttered under his breath as he stepped carefully out into the lot. He kept a hold on Thea but positioned her partially behind him.

That's when the first shot fired.

Conall was a blur of movement as he turned to cover her body with his. She felt him jerk and grunt seconds before he pushed her behind a car.

Shocked, Thea stared at his strained features as he slumped against the wall. He'd taken a bullet for her.

What …

More bullets punched through the wall above them as Conall growled. He tried to get up but pain darkened his eyes as he collapsed.

Okay.

Maybe he took more than one bullet.

"Stay," she ordered, turning toward the gunfire.

Two different directions.

Two gunmen.

"Dinnae." He grabbed her wrist, his hold still strong. "Dinnae even think about it."

She wrenched her arm away as he struggled to stand. "We're sitting ducks."

Conall slouched over, the color draining from his face. "Silver." He winced in agony. "The bullets are silver. Know … know I'm a werewolf."

Thea had read books on supernaturals and in some, they stated silver was poison to a werewolf. She'd always wondered if it was true and if so, why? Guess this was proof. But she still didn't understand the why.

Not that it mattered.

It just meant it was up to her to deal with the shooters. Whoever they were.

Peeking around the car she saw a shadowed fighter behind a white sedan less than a hundred yards away. Thea pulled back as he fired again.

She braced herself, one hand to the wall, one to the car. And then she pushed off, a streak of movement so fast, not even the quickest supernatural could hit her.

Although Conall had certainly been fast enough to grab her, she remembered, disconcerted. But that was a worry for another time. She had more immediate problems.

One second Thea was behind the car.

Next second, she was behind the shooter, ripping the gun out of his hand and pressing it to his temple. She used his body as a shield against the other gunman somewhere on the opposite side of the lot. She peered around him, searching, and found a woman with a gun pointed at her.

"You're both human." Thea dug the gun into the man's head.

She felt him tremble. "Don't kill me." He was English. Huh.

"Weird request coming from a guy who just tried to kill *me*."

"Not you. Silver bullets won't kill you. Our client said so. Those were for the wolf … to get him out of the way."

"Willis, shut up!" the woman yelled.

Sirens filled the air in the distance.

Thea bit out a curse. "Looks like we don't have a lot of time. Who sent you?"

"I can't. They'll kill me."

Frustration ripped through Thea. The sirens were getting closer, and she had no time to interrogate the humans. With a growl of anger that would have impressed even Conall, she took the butt of the gun and cracked it across the back of the shooter's head. He crumpled to the ground.

The female fired at Thea as she dashed across the parking lot, but no one could hit a target that moved as speedily as she did. Thea snapped the gun out of the shooter's hand and threw a punch with enough strength behind it to knock out a guy Conall's size.

After, she wiped down the gun and left it by the unconscious woman's side, deciding to leave the shooters there as a gift for the Polish police. It would give Thea time to get out of Dodge.

With those sirens growing steadily closer, Thea glanced back at the car where Conall laid injured. The facts were that the wolf was trying to deliver her to her greatest enemy.

However, he'd also put himself in front of her when bullets began flying.

She knew it wasn't because he cared.

He needed her alive.

Still … if she left him, he would die.

"Not your problem," Thea said through gritted teeth and started to walk away.

The guilt stopped her three strides in.

"Oh, fuck!" She spun around and raced back to where he was lying, eyes shut, beads of sweat rolling down his temples. "Wolf Boy?"

His eyes snapped open. They were mostly icy gray except for the rim of dark gray around the edge of the iris. Wolf eyes. Compellingly vivid. "I told you … dinnae call me that," he grunted.

"Can you get up if I help?"

Conall's expression was suspicious. "Why would you help?"

"Do you want to die here or not?" she snapped, bending down to slide an arm around his wide, strong back. His shirt was wet with blood. She pulled him up to his feet, and he grunted, sounding surprised.

"Fuck, you're strong," he grunted, clinging onto her.

She got him across the lot and opened the back door of his car. When she pushed him in, she winced at his blood-soaked shirt as he sprawled on his front. His legs were way too long. She searched his pockets for the car keys and as she wrenched them out, she said, "You need to bend your legs to fit in the car." Thea pushed at them. "Now, Conall!"

He snarled several curse words but did as she asked.

Thea wiped her blood-smeared hands over her dark jeans and got in the driver's seat. And then they were thankfully on the move.

Just as she was turning at the top of the street, she saw police cars and ambulances in her rearview mirror. Forcing herself not to speed, Thea sighed with relief when they veered into the hostel lot and she took off for the freeway.

"How many times were you shot?" She glanced into the back seat.

The wolf looked unconscious but answered, "Three."

"How long can those bullets be in there before …"

"Before I die?" He coughed and shifted with a wince. "It takes a while … But I'd rather … not wait that long."

"Do you have a first aid kit in this car?"

"Boot."

She knew from having grown up with British parents that the boot of a car was the trunk.

"Oh. Okay. Good." She threw another glance into the back and saw his eyes were open and watching her. Thea turned again toward the road. "If I save your life … will you let me go?"

He was silent so long she thought he'd passed out, but when she glanced back, he was still watching her. "No, lass. I cannae promise you that." He coughed and grimaced in pain. Letting out an exasperated sigh, he continued, "It would mean breaking a promise I vowed I'd die to keep."

Thea wondered about the person who had elicited that kind of loyalty from the wolf, and bitter envy flooded her chest with a dark, burning heat. There was no one on this planet willing to die for her because they cared that much.

Oh sure, they'd throw themselves in front of bullets to keep her alive … but that was always because they wanted something from her.

Shaking her head in disgust, Thea was furious at herself. She should have left the wolf to die and now she was taking the chance that if she helped him, he really could track her down again.

"But no," she muttered to herself. He was bluffing. An ability to track someone with their scent no matter where they were? It was ridiculous.

She'd help him, her conscience would be clear because she wouldn't owe him anything anymore, and while he was recovering, she'd take off, never to see him again.

They'd been on the freeway a little over an hour, Thea's panic mounting that she wouldn't be able to find somewhere to stop, when she saw the sign for accommodation.

The place referred to the accommodation as apartments but as she pulled off, following the signs, the building she pulled up to reminded her of a motel. Although it was getting dark, there weren't any other cars in the lot. Perfect.

Her hands were slightly streaked with Conall's blood, but it almost looked like streaks of dried-in reddish mud. Reaching into the back, she realized Conall was unconscious, but his chest was still rising and falling. It was strange to see someone so mammoth and powerful, crumpled into this tiny car, covered in blood and weak as a lamb.

The dark voice in the back of her head told her she should leave him, protect herself.

But … she couldn't.

"I will get myself killed one of these days," she grumbled as she tentatively patted Conall's pockets for his wallet. She ignored the rock-hard feel of his ass as she slipped her hand into his tight back pocket to pull out the leather wallet.

Fast as a whip, Conall's hand clamped around her wrist.

Heart pounding in surprise, Thea's eyes flew to his face.

He stared at her balefully. "What are you doing?"

Annoyed that he'd once again been able to take her off guard (seriously, what was that?), she yanked out of his grasp, taking the wallet with her. "I need money to pay for a room. And I need a room to see to your wounds."

The wolf still appeared incredulous, but he had no choice but to trust her. Thea scooted out of the car and strode with an air of casualness into the small reception. There was a refrigerator with drinks in it and a large display with snacks. An older woman sat behind the desk, her back to the door, watching—

Thea raised an eyebrow.

She was watching porn.

Or a very sexually graphic romantic drama.

"A room, please." Thea leaned against the high counter.

The woman glanced at her and then at the TV. She sighed in frustration and turned to Thea. "One hundred *zloty* for the night."

Thea nodded and wandered over to the drinks' cabinet. She pulled out two large bottles of water and grabbed a couple bags of chips and candy bars. "These too. And I'd like your room farthest from the road."

The woman didn't even flinch. She took the money and handed over a key. "Checkout is at eleven." She turned back to her sexy movie, summarily dismissing Thea.

Grateful fortune had delivered her a room and a motel owner uninterested in her existence, Thea grabbed the bottles and food and tried not to drop it all as she carried it to the car.

She parked around the corner out of sight. Once she'd dumped the stuff inside the basic but clean little motel room, Thea searched the trunk for the first aid kit. Not only did she find a large first aid bag, she found bottles of water, protein bars, and a rucksack with a change of clothes for Conall. She grabbed it.

Once the kit and rucksack were inside the room, Thea returned for Conall.

"Right, big guy." She opened the rear passenger door thinking it might be less painful for him if she pulled him out feet first. "Here goes nothing."

Thea couldn't get her hands all the way around his calves, they were that thick with muscle. Jesus, this guy was huge. "What do you eat?" she murmured, hauling him out and ignoring his groans of displeasure. "Steroid Popsicles?"

Conall stumbled on his feet as Thea wrapped her arm around his back to hold him up. He was worse than before, falling heavily into her, giving her his entire weight.

"Holy crap." She braced against him. His weight wasn't the issue, it was his size. He was at least nine inches taller than her and made of solid muscle. Unless he wanted her dragging his legs across concrete, she'd need a little help. There was only one way Thea knew how to make him angry enough to come around. "Wolf Boy, help me out here, yeah?"

His head snapped up, his eyes opening to little slits. "Brat," he grouched, but it did the trick.

Curse words Thea had never even heard before filled her ears as she helped Conall into the motel room. Not wanting blood on the sheets, she took him into the small bathroom and tried to lay him gently on his stomach ... but he kind of hit the ground. Hard.

"Sorry." She winced before she hurried to lock the door and grab the first aid kit.

Inside she found scissors and began to cut off his shirt.

"What are you doing?"

"Cutting off your shirt."

"You're ... helping me?"

Thea snorted. "Just catching up, huh?"

His hands lay near his face, palms to the bathroom floor, but they curled into fists. "Why?"

She'd been asking herself that for the past hour. "You covered me back there. I know you did it for your own selfish reasons, but I owe you. I don't like owing anyone."

After that Conall was silent. Thea spread the cut shirt off his back, revealing three bullet holes in an uneven triangle near his right shoulder. The holes were inflamed around the outer edge and silver veins amassed like spiderwebs around the wounds.

That didn't look good.

Thea felt a pang of sympathy.

"Okay." She folded out the kit, which was supplied with scissorlike forceps, the kind surgeons used. "I'm going to pull out the bullets. Don't worry. I've done this before."

In Thea's experience men had a lower pain threshold than women. She'd seen men grump and groan like babies over a flesh wound that a woman would have brushed off as a scratch. So she was a little taken aback when Conall barely responded to her digging the forceps into his wounds. His body jerked at first, but he merely clenched his jaw and didn't make a noise as she dug around for the bullet. This guy was tough. A worthy opponent.

That wasn't worrying.

Finally, Thea clamped down onto the squashed metal and pulled it out. Sure enough, beneath the blood smears, the metal shone silver in the light.

"Why silver?" Thea asked, thinking maybe it would distract the wolf as she went in for the second bullet.

"Why … what do … you mean?"

"Was it silver that caused your scar?"

His right cheek pressed to the floor so his left, scarred side faced toward her. As far as Thea knew, werewolves had amazing healing abilities. If someone slashed his face, it should have healed.

"Aye. Silver … is like poison to a wolf."

She pulled out the second bullet. "You're not the first werewolf to come after me, you know. Ashforth sent a werewolf after me about three years ago." Thea dug in for the third and final bullet. "The bastard tried to rape me … so I broke his neck."

Conall grew unnaturally still beneath her and she didn't know if it was because she used the *R* word or because she'd admitted to trying to kill one of his kind.

"Realized that didn't work when he caught up with me about a year later." Thea pulled out the bullet, her stomach churning as she remembered he'd brought the syringes too. Only he hadn't been fast enough to inject her like Conall had. Remembering Conall had hurt her, Thea yanked the last bullet out none-too-gently. "Silver isn't the only weapon against you."

"What …" He turned his head slightly to look at her. "What did you do?"

Thea refused to meet his gaze, searching the kit for bandaging. The bullet holes were closing but nowhere near as fast as hers would. "I ripped out his heart," she said nonchalantly. Like she couldn't still feel the sickening hot, wet lump of muscle in her palm.

"He deserved it. But you kill so easily."

It wasn't a question.

It was a statement. Like he knew her.

Enraged, Thea cut him a dark look. "Oh yeah," she said, her voice filled with venom. "It's so fucking easy."

After that there was silence between them. Thea cleaned up his back and taped bandages over the bullet wounds. There was no more blood, however, and the silvery veins had all but disappeared.

Conall shifted on the floor. "I can sit."

Thea stood and retreated as the werewolf sat up and leaned against the bathtub with a groan. He was one of the biggest men she'd ever met and every inch of him was hard and smooth. His broad, muscled chest was surprisingly so. Thea would have thought as a wolf, he'd be covered in hair. However, there was only a light dusting of a happy trail down his incredibly roped six-pack.

And I need to stop staring at the half-naked, angry werewolf. "Okay. Well … I'll go get your rucksack so you can change out of those bloody jeans."

Afterward she left Conall to dress in the bathroom and she wandered outside. There really were no other cars in sight. Just Conall's.

It would have to do for now.

Stepping back inside the motel room, Thea halted as Conall came out of the bathroom. His height caused a logistical problem for her next move.

Although his color hadn't fully returned to normal, the wolf was looking much stronger. She didn't know if she could take him in a fight when he was at full strength, which was more than a little concerning. As if he'd read her mind, he cut her an expressionless look. "You should have left me to die, lass."

"Probably. I guess I'm just going to have to take the chance you were bluffing."

He frowned and opened his mouth to question her, but Thea had already made her move.

Before he could comprehend it, she was on the bed behind him and reaching for his head before his weakened reflexes could catch up.

The crack of his neck echoed around the room, causing a sick lurch in Thea's stomach.

For some reason, stupid tears stung her eyes as she watched his body hit the ground with an almighty thud. Why should she care? It wasn't like he was dead. She'd knocked him out. For … however long he took to heal.

And he had stuck her with that goddamn injection.

Speaking of …

Thea jumped off the mattress, avoiding Conall's body. Earlier when she'd been treating his wounds, she'd spied the syringes in the first aid kit. Grabbing them, Thea hurried out of the motel room and toward the fields beyond. Quickly she dug a hole with her bare hands and buried the syringes. Hurrying back, she avoided staring at Conall because he looked very much dead.

She grabbed his wallet and as she took his money, leaving him his credit cards, a folded-up photograph caught her attention. Curiosity got the better of her and she pulled it out. Smoothing her fingers across the picture, she spotted who she thought was Conall only to realize it wasn't. The man who looked like him was standing next to a much younger Conall, and Thea deduced it was his father. The younger Conall had his arm around the waist of a small, redheaded girl buried into his side. And beside the man she'd mistaken for Conall was a beautiful redheaded woman.

Was this Conall and his family?

They were standing on a rocky beach, a beautiful lake and mountains behind them.

Thea wondered which one of them was sick. Which of these people was he willing to sacrifice her for?

Memories of her own parents swelled in her throat, burning and screaming to get out. But Thea shoved them back down as she shoved the photograph into his wallet.

There were times she pulled those memories out and let herself swim in the pain because it was worth it to remember the happy moments.

But now was not the time.

With a ruthless supernatural sure to wake up from a broken neck wanting to kill her, and some unknown entity out there hunting her too, now was very much the time to go.

9

IN THE DARKNESS CAME THE PAIN. IT CUT THROUGH, AWAKENING HIM, until he laid immobilized by what felt like a sword through his neck.

He drowned in confusion, the agony making it hard to swim out. But there, a glimmer on the surface, was the memory.

She'd broken his neck.

Conall's current awareness told him he was already healing and knitting back together, but an injury like this could take time if he just laid there.

No. He'd have to shift to accelerate the painful healing process. He didn't want anyone to find him like this. And he had a brat to hunt.

He pushed the shift, unconsciousness threatening as he strained his injuries, attempting to feel the first tingle of transformation. Finally, he felt it in his fingertips, his growls garbled and low in his ears as he forced himself to continue through the misery. Usually shifting was akin to stretching his body after hours of being cramped in one position.

Not today.

Today it was like fire scoring down his spine.

Still, it had to be done.

His muscles burned, his bones cracked. Fur pierced through his skin like goosebumps.

And then as his spine changed, as the wolf took over, he almost blacked out from the pain as his neck snapped back into place.

After a few seconds of panting, he opened his eyes and took in the room as a wolf. Despite the darkness of night, he could see better than in his human form, especially in his peripheral. He could hear the traffic of the motorway in the distance as if it ran right outside the room.

Stretching, he finally stood on all fours and gave a breathy huff.

The small room was empty except for his rucksack.

Smelling blood, he turned toward the bathroom and saw the floor tiles smeared with his from the bullet wounds. That would need cleaning up before he left. Sniffing around the room, he caught her scent on the first aid kit and bared his teeth, a growl rumbling from his belly.

Padding across the room, his nose to the ground, he could smell her everywhere.

He stared at his tattered clothes on the floor and then at the room's closed door. If it were up to him, he'd take off after her like this. He'd knock out the motel room door like a battering ram and run along the motorway to get to her. Unfortunately, it was too dangerous.

With one last snarl, he pushed on the shift. This time it was far more pleasant.

As the room darkened and cool air blew across his skin, Conall sat back on his heels and instinctively rubbed a hand over the nape of his neck. There was no pain and no inflammation. It was as good as new. Standing, he felt relief to realize he was stronger than before Thea had broken his fucking neck. He strode into the bathroom and turned to look at his back in the mirror above the sink. There were three tiny scars because the bullets had been silver, but otherwise the wounds had completely healed.

He walked back into the bedroom and pulled his last clean pair of jeans and shirt out of the rucksack. As Conall dressed he tried to make sense of what had happened that day. He assumed it was still the same day or the motel owner would have shown up to kick him out.

Thea had saved his life.

Instead of leaving him to die in that car park, she'd saved him.

And then she'd broken his neck, knowing it wouldn't kill him, but that it would give her a head start.

He felt out her scent and knew instinctively, as always, which direction to take to find her.

Instead Conall slumped on the bed.

The wolf in him wanted to hunt her, to pin her and force her to show her belly in submission and admittance of wrongdoing. Another alpha might want to force her submission in other ways that made Conall's skin crawl. Like the werewolf Thea said had tried to rape her.

And where she'd learned that breaking his neck wouldn't kill him.

Warring between his anger and confusion, Conall glared at the blank wall, trying to make sense of this information.

Why had she not left him to die?

Was it a manipulation? So that if he found her again, he'd show mercy, or worse, be lulled into a false sense that maybe Thea Quinn wasn't the villain Ashforth had made her out to be?

But no. She'd admitted to ripping that wolf's heart out. Not that he didn't deserve it, but she said it like it wasn't the first time she'd done it. And they both knew her victims weren't always psychopathic rapist werewolves, but innocent people.

She was manipulating Conall.

On the off chance that his tracking ability proved to be real, she'd saved his life to soften him.

Well, it would not soften him. Not only did he need to find the murderous brat, he had to find her before whoever sent those humans after them, found her.

Someone else knew the value of Thea, which meant Conall was now hunter *and* bodyguard. He huffed at himself as he stood. Some fucking bodyguard. He'd never been so caught unawares as he had been these last twenty-four hours. But now he was more prepared.

(A) There was someone after Thea and they knew Conall was a wolf, so he'd avoid bullets from now on.

(B) Thea Quinn was the fastest fucking supernatural he'd ever come up against.

Conall gathered his stuff into his rucksack and as he grabbed the first aid kit, he discovered the syringes were missing. Not that it mattered. Drugging her was too risky. They were useful in bringing her to heel and Conall no longer cared about causing her pain, but they weakened the connection. She probably thought she'd gotten one over on him, taking the damn things.

Things got slightly more difficult when he discovered she'd taken all his cash. Thankfully, she'd left his credit cards. The car was missing and with it his phone. However, he had his passport and her fake one in the rucksack.

After sniffing around outside the almost-deserted motel, Conall found a locked door that led to cleaning products. Keeping his head low in case there were any cameras, he broke in, grabbed what he needed, and cleaned the bathroom floor of his blood. Once he'd wiped down the room, he returned the cleaning products and went to the motel room reception.

It was closed.

Conall posted the room key through the door and began to walk toward the motorway. He'd been out of it when Thea drove them here so he could only hope there was more than a motel around.

His relief came soon when he discovered the petrol station. Walking inside, Conall could feel the tension of the man behind the counter as he took in Conall's size and countenance. He was an older man, tall, and well built. But no matter how congenial Conall was, humans seemed to sense they were no longer the top of the food chain when he was around.

"Pay phone?"

The man frowned in confusion.

Fucking great.

Conall held his thumb and pinky to his mouth. "Pay. Phone."

His brow cleared. "No."

"Do you have one I could borrow?"

Another frown.

Fuck.

He mimed some more, feeling like an arse, but the man cottoned on and pulled his phone out of his pocket and gestured to Conall. Grateful, Conall thanked him and took the phone. He didn't know Ashforth's number, but he knew James's.

His beta didn't pick up.

Conall was just about to throw the stranger's phone at a wall in disgruntled impatience when the phone rang again. It wasn't James's number, but it was the UK country code. "Conall," he answered abruptly.

"What happened to your phone?" Ashforth asked.

That man's voice was beginning to goddamn grate. Conall moved away from the cashier. "Why is James not answering his?"

"I told you I want to be in control of this, Conall. I can't have you communicating with your beta behind my back. James agreed to the confiscation."

Outrage rose from his gut, but Conall stifled it. Now was not the time. "My sister is okay?"

"She's as well as when you left her."

"I'll want to speak to her and James in the morning. That's not a request."

Ashforth hesitated but then, "Of course. Now will you tell me what has happened?"

"Someone who knew what I am attacked us. Thea got the better of me in the confusion. I came to and the car, my phone, and my money are missing."

"Someone else is after her?"

"Aye. Now I know that, I can be more vigilant."

"I told you she was tricky."

"Aye, an understatement. I need a car, money, and a new phone."

"Find out where you are, and I'll arrange everything. I'll also track down the other car. She probably abandoned it, but it'll give you a starting point."

Conall curled his lip, impatient to catch up with the lethal brat. "No need. I know where she is."

"Of course." Ashforth sounded extremely satisfied, gloating almost. "It's wonderful to know she'll never be able to outrun me again."

Outrun me, Conall corrected inwardly. *She'll never be able to outrun me.* That knowledge created an unexpected feeling of satisfaction for Conall too.

"I'll see if I can find out who might be after you," Ashforth continued. "Now, where are you?"

Conall returned to the cashier to ask where they were. Finally, after a long moment of miscommunication, they figured it out.

Conall waited at the petrol station for an hour; he felt the cashier's eyes constantly on him. Just as he was sure the guy was readying to call the police, two cars pulled up outside, and a stranger got out of the first. The man strode inside, his eyes going straight to Conall's.

"Chief MacLennan?" he asked in a thick, Polish accent.

Conall nodded.

"Come with me?"

Following the man outside, he huddled next to Conall and handed over the car keys. He then discreetly passed over a wad of cash, along with a new phone. After Conall thanked him, the man nodded, walked to the second car, got in, and the car drove off.

Conall pondered this, wondering at Ashforth's connections, that he could pull this off in a little over an hour. He threw his rucksack into the car and turned back to the station. Grabbing some food he could snack on as he drove, he paid for it and then added extra as a thank-you for the use of the phone.

The cashier remained unsure, but he smiled his thanks and Conall tried his best not to hurry. Neither he nor Thea needed the police joining the hunt as a second outside entity.

As he pulled onto the motorway, steering with one hand and holding a protein bar with the other, he ripped open the packaging with his teeth and made a sound of anticipation in the back of his throat. Thea Quinn would be back in his grasp and he would enjoy the moment she realized he hadn't been bluffing—when it finally sunk in that no matter where she ran, he could find her.

It would be interesting to see if she gave up on the manipulation and decided the solution was to rip his heart out.

Not that he would ever give her the chance. He was far more understanding of her capabilities now.

Conall frowned as he followed her scent, realizing she'd turned southwest instead of west toward Germany.

She was in the Czech Republic.

"Fuck," he grunted, pressing harder on the accelerator. There was someone else after the lass and Conall was determined to find her first.

And this time, he'd know better than to turn his back on her.

10

Wolf Boy's car was somewhere in Lubawka, Poland. Thea had dumped it a thirty-minute walk from the train station, where she'd then boarded a train to Prague. Nervous energy filled her. She had a huge Scottish wolf after her—and a mystery hunter.

It wasn't Thea's first time in Prague. It was one of the first cities she'd stayed in after she'd escaped Ashforth, so she was familiar with it. She'd exchanged all Conall's *zlotys* at the train station for Czech *koruna* and asked the cab driver to recommend accommodation. He'd dropped her off at a three-star hotel on a tree-lined street where neoclassical buildings towered symmetrically one after the other. In the middle of all the light sandstone, a block was painted in the palest of pinks.

This was Thea's hotel.

Although basic, it was the nicest place she'd stayed in for a long while. After discovering her in a hostel, it concerned her that Conall might look for her in the cheaper hotels if he managed to catch up with her in Prague, so the three-star was a necessary "luxury."

The hotel was only ten minutes from the historical center of the city and Thea reluctantly stepped out into the world the next day in search of work. Instead of finding work, however, she bought clothes she wouldn't be able to afford if she didn't find a job soon. But clothes were now a necessity, since Conall had dragged her out of Kraków with only the clothes on her back.

Buying two pairs of jeans and a few shirts was easy.

Finding a job was not.

Wearily, Thea returned to the hotel after a day of searching, anxious about paying for another night but doing so for her safety. The next morning, however, she checked out, realizing she'd just have to risk a cheaper place for fear of running out of funds. Thea was betting on the fact that both her pursuers would guess she'd get the hell out of Europe, or at least travel farther than the Czech Republic.

Having bought an inexpensive backpack the day before, Thea put the little she owned into it and checked out of the hotel. It was a warm spring day; the sun beat down on her face. She longed for her sunglasses and baseball cap she'd left behind in her shitty apartment in Kraków.

At least Prague was beautiful. She hadn't stayed long during her previous visit. The historical center and its mishmash of architectural styles charmed her. There was Romanesque, Gothic, Renaissance, Baroque, neoclassicism, all mixing in with art nouveau, cubism, functionalism, and the stern, gray, concrete architecture of the Communist era. Thea would walk past a neoclassical building and standing right next to it would be the modern prefab, glass-walled buildings that went up in the latter half of the twentieth century.

The only reason she knew anything about architecture was because every city she stayed in, she'd roamed the libraries, spending any spare time she had educating herself on subjects she missed out on growing up, and then some.

Like all the cities she'd spent time in in Europe, Thea was drawn to the old towns with their cobbled or brick-paved streets, trams and the bustle of tourism. It wasn't just that she loved the centuries of life those places had witnessed—it was being able to disappear among the crowds. To feel like a normal young woman. A number among many.

Instead of what she was.

As the day wore on, a ceiling of clouds blew in over the city, and Thea grew more concerned. She'd asked at a lot of bars and restaurants, but she couldn't find someone to hire her who didn't need all the legal crap. Thea had snacked as she walked but she was still ravenous. Perhaps it was the excitement of the last few days. She'd probably expelled more energy than she'd thought. Deciding it was maybe time to give up and find a hostel and somewhere she could buy cheap vendor food, Thea walked down a busy street as night fell.

The booming bass of music and the chatter of partygoers outside a building in the middle of the shopping area drew her attention. Thea slowed to a stop in front of the place and looked up. It was a building she'd visited yesterday and many times during her last stay in the city. Called Lucerna Palace, it was an art nouveau building designed for a former president. It was now a shopping mall of sorts, and housed a cinema, shops, restaurants, bars, and cafés. And she knew from her wanderings inside it seemed to be particularly famous for its music bar. It was the one place she hadn't asked if they were looking for a bartender.

Her eyes drifted over the people walking in, some dressed to the nines, but most casual in jeans and shirts. A lot of English language tourists passed her by, which meant the Lucerna Music Bar was more than likely keen on English language bartenders.

What the hell, Thea thought, ignoring her grumbling belly. She might as well check it out.

Following people as they followed the music, Thea's boots echoed across the checkered floor, the sound muffled by the bass in the distance. She passed a statue suspended from the ceiling of a guy riding an upside-down, dead horse. Every time she'd seen it, she'd wondered at its significance and so eventually looked it up. It was supposed to be a satirical version of the statue of King Wenceslas on Wenceslas Square.

Continuing down the hall, the bass led everyone to the left.

At the coat check, Thea risked her worldly belongings and checked her backpack. She took off her shirt and stuffed it into her bag, leaving her dressed in a pair of the new, dark blue jeans she'd bought and a dark green T-shirt. The shirt had a V-neck and showed off her generous cleavage. As wrong and sexist as it was, she found she always got further on the job hunt if she showed a little skin.

Fuck my life, she griped to herself, wondering when it would change. Thea pulled her long hair into a ponytail and handed her bag over at coat check, pocketing her ticket.

She supposed she could use her gifts to live in the lap of luxury and never have to worry about being sexually objectified again, but it would mean hurting people more than she already had.

And Thea was pretty sure she'd filled her quota on that.

Simple Minds' "Don't You Forget About Me" filtered out from the music hall and she overheard two English girls saying it was eighties night. Great.

Thea raised an eyebrow as she walked into the dark, smoky room and turned around, looking up. Above was a galleria where more people congregated. The dancing crowd surrounded the stage as the band played a cover. It was smaller than she'd expected. And claustrophobic. Thea stealthily made her way through the crowd, heading toward to the bar when out of nowhere, someone grabbed her wrist.

"What the—" Thea huffed as a young woman hauled her close in the swarming, hot darkness. The stage lights suspended on the ceiling flickered over the girl's stunning elfin face.

Round, penetrating eyes stared intensely into Thea's and the air filled with static. The hair on Thea's neck and arms rose, and she froze in unexpected stillness.

"You don't fear him because there's nothing to fear," the woman shouted in accented English over the music, her expression earnest and almost … frantic.

Goosebumps pricked Thea's skin. "Excuse me?"

The woman's hold on her tightened. And then to Thea's utter disbelief, she heard the woman's voice in her head. In. Her. Head.

Her rich Irish brogue filled Thea's mind as they stared wordlessly at each other. *He's important. His future affects your future. He's important, Thea.*

Shocked to her core, Thea pulled against the young woman's grip, but she was strong.

Too strong.

Foreboding and incredulity ran cold through her. "Who the hell are you? How do you know me? How are you doing this?"

Concern brightened the woman's eyes. Her voice filled Thea's head again. *You should leave. Night children run this place and they're waiting for you.*

Suddenly a tall, dark-haired man jerked the woman away from Thea. He seemed to berate the girl in a language she couldn't pinpoint. Irish, maybe?

What the hell?

Thea's heart pounded hard in her chest as the woman peered past the man. A connection unlike anything she'd ever felt before soared through Thea. What was this woman? Who was she?

Was this a trick and Ashforth had found her?

But then how did the woman speak into her mind like that? What kind of supernatural could do that?

Thea bulldozed the man out of the way and grabbed the young woman's arm. "Who the hell are you? How do you know me?"

She pressed a reassuring hand to Thea's face and a sense of calm flooded her. "I'm not your enemy." Her voice was low, yet Thea could hear every word. "And neither is the wolf."

"What?"

The man pushed Thea away, towering over her. "You leave her alone."

"Hey, dipshit, she grabbed me." She looked past him at the woman who was already disappearing through the crowd. "How does she know me?"

The man glared at her, but she saw the flicker of something like worry in his eyes and she realized they were the same eyes as the woman. Brother, perhaps? "She knows things she should not know. She means no harm. You leave her alone."

Before Thea could argue, he turned and pushed through the heaving bodies of dancing clubbers.

"What the goddamn hell was that?" she muttered, stunned.

And a little freaked out.

Determined to find out more, Thea moved to pursue the woman

and her protector when the warning tingle burned the back of her neck, her stomach filling with dread.

Oh shit.

She turned, searching the crowds, feeling the humans out.

Which one of these is not like the other? she thought, exhausted by the mere idea of fighting.

There.

A good-looking guy stood in the middle of the dancing bodies staring at her.

Thea felt the surrounding air just as he turned his head. The light caught the mercury of his eyes and she froze.

Night children run this place and they're waiting for you.

Double oh shit.

Thea waited as the smirking vampire strolled casually toward her.

Vamps had been a growing problem for Thea over the years. She preferred to stick to cities, but so did they. She preferred Europe, but so did they, it seemed. When she first escaped, it was months before she had an encounter with a vamp but as time wore on, Thea seemed to bump into one every other month. Mostly she escaped a skirmish because she was fast and good at avoiding them. But sometimes she had to fight because whatever she was made them curious about her.

And all blood-lusty for her too.

Maybe it was time to move. Perhaps northern Alaska where there was constant daylight and a hundred percent chance of no vamps.

Pretending not to know what he was, Thea gave the vampire a flirty smirk as he circled her, dragging his eyes all over her in curiosity. He was feeling her out. Wondering what she was. Or, if the girl was right, he already knew she was something different. He'd been expecting her.

But how?

Taking hold of her hand, he leaned in to whisper in her ear, his words musical with a European lilt, "Dance with me."

Contrary to popular belief, vampires weren't dead. They were immortal. Their hearts beat and they had a breath. Although from what she'd gathered, humans could sense they were different, and there was no way of knowing just how deadly they were. That "different" meant they were a predator and humans were their prey.

Thea let the vampire pull her into a dance, her mind racing. If she'd refused, his curiosity would only compel him to hunt. She needed to lull him into a false sense of security so she could escape.

Discomfort flooded her as he rested his hands on her hips and rocked his against hers. She forced herself to gyrate with him, when all the while it felt like little ants crawling all over her skin. It had been a while since anyone had held her this close but when she let the deepest, darkest parts of her mind imagine how it would feel again, it was nothing like this.

Her stalwart control meant she relaxed into the vampire's embrace and met his penetrating stare. He bent his head toward her neck, and it took everything within her not to tense. The bastard nuzzled her, sniffing. "You smell amazing." His words were guttural.

Hungry.

Fuck.

If she kneed him in the balls and ran for it, she could probably get out of there, but then she would leave behind her bag and it had all her worldly possessions in it.

And there was the matter of the strange young woman.

Thea huffed to herself. The girl had made no sense. And yet, Thea still fought the urge to go after her. There was something familiar about her. As though they'd met before. More than that … her presence was *comforting*. When she'd cupped Thea's face in motherly reassurance, it was the first time in years Thea had felt safe.

Horrified to realize there were tears burning in her eyes, Thea blinked and looked down at the clasp of the vampire's body against hers. She was being ridiculous about the woman. Childish even.

Focus, Thea.

"Have you been to the theater yet?" The vampire's lips brushed against her ears.

She shivered in distaste but the tightening grip of his hands on her hips suggested he'd confused the shiver for desire. "No."

"It's closed tonight. Would you like a private tour?"

Considering this, Thea decided ultimately it was best to get him away from the crowds. She didn't want to kill the vampire, but she would disable him if he attacked first.

Thea nodded, and he smirked in satisfaction, releasing her hips to take her hand in his. She let him lead her out of the music hall and then tugged on his hand. "I need my stuff." She gestured to the cloakroom.

He frowned. "Get it after."

She stroked her thumb over the top of his hand and smiled prettily. "It'll take two seconds."

The vampire scowled. "Fine."

The young woman working the coat check handed over her backpack, her eyes wide on Thea's companion. She'd gone pale as soon as she'd seen him and had given Thea a look of pity.

Hmm.

Her telepathic friend from earlier had said the "night children" ran this place. As she let the vampire take her hand, she wondered how big his coven was, how far up the hierarchy he was, and if killing him would lead to a shitstorm for her here in Prague.

Seriously, fuck my life.

The theater-turned-cinema wasn't huge either, lights blaring to life to reveal the ornately carved galleria that wrapped around the central seating facing the old stage and screen. "It's beautiful," she murmured, coming to a stop beside him.

The vampire gestured for her to go ahead but there was no way she was turning her back to him. She stared at the rows of dark peach velvet seats and then turned around so her back was facing them and not him. Thea took a few steps away from him.

They were alone.

There was no need to pretend anymore.

She dropped her smile. "What do you want, bloodsucker?"

Surprise slackened his features. "Clever girl." He took a step toward her. "So, you know what I am? But I still don't know what you are."

"I'll tell you what I am … a bad investment of your time. You should have chosen a weaker victim."

"You don't look so tough." He bared his teeth and his incisors lengthened.

Thea widened her legs, hands on her hips. "Was that supposed to scare me? Because I've seen bigger."

His lips nearly vibrated with his answering snarl. "I'm supposed to keep you alive, but I won't if you piss me off, little girl. Instead, I'll rip into that pretty fucking throat and drink you dry."

Alert, Thea cocked her head. "Who asked you to keep me alive?"

"Someone you don't say no to. That someone asked me to watch out for your arrival."

Was it Conall? Did he have vampire connections? Or was it the mysterious person behind the humans who'd shot at them?

Thea supposed it didn't matter. It looked like it was kill or be killed because she would be no one's captive. Ever. Fucking. Again.

The vampire shot across the space toward her, a streak of movement shockingly fast.

She was faster.

She ducked him, a lightning-quick shadow, and moved across the room toward the door.

Which was barred by two new vampires.

Shit.

She backed down the aisle toward the stage.

Her attacker watched her in consternation. "How do you move that fast? What are you?"

All the hair on Thea's neck rose, and she looked up.

Two more vampires stood above on the galleria, teeth bared, incisors out.

Five vampires.

A knot of worry tightened in her gut, but she forced herself to ignore it. She was strong enough to fight all five.

She had to be.

"I'll tell you what I'm not. I'm not your prisoner or your walking blood bank." Relying on the element of surprise, she dashed behind one of the thick pillars holding up the galleria, and was nothing but wind under the balconies as she headed past the vamps toward the entrance.

Suddenly, however, someone grabbed her throat and slammed her hard against the wall, the impact of which would have knocked out a lesser being. Instead Thea shook off the confusion and glared into the face of the vampire she'd been dancing with. Her neck was clasped in his strong hand as he held her suspended above the ground.

The son of a bitch was fast and strong. He had to be pretty freaking old to rip her out of her top running speed.

Goodie for me, she huffed.

His grip tightened around her neck and although uncomfortable, it didn't elicit the panic he was hoping for. Instead Thea grabbed his wrist and twisted with all her might, the answering crack extremely satisfying.

The vampire dropped her with a roar, and she darted by him only to encounter his companions. They were on her before she could run. Ducking and diving their punches and kicks, Thea blocked where she could and swiped one off his feet. As much as she was holding her own against the bastards, they were pushing her farther and farther away from the entrance.

Finding a gap in their attack, she dove between two of them and tumbled into a roll, shooting up onto her feet and into a run, eyes to the door—

His leg came out of nowhere.

A roundhouse kick to her chest.

She heard something crack, she couldn't breathe, and it wasn't because she was soaring through the air like a fucking bird. Pain cracked up her spine and her neck rolled before she was grounded again.

As quickly as she hadn't been able to breathe, air flooded her lungs, and the pain dissipated. She got to her feet on shaky legs, realizing the vampire she'd danced with had kicked her as if she were merely a football, and she'd hurtled through the air and slammed into the edge of the stage.

Outraged by his show of strength, unnerved even, Thea fell into a defensive stance, glaring at him as he moved through his vampire friends. She'd picked up most of what she knew about other supernaturals during her time with Ashforth, since the man was obsessed with the paranormal. She'd met her first vampire at Ashforth's and from him, she'd learned that the older a vampire was, the stronger they were.

This guy had momentarily collapsed Thea's lung. With a mere kick to the chest.

So, he was old.

He cocked his head, eyes narrowed on her chest. "I heard the damage … now I hear nothing. You healed instantly. What are you?"

"I'm out of here." She saw an exit door off the right side of the old stage and made a feint toward it. They chased and Thea leapt with the grace of a cat; she pushed her feet off one of the galleria pillars, using the height to jump over their heads in the opposite direction. Her landing was just as graceful, but two of the vampires ruined the suaveness of the entire maneuver by catching her. They pulled her into a brutal fight, growing more and more frustrated that she was landing hits while they failed to.

Becoming impatient, Thea sought to end it, to incapacitate, and so she snapped the neck of one of the vampires, knocking him out cold.

"Oh, you're dead now, little girl," the other vampire threatened. "We will fuck you up and have a lot of fun doing it. Ever been tortured? You will not like it, I assure you."

Memories flooded Thea at the threat.

Nightmares that unfortunately were real.

And just like that, the savagery of survival instinct took over. First, she disoriented him, moving this way and that until his back was to her. Then she leapt with a light grace onto the top of a theater chair and used it to propel her onto the vampire's back. Before he could even react, she punched her fist through his back with every ounce of supernatural strength within her, gripped tight to his heart, and ripped.

The hot muscle in her hand crumbled to ashes seconds before his entire body obliterated into dust. Thea dropped to her feet as the three remaining vampires stared at her in mounting rage.

Three blurry streaks sped toward her, surrounding her so she couldn't find a way out. Outrage and fear flooded her as she found herself captured by two of the vampires. They held fast to her wrists, holding her outstretched. As much as she strained, she couldn't detach them. Her original hunter stepped toward her, his eyes pure silver.

"It was never stipulated whether I was to keep you alive," he snarled. "So, you're dead now, bitch."

It was difficult for Thea to feel anything approaching the word agony. Pain, yes. Agony, not so much. Ashforth was the only one who seemed to know how to inflict it.

But until that point, no one had come close to hurting her like he had.

Until this vampire pulled back his arm and thrust it like a sledgehammer through brick into her chest.

She gasped at the indescribable horror of feeling his hand curl around her heart.

He squeezed, and it was excruciating, but she still enjoyed the way his eyes rounded in horror when he realized her heart was uncrushable.

Her heart was uncrushable.

Jesus fuck.

Fury and disbelief tightened his features, and he gave her heart a yank. She muffled a gasp at the sickening sensation as her heart tugged but could not be removed.

"What the hell are you?" he breathed. "Are you—"

Flecks of coppery-tasting fluid splattered Thea's face as the vise on her heart released.

She sagged in relief and confusion until she looked through a cloud of dust into Conall's fierce face. His canines were out as he towered over the gathering, his arms spread wide, his claws protracted and wet with blood.

He'd just decapitated the vamp with his bare hands.

Holy shit.

A sickening ache filled Thea's chest as it began to heal and she found herself on her knees, unable to move as she knitted herself back together.

Not that her help was required.

A mix of fear and admiration filled her as she watched the alpha fight the remaining vampires. Their deaths were appallingly quick as they came at Conall. He seemed to brace for them as they rushed him on either side, a blur of movement, hard to track.

But track them he did.

Conall punched out, claws sharp, and the vamps speed, meeting his, inadvertently caused their deaths with the force of impact. His fists slammed through their chests and he ripped out their hearts.

The next moment they were dust.

Thea tried to reassure herself that if she'd just given into killing the vampires in the first place, she could have killed them faster than even Conall had.

Still, this wolf was worryingly strong.

And he'd found her.

Which could only mean one thing.

He really did have a tracking ability.

She watched as he approached the vampire passed out cold and punched a hole through his chest, removing his heart, until he too was nothing but dust. Conall stood and glared at her. "No witnesses," he explained.

Weariness consumed her as he came to her, his claws and canines retracting as he lowered to his haunches. "Are you all right, lass?"

She gave a huff of laughter, amused that he would ask when the last time they saw each other, she'd broken his neck. "Oh, I'm super." Groaning, she got to her feet and scowled at the torn fabric of her shirt, trying to cover up as best she could. "Guess I know how that feels."

"That was a close call."

Thea looked into his eyes. He thought he was saving her life. Even if she was never truly in danger, his intention was to rescue her, so did that mean she owed him her life? Again?

You don't fear him because there's nothing to fear.

Suddenly the telepathic girl's words made sense. When Conall first approached her, her body didn't respond in warning before he revealed himself. Again, when she was hiding in the hostel in Wrocław, she hadn't sensed him until he was outside her door.

And in the theater.

Sure, she'd been a little preoccupied with the guy who had his fist in her chest cavity, but she'd felt the vampire in the music bar, yet she hadn't felt Conall. Wouldn't she have felt him as soon as he entered Prague if his goal was to hunt her?

Which it was.

He's important. His future affects your future. He's important, Thea.

She'd said, "The wolf." Did that even mean Conall?

And should Thea drive herself crazy trying to figure out the vague prophetic words of a stranger?

One thing was for sure, Thea could never outrun this werewolf, and he'd proven he was a force to be reckoned with.

She glowered at him, hating him for believing Ashforth's lies. Or maybe he just *needed* to believe them. "Who is it?"

The wolf's brows drew together. "What?"

"Who is the person you're trying to save with my blood?"

Conall's face blanked, and he crossed his arms over his chest. "This isnae the time or place for that discussion. We need to get out of here. Are you healed?"

"Completely."

He shook his head. "I've never met a supernatural who heals as quickly as you."

Remembering his broken neck, Thea eyed his strong throat. "You seem to heal fast too."

"I shifted." He reached out to take hold of her biceps. "The wolf in me is stronger. Shifting accelerates the healing process."

Letting him lead her up the aisle, she eyed his broad back. "So the bullet wounds are healed too?"

"Aye."

Thea tugged on his hold and he stopped, turning to her. "Dinnae fight me, lass."

You don't fear him because there's nothing to fear.

"I owe you my life again."

Conall smirked. "Aye. I know how much you hate that."

"I also know that it wasn't altruistic."

"Correct." He leaned toward her. "You mean one thing to me."

"Living, breathing, blood transfusion."

"Exactly." He hauled her more roughly down the aisle. "For that, you're lucky. Few people would get away with breaking my fucking neck."

Panic rose in Thea as she swiped up her dropped backpack and let the wolf hurry her out of the theater and into the main part of the old palace. She tried to get a hold on that anxiety, to think fast.

If Conall could track her, there was nowhere she could go to escape him. But if he didn't mean to hurt her, only to use her blood, then perhaps there was a way for her to get out of this. She knew he had some kind of contract with Ashforth, and one he wasn't willing to break for Thea because he believed Ashforth's lies.

The obvious option was to trust the werewolf with the truth.

Thea shuddered at the thought.

No. It was out of the question.

She never allowed herself to go back to that place, and she didn't trust the wolf to take him there with her.

The only thing to do was to bide her time.

An insidious voice whispered in her ear that it wasn't the only option available to her. If she killed Conall, she would be free again. Surely he knew that?

He's important. His future affects your future. He's important, Thea.

Thea attempted to throw away the young woman's prophetic words.

For now, the goal was to make Conall believe she needed him somehow. Men always thought women *needed* them. Maybe she could eventually convince him to work alongside her and they'd both get what they wanted.

If not … well … if it came down to her or the person he was trying to save, Thea was choosing herself.

Ultimately, if she had to, Thea *would* kill Conall, if it meant her survival.

11

CONALL FLICKED A LOOK AT THEA AS HE TOOK HER TO THE FOUR-STAR hotel he'd checked into upon his arrival. They'd taken the time, and therefore the risk, to clean the blood off her face and his hands in a public restroom in Lucerna Palace, and she'd changed her shirt. Luckily, no other vampires had sought them out.

Conall wasn't afraid of Thea running because he saw the moment in her eyes when she realized she could *never* run from him.

And he also knew the moment she'd realized her only option was to kill him.

That meant Conall was on high alert.

She was silent as she walked calmly at his side into the elevator. He watched her in his peripheral vision. Thea observed everything about their surroundings. At first, he thought it was because she was plotting but when they walked into the hotel room, he began to think otherwise.

Her steps slowed as she took in the room and her fingertips whispered across one of the luxurious twin beds. There was something vulnerable in her expression as she turned to him.

"This is nice." Her eyes darted away and she sat slowly down on the bed she'd touched. She looked uncomfortable.

She'd known poverty for a long time.

Remembering the shitty apartment in Budapest and the hostel where he'd found her in Wrocław, Conall felt a pang of some unknown feeling in his chest. Then, as he watched her smooth her hand over the bedding, her movements unconsciously graceful, he felt something else stir inside him.

Pity for the hellion was the last thing he needed.

She'd broken his goddamn neck, for Christ's sake.

She was a murderer.

And as she'd so eloquently put it, she was his sister's blood donor. Nothing else.

"You're acting as if you've never seen a nice room before and we both know that's not true. You must have been living in the lap of luxury as Ashforth's ward."

Her head whipped toward him and he saw outrage flicker in her dark eyes before she banked it. Whatever she'd momentarily wanted to say, she stifled the urge and stared at him.

It was unnerving.

Even more so since he felt a prickle of guilt he did not understand.

Eventually, she turned to the window, gazing at the dark world outside, her delicate profile at odds with the strength contained within her. "Since it looks like you're going to be sticking around, you should know those vampires were hired to capture me. I'm guessing by the same person who hired the humans who attacked us."

This unknown hunter was a concern. Conall nodded and sat down on the other twin, hungry and weary. He didn't want to be in Prague. He wanted to wake up to the sounds of a loch lapping at the shore, to the sight of the sky reflected in the tranquil waters.

Instead of to a bustling city and an enigmatic Thea Quinn.

On that thought, Conall realized he wouldn't be sleeping tonight.

She might murder him in his sleep.

"Ashforth is looking into it," he said, rubbing a hand over his tired eyes. "Whoever it is, he must have alerted local contacts to your possible arrival. Your energy, your scent, make you an easily identifiable target to supernaturals."

"Lucky me." She shot him a wry look. "So, what now?"

"I take you back to Scotland and we try to evade this mystery man until Ashforth gets to the bottom of it. Once we're in Scotland, you're his problem, not mine."

"How do you know I won't kill you?" she asked.

"I dinnae."

"I don't want to kill you, Conall."

He bristled at the sound of his name on her lips. "You'll never get the chance, lass."

There was silence between them until her belly grumbled. When he raised an eyebrow at her, she smirked. "Does my internment come with room service?"

Sighing, he got up off the bed and searched for a menu. Finding one, he handed it to her. "Pick something."

She browsed it and he watched an attractive flush crest her cheeks. "Anything?"

"Aye, anything."

Something like anticipation filled her expression. Conall ignored the appealing sound of the smile in her voice as she said, "I'll have the filet."

He ordered them both steak and immediately regretted it when the food arrived. Thea took her time over the meat, seeming to savor every second. As he watched her, it became harder to quiet the doubts in the back of his mind. Doubts, that if he were honest with himself, had been there from the beginning.

If Thea had the gift to make anyone believe whatever she wanted, if she was as strong as Conall knew she was, as fast, as goddamn powerful, then why was she living in poverty?

And why did the vampires in that theater get the better of her unless she'd been trying *not* to kill anyone?

Just as she'd broken his neck instead of killing him.

Why was she biding her time with him now? Why let him bring her to the hotel when she could have fought him in the theater?

Was it about owing him?

Or was there more to her story than Ashforth was telling?

Conall dragged his gaze away from her. The image of Callie's face as they said goodbye floated across his mind's eye, heavy with the hope and faith that he could find the cure to save her life.

Thea was Ashforth's problem. She'd murdered his family. She deserved his revenge.

And Callie deserved a chance at life.

That was all that mattered.

His doubts be fucking damned.

"If you think you can change my mind, think again," he told her abruptly as she finished her meal.

Her cognac eyes bored into his with so much soul, he had to fight a war inside himself. Conall wasn't sure if the side of his conscience that was winning was the selfish or the righteous.

"I need your blood to save my sister. She's dying from a lycanthropic disease called apogee. And I'd take on an army to protect her. Nothing else matters to me. Do you understand?"

Her expression was granite as she placed her empty plate on the sideboard and walked back to the bed. "I'm tired. A vampire tried to rip my heart out today, so I intend to sleep." She looked him directly in the eyes. "I don't have any plans to kill you tonight, Wolf Boy, so catch some z's too."

Despite the flare of irritation he felt at the ridiculous nickname, Conall also felt more than a flicker of amusement. "But you plan to kill me eventually?"

She was silent a moment and then answered, and his instincts told him she was being honest. "I don't know. What I do know is that there's someone else after me and you've saved my ass twice. I can't get rid of you, so I may as well make use of you."

Her words caused a stirring somewhere they shouldn't. Poor word choice on her part. "Make use of me?" His voice was gruff.

She flicked him a casual look as she kicked off her shoes and got into the bed, fully clothed. "Bodyguard." She reached up and switched off the lamp at her bedside.

Surprised, Conall snorted. "And here I thought you didnae need a bodyguard."

"Me too. Until a vamp punched a hole in my chest." Although she tried to hide behind levity, he heard the slight tremble of uncertainty in her words.

"Is that the closest you've come to death, lass?"

"No," she whispered, the duvet rustling as she turned her back to him. "Death and I are old friends."

DESPITE HER ASSURANCES, CONALL REFUSED TO SLEEP. INSTEAD, HIS MIND returned him to the events of the night, to the moment he'd tracked Thea's scent to the theater, when he walked in and saw the vampire punch a hole through Thea's chest as the others held her captive. Panic unlike anything he'd felt suffused him, and he'd acted on savage instinct.

One minute he'd been at the theater door, the next he was across the room, claws and teeth out. He'd swung his arm toward the vampire's neck with the force of an axe, pouring his rage into it.

He could still feel the moment his claws severed through skin, muscle, and bone, the impact juddering up his shoulder and into his teeth.

It was Conall's first vampire kill, and three more had followed. Guilt didn't come to him, however, as he laid staring at the hotel ceiling, listening to the almost imperceptible sound of Thea breathing.

Conall had vampire acquaintances, a few he even considered friends. They were based in Glasgow, though like most vamps, his friends liked to travel. Although Conall knew many vampires had no qualms about killing humans, they tended not to. A quick bite here and there was usually the extent of the damage they caused. But the older they got, the less empathetic many of them seemed to grow toward humans. And there were always the psychopaths among any species.

Mostly, vampires and werewolves kept their distance from one another. It was instinct. Some believed the reason for the natural discord was rooted in their origins, but then Conall didn't believe in the origin stories.

It was his opinion that vampires were generally arrogant, superior fuckers who thought they were better than wolves and *that* was the cause of their natural discord. Moreover, wolves tended to have more respect for human life because they too were mortal.

Still, Conall had never been moved to kill one before this evening. But killing those vampires had been easy as a possessive, protective instinct roared through his body at witnessing Thea's capture.

It wasn't because of Thea.

Seeing her close to death had made him realize how close he was to losing his last hope to save Callie. He turned his head on the pillow to stare at Thea in the dark.

Aye, that's all it had meant.

Being able to last longer on little sleep than a human was a major advantage when you didn't trust your companion not to kill you. Conall forced himself to sit up in bed, worried that the soft sounds of Thea breathing would lull him to sleep. Grabbing the phone Ashforth had given him off the nightstand, he downloaded a word search app Callie had gotten him addicted to and kept his brain awake with the distraction.

Minutes from dawn, Conall noticed the change in Thea's breathing. It stuttered and hitched, and he looked over at her, frowning. After a few seconds of nothing, just when he was about to turn back to the phone, she began to whimper.

He immediately suspected she was trying to trick him and silently swung his legs off the bed. As he did so, Thea made a garbled, choking sound, like she was in pain and holding it in. Hovering over her, Conall realized it wasn't a trick when he saw her hair sticking to her temple with sweat.

She'd screwed up her face in anguish in her sleep, her pretty lips pinched together in pain.

"Jesus," Conall muttered as she began to writhe. He reached out a hand to her shoulder to shake her awake. "Thea, wake up. It's just a dr—"

The room transformed into a blur of its muted colors and his breath was abruptly knocked out of him. The feel of Thea's warm body straddling his to the floor disoriented Conall until she wrapped her hands around his throat and began to choke him.

There was a glazed look of fury in her dark eyes as she squeezed.

Realizing she was locked in her nightmare, Conall rolled them. It wasn't easy. In fact, it took most of his strength. Her grip on his throat loosened as he flipped them and he grabbed her hands, pinning them to the floor at either side of her head. "Wake up, Thea!"

She struggled against him, her thighs tight around his hips, and shock moved through him as she snapped at his wrist like a wolf. Heat pooled deep in his groin where it pressed flush to hers.

Fuck!

Conall pushed off her, springing back on his haunches and just like that, she grew still except for the heaving of her chest. The neckline of her shirt had pulled down during their tussle and sweat glistened across the swell of her breasts.

He forced his eyes to her face, shaken by his response.

Angered by it.

"Jesus, fuck, woman, remind me never to wake you up from a nightmare again," he snapped.

She blinked rapidly. Confusion filled her low, melodic voice. "Conall?"

"Aye, it's me." He stood up and reluctantly held a hand out to her.

Thea eyed it suspiciously and sat up. "What happened?"

"You were having a nightmare. I made the mistake of trying to rouse you and you choked me."

Ignoring his outstretched hand, she rose to her feet, straightening her clothes without meeting his eyes. She brushed the long strands of her soft hair from her face and moved toward the bed, slumping down on it with a weary exhalation.

Curiosity got the better of him. "What was the nightmare about?"

Thea shot him a sardonic look. "Would you believe me if I said it was you?"

He grunted. "It pains me to say, but I think you fear me as much as a shark fears a wee fish."

Her lips twitched and the laughter that glittered in her eyes took Conall aback. "Not quite."

The basic ringtone of his temporary phone blasted, cutting off his quest to ask more about her nightmares. Striding across the room, Conall answered, his voice impatient and gruff with self-directed frustration. "This better be my sister."

The sound of Callie's gentle laughter soothed him. "Then thank goodness it is."

He hadn't realized until that moment how tightly wound he was about leaving Callie with Ashforth. Hearing her voice was a balm to the guilt he carried about letting his sister be used as a pawn in this hunt for Thea. Flicking a look at his prey, he noted she was watching him and listening in.

Fine.

He didn't care.

She should know how important Callie was to him. Understanding that would make her understand the hopelessness of her position. *This only ends one way*, he silently reminded her with his expression.

Or was he silently reminding himself?

"Are you all right?" He turned from Thea's intense regard.

"I'm fine. Some guards complain a lot among themselves. Apparently, our food is horrible, and the castle is cold."

Conall smirked. Wolves ran at hotter temperatures than humans and so the cold didn't bother them. Luckily for them because winters in the Highlands weren't exactly a Caribbean paradise. "Where do these guards come from?"

"There's a mingling of accents."

Conall nodded, thinking he'd get strategic information from James instead of grilling his sister. Once upon a time, as lead warrior, it had been her job to compile that kind of information, but Conall didn't want to tire her out. "But you're comfortable? They havenae done anything to you?"

"I'm very comfortable," she assured him. "He's given me the nicest bedroom in the castle and I have free roam of the place as long as a guard accompanies me. And James is always with me."

"Always?"

She chuckled. "He sleeps in a cot at the bottom of my bed. The perfect gentleman, to my great frustration."

"You didnae just say that to your brother," Conall heard James complain in the background.

Callie laughed, and he closed his eyes against the sound. That was all it took. It reminded him that if he didn't succeed in bringing Thea back to Castle Cara, there would be a short limit to the times he'd hear Callie laugh.

"Put James on, sweetheart."

"Okay. I miss you, big brother."

"I miss you too. I'll be home soon."

After a shuffling noise, his beta's voice filled his ear. "Conall?"

"She's doing okay?"

"Callie's fine. We're the best-treated prisoners in the world."

Conall bared his teeth. "Aye, not for long. How many guards?"

"It's not their numbers that worry me. Several of the night guards are vampires and Ashforth has lone wolves on the daytime guard. A few of them are big, mean buggers."

"Vamps and wolves?" He frowned. "I'd like to know how one human man can amass so many contacts in the paranormal community."

"Money. I've overheard the guards talking and they're being paid extremely well to guard us."

"Dishonorable fucks," Conall sneered. It was one thing to take the risk of going into business with a human who was emotionally blackmailing him to save his sister's life. It was another thing entirely to act as a prison guard against your own kind for the sake of something as fleeting as money.

But that was lone wolves for you.

"You doing okay, Chief?" James asked.

"Things … are a little complicated. It seems I'm not the only one after Ashforth's ward. But we'll be in Scotland in several days if all goes to plan."

They hung up with assurances to speak again soon and Conall looked over at Thea. She was standing by the window, the morning sun casting her in a halo of light as she stared out into the city. Feeling his regard, she glanced over at him. "I'm not Ashforth's ward. I'm not his anything, and you can't trust him."

Conall glowered at what he was sure was an attempt to manipulate him. Finally. He'd been waiting for her to take this path and was relieved he hadn't misjudged her. "And I suppose I should trust you instead?"

Thea shook her head. "You shouldn't trust anyone who can never trust you in return."

Struck silent by the weary wisdom of those words, Conall's scowl deepened. He wanted her to attempt to manipulate him. To fill his ears with lies about Ashforth. Instead, she continually surprised him.

The urge to *ask* for her side of her story was great, but he refrained. Conall now doubted Thea would tell him. She would have done so by now. There was a moment he thought she was going for it, and instead she'd chosen silence. That was frustrating for many reasons, mostly because he appreciated that she wasn't trying to manipulate him, just as much as he wished she fucking would.

The phone rang again and this time when Conall answered, it was Ashforth.

"I trust you're happy that your sister is being well cared for?" he asked without preamble.

"As much as I can be."

"And Thea? I assume you've caught up with her?"

"I have. Unfortunately, she was in a bit of bother with a few vampires who told her someone hired them to grab her. Any news on who this unknown hunter is?"

"There are rumors that a coven is after a young woman with healing blood and are willing to pay a reward to anyone who brings her to them. Thea's description has been passed along to several contacts throughout Europe." Anger was clear in Ashforth's words.

"She's still a needle in a haystack," Conall mused, not overly concerned. "What's the name of the coven?"

"The Blackwoods. They're a wealthy group of witches and warlocks from Maine. I came across them in my research years ago … but I have no idea how they could have discovered Thea's existence, let alone her abilities."

Conall sighed. "There's nothing to be done about it now. We'll avoid major cities." His eyes flickered to Thea who was staring at the floor. Her tense body language told him she was listening in. "Of course, this would be easier and faster if we could just take a plane back to Scotland."

Her gaze flew to his, and he marveled at how such warm, dark eyes could turn to black ice in an instant. "I guess plummeting to death *would* be faster than a road trip across Europe."

Amusement tickled his lips, but it instantly fled when Ashforth whispered, "Was that her? Is that Thea?"

There was something like reverence in his voice, except darker, desperate. It was not the tone of a man bent on revenge but something else entirely. Confused, Conall asked, "Why would this coven be interested in Thea's blood? If it's about her healing abilities, surely they could find a way to become an immortal; get bitten by a vampire. Or even a wolf if all they're interested in is some longevity and strength. They've got enough between them to pay supes to do it."

"Well, vampires are not true immortals," Ashforth's tone returned to normal. "They can still be killed."

"None of us are truly immortal."

"Yes, well, I don't believe immortality is the coven's goal, but I'm also not sure what is their goal."

Exasperated by what sounded like a lie, he replied shortly, "We'll drive through Germany, avoiding the cities if we have to stop. I willnae give you an estimated time of arrival since things arenae exactly going to plan at the moment."

"That's fine. Call in tomorrow at the same time. And tell Thea I'll see her soon."

Conall hung up, scowling at the phone.

"Hard for an alpha to take orders, huh?"

He half expected her to gloat. Instead, she eyed him like she was trying to figure him out.

"What was your nightmare about?" he asked before he could overthink his curiosity.

She held his gaze for a few seconds and Conall thought she might answer. Instead she moved away from the window and grabbed her small backpack off the floor. "I'm going to use the bathroom and then I could eat before we leave, if that's okay."

He pushed. "The nightmare, Thea?"

She sighed, a long, slow exhale. "You don't really want to know, Conall. You need to believe I'm your enemy, for your sister's sake."

"And you telling me about your nightmare … you think that will change things, do you?" Why the fuck was he pushing this?

"You said it yourself. *Nothing* will stop you from saving her life."

She was right. "Nothing, lass." He stood up slowly and Thea took a wary step back. "I'll protect you until we reach Scotland. Where I fully intend to hand you over to Ashforth as soon as you save my sister's life."

Thea didn't seem particularly upset by any of this but Conall suspected she was very good at hiding her feelings.

Not long later, after Thea had freshened up and pulled the masses of her rich, dark hair into a ponytail, Conall took the risk of using the bathroom to relieve himself but nothing more. He needed a fresh change of clothes; however, it would have to wait.

Leaving the hotel room, Thea fell naturally into stride beside him and he ignored the urge to look at her. When they stopped at the elevator, she reached to press the down button and when she lowered her arm, the back of her hand brushed against his. His skin tingled at the touch and he frowned at her.

"Sorry," she muttered, avoiding his gaze.

Consternated by his hyperawareness of her, Conall faced forward and scowled.

Thankfully, the doors opened with a musical *bing* and an older couple started to smile at them until they took in Conall's size. They shrank back against the elevator. Conall was immune to this kind of reaction and gestured for Thea to enter first, crowding in behind her.

As the doors closed, he glanced at her. Her eyes were downcast beneath her thick, sooty lashes. "So, no plans to kill me today?"

The couple sharing their elevator exchanged a wide-eyed look and Conall realized they spoke English. Oh well.

Thea looked up at him and her lush lips parted into a slow smile. "Not today." The elevator jolted to a stop, and she moved past him with a nonchalant shrug. "But there's always tomorrow."

12

THERE WAS NOTHING BUT THE SOUND OF THE ROAD WHOOSHING BENEATH their tires and the whir of cars passing by. The wolf apparently didn't like to listen to the radio. A little over an hour outside Prague, they'd driven directly through a border point to Germany without being stopped and were now taking the freeway just outside Dresden. Conall had barely said a word to Thea from the moment they'd stepped out of the elevator at the hotel. In fact, he'd been gruff throughout breakfast.

Thea wasn't oblivious. A big part of surviving the life she'd been living since she was nineteen years old was being able to read people. She'd studied body language and the way it betrayed even the most stoic. Of course, her spooky supernatural heightened instincts helped a lot.

The alpha, however, wasn't that easy to read. Yet she'd learned some stuff in one morning. Thea had learned his entire demeanor changed when he was talking on the phone to his sister. His harsh expression softened, and his voice heated from a cold gravel to a warm rumble. Thinking of the photograph she'd seen in his wallet, Thea wondered where his parents were in all of this. Were they dead? Was his sister the last of his family?

Thea also learned that Conall did not like Ashforth. She wasn't even sure the Scot was aware of his dislike for the American, but he wore this sneer on his face when he was talking to the bastard who had fucked up her life.

Finally, Thea observed something else about Conall over breakfast at the hotel. When she spoke, he watched her mouth. When she wasn't looking, she could feel his eyes on her face. When she first got into the car and leaned into the back to put her rucksack on the passenger bench, she caught his gaze moving swiftly away from her breasts. There was a barely perceptible flex of the muscle in his jaw as he stared mutely ahead.

If she wasn't mistaken, the wolf was attracted to her.

And he really, really didn't want to be.

The suspicion caused a strange fluttering in Thea's belly anytime she looked at him. She hadn't encountered anyone like Conall and wasn't exactly sure how to feel about his possible attraction to her.

She could try to use it as a weapon. Seduce and manipulate him. Thea flicked a look at him, her eyes traveling up his strong arms to his broad shoulders to his face. There wasn't an inch of softness to him. Not an ounce of fat anywhere. His jawline was strong and angular. He had high, severe cheekbones and a proud Roman nose. His scar was on the cheek facing away from her, but she could visualize it and the way it only added to the aura of mean fierceness that surrounded Conall.

His gray wolf eyes were shockingly pale compared to his unruly dark hair, and he was sporting stubble on his cheeks after days on the hunt across Europe.

The massive height and broad shoulders, not to mention the dark clothing and biker boots, screamed danger, and Thea had noted the way most people at the hotel had taken a wide berth around the alpha.

She got it.

He was scary on first impression.

However, during breakfast his scar seemed to lose its harshness, becoming a part of the interesting features that made up his masculine face, and Thea enjoyed studying him, trying to figure him out.

Her eyes moved to his mouth where his lips pressed together in concentration. Or was that annoyance? Because she knew he could feel her study. She wondered what he'd do if she suddenly kissed him. Thea felt a flutter much lower than her belly and yanked her eyes away in consternation.

What was that? she grumbled to herself.

There was no way she was attracted to this belligerent werewolf who was determined to hand her over to her number one enemy without a goddamn care what it meant for her.

She curled her lip in disgust at the thought.

Jesus, she had more self-respect than that.

Well, that was that. She would *not* seduce the wolf onto her side. She couldn't, anyway. He'd see right through the manipulation, the paranoid asshole that he was.

That didn't mean he *couldn't* be manipulated.

Thea had to admit she was curious about Conall and his sister and the pack he led. She knew only what she'd read in books about werewolves but knew little about the realities of pack life. She'd never been to Scotland, yet she'd met a lot of Scottish tourists and most of them could wax lyrical about Scotland for hours.

People, she discovered, loved talking about the things that made them happy. Perhaps if she found out more about Conall, if she showed an interest, that—along with her pretending she needed him to protect her—might soften him a little.

Friendship, Thea realized.

What she was suggesting was something akin to friendship.

Afterall, it was hard to hand over a friend to her worst enemy.

Would Conall see through it?

There was nothing Thea could do but try.

She looked over at him again and he shot her a quizzical look. "What is it, lass?" he asked impatiently.

"Ashforth is holding your sister prisoner, isn't he?"

"How clever of you to deduce that from your eary-wiggin'."

"'Eary-wiggin'? Does that mean listening in?" she asked, genuinely curious.

"Aye." He flicked her another impatient look. "Earwigging."

"It was hard not to. We were in the same room."

He grunted.

Thea tried not to smirk. He had serious caveman qualities. "Tell me about her. About your pack. How does that work?"

Conall's expression grew tight with obvious suspicion.

Jesus, he really was paranoid. Thea felt a prick of something that almost felt like hurt. She shouldn't be. Hurt, that was. Why should he trust her with anything when she didn't trust him?

And she definitely didn't trust him.

However, she was wondering if maybe she'd stopped fearing him. Okay, she feared where he was taking her, whom he was taking her to, but Conall? No. She didn't think so.

God, she was an idiot—listening to the words of a strange girl in a club and letting them dictate her feelings toward this werewolf. An image of him punching his clawed fists through the two vampires' chests as if they were made of polystyrene instead of flesh and bone came to her. Never mind the fact he'd decapitated a powerful vampire with one swipe of his claws.

She needed to remind herself the bastard was just as deadly as she was.

More so. She'd tried not to kill the vamps. Conall had taken them out without even thinking about it.

"We're going to be stuck in this car a while," she said, the words flat, "and since you refuse to put on the radio, I thought a little conversation might pass the time."

"Chart music is shite," he offered as an excuse for the lack of radio.

"Well, it's music or conversation. Those are your choices."

"I choose the lesser of two evils … My pack is the last in Scotland."

"And you're the alpha." It wasn't a question. She'd never met a wolf with more alpha in him than Conall.

"Aye. We're also one of the last clans in the Highlands that still operate like a traditional clan. I'm the chief. But that's hereditary. It has nothing to do with my wolf."

"Your wolf? So, do you think of that part of you as a separate being?" She was genuinely curious to know.

"Aye and no. It's complicated." His tone was brusque. "Next question."

Thea studied him thoughtfully, wondering if she should ask what was on the tip of her tongue. Finally, she went for it. "If you're the chief, then I take it your mom and dad aren't around anymore?"

His fists tightened around the steering wheel, the action betraying emotion his face sought to hide. "My dad invested in shares in oil and was invited to tour some rigs in the North Sea. He was on the platform of one when the rig exploded, killing him and many of the workers." He let out a huff of bitter laughter. "He was Clan MacLennan's strongest alpha in centuries, and he was felled by an oil rig explosion."

"I'm sorry," she whispered. And she truly was. If anyone knew what it felt like to lose someone in such a horrific way, it was Thea.

"Aye, well, my mum was devastated. She was an alpha female, so she advanced not only to pack alpha but to chief of the clan. Predators came out of the woodwork to take advantage of her grief."

"What do you mean?"

"Any alpha can challenge another for control of their pack."

"Any? From anywhere? How is that fair?"

He smirked at her indignation. "It's the way of things. Most packs dinnae suffer from strangers challenging their leadership. But Pack MacLennan is not only the last pack in Scotland, we're also the owners of GlenTorr Whisky and a profitable fishing company."

Thea raised an eyebrow. GlenTorr Whisky was one of the most famous whisky brands in the world. She'd served more than a few glasses of the stuff in her time as a bartender.

"These greedy bastards came in and challenged your mom?"

"Aye. And a challenge cannot be unmet."

Realization dawned. "One of them killed your mom."

Conall looked at her again and Thea's breath caught at the fury in his eyes. Oh, this wolf carried a lot of anger. *I know the feeling, Wolf Boy,* she whispered to herself, feeling a sudden affinity with him.

"I think she wanted to lose." He looked away, that muscle ticking in his jaw again. "I dinnae think she could bear life without my dad."

For some stupid reason, Thea felt her throat thicken with emotion and she turned to look out the window while she tried to control the feeling. It was just … She couldn't imagine what it must be like to love that deeply. Or to be loved like that.

Her parents had loved her.

She clung to that. Always.

But it differed from romantic love. Thea wasn't much for romance. She curled a lip at the thought. Nah. It wasn't something she'd ever encountered or ever expected to even if she lived forever.

The sudden thought of eternity made her shudder, like always.

"She barely took her last breath when I challenged the wolf who killed her," Conall continued. "I became alpha to the relief of the clan, but I was challenged many times. Remaining undefeated for so long finally settled things. There hasnae been a challenge to the leadership in four years."

"You killed them all?"

"A wolf can give in during the challenge by showing his belly. It's an act of submission. They leave the fight in dishonor, but they leave alive. I only had to kill a few. And only one of them left a parting gift."

Her eyes flew to him and he turned to her, revealing the deep scar that scored his skin from the tip of his eyebrow to the corner of his mouth. He ran a thumb down the scar. "He used a silver blade before the shift." He returned his attention to the road.

Thea curled her lip in disgust. "Cheating bastard."

Conall gave a snort of laughter. "Aye. But I was stronger than him."

"You won. Obviously."

"Aye, but not just because I was stronger." His expression was hard, fierce. "I won because I care more. All he wanted was power and money. I want to protect my pack. The pack is everything to me. *Family* is everything to me. I'll never stop protecting what's important to me, even if I have to die doing it."

Thea stared at him, transfixed for a moment.

If his vow didn't mean handing her over to the worst piece of scum who ever lived, Thea would admire the heck out of the wolf for his passionate dedication.

"And word reached the supernatural community of my ability to track." Conall shot her a pointed, challenging look. "Few people want to piss off a wolf who can find you wherever you hide."

"Hence why I'm stuck with you." She shot him a dirty look and leaned her elbow on the door. Resting her chin in her palm, Thea watched the cars and the German countryside pass by. "Are the Highlands as beautiful as they look in pictures?"

Conall was silent so long, she turned to see if he'd heard her question.

He glanced at her, something warm in his eyes, a little curl to the corner of his mouth that caused an inexplicable feeling of nervousness in her stomach. "Lass, my Loch Torridon holds a beauty unlike anything you've ever seen."

Another flutter of nerves unsettled her as she realized she wanted to see it. She wanted to visit the place that could crack Conall MacLennan's ice-cold facade and put that too-attractive boyish wonder in his eyes.

Remembering she would see it when he handed her over to Ashforth killed the stupid fluttering, and she yanked her eyes from his to stare out the window. "I wonder if there'll be a window in my Scottish prison cell. I'd so hate to miss out on the scenery."

The car filled with immediate tension she didn't understand until Conall bit out in irritated dryness, "You're a wee bit optimistic, Thea Quinn."

She frowned. "How so?"

His eyes hardened. "You killed his wife. I doubt you'll live long enough to see a prison cell once I hand you over."

Years-old grief sliced into her gut. God, he was an idiot. She laughed bitterly and turned away, suppressing the urge to tell him that death would be a blessing over what Ashforth intended for her.

Silence fell between them again and this time Thea let it. She decided she couldn't even feign friendship with an asshole who couldn't see Ashforth for what he really was. The guy was holding his sister captive in exchange for Thea's blood, for God's sake! Did that not clue Conall in, even a little?

Werewolves.

More brawn than brain.

The thick tension that had fallen between them felt suffocating in its silence, but Thea was too pissed to engage him in any further conversation.

She guessed they were around thirty minutes outside Dresden when she felt a warning tingle on the back of her neck. Her heart began to race, and that familiar feeling of dread settled in her gut.

Oh shit.

She glanced in her wing mirror, eyes dancing over the cars behind them. A black sedan that weaved in and out of the fast lane in the distance caught her attention.

"Wolf Boy."

"If you expect me to answer to that, you've got another thing coming."

"Fine. Wolf Dude, we're being followed."

Conall shot her a look of surprise. "What makes you say that?"

"Call it a hunch." The sedan was getting closer. "Black sedan. Czech license plate."

He glared into the rearview mirror. "You're sure?"

"You know how you have that creepy smelling talent?"

Conall's low growl almost made Thea laugh.

"Well, I have a talent for sensing when I'm in deep shit." She turned around to stare out the back window and saw the black sedan getting closer. "And I'm sensing a huge pile of manure heading my way."

"How the fuck did they find us?" He hit the gas pedal and swung out into the fast lane to overtake.

During breakfast Conall had filled her in about the Blackwood Coven. "How did Ashforth know about the coven? Contacts, right? So maybe he let something slip to the wrong person."

"Aye, maybe." He bared his teeth as he stared into the rearview mirror. "And our license plate would have been tagged at the border point. They're gaining us. We need to get off this motorway and dump this car."

"Keep driving." Thea touched the sat nav screen Conall was using to drive them to Calais and widened out the map.

"Fuck!" Conall swerved hard and Thea fell against the passenger door. "Sorry, lass. Fucking lorry."

Making the decision that ignoring the road and Conall's driving was better for her heart, Thea concentrated on the map. Just because she couldn't die in a car crash didn't mean she wanted to experience one. "Okay, we're coming up to a slip road. You come off it, go around a traffic circle, and back under the freeway. There's a town about ten minutes behind us where we can hide," she said, urgently. "Now!"

Conall swerved off the freeway, the car skidding down the slope that led to the traffic circle. Thea held onto the dashboard and door as he swung them around, kicking up dust. "Dinnae tell me you're afraid!" He threw her a smug look as he thrust the vehicle forward under the freeway.

She grimaced. "A car crash won't kill me, but it might kill someone else."

He frowned but kept pushing forward at high speed. "They're still on us."

Thea glanced in the wing mirror, seeing the black sedan gaining on them. Her heart pounded. "Conall …"

"I see them. I'm going as fast as this fucking shithole of a car will let me."

Thea braced as the black sedan flew up beside them. The blacked-out driver's side window rolled down and a woman wearing dark sunglasses appeared. She smirked, lifting her hand. "Conall, gun!"

He let go a flurry of curse words mixed in with thick Scots she couldn't understand as he swerved into their pursuers, trying to shake them off the road. But they were determined.

When a red car appeared out of nowhere on the oncoming side of the road, everything changed. The new arrivals beeped their horn at Thea's pursuers and dread filled her as she realized the black sedan had no intention of getting out of the way.

Thea watched the couple's faces in the oncoming car as they realized too. Pure horror. The driver swerved too late, surprising their pursuers. The black sedan veered to miss them; it flew past the trees and bounced with such force into the field beyond, it flipped over. Good fucking riddance.

Behind her Thea heard the sickening sound of metal crunching. It was a sound she knew all too well. Looking back, she saw the red car had driven with full force into one of the many trees that edged the freeway. The passenger door opened, and a body tumbled out just as the front of the car went up in flames.

A small, terrified face appeared in the back window.

Shit.

"Conall, turn back."

"We cannae."

"There's a kid in that car!"

Cursing, he wrenched the steering wheel and the vehicle almost skidded off the road into the field. "That car will explode at any moment, Thea."

Ignoring his warning, she threw open her door before he'd come to a complete halt and was a shadowy blur across the roadway. A woman lay unconscious on the ground by the passenger door, but Thea's priority was the little girl crying in the back of the car.

She wrenched open the back-passenger door, feeling the heat from the flames that had consumed the crumpled hood. She reached for the terrified girl. "Come on, I got you." She tried to sound encouraging, not even sure if the girl spoke English.

"Rette meinen Papa. Du musst meinen Papa retten!" The kid fought against her as one word made itself clear amongst the German.

Papa.

Looking into the front, she saw the man's body. He was either dead or unconscious. Oh shit.

"Okay. I'll get your papa," she promised. Done letting the kid struggle, she wrenched her out of the car against her will and turned to watch as Conall pulled the mother to safety. She shot across the roadway to him and held out the girl.

"Where are you going?" She heard him yell as she returned to the crash.

Flames lashed out at Thea and her heart raced. The car was ready to blow. Rounding the driver's side, she held up an arm against the heat and saw the dad was alive. His eyes were shut, blood trickled down his temple, and his legs were mangled where the front of the car had crushed into him, but he was groaning in his unconscious state.

The metal handle was hot to the touch, but Thea would heal

quickly from any burns. She wrenched open the buckled door, and it fell off the hinges with the strength of her yank. Flames licked at the cracked windshield, warning her of imminent explosion.

Unbuckling the guy's belt, she eyed his legs. They were trapped.

"Jesus Christ."

Pressing her hand against the melting dashboard, Thea winced against the burns that would have agonized a normal person and pushed with all her might. The mangled car slowly began to give under the force of her will.

A popping sound made her heart stop. Pushing the crumpled machinery could cause it to explode even faster.

"Oh, come on, come on," she muttered frantically, begging the car to budge just a little more.

She heard Conall roaring her name just before she felt him at her back.

"Thea, we need to get back, now!"

"Back up!" she yelled over her shoulder.

The car creaked one last time.

It was enough.

"Thea!"

"I've got him." She slid her arms around the man and struggled to pull him out. His legs were a mess. She turned to find Conall still waiting. He looked like he wanted to kill her, but he said nothing, instead taking the injured man from her with ease.

Together they were streaks of movement up the road to the waiting mother and daughter.

The explosion behind them caused a gust of wind to blow Thea's hair up and around her face, momentarily blinding her. She smoothed it down impatiently, glad to feel the burns on her palms had already healed.

Crying over her mother's unconscious body, the little girl didn't even acknowledge the car's explosion. Her eyes were on her father, whom Conall laid on the road beside her. His daughter fell over him, crying in relief.

Thea felt something settle inside. Feeling Conall's attention, she looked up to find him staring at her as if he'd never seen her before. It was intense. Really intense. Another flutter of nerves made themselves known in her belly.

Just as she was about to ask him what his problem was, the sounds of sirens filled their ears. Someone had called the emergency services.

"We need to leave." Conall seemed torn about it as he glanced from the injured family to the black sedan lying upside down in the field. "If the people inside that car arenae human, we dinnae have much time to get out of here."

The words were barely out of his mouth when the back-passenger door of the sedan heaved open, an arm appearing.

"Yeah, we need to go." She nudged him toward the car and looked down at the little girl. Guilt suffused her but the sirens were growing ever closer. The kid would be fine. Just as long as her mom and dad woke up.

Things didn't look good for her dad.

Thea's heart ached but she shoved down the pain as she and Conall grabbed their rucksacks and belongings, abandoned their vehicle and ran into the cover of the forest that ran beside the freeway. Thea sent a prayer out into the universe. She wasn't certain she believed in God, but if He did exist, she asked Him to watch over the kid, to make sure she didn't end up alone.

THE TREES CAMOUFLAGED THEM AS THEY RAN AT FULL SPEED. THEA WAS faster than Conall, but he did an admirable job of trying to keep up. There was forestation all along the freeway, toward the town Thea had intended Conall to drive to, which provided much-needed cover.

Given their speed, they arrived quicker than they would have in the car. The tingling never abandoned Thea's neck, so she knew her pursuers were still after her. She and Conall cut southeast through fields and trees, and she'd never longed for the dark of night more.

"I can hear them. They're werewolves." Conall grabbed Thea's biceps, pulling her to a halt. "We cannae lead them into a town if they're armed. We've caused enough damage." He searched the fields in the distance and Thea saw her own guilt mirrored in his eyes.

"There." He pointed to what looked like industrial farm buildings.

They fled across the fields and stopped within the protection of the trees surrounding the largest of the buildings.

Conall held a finger to his lips, and she stayed silent. Her hearing was good. His was better.

Finally, he looked down at her. "Empty."

"I'm guessing this is a kill-or-be-killed situation."

"Aye." He took off his rucksack and urged her to do the same. After hiding them behind a tree, he nudged her in front of him and they crouched low as they broke out of the trees and dove against the building. Conall pulled the large double doors open and Thea followed him inside.

It *was* entirely empty.

There were stalls and chunky metal gates everywhere but no animals and no people. There wasn't even a strong smell of animal waste in the air, just a musty scent and sparse bits of old hay scattered about.

Her eyes swept over the disused barn.

Unfortunately, there was nowhere they could set up a defensive position. Everything was out in the open.

The thought had barely processed when the tingling on her neck increased. "Conall—" She whipped around as two female wolves stormed into the barn, handguns blazing.

Thea's body moved before she could think, instinct fueling her speed as she jumped in front of Conall and felt the bullets ricochet through her like hot stings. She shoved the Scot with such force, he flew into the air out of the way of the spray.

Thea turned as the wolves reloaded and she thanked fuck they weren't packing automatics as she pushed through the awful feeling of having metal foreign objects lodged in her back. Two were through and through. Three were not.

Dipshits.

It took seconds to kill them.

Break wrist holding gun. Tear heart out of chest. Rinse and repeat.

A deep sadness filled Thea as she stared down at the two women, but she knew she had to kill them. If she'd merely knocked them out, they would have come after them again, and Thea needed time to take care of the three bullets inside her.

Whoever this coven was, they underestimated her. They weren't exactly sending their finest to fight her. Well, except for the strong vampire in Prague who Conall had annihilated. Speaking of which ...

Groaning, she bent down and picked up the handgun, releasing the magazine. Silver bullets winked in the light. Just as she'd suspected. These weren't for her.

Hearing Conall moving across the barn toward her, she turned and showed him.

He stared fiercely at the bullets and when his eyes finally met hers, she saw confusion and something she didn't quite understand burning in his pale gaze.

Feeling a bullet lodge itself a little deeper into her back, hot blood soaking her shirt, Thea dropped the gun. "Uh ... we need to get to a bathroom."

Conall reached for her, spinning her around. "Jesus fuck, Thea. How many?"

"Five, but one in my arm and another in my shoulder were through and through. There are three in my back."

He reached for the hem of her top. "Let me—"

"No!" Panic suffused her at the thought of him tending to the wounds. "I can do it."

Anger radiated out of the wolf and he gave her a clipped nod. "I need to bury the bodies in the woods. Can you wait?"

Waiting sounded a whole lot of not fun, but Thea knew they needed to cover their tracks. She nodded.

Conall was remarkably fast and efficient, though he wore a grim expression as he buried the wolves who had been sent to specifically kill him and capture her.

He came back, their rucksacks in hand, looking pissed and distracted at the same time. "Let's go."

Sweat trickled down Thea's temples as she followed him out. As they walked into the yard, she could feel a bullet move deeper with every step. She wasn't going to make it into town.

"We need to find an empty farmhouse or something." She ignored the pinching pain all over her back.

"Aye, your back is soaked in blood." He grimaced. "If someone sees you, we're done for."

"Well, it looks like it might be our lucky day," she said with more glibness than she felt as they walked out of the farmyard to encounter a road. It appeared to lead straight into town and across it were two houses nestled among the trees.

Conall hurried them toward the houses and pushed her behind a tree. "Wait here while I check things out."

As she waited, Thea reached a hand behind her neck, sliding it beneath her shirt where she felt a bullet in her shoulder. Tweezers would be good, but this bullet wasn't lodged too deep. She dug her fingers in, wincing. Thea yanked it out just as Conall reappeared.

He eyed the squashed silver bullet in her blood-covered hand and shook his head.

"What?" she snapped, growing irritated by the pain in her back. Her irritation, however, fled at the expression in Conall's usually icy eyes. There was something warm in them.

"You're tough as leather, lass."

Annoyed by the prickle of pleasure she felt at his words, she rolled her eyes. "Admire me later. Do we have an empty house?"

"Aye. This way. But we best be fast."

"It would really not suck if you'd stop stating the obvious." She hurried after him, up a gravel drive toward a quaint family house with a red-tiled roof.

He pushed open the front door, which he'd clearly broken during his reconnaissance of the property. "No alarm, if you can believe it."

Thea studied the cream carpets as he strode right on in. "Well, some people aren't expecting a werewolf and whatever the hell I am to break into their house." She wrinkled her nose. "Where's the bathroom?"

"Come in and see."

"No. I need to *whoosh* there, so I don't get blood on the carpet."

Understanding, Conall strode farther into the house and returned seconds later. He handed her a small black cloth bag. It was his first aid kit. "Down the hall, last door on the right."

Thea found what she needed in the kit. She used forceps scissors to dig all but one bullet out. Sweat coated her skin as she tried to bend her body to reach the bullet that had lodged deeper than the others right in the middle of her back. Realizing they were running out of time, she decided she'd have to leave it until they got to safety in a hotel somewhere.

The other bullet holes closed over and she cleaned them up as best she could. Bandaging over the hole made by the bullet she couldn't get to, Thea then searched her rucksack for her last shirt. She pulled it on and stuffed the bloody one into the backpack. Once she'd dressed, Conall came into the bathroom to help her clean up any evidence of their presence.

Her heart rate kept up a fast pace as they hurried into the town. The Scot had to remind her to slow her steps. They had to appear casual. Thea thought it a shame they were venturing into the picturesque Saxon town of Wilsdruff under such circumstances. As they walked across the cobbled town square, she ignored the way people stared at them. Or Conall, to be specific. There was no way to make him inconspicuous.

"We need to get out of here," he grumbled. "And I dinnae want to steal a car."

"You may have to abandon your scruples on that one if they don't have a bus station." Thea winced as a sharp pain shot through her back. A sign for accommodation caught her eye. "We need to stop, anyway."

"We cannae," he said, matter-of-fact and annoyingly bossy. "We need to keep moving in case the girl gives our description to the authorities. I wouldnae blame her after what we did to her parents."

"We didn't do it." Thea ignored the aching pang in her chest. "Those asshole female wolves did it. As for us, we need to move, yes. But first I have to stop somewhere with a bathroom. And I need time."

"Why?" He halted, turning to her.

Anyone else might have been intimidated at the way he towered over her, his expression forbidding, his scar stark against his tan cheeks.

Thea was too pissed to be intimidated.

The bastard hadn't even thanked her for saving his goddamn life.

"Because one of the bullets I took for you is still lodged in my back and I need time to get it out."

His scowl deepened. "I can do it."

Her stomach lurched at the thought. "Uh … no thanks." She swerved around him and kept walking. "This sign says there's a hotel somewhere."

Conall didn't argue. "Fine, but we cannae stay long."

"You can go out and find either a bus station or a car while I deal with the bullet."

The rest of their walk was silent as the wolf stewed at her side. The accommodation turned out to be a stone-built hotel on the outskirts of town. It was quaint and far nicer than Thea would have preferred. People who ran nice hotels paid attention to their customers.

The owner looked terrified of Conall, and Thea cursed him for being so easily recognizable.

"It's like trying to hide a *T. rex* behind a MINI Cooper," she grouched as they walked down the red-carpeted corridor to their room.

"Well, if you'd let me help you with the bloody bullet back at the house, we wouldnae be here, showing my scarred face to potential witnesses," he snapped back.

She frowned. "It's not your scar that's the problem. It's your size." She led them into the room. It was small with two tiny twin beds they, unfortunately, wouldn't be using.

And an even smaller bathroom.

Instead of leaving to see about transportation, Conall insisted on waiting while Thea got the bullet out. She stood in the cramped bathroom, feeling him too close to her on the other side of the door, wishing he'd get the hell out of the room so she could muddle along by herself.

Pulling her shirt up and over her head, she glanced at her back in the mirror, reached behind her to rip off the bandage, and then opened the first aid kit for the forceps.

Angling her arm this way and that, Thea could touch the bullet hole with the medical scissors, but she couldn't seem to stretch quite enough to dig in.

Grunting, she was determined to do it.

But try as she might, she could not get the goddamn bullet.

Frustration got the better of her and she let out a low growl.

"For fuck's sake"—the door flew open—"let me see the—" Conall slammed to a halt as his eyes drifted down her bare back.

Thea's stomach pitched, nausea welling inside her as the wolf gobbled up the sight of her in all her messed-up glory.

13

CONALL COULD HEAR THEA struggling inside the bathroom and it was pissing him off. His mind hadn't stopped racing since the car accident.

First there was the guilt of involving innocent civilians in the hunt, and of then having to leave the wee lass and her broken parents behind. But protecting his world, his pack, was the priority, even if it made him feel like the biggest wanker on the planet.

As for Thea …

Conall considered himself a good judge of character but walking through the small German town with Thea by his side, he questioned everything she'd done in the last hour.

Why had she gone back for the little girl in the car and then risked a lot of pain to save the girl's father?

Why had she shoved Conall out of the way of the spray of silver bullets and taken five shots to the back in the process?

Was it all some grand manipulation to win him to her side?

And even if it was … fuck, he'd never met anyone as tough as this woman.

Hearing her struggle to get the last bullet out pricked at Conall's guilt. Manipulation or not, she'd saved his life, and it pissed him off she wouldn't let him help her in return.

Finally, when she let out a low growl of frustration, Conall's patience died. If she was afraid of him seeing her seminaked, she needed to get over it. They had to get the hell out of this place in case the little girl gave their description to the authorities.

"For fuck's sake," he snapped, pushing into the bathroom, "let me see the—" His words cut off at the sight before him.

Thea stood at the small bathroom sink, shirtless, with her arm twisted up her back, a bloody pair of medical scissors fisted in her hand. It wasn't the seeping, inflamed bullet hole in the middle of her upper back that shocked him into silence.

Conall's gut twisted as he took in the mass of scars that crisscrossed Thea's slender back. It looked as though someone had taken a whip to her. Brutally. Many, many times.

Confused, he shook his head, trying to make sense of it. Thea's healing abilities were second-to-none … What could have caused permanent damage?

He thought of his own scar, created by a wolf's one weakness.

Silver.

So what was Thea's weakness?

The black concoction in the syringes came to mind.

The syringes Ashforth had given him.

An unexpected rage began to build in Conall as he lifted his gaze from evidence of abuse on Thea's back to the horror that darkened her eyes to black. "How did this happen?"

"Now that you've barged in without an invitation," she said, glaring and covering her breasts with one arm while she held out the scissors with another, "you might as well try pulling out the bullet."

Stunned to silence by her seething anger that dared him to question her further, Conall could only stare. What the fuck was going on here?

"If you aren't going to help, get the hell out."

Scowling, Conall took the scissors. "Face forward," he said gruffly. He dug the small forceps into her back and other than the rigid line of her spine, Thea gave away nothing of her pain. Just when he worried the bullet had moved too deeply inside her, Conall felt it. She made a low sound in her throat as he tried to catch hold of it.

"Sorry, lass, this one is tricky."

She merely nodded.

Finally, Conall got hold of the misshapen bullet and pulled it out. He watched in awe as the bloody, swollen hole in her back closed over, good as new, as if it had never been there. Their eyes met in the mirror and he held transfixed, watching her pallor brighten to a healthy glow.

What the hell was she?

"I'm naked here."

Conall glanced down at where she had her arms wrapped around her bare breasts. She covered her nipples well enough, but her arms were too slender to cover much else of their full lushness.

Heat flushed through him and he wrenched his eyes away, dropping the forceps and the bullet in the sink. He gave his hands a quick wash and turned from her.

"I'll see about transportation." He strode out, willing the sudden and throbbing need from his body. To do so, he mentally forced his last image of her out of his head and replaced it with that of her scarred back. Just like that, the heat transformed from desire to rage. The vehemence of it took him aback but he couldn't deny he felt it.

It was obvious Thea didn't want to talk about it, but as much as Conall wished this whole fucking situation between her and Ashforth was black and white …

Och, it wasn't.

Before he returned her to Ashforth, he needed to know who whipped her so brutally her back was a checkerboard of scars. Then Conall had to find out what Thea was. The clue would be in whatever was used to harm her. Whatever was in those syringes. Her weakness would lead them to her origins.

Gritting his teeth in frustration at the mess he'd found himself in, Conall pulled out his phone as he exited the hotel and googled the nearest bus station. It was a two-hour walk toward Dresden. He'd have to go back for Thea but first, Conall wanted to check they had the all clear out of town.

Following his phone's directions, Conall approached the exit onto the road that would lead out of the typical Saxon gingerbread town and abruptly retreated. There were two police cars stationed on the road out of town. Cursing under his breath, Conall disappeared up a side street.

The girl had probably given their description to the police. He didn't blame the wee lass.

He considered their options. There was a huge possibility the police were stationed at all exits. After all, they were looking for not just two but four suspects. It would be a shitshow if anyone dug up those bodies before Conall could tell Ashforth about them.

Ashforth.

As much as he hated asking for help and especially asking that arsehole for aid, they were trapped. Conall needed to get on the road again so he could work out what the fuck was really going on.

It shouldn't matter, he knew that.

All that should matter was Callie.

But if Thea wasn't who Ashforth said she was …

"Fuck," he bit out. Since when did he overanalyze shit? *Indecisive arsehole*, he huffed at himself. He called Ashforth, and the man picked up on the second ring.

"Is something wrong?"

"Aye, you could say that. Someone knew what car we were driving, Ashforth, so someone betrayed you."

The man was silent for a moment. "I … see."

"No, you dinnae see. They chased us off the motorway and caused a civilian accident. It was two female wolves. Thea killed them and I buried them in the woods. I'll text you the coordinates and I'll need you to clean that up."

"Very well."

"We're also trapped in a town called Wilsdruff. There were witnesses and now the police are manning the exits out."

"Witnesses? Who?"

Something made Conall hesitate. "I dinnae know who or how many," he lied, "but it was quite a scene we caused."

The usually stoic businessman let out a string of curses.

"Where are you now?" he finally snapped.

That rage simmering inside Conall began to build, and the wolf revealed itself in his voice when he replied, "I'd be very careful how you speak to me."

Ashforth cleared his throat. "I apologize. It's just a little bit of an inconvenience."

"Can you get the police off our backs here or not?"

"Yes, but it may take a few hours. Do you have somewhere to hide?"

"We're staying in a small hotel on the edge of the town but if the authorities come calling, the owner will identify me right away."

"It's a risk you'll just have to take. I'll call you when the coast is clear."

Conall hung up and walked back the way he came, sticking to the shadows. He tapped into his connection with Thea without even thinking about it, and he took a second to realize that she wasn't bloody where he left her.

Growling under his breath, Conall felt his wolf tremble for release.

She was trying to run from him.

Again.

The knot in Thea's gut wouldn't loosen. It just seemed to wind tighter as she hurried along the edges of town, hoping against hope she didn't bump into Conall.

Rationally she knew that he could find her but the hope she was wrong about his ability to track her kept her moving. She couldn't face him again. She couldn't face the inevitable questions about her back.

And not because she didn't want to tell him, warn him, just how evil Ashforth was, but because she thought he might not believe her if she did.

Why did he have to see her scars? Did they repulse him?

Oh, who gives a shit. She never had before.

Throwing the thought away, Thea realized she was wandering aimlessly. She had no idea where the bus station was or if there was one. She turned left down a street she was sure was only one or two over from the main square, thinking how glad she was to be without Conall—for many reasons, most important of which was that he was beyond conspicuous—when she felt the hair on her neck rise.

Too late.

A strong hand clamped down on her biceps and she looked up into Conall's angry face just as he dragged her between the dark alley of two stores. "What the hell?" She ripped her arm from his and stumbled against the wall.

Damn his goddamn tracking weirdness!

The wolf glared at her.

He was a volcano of intimidation, but she refused to quake beneath him.

Thea threw up her hands. "Oh, come on. I just thought I'd test out your little nose trick; make sure there wasn't any permanent damage to it from the car accident. But it looks like it's still working." She dared to slap his upper arm. "Congratulations."

The muscle in his jaw flexed so hard, the scar on his cheek rippled. *Okay, so that's a little intimidating.*

"Do you think this is a joke? There are police all over this town looking for us, Thea. They've blocked the exits. And you're trying to fucking take off again!"

Narrowing her eyes, Thea stepped toward him. "Well, if there are police hunting us, maybe you should keep your voice down."

He lifted his hands and clenched them, like he was dreaming of fisting them around her throat. "I have enough on my plate without you running off, especially when you know it's fucking futile."

"I went for a walk," she lied.

Conall bent his head toward her, his nose almost touching hers, his eyes hard with knowledge. "You ran away so you wouldnae have to explain your back."

Thea felt her anger and fear building and building, reminding her of all the times she'd lost control. She clenched her own fists, trying to even out her breaths.

"Thea." Conall took hold of her shoulders, concern stealing the irritation from his expression. "Your eyes."

Realizing they'd probably turned golden, Thea tried harder to control the energy that was rising inside of her.

"Why are you afraid?" Conall whispered.

She shook her head frantically. "I'm not afraid." And telling her she was wasn't helping.

"I can smell it, lass," he said. "I'm not going to hurt you."

"It's not"—she shook her head again—"it's not that …"

Conall's grip on her shoulders turned bruising. "Police," he bit out, before he shoved her up against the alley wall, pressing the full length of his body to hers.

The action pulled her from her mounting panic, distracting her. Thea listened and could hear the approaching footsteps and the sound of conversation over a police radio. Finding her control again, she mentally reached out to the shadows and felt Conall stiffen against her as she cloaked them.

She looked up at him, her heart stuttering at how close his face was.

What are you doing? His eyes asked.

Trust me.

The footsteps stopped at the alley and Conall looked over his shoulder, his body rigid, ready for a fight. Thea grabbed his waist, restraining him, and he looked down at her. She shook her head.

They heard the two officers exchange a few words before they spoke into the radio. And then they disappeared.

As soon as they were gone, Thea felt Conall relax and in doing so, she became aware of the fact that almost every inch of his hard body was touching hers and that she was gripping onto his waist. The heat and power of him was overwhelming and …

A tingling of heat between her legs increased in intensity by the second.

She flushed at the embarrassing realization she was getting turned on.

Conall let out a guttural sound of disbelief and Thea's eyes flew upward. His nostrils flared, his lids heavy over his eyes as he stared down at her in realization too.

Oh shit, could he smell that she wanted him?

Horrified by the thought, Thea dropped her hands from his waist. "You can get off me now."

After a moment's hesitation, he pushed off from the wall and took a few steps back. "What was that?"

The blood in her cheeks turned hot. "Uh … what?"

If she wasn't mistaken, the wolf looked like he was trying not to laugh.

If he laughed, she'd kill him.

"The shadows," he said pointedly, an arrogant smirk quirking his lips.

Oh crap, he definitely smelled her.

That was disturbing.

Turning away from him so he couldn't see how mortified she was, Thea shrugged. "It's just something I can do."

"It's something vampires can do too."

Thea whipped around to glare at him. "I'm not a vampire."

"I know that. So what are you?"

"I honestly don't have the answer to that."

Conall took a step toward her, his expression unexpectedly tender. "Aye, you do. The answer is on your back."

Her stomach tightened into that ugly knot. "How do we get out of here if the police are crawling all over the place?"

To her surprise, Conall allowed the subject change. "Ashforth is dealing with it. All we can do is hide out at the hotel until he calls to tell us we can leave."

They peered out onto the street, saw the coast was clear, and made their way back to the hotel. "You don't strike me as someone who particularly enjoys having to rely on anyone else."

Conall sighed. "You mean Ashforth?"

Thea nodded.

"Aye, I dinnae. But there was no other way out of here."

A sudden worry hit her. "What about the werewolves? Their bodies?"

Conall's features hardened. "Ashforth's dealing with that too."

The Scot was so quiet after that, Thea almost began to hope that he wasn't going to subject her to an interrogation. The reception desk was empty when they passed it again, and they snuck back into their room without being spotted by anyone. Conall locked the door and Thea immediately slumped on the bed.

She glared at the rucksack on the floor, realizing she'd been in such turmoil she'd left without her stuff. What an idiot.

"I'm hungry." She blew out a weary breath. "How long do you think we'll be here?"

When he didn't answer, Thea looked up to see Conall standing in front of the door, legs spread, arms crossed over his wide chest, his expression implacable.

Oh no.

"Food can wait, Thea," he said, his voice filled with an innate authority that pissed her off. "You will tell me who did that to your back and with what."

Thea crossed her own arms over her chest. "I dinnae have to tell you anything, Wolf Boy," she mocked.

His eyes turned to ice chips. "My sister is currently under the house arrest of Ashforth. Now," he said, stepping toward her, "I need to know if I've put her in danger."

The rebelliousness leaked out of her. Behind the hard ice in his eyes was bleak powerlessness. It was the same look on the little girl's face when she realized her dad was trapped. And Thea was sure it was the same look on her own face as she stood outside the burning wreckage that had incinerated her parents.

Family was everything.

Even someone as fucked up as Thea knew that.

"Conall …" She shook her head, worried for him, for his sister. "You should never have made a deal with Ashforth."

The muscle in his jaw flexed. "Did he do that to your back?"

She could still hear the lash hitting her flesh, could still feel the agonizing, burning pain of every slice into her back. She could smell the blood. Could feel it underfoot as she slipped in it. Could remember when darkness finally came.

And the moment she realized there was no relief of death for her.

It wasn't the worst thing he'd ever done to her … it was just the only thing that truly physically hurt.

"Yes," she choked out.

"How?"

The words stuck in her throat. As much as she longed to trust someone, and wished she could trust Conall, she just couldn't. "I can't tell you."

"Why?"

"Because it's my only weakness."

Silence descended over the room. Finally, Conall let out an exasperated huff. "And you dinnae trust me enough to tell me."

Thea cut him a look. "You're taking me to Ashforth. A man who brutalized me. Why the hell would I trust you?"

Conall glowered as he lowered onto the bed next to her.

Tension thickened between them, time slowing down, passing in awful increments. Feeling heat on her face, she looked over to find Conall watching her. His intense study caused a fluttering in her belly she tried to squash.

"What?" She frowned.

"Tell me," he said, his voice soft. "Tell me everything, Thea. Your side of the story."

Thea chuckled, the sound bitter and hard. "And have you *not* believe me? No thanks."

Conall's expressed hardened. "Do you think I wouldnae rather pretend you're the bad guy and he's the good guy? I do that, I hand you over, I save my sister, and I can forget this whole bloody nightmare."

Hurt she hated she felt suffused her. "Well, you do that, Wolf Boy. I'm not stopping you."

"I've seen your back, so I'm no longer buying that. There's no fucking way you will let me turn you over. I dinnae know what your plan was here, with me, but it wasnae to let yourself be handed over to a man who did that to you." He leaned toward her. "Here's what I do know. You saved my life because I jumped in front of those bullets in Wrocław. You didnae need to do that because we both know I didnae technically save your life."

"You thought you were saving my life when you did it."

"Exactly. So you still believed you owed me." He cut her a dark look. "You broke my neck to get away from me ... but you didnae kill me. And we both know you should have."

Thea's irritation mounted as she grew increasingly vulnerable. "Point?"

He ignored her snippiness. "You were trying not to kill those vampires in Prague and it nearly got you killed."

"Not true ... I was trying not to at first and then I killed one before you got there."

"They would have all been dead if you'd made the decision to kill them from the get-go. Instead, they almost killed you."

"But you saved me."

"Did I?" Conall eyed her suspiciously. "Were you really in danger, Thea?"

She swallowed hard and looked away. "I thought there was a point to this?"

"Aye. You went back for that wee lass ... why? Because she reminded you of you? When your parents died?"

Thea whipped her head around so fast, she felt a burn score up her neck. How did he know that? She glared at him. "Stop it."

He shook his head, and she hated the pity in his eyes. "You risked us to save that family and then you pushed me out of the way of those bullets. Now I tried to convince myself that it was all a manipulation, to get me on your side—"

"It was," she hurried to cut him off. "It was, Conall. I pretended I needed you as a bodyguard. We both know I don't."

He smirked wryly. "Too right. I've never felt so emasculated in my life as when you pushed me in that barn."

She rolled her eyes. "You decapitated a vampire with your bare hand. *Hand.*"

"That *is* true." He mused. "That makes me feel slightly better."

Despite herself, she laughed.

His expression intensified. "Why do you not want me to be on your side?"

She shrugged. "Two reasons: What happened to me is so fantastical, no one would believe me, not even you. I'd have shared all the horrible crap for nothing. And second ..." She looked deep in his eyes, seeing only his determination for his sister. "It won't change the fact you need to turn me over to save your sister."

Conall shook his head slowly. "I cannae tell you the future, or what will need to be done to save Callie. And I realize you dinnae owe me anything, but I'm also beginning to think Ashforth is the real enemy here. *That* was the point I was trying to make. I've had doubts about the man from the moment we met but all I cared about was saving Callie. Meeting you … I have good instincts, Thea, and I've been fighting them." He rested his arms on his knees and dropped his chin in weariness. "I have to know what this man is capable of and I need to know who I'll really be turning over to him to save my sister."

Tears filled Thea's eyes, and she looked quickly away so he wouldn't see. "Why? What will it change?"

"It depends on what you tell me," he said, his words soft. "But I'll tell you this. I dinnae have it in me to hand over an innocent woman to her abuser to save my family. Callie wouldnae be able to live with that either."

Hope was a dangerous thing. Thea had discovered that the hard way. She'd given up on feeling it for so long that the prickle of it in her chest frightened the shit out of her. Turning to him, she watched his expression soften at the sight of the tears shimmering in her eyes.

"If I tell you …" She pushed off the bed and glared down at him. "If I tell you and you betray me to Ashforth anyway, I'll kill you, Conall. No hesitation this time."

He nodded slowly. "Aye. I believe you, lass."

14

NEW YORK, SIX YEARS AGO

Posters covered the white walls, images that reflected who Thea had been before this madness had descended. There were rock bands she knew Amanda detested but allowed her to listen to. Photos ripped out of magazines of Caleb Followill and Ryan Gosling. There was a poster of the movie *UP*, an animation that made her sob her heart out in the first ten minutes.

Photographs of her classmates from the ages of twelve to fifteen.

Thea often wondered what Ashforth had told the school and her friends about her. What he'd told her therapist. She'd finally gotten the courage to ask Devon, and he'd said his dad had told everyone she'd gone back to England to live with her mom's family. And no one questioned it. No one ever questioned Ashforth.

That had made her laugh for about two seconds before the laughter turned into hysterical sobs.

No one who might care knew where she was.

No one was coming for her.

Although there was a wall of books and DVDs and an old-fashioned TV and DVD player in the corner, Thea rarely left the big luxurious bed. The entire room was lined with this stuff that burned the crap out of her when she touched it, and proximity to the amount in the room left her feeling weak, almost flu-like. Or at least what she assumed flu felt like.

Hearing the click of a lock, Thea turned her head on the pillow and watched as the heavy, armored door opened and Devon walked in. A werewolf guard followed Ashforth's son and stood at attention by the now-closed door.

Whenever one of the Ashforths visited, a werewolf or vampire always attended for their protection.

Last month Ashforth had taken so much blood from Thea, she'd been so weak she couldn't keep her eyes open. One guard, a human, had tried to take advantage of that. He climbed into her bed at night. She didn't know where she found the strength to fight him off, but in her fear and rage, she'd punched a hole through his chest.

He was the first human she'd ever killed.

Ashforth had cleaned up the mess like it was no big deal. He'd given her a fatherly smile and praised her strength. It had horrified Amanda and Devon and he'd promised nothing like that would ever happen again.

But they'd allowed it to happen by letting Ashforth keep her here. A prisoner. A science experiment.

A torture victim.

For four fucking years.

She turned her head away from Devon, unable to bear looking at him.

The night before, Thea had escaped. Again. It took a lot of strength, most of which was zapped by the room, but she was determined to get the hell out of there. Unfortunately, the last two times she'd tried she hadn't even gotten out of the house before someone shot her in the back with a dart. It contained that black substance Ashforth used to weaken her whenever she was out of the room.

"Dad's furious, Thea." She could hear Devon pulling a seat over to the bed.

Yeah, she kind of guessed that when he hit her.

She'd escaped the house the previous night. But a vampire tackled her on the tennis court and injected her. The last thing she remembered before she blacked out was Ashforth's enraged expression as he punched her in the gut.

"I'm worried about you. I've never seen him so angry."

She scoffed and turned to look at her adoptive brother's handsome face. "If you were really worried about me, you would have gotten me out of here a long time ago."

Remorse darkened his expression. "He has too many men. He's too powerful."

Yes, Jasper Ashforth had used his money to surround himself with supernatural guards at his island estate. He'd bought the small island on the Lawrence River, just off Lake Ontario, a few years ago. It was far enough from the other islands that dotted the river to afford complete privacy. He'd converted the house for his purposes and as far as Thea knew, he invited no one but family onto the island. For example, none of his wealthy business acquaintances or friends knew he'd kept his ward in the basement of his island house for the last four years.

"I saved you," she whispered.

Devon nodded, eyes bright. "I know. You don't know how much I wish I could return the favor. But I'm not strong enough to fight him. I'm sorry."

Thea's mind flew back to those first days after the plane crash. After what she'd experienced, the terrifying plummet out of the sky, the screams of terror she could still hear in her head, the horror in her parents' eyes when they looked at her for the last time …

And the crash itself. She remembered the noise, pain, and burning all over her body. She could remember the awful smells, but she couldn't remember getting out of the wreckage. One minute they'd crashed, there was darkness, and the next Thea was on the ground outside the wrecked plane.

Her therapist said it was a saving grace, and Thea agreed. There were some images a person didn't need in her head.

The Ashforths had been worried she wasn't talking and so they'd taken her to the therapist, but she refused to speak at first there too. It wasn't until a week later when Devon, only a year older, found her sitting alone in the gardens. He sat down and talked to her about this video game he was playing. Thea had listened to him chatter away, and it was the first time she'd felt a modicum of normality. When he'd eventually asked her if she wanted an ice cream, she'd opened her mouth and said yes.

Devon had taken her hand and led her into the house.

The years between twelve and fifteen hadn't been easy. But she believed she was protected. Ashforth kept the media frenzy at bay. Everyone wanted to know about the miracle child who'd survived a plane crash. But she also later discovered the government had come knocking, wanting to look at the little girl who walked away from a plane crash almost unscathed, and Ashforth used every ounce of his influence and connections to keep them away. There were overzealous religious people who wanted to get near her because they believed God had touched her.

He kept them all away.

And she'd been grateful.

Thea had been secretly terrified of anyone finding out she was different. Her parents had been so careful to protect her secret.

Kids at her new private school were distant at first, but Devon was popular there and he forged a path for her. She made friends; she did well at school, and every week she visited a therapist to make sure she was dealing with the trauma of losing her parents the way she had. Except for being careful not to show her true strength, her healing abilities, or any of the weird things she could do that her parents had taught her to control and hide, Thea was as happy as a girl who'd lost her parents could be.

There had been moments of near misses with the Ashforths. Cuts that healed immediately. A broken leg on a skiing trip that miraculously was no longer broken by the time they got her back up the hill.

Still, she thought she'd gotten away with it.

Two years later, on her fourteenth birthday, Ashforth tried to get her on a private plane for the first time for a family holiday to Italy. Thea had lost control in front of the family who sat in the limo waiting for her to get out onto the tarmac. During the struggle, she remembered the air crackling and the Ashforths staring at her in horror, asking her what was wrong with her eyes, and then …

Thea remembered the explosion of glass

To this day, she still didn't know how she'd done it … how she'd caused the front windshield of the plane to shatter … but she had. She was grateful the pilot and flight attendant hadn't been hurt.

However, everything changed in that moment. Ashforth realized what it all meant. Her surviving the crash, her broken leg healing, and so, like the naïve idiot she was, she'd told the Ashforth family about the abilities she'd had as long as she could remember. That her mom and dad had protected her, helped her hide them.

"And they didn't know what you are?" Ashforth had sounded exasperated. *"You're extraordinary, Thea, and they didn't want to know why?"*

"I'm their daughter. They were human. How could I be anything else?"

Ashforth was in awe. Even as a fourteen-year-old kid, she knew for him it was all about power. He'd amassed a lot of it over the years, but Thea had her own kind of power. A power he coveted. Ashforth became obsessed with understanding it.

The first year of the family knowing wasn't too bad. Amanda worried about her and insisted she continue to hide her abilities, scolding Devon when he goaded Thea into a sprint race he had no hope in hell of winning. He just wanted to see her move like a blur. Devon had the typical attitude of a fifteen-year-old boy who found himself living with the equivalent of a superhero sister. He thought it was awesome.

Thea knew Ashforth had begun researching her. He came to her with his findings and opened her eyes to the world of the supernatural. Werewolves, vampires, and witches were real. And yet, Thea wasn't any of those things. So, he kept researching.

And as the months passed, Devon grew ill.

Leukemia.

"My son is dying, Thea." Ashforth had stormed into her bedroom one night, a manic wreck. He fell at her bedside. *"You have to help."*

"How?" she whispered, terrified of losing another person she loved.

"Your blood. I've tried vampire blood. I've tried werewolf blood. They heal quickly but their blood doesn't do the same for humans."

He'd fed creepy paranormal blood to Devon? She'd been shocked.

"Don't look at me like that. I had to try. And you have to let me try yours."

An ugly knot formed in her gut, a strange foreboding, but she nodded her agreement.

It had worked.

It saved Devon.

But Thea's life changed.

She'd known the very next day because the warning burn she'd felt on the back of her neck the day her parents died, the inexplicable racing of her heart, the feeling of dread, she'd experienced it all as Ashforth walked into the kitchen that morning.

At first, he just wanted to take more blood. He had people he could trust analyzing it. But Thea soon started to realize that he'd learned more about her than he'd let on.

"I want to test the limits of your capabilities."

He'd made her train to fight werewolves and vampires he'd hired. Supernatural men and women whom he then kept on at the estate. He said they were her trainers, her bodyguards, but Thea knew they were prison guards. As he'd hoped, she soon surpassed them in their fight sessions until it became less about training and more about testing her speed and strength against the strongest supernaturals he could find.

She no longer went to school and was homeschooled by Amanda because Ashforth refused to allow a tutor onto the island. Thea overheard arguments between Ashforth and Amanda about his treatment of her, but he promised his wife he'd never hurt Thea.

Thea knew it was a lie.

The burn up the back of her nape told her so.

Her suspicions were proven true the first time Ashforth allowed a vampire to break her neck. The evidence was insurmountable when a wolf took a knife to her gut. It became a sick kind of torture when a marksman shot at her while she ran an obstacle course.

As Thea plotted her escape, stealing money from the house where she could and keeping it hidden under her mattress, she was unaware that Ashforth had discovered something important about her.

One day he killed any affection she'd had for him when he came to her with a blade made of a metal the color of mercury. She'd braced herself but nothing could have prepared her for the agony that tore through her lower gut when he plunged it into her.

The whole time he'd studied her reaction like she was a science experiment.

Thea had laid stunned on the floor, having never experienced such pain before. Not even the burns from the plane crash had hurt like this. And it took much longer for the wound to heal.

Amanda had walked into the room unawares.

Thea could still hear her screaming in horror at Ashforth. Amanda thought he'd killed her.

There were so many times she'd cursed herself for waiting to run. In the time she'd procrastinated, her so-called guardian had the basement converted. He'd lined it with the same metal as the blade he'd stabbed her with.

Over the years, he'd developed a drug that weakened her and weapons from that he never used but lorded over her to force her submission. All pretense was over. Ashforth wanted to be like her. The transfusion of blood didn't change his DNA, it merely healed, but he'd lost all reasoning in his obsession for power. He would keep her locked up until he found a way to become what she was.

Four years she'd been a prisoner in that basement while he stockpiled her blood and experimented on it, searching for her source of power, searching for a way to become like her. He was like some fucking fantastical villain from a comic book.

No one would believe this shit even if she did escape.

"You can't try to escape again, Thea," Devon pleaded. "I'm afraid of what he'll do to you."

She laughed bitterly. "Like he could do anything worse to me."

The words had barely left her mouth when the door opened. Lifting her head off the pillow, that burn scored down her neck and her pulse escalated.

Ashforth strolled in, his face blank, calm. At his side was a vampire called Morton. He'd worked for Ashforth for almost three years and was built like a werewolf, big and bruising. But Morton had the speed and reflexes of a vamp.

In other words, he was deadly.

And in his hands was a cat-o'-nine-tails.

The special kind.

The strips of the whip weren't leather. They were strips of familiar silver-gray metal.

True fear filled Thea's mouth.

"Dad, what are you doing?" Devon stood up from the chair, blocking her view. "What the hell is going on?"

"Son, get out of my way."

To her surprise, Devon got into a fight with his father—he even threw a punch—but the werewolf guarding the door easily wrestled him out of the room. His horrified gaze locked with Thea's before he was expelled.

Leaving Thea alone with Ashforth and the vampire and the weapon.

"You shouldn't run, Thea," he said calmly, like they were discussing the weather. "I never wanted it to come to this, but you need to know what the consequences are if you try to run again."

The werewolf returned to the room with a friend to help secure her. She fought through the fatigue the room cast over her, but she wasn't strong enough. She refused to scream though. She clenched her teeth and struggled with all her might, knowing it was futile as they held her between them. Their hands locked tight on her arms, splaying them out like a cross, and they tore her shirt down the back. The fabric fell away, exposing her skin.

It was pain unlike anything she could have imagined.

Tears streamed down her face as she stuffed her screams deep inside. Thea tried to keep on her feet as the biting lash ripped into her flesh, tearing and tearing until there couldn't possibly be anything left.

To her despair, the fog of agony descended, her knees buckled, and she slipped in the blood and bits of flesh beneath her.

But then hope lingered in the dark. Hope that perhaps this was the end. Ashforth had told her he suspected her invincibility meant she was immortal.

She'd never die.

That's why he was so obsessed with the idea of being like her. He didn't want to be a vampire whose immortality came with compromises. Where death came too easily.

He wanted to be like Thea.

A true immortal.

God, she hoped he was wrong. She hoped the darkness descending over her was the end and somehow a hand would reach out for her and she'd finally be with her mom and dad again.

"I'M SO SORRY, MY DARLING GIRL," A VOICE WHISPERED THROUGH THE dark, through the burning pain. "I'm going to get you out. I promise. I won't let this happen again."

"Mom?" she croaked.

A sob sounded in her ear. "No, darling, it's Amanda."

The pain intensified and Thea could feel her body, could feel her eyelids. She pushed them open, and her blurred vision came into focus.

Amanda Ashforth's tear-streaked face filled it as she bent over Thea.

"Alive?"

Amanda's face crumpled, and she nodded.

"No." Thea shuddered, the movement hurting her back. "No." The tears came before she could stop them and her adoptive mother took her hand, holding it in comfort as Thea sobbed out all the pain of the last seven years.

When finally she stopped, she was exhausted. The taste of salt from her tears filled her mouth.

"Your back is healing slowly." Amanda looked green. "But I don't know if the scarring will fade."

It wouldn't. Thea still had a scar from where Ashforth had plunged the knife into her gut all those years ago.

The door creaked open behind her.

"Time's up," a female voice Thea recognized as one of the vamps cut through the room.

Amanda glared in the door's direction. "Time is up when I say it is up."

"Time's up when Mr. Ashforth says it's up. He said fifteen minutes with Miss Quinn and no more."

"I'm coming." Amanda raised an eyebrow. "You can leave."

The door shut and Amanda bent down to Thea. She felt her adoptive mother's lips on her ear. "I will get you out."

That awful hope glittered inside Thea's darkest hiding place. Amanda had often apologized for her husband's behavior, but she'd never dared to promise Thea an escape. And although Thea didn't know how it could be possible, the hope that someone might care enough to save her still existed.

TWO WEEKS LATER

Staring at her back, Thea felt foolish for the shallow worries that filled her head. When she finally had sex, what would the guy think about those awful scars? Would he see the scars as she did … as a failing? As a weakness? As proof she wasn't strong enough to protect herself? Would they repulse him?

Maybe she could have sex without removing her top?

She scoffed at herself as she pulled on a shirt. She couldn't wear a bra yet because her back was still too tender. Going braless was a nightmare. She was too full in the chest to go without a bra and she hated the way some guards watched her like she was a piece of meat.

Guards, she reminded herself.

In her prison.

Where she was unlikely to ever meet someone she was attracted to in order to lose her virginity.

God, would she die a virgin?

Oh, right … possible immortality.

If that was true, she just had to survive this nightmare until Jasper Ashforth died. Unless he became like her.

Thea felt rage churn in her gut at the thought. No way was she staying stuck down here for another fifty fucking years. Or worse, forever.

Right on cue, the door to the room opened and Amanda walked in with a human guard (armed with a dart gun) at her back. She smiled sadly at Thea. "I've been granted permission to walk with you around the grounds for an hour."

That tickle of intuition, of hope, bloomed in Thea and she nodded carefully before pulling on a pair of sneakers to follow Amanda out.

To her surprise, the human guard and a werewolf, who Amanda called Sarah and Jack respectively, trailed them. No others. They kept a polite distance as Amanda led Thea down the basement corridor; right led up to the house and left led out into the gardens.

Another guard opened the exit and Thea blinked against the natural daylight as she walked up concrete steps to the outside. The sun felt amazing on her face after spending weeks in a windowless room.

The large house was surrounded by the island's forest, which acted as a natural perimeter on three sides. The grounds also housed a tennis court, indoor and outdoor pools, a guest cottage, and perfect lawns that led down to their beach.

Amanda slipped her arm through Thea's and huddled close. "How are you feeling?"

"Still weak," she admitted. "The effects of the room take time to wear off."

"About an hour, right?"

Thea fought to stay relaxed. "Yes, about an hour."

"We're going to walk around the grounds for an hour," Amanda said, lowering her voice. "And then we'll take a walk on the beach. Jack and Sarah are *my* personal guards, Thea."

She looked into Amanda's eyes. "How?"

"There's a boat," she whispered. "Jasper is in Australia on business, and I've told about a hundred lies to get guards out of the way for the exact moment when the boat will arrive. You have to be on it at exactly one fifteen or we could get caught."

"What will he do to you?" Thea asked, fear for Amanda stalling the anticipation of flight.

"I'm his wife. He won't hurt me. He'll be furious with me, but he won't hurt me."

Thea cut her a dark look. "He's a bad person, Amanda."

Her green eyes filled with tears. "I know," she whispered bleakly. "And I'm … stuck … but I can't let you be. I loved your mother. She was my best friend."

Tears momentarily blinded Thea. "Come with me."

"I can't leave Devon."

"He's at school. He's grown up."

Amanda smiled sadly. "He'll be fifty and I'll still think of him as my little boy. I can't leave him alone with Jasper. I just … I can't."

They fell into silence as they walked by the pool, not acknowledging the guard placed at the entrance to the lounge area.

When they were finally out of earshot, Amanda whispered, "There's a backpack with a change of clothes and ten thousand dollars on that boat. You can't use a passport or he'll find you …" She tightened her hold on Thea. "You're going to have to use your gift."

Thea shook her head. "No."

Ashforth had made her use it on people and his experiments had brought the realization she couldn't use it on supernaturals. But she could mind warp the hell out of humans, and it was awful.

The first time she'd become aware of the gift was when she was just a kid. She'd broken one of her mom's favorite vases and had unintentionally wished her mom wouldn't see it. And then her mom couldn't. Her dad, however, could, and he thought Thea's mom was going crazy until they realized their special daughter might be even more special than they'd thought. After testing the gift among the three of them, they'd discovered Thea could make people see anything she wanted them to see.

William and Laura Quinn had forbidden her from ever using it again.

As a child, she hadn't understood what a violation the "gift" was, and her parents never knew she'd continued to use it.

It was only now she understood that it wasn't a gift. It was a terrible power she did not want to use ever again.

"I can't." The thought of stripping someone of their free will disgusted her after her imprisonment.

"Darling girl." Amanda suddenly looked fierce. "You will have to give up a few morals to survive. My husband has almost unlimited resources and he will use them to find you. So you need to be as far from here as possible. The boat will take you to New York. You can't get on a plane, so you need to find a ship that's sailing far away. And to get on that ship you're going to need the right people to think you have a passport."

Although the thought made her sick, Thea nodded.

The tension thickened between them as time moved on and Amanda led them toward the beach. "I can never repay you for saving my son's life and I will never forgive myself for not taking the risk to help you sooner. I will live with that regret to my dying day." She turned to Thea and took her face in her hands. "So much has happened to you. You have the kind of strength that is awe-inspiring, Thea. Never forget that. I know horrible things have been done to you and I have no doubt that out there alone, you'll come across more bad things this world has to offer. But don't ever forget that there's love and kindness in this world too. Your parents loved you. *I* love you. Remember that. Don't forget … because if you forget, you'll forget to love." She gripped Thea's arms now. "Power like yours in the hands of someone who no longer cares or loves beyond themselves is a dangerous thing. Promise me you won't forget. Even if it hurts to remember Will and Laura. Even if it hurts to remember me. Promise you won't forget."

Thea nodded, holding back the tears. "I promise."

Satisfied, Amanda hugged her hard.

They stood there so long, a throat cleared behind them. "Mrs. Ashforth," Jack interrupted. "It's time."

From there they let go of one another and hurried down to the beach. Anticipation caused a mad flutter of butterflies in Thea's belly when she saw the speedboat, manned by a guy with an automatic rifle and another who was steering the boat.

Amanda followed her down onto the private jetty with the guards at their backs. Thea gave her one last hug. "Thank you," she whispered. "I won't forget."

Shouts rang out just as Thea stepped into the boat. She turned around as the sound of bullets ripping through the air filled her ears.

"Go, go, go!" the guy with the automatic rifle shouted as he fired back.

Thea huddled, peering over the edge of the boat when the water sprayed up out the back as it peeled away from the dock. Sarah was down and Jack was guarding Amanda with his body.

Bullets pinged off the stern and Thea gave a muffled shout as she saw Jack's body jerk several times before he fell off the dock. Her heart in her throat, Thea watched as Amanda went to stand up, empty hands raised, and her body jolted, blood spraying out the back of her head.

She fell like an anchor into the water.

"No," Thea whispered, choking on sobs as she turned, cowering in the boat as it tore across the river to safety. "No."

"Hey."

She looked up to see the guy with the rifle bending down on his haunches to peer at her.

"You hurt?"

She shook her head.

His features softened with concern. "Sorry about the lady. She paid real well."

Thea glared at him, waiting for the questions to come.

He shook his head as if reading her thoughts. "She didn't pay me to ask questions. I just do the job. We're dropping you off at Henderson Harbor where there's a guy with a car waiting to take you where you want to go. Here." He dumped a backpack at her feet. "This is yours."

She was silent as the boat bounced across the water, trying to bury her grief over Amanda. She'd dig up that grief later, when she was far, far away from Ashforth.

"Where do you think you'll go?" the guy with the gun asked.

She thought of England. Her dad's parents were Irish, but they had raised him in London, while her mom had been raised in Cornwall. Growing up, Thea had seen photos of Cornwall and thought it looked beautiful.

But it would be the first place Ashforth would look.

Thea shrugged. "Somewhere that's not here."

The guy grunted. "Right."

The man waiting at Henderson Harbor was human, but he was tall and muscular and looked like private security. Thea told him to take her to New York Harbor. It was a five-hour drive, and it felt like it took forever. There were two werewolves sniffing around the harbor when she got there and she knew Ashforth had sent them.

However, the ship leaving the harbor minutes after her arrival was bound for Southampton in England. Her driver was apparently paid to be more than just a chauffeur. He'd spotted the wolves too and told her he'd distract them while she boarded the ship.

Thea reluctantly used her mind trick to secure her way onto the ocean liner.

She stayed in her small cabin for much of the seven days it took to cross, wishing the goddamn ship would speed up. Thea had visions of Ashforth sending out cops to stop the ship, but she knew he'd rather let her get away for now if it meant leaving the authorities out of it. And he also knew she could make the police see whatever the hell she wanted them to see, including a girl who looked nothing like Thea Quinn.

Having cried herself to sleep most nights over Amanda, Thea landed in England with a renewed attitude. She'd keep her promise to her adoptive mother to never forget, but she was done crying.

She was alone now, and all that mattered was surviving and staying out of Ashforth's hands.

The claustrophobia that had tightened her chest since she'd become Jasper Ashforth's little science experiment all those years ago finally released as she stepped onto the cruise ship that would take her to Greece.

And from there … well, from there she could go anywhere.

15

Conall wasn't sure how much time had passed as he sat in the hotel room, listening to Thea's melodic voice. Darkness had fallen but neither of them had moved to turn on the lights. She sat on the floor, her back to the wall, sometimes meeting his eyes, but mostly staring out the window at the darkening sky.

Conall heard the love and grief in her voice when she talked about her parents, of Amanda, and even of Devon, but there was more than hatred in her tone as she spoke of Ashforth. The musky, coppery scent of fear filled the room and made Conall's gut twist. Thea was possibly the most powerful being he'd met, and yet she was afraid of a human man because of the abuse he'd perpetrated on her.

Processing her tale, disgusted with Ashforth, awed by Thea, he realized with great regret that desperation had caused him to make a deal with the devil.

Putting all the pieces of the puzzle together from Thea's story and from what he knew in his gut, Conall believed her.

Jasper Ashforth was a piece of shit.

As Thea fell silent, looking out the window, Conall's eyes drank her in. Her lips were parted, carefully relaxed, no tension in her jaw. But when his gaze traveled down her body, he found her inner anxiety reflected in the tight fists her hands made in her lap.

She was waiting on his disbelief.

Conall returned his study to her face. He hadn't looked away from her for hours and he willed her to finally turn her eyes upon him. As if she'd heard the thought, Thea met his stare with that neutral countenance she often donned as a mask. She'd never mastered the art of a blank expression. She thought she had. But those cognac eyes were soulful. More often than not he didn't know what she was thinking, but that didn't mean he couldn't see who she was in their fiery depths. They were dark pools of experience and of all the empathy and compassion the world—Ashforth—had tried to rip out of her.

He thought of her demanding that he turn the car around so she could save that bairn and her father.

Of the way she'd saved Conall from the silver bullets.

All the lies he'd believed about her seemed ridiculous now. Feeling his chest ache with a strength of emotion that surprised him, his heart beating a wee bit faster than usual, Conall cleared his throat. "There was a shopkeeper in Budapest."

Thea narrowed her eyes and nodded.

"Did you kill him?"

Disbelief slackened her features. "What? No." She shook her head. "I liked the old guy. He was always lecturing me about walking around by myself at night. Strangers rarely care about other strangers, but he seemed genuinely concerned for me. That night someone came in to rob the store while I was there. I got that feeling I told you about … my internal alarm system that warns me of danger. The gunman was going to harm the shopkeeper, so I stupidly stepped in, even though I knew *my* kind of activity sends up a flare in the supernatural community. Ashforth has eyes and ears everywhere, apparently. The gunman shot me and seeing me react inhumanly caused the old man to flee. The gunman fled too."

She shrugged, her tone defensive. "I knew I had to leave the country after that, but I didn't have enough money, so I stole from the cash register. I'm not proud of that but I considered it payment for saving the shopkeeper's life."

Fuck.

Conall sighed, hating to impart the news. "He's dead, Thea. The shopkeeper's dead. Ashforth showed me photographs. Of him and of others. And he told me they were your victims."

He watched the color drain from her face as she pushed up onto her feet, giving him her back. The shadowy room filled with static and then the lights flickered on before blazing to life.

Conall bit back a curse at the show of power and studied Thea's slender back, remembering the scars he'd seen beneath her shirt. That ache in his chest flared, the knot in his gut tightened again, and he wished Ashforth was in front of him so he could rip his fucking heart out.

The intensity of the feeling was overwhelming.

She turned to him, desolate. "I've never intentionally harmed a human. Not since that guard back at Ashforth's island house. He's lying. About all of them. I would never hurt an innocent or someone who can't fight back."

Conall nodded, thinking of the atrocities Ashforth had committed to keep Thea's existence a secret. "He's killing witnesses to cover your trail."

She pressed a hand to her mouth. "Oh my God." She looked sick as the magnitude of Ashforth's crimes set in. Her hand dropped limply to her side, her expression stark. "Maybe I should have stayed with him. All those people would be alive. They died for my freedom."

Angry at her self-directed and misplaced guilt, Conall stood and glowered down at her. "No. Their deaths are not on you. You're not responsible for Ashforth's actions. He's a psychopath."

She made a harsh sound of strangled laughter. "Actually, I don't know if he is. I looked up the definition of psychopath and Ashforth isn't emotionally shallow or without conscience. He has the ability to love, to care. He loved his family. But, ultimately, he loves power more. Ashforth is a *megalomaniac*. And that unnatural drive to obtain power has warped him. It's an obsession. It makes him justify all the bad things he's done. And somewhere along the way, I think it just became easier for him to stop seeing me as a person, as Thea, and more as an object of power. Killing innocent people"—she shook her head—"he's so far gone now. I can only imagine Amanda's death was a catalyst. Something's snapped in his mind."

Conall thought that made sense. He nodded. "He needs to achieve what he set out to achieve, otherwise her death was for nothing."

"Yes."

"I'm sorry I believed you killed Amanda."

He saw the harsh grief mar her face before she hid it beneath her rage. "The first hunter he sent after me was a mercenary for hire, armed with a dart gun and Ashforth's drug. He said he didn't know why Ashforth wanted me back alive, that if I had killed *his* wife, he'd take his revenge on the spot. And that's when I knew he probably told Devon that I murdered Amanda. I wanted to kill Ashforth for that. Everything he'd done to me … and somehow," she said, her jaw tensing as she blinked, fighting back tears, "somehow that was the worst."

His throat thickened, watching her battle her emotions and win. There was a part of him relieved that she won. Conall wasn't sure how he'd cope with Thea crying.

"Thea, what is the weapon he used against you?" He sounded gruff, impatient. However, his frustration wasn't just with her. He was frustrated with himself for believing Ashforth's lies. And he wanted Thea to trust him.

Wrong.

He *needed* her to trust him.

"I can't tell you." Her tone brooked no argument.

A fury the situation hardly warranted rushed like a burning heat through his blood and he felt his gums and fingertips tingle with the shift. Jesus fuck. He took a calming, slow exhalation. Thea's eyes narrowed on him.

"Are you okay?"

No, he was far from okay. He was disappointed and angered beyond measure by her lack of trust in him and yet how could he blame the lass? Hadn't he spent the last few days holding her captive, to return her to a man who had brutalized her?

Still, she knew his weakness, and he was giving her his trust by believing her over Ashforth. "You know I'm weakened by silver. What's the difference?"

Thea crossed her arms under her chest, drawing his attention. The heat within him changed in an instant before he fought it and dragged his gaze back to her face. If she noticed his wandering eyes, she didn't acknowledge it. "Every supernatural on the planet knows silver is poison to a werewolf, the same way every supernatural knows a wooden stake to the heart will turn a vampire to dust. But no one knows my weakness except Ashforth, and that's as big as I want to make that circle of death."

Conall's frustration mounted. "If you tell me," he bit out sharply, "maybe I can help you find out what you are, why you have the abilities you have."

"I'm not interested in knowing."

He raised an eyebrow at her mulish expression. "Ashforth knows, Thea. If we know what he knows, we'll have a better chance of understanding what is driving him."

"Power. I told you that. Absolute power." She sneered. "Do you know before he found out about me, he was gearing up to run for president? Of the United States. *President.* So he could be immortalized forever in world history. But then I came along." She took a step toward him, her intoxicating mix of fresh, floral, heady, sweet scent thickening in the air between them. "Why be immortalized in history when you can be immortal? He thinks I'm a *true* immortal. Whatever that means."

Ashforth's voice filled Conall's mind. *"Well, they're not true immortals. They can still be killed."* "He thinks you're indestructible."

She slumped down on the twin bed next to her. She was the perfect image of youthful weariness, like a thousand-year-old vampire that had stopped aging at twenty. "The vampire who punched me in the chest …"

Conall sat on the other bed. "Aye?"

"My heart wouldn't budge, Conall."

His heart raced a little harder at the sound of his name on her tongue. He forced himself to concentrate on the words that had come before it.

"He couldn't pull it out of my chest, and he couldn't crush it." Her voice dropped to a whisper. "I don't want to be immortal. I don't want to live forever."

Her pain affected him more than he'd like so he covered it with his usual brusqueness. "The only way to find out one way or the other is to discover what you are."

"And you have no inkling?" She cocked her head in thought. "You've never heard about someone like me?"

"No. The only beings that come remotely close are myths and legends. Some supes think of them as our origin stories, a religion. But I've never believed in them. I believe in facts and evolution."

"Then how do you explain me?"

"Evolution."

She cracked a smile and his eyes lingered on her mouth. "Like X-Men?"

Conall flashed her a wolfish grin. "Aye, why not?"

Thea laughed and shook her head. "If only it were that interesting. I've read about those origin stories too. They sound like fairy tales."

"Aye, well, some people need to believe in fairy tales but it's a waste of time."

"Let them have them, Conall," she whispered sadly. "If it helps them deal with how shitty the real world is, let people have their fairy tales."

"I'm happy to." He nodded. "But there are people like Ashforth whose beliefs become a justification for evil. That's where I draw the line."

Her eyes filled with wariness. "What does that mean?"

The blaring ringtone of Conall's temporary phone made him bite back a curse. Pulling it out of his pocket, he saw it was Ashforth. He looked at Thea. "It's him."

"Answer it." Her expression hardened. "He still has your sister."

The thought of Callie anywhere near the slimy fuck made Conall murderous. A growl erupted from the back of his throat before he could stop it.

A gentle hand on his arm brought his head up from the phone. Thea was touching him. "You can do this. For Callie."

A calm moved through him and then a sense of loss when she removed her hand. Ignoring the latter, he answered Ashforth with a curt, "Conall."

"Good, you're still alive." Ashforth's cool, cultured voice threatened to obliterate Conall's calm but he kept himself under control.

"Aye. Is the town clear?"

"Yes. And the bodies dealt with. I'll arrange for another vehicle. Where are you staying?"

"No." Conall needed time to think, which meant he needed space from the bastard. "Someone within your circle is leaking information to the Blackwoods. I think it best I arrange transport and call you when we're on the road again."

"Fine. But I'm working on finding out who that rat is."

God help the traitorous little rodent.

"I'll be in touch." Conall hung up abruptly without asking for his sister. He didn't want Ashforth even breathing her name. Thank fuck he'd sent James with her.

Conall stood from the bed, towering over Thea who had returned to watching him with a guarded expression. He'd do anything to rid her of that wariness forever.

His breath stuttered at the thought.

"Well?" she asked.

Clearing his throat, he held out his hand to her. "I'm not going to turn you over."

Instead of the gratitude he was hoping to see, instead of feeling her hand in his—something he'd anticipated more than he should—Conall watched her shut down. Thea pushed off the bed, ignoring his outstretched hand. She seemed to bristle with outrage. Her teeth clenched together, and she bit out, "You have to. For your sister."

"My pack will help me free Callie and James from Castle Cara." They would but he knew that wouldn't be the end of their problems with Ashforth. Conall may have to kill the bastard. He'd never killed a human before. Then again, the man who'd tortured Thea barely qualified as human.

"Conall, Ashforth is more powerful than you seem to understand. He's killed people and gotten away with it. He'll have your sister flown out of Scotland before you can ever hope to get to her. And she'll die. In his hands." Her words pierced straight through him. "We're stuck. You can't let me go and I can't hide from you. He knows that now. And he'll hurt everyone you care about if you don't bring me to him."

Impotence churned his insides to hell, and he let out a low growl of outrage that made her nostrils flare. He gave her a sharp shake of his head so she'd know his anger was not directed at her.

Her answering smile was melancholy. "It was always going to come to this."

"To what?"

Thea flexed her hands, her eyes shadowed. "I have to kill Ashforth."

"Thea—"

"We make the exchange." She stepped close to him, tilting her head back to hold eye contact. Sincerity and determination rose to the surface of her eyes. "We heal your sister and you get her out of there. I'll deal with Ashforth. He thinks he can best me, but I'm stronger than I used to be. His drug isn't as effective outside of that special room of his. After that" —she shrugged, looking away—"we go our separate ways."

Conall hated the plan. Every part. "And the Blackwood Coven?"

Thea strolled over to the bed to pick up her rucksack. "They're my problem, not yours."

Her words needled and as Conall followed her out of the hotel room, letting her lead him into the first phase of a plan that should have satisfied him, he grew angrier with the lass, and her lack of trust in him, by the second.

16

Trusting Conall was difficult for Thea. She knew he thought she didn't trust him, but she'd shown some faith in him just by telling her story. It was more than anyone else got these days. Yet, it was hard to deny there was something about Conall that made her want to trust. A genuine decency.

Not only was it strange to feel like they were no longer at war, it was odd because she almost felt like they were a team now. Not totally, but almost. For so long she'd been alone, unable to confide in anyone about her abilities. Conall knew the truth, and being different himself, he seemed to accept her. It was kind of nice.

She knew she should resent the hell out of him for coming into her life and making it impossible for them to escape Ashforth's machinations, but she couldn't resent the guy for doing something she would have done too. She'd put her trust in Ashforth by allowing him to take her blood in the hopes of saving Devon.

And she would have given anything to anyone to have saved her parents from that plane crash.

It wasn't any different from Conall joining forces with Ashforth to save his sister.

These were her thoughts when they reached the international bus depot in Dresden. Conall thought they should get the bus to Düsseldorf where he would then acquire a new car.

"It's better we travel alone by car. If someone else comes after us, I dinnae want any more innocent people caught in the crossfire."

Because she agreed, Thea got on the bus with Conall, feeling his overwhelming presence at her back. It was around two thirty in the morning but the bus to Calais was busy. It would make several stops, including Düsseldorf. When Thea asked, "Why Düsseldorf?" Conall had merely shrugged and said he'd been there before. It would do better than most for somewhere to gather their wits.

Thea usually never made eye contact with anyone when she traveled, yet she couldn't help but notice passengers were staring behind her as she walked down the aisle, their nervousness obvious.

Somewhere along the line she'd stopped seeing Conall as meanlooking, but she guessed he still scared the shit out of people. She spotted two empty seats near the rear and dropped into the window seat. Conall was so big his knees touched the back of the seat in front of him and his shoulders pushed into her space.

"Sorry," he muttered, frowning in annoyance as he tried to hunch to make himself smaller.

Thea felt a smile prodding her lips and a feeling in her chest that was almost akin to affection. She shimmied over, pressing up against the window. "I don't take up much room, you're fine."

He shot her a look. "Another reason we need to get a car."

She nodded, grinning.

Conall's eyes dropped to her mouth before he quickly looked away.

Thea leaned into him to speak but when he turned to her, she became aware of how close his mouth was to hers. And she knew the moment he did to.

A thick tension sprung between them as their eyes met, their attraction palpable.

Shit.

A complication she did not need.

Thea pulled back a little. "Do people always look at you like that?" she whispered, staring over the top of the bus seats. "Like they fear you?"

"Aye," his answer was gruff. "It makes no matter."

"It doesn't matter?"

"No, it doesnae."

Thea slumped against her chair, annoyed Conall accepted that people judged him before they got to know him. "They're idiots."

His lips twitched at the corner. "What's new, lass?"

She chuckled, and they shared a look of affinity that made her breathless. Uneasy, she dropped her gaze and turned into the window. "I think I'll catch some z's." The journey to Düsseldorf would take around six hours.

"You do that."

What made Thea realize that she'd begun to trust Conall, just a little, was waking up almost six hours later to find herself snuggled against his hard chest. His scent wove its way into her consciousness first and not fully awake, she wanted to bury deeper into the smell. It was amber and cedar and the peppery aroma of ginger. Earth and spice and incredibly male. In the sleepy corners of her mind, it wrapped her in an embrace that offered comfort and sex at the same time.

Slowly cognizance returned, telling her the hard, warm cushion underneath her was rising and falling. That the gentle breathing she could hear wasn't her own.

Thea's eyes flew open.

Her head was definitely resting on Conall's chest. One hand was beneath her cheek while the other laid on his flat, taut stomach. She could feel the ridge of abs between her hand and the fabric of his shirt.

Then the weight resting along her back became apparent.

He had his arm around her. His hand was cupping her hip.

What the hell?

Never could she have imagined trusting Conall enough, even in her unconscious state, to snuggle with him.

Snuggle.

She hadn't snuggled with anyone in years. The last snuggle she'd had was with her mom.

Tears pricked Thea's eyes as she realized how much she'd missed the basic human comfort of a hug.

You're being ridiculous.

The werewolf was turning her into an emotional wreck, and she couldn't be an emotional wreck. An emotional wreck would not win the war against Ashforth.

Thea pulled out of Conall's embrace and he grunted. She looked up at him as she retreated and saw him blinking awake. Well, at least he'd been asleep too. He didn't seem nearly so disconcerted that they'd been snuggling as she did. Conall rubbed a hand over his face, the bristles of his unshaven cheeks sounding rough against his palm.

"Are we there?"

Thea glanced at the digital board above the exit. It said Düsseldorf was the next stop in twenty minutes. "Almost."

They both stretched their necks trying to work out the kinks, and Thea scowled at their synchronicity.

"You slept?"

She nodded, flicking him a wary look. "You did too."

"Aye, a little."

"I'm sorry if I …" She gestured uncertainly between them. "Forced you to …" Thea absolutely could not use the word "snuggle" in front of Conall.

The werewolf waved off her concerns. "It's fine."

An awkward silence fell between them, probably only made awkward by Thea. And then Conall surprised her. He turned to her, his voice low, and he said, "No nightmares this time."

Feeling vulnerable about her nightmares, Thea frowned. The Scot had probably deduced now that the nightmares were about her time with the Ashforths. Surprisingly, they were rarely about the whipping she'd taken. They were about Amanda's death or about Ashforth finding her.

She stared out the window, hating that the bad dreams made her weak.

"Hey …" Conall's breath whispered against her ear and her own breath caught in her throat at his nearness. She didn't dare turn her head because if she did, her lips would brush his. "I didnae mean to upset you."

He pulled back, and she almost exhaled with relief.

His expression was ... tender. "After everything you've been through, it's amazing how together you are, Thea. I think you're exceptionally strong." He gave her a sharp nod. "And I dinnae just mean physically."

Something welled up inside Thea's chest, something that felt too big to contain and she wondered if that feeling was in her eyes for him to see.

Don't betray me, Conall. Please don't betray me. Not you too.

And then Thea smiled sadly. Because of course he would betray her. That was the plan they'd decided on together. Conall had to hand her over to protect the people he loved.

Questions filled the wolf's eyes as he studied the play of emotion across her face, but thankfully, they were suddenly in the city.

"We're almost there," she said, avoiding his gaze.

"We need something to eat and a change of clothing," Conall decided. "There's a shopping area I remember from my last visit. Callie dragged me to what felt like a million stores that day."

That got her attention. "You visited with Callie?"

He pinched his lips together before saying, "She'd been talking to ..." He lowered his voice. "A wolf. Online. On a dating site."

Thea's eyes widened. "There are supernatural dating sites?"

Conall grunted. "Aye. She met one from Düsseldorf and arranged to meet him. It was more to piss off my beta, James, than anything, but she was adamant. And I couldnae let her go meet this arsehole alone."

Amused at Conall flying to mainland Europe to chaperone his little sister on a date, Thea tried not to chuckle. "What happened?"

Conall sighed. "We got on the plane and when we were in the air, she burst into tears. She couldnae believe James had let her get on the bloody plane. I dinnae think even she realized how much it had been about trying to force him to admit there was something between them. She canceled the date, but I decided we should stay anyway. She needed a break from James, so I let her torture me as she dragged me from shop to shop around Düsseldorf."

That feeling in Thea's chest was about to explode. It had to be. It ached so badly. "You're a good brother."

They shared a look, and he sighed. "It's what family is supposed to do."

"But they don't always. You know that." She shrugged off her melancholy. "Isn't James the guy with Callie at Castle Cara?"

"Aye." Conall frowned. "He finally pulled his head out of his arse but Callie was diagnosed before they could be together. I've forbidden a relationship between them."

That seemed out of character. "Why?"

"Because it'll only cause them more pain in the long run." His voice was gruff with emotion. "If we lose her ... if he loses her, at least he doesnae have to live with the torturous memories of what it was like to be with her."

"And what about her?" Thea found herself angry.

Conall turned, surprised by her tone. "What do you mean?"

"She's dying, Conall, and you're denying her the chance at the only happiness she'll ever have."

"That's not what I'm doing. I'm protecting them."

"You've never been in love, have you? If you had, you'd know you're wrong."

He scowled down at her so ferociously, anyone else would quake in their seat but Thea was too pissed to care if he was annoyed.

"And have you been in love? Fallen for some Italian arsehole on your escape across Europe?"

She huffed in disbelief at his insensitivity. "No, I've never been in love. I don't trust anyone that much. But I know what it's like to lose people I love. So do you. Are you telling me you would rather you hadn't given them all of your love knowing they would die?"

"Of course not."

"It's the same thing, Conall."

Thea knew her words had penetrated because he was glowering fiercely at the seat in front of him like he wanted to punch through it.

"I think you're so used to managing people's lives, you don't know when you should stop."

His head whipped toward her. "And apparently, you dinnae know when you should stop talking."

Thea grabbed her backpack from the floor as the bus pulled into the station. "Yeah, well, the point is moot. I'm going to save your sister's life, Wolf Boy, but to do that we need to move."

Growling under his breath, Conall grabbed his own backpack and stood up, stretching to his full height. "I've got six years on you, lass. Stop calling me boy."

Thea thought it was amusing he wasn't averse to the wolf nickname, merely the boy part. She considered adjusting the nickname but decided she enjoyed needling him too much to bother.

A young woman a few seats down glanced over her shoulder, spotted Conall, and her eyes widened. Then she dragged her gaze up and down his body. She *did* not look scared of the werewolf.

She looked something else entirely.

Thea felt a sharp burn as she glared at the young woman who gave Conall a flirty smile. Conall didn't return the smile, but it didn't lessen Thea's unexpected annoyance. In fact, she pushed in front of him and shot the woman a death stare that made her blanch and turn away.

Suddenly she felt the wolf's heat right along her back and then the whisper of his breath on her ear as he bent down, amusement in his words, "What was that, lass?"

She stepped away, needing space, and cut him a dirty look. "We don't need anyone staring too hard or remembering the big guy on the bus from Dresden to Düsseldorf."

Conall's lips twitched, his pale grey eyes dancing.

"What?" she huffed.

He shook his head, looking far too pleased. "Nothing."

It was probably a good thing everyone started to get off the bus before Thea could punch him in the nuts. They were supposed to be allies after all.

HAVING GRABBED A QUICK BREAKFAST AT A CAFÉ NEAR THE BUS STATION, Thea felt somewhat rested and fed. Conall had insisted on buying toiletries for them both so they could have a quick wash in a public restroom. Afterward he said they both needed a change of clothes.

If he thought they had time to waste, Thea wasn't going to argue with him. Used to traveling dirty sometimes, the smell of sweat and bus breath didn't bother her too much, but it clearly bothered Conall. It was kind of cute, actually. If you could call anything related to Conall "cute."

Since she really was just following him around, she let Conall lead them to a pretty tree-lined street in the middle of the city that seemed to be the central shopping area. She insisted on him doing what he needed to do first and so she waited while he bought a pair of new jeans and a few T-shirts. The cold didn't appear to bother him, and Thea suspected that the rumor werewolves ran at a higher temperature than humans was true.

Paying closer attention to the shop assistants, Thea realized that while there was definitely wariness emanating from them as they watched or interacted with Conall, there was also a heavy fascination from both men and women. When he gave a pretty shop assistant a brief smile, Thea felt something twinge in her chest. The same something that had bothered her back on the bus with the flirty woman.

She ignored the feeling because with it came with a vulnerability she feared.

After Conall had what he needed (she'd wandered away when he started looking at boxer briefs), he stopped in a public restroom and changed into his new clothes. He'd packed the other new shirt and old clothes in his backpack. When he came out of the restroom, he didn't seem surprised Thea was outside waiting for him. It relieved her to realize he trusted her word that she'd stay to see this through with Ashforth.

Now it was time for her to buy a change of clothes. It was weird wandering around shops with Conall. One assistant had even mistaken him for Thea's boyfriend.

Confused by the messy emotions roiling inside her, Thea grew impatient as they searched for clothes. She had basic requirements—

jeans for bottoms and tops that covered her back. Somehow with Conall beside her, she couldn't think, and the thirty minutes they'd been looking felt like hours.

Finally, she grabbed a pair of jeans and a black, long-sleeved Henley to try on. Conall insisted she pick out more than one shirt.

"I have a wardrobe of clothes to return to. This is all you have."

"I don't need you to buy me clothes."

"I can afford a couple of shirts."

Seeing his mulish expression, Thea picked up a silky black shirt for the warmer weather. Conall took it out of her hand, checked the size, and then exchanged it for the same shirt in forest green. She stared at him questioningly as she took it.

Why did he have to make her feel like she was the only one in the room when he looked at her?

He shrugged. "The color suits you."

Thea felt a flush beneath her skin and accepted the green shirt. On the way into the changing room, she spotted a green T-shirt with a V-neck and grabbed it too. He *was* buying.

Her intention had been to get in and out of the changing rooms as fast as possible.

However, sometimes she had an issue with jeans fitting because she was small in the waist and legs but fuller around the ass area. The jeans she'd selected didn't fit well.

"How's it coming along?"

She jumped at the sound of Conall's voice beyond the curtain.

"Uh … the jeans don't fit."

"Right …" His footsteps faded and Thea peeked around the curtain to see Conall had flagged down a store assistant and was bringing her to the changing cubicle. Thea closed her eyes in annoyance. She hated dealing with people and would rather figure shit out on her own.

"How can I help?" the German shop assistant asked in perfect English.

Thea shot Conall a look of irritation that seemed to fly straight over his head and then pushed back the curtain. Making sure her shirt was covering her back, she indicated the massive gap between her back and the waistband of the jeans.

"They fit everywhere but the waist."

"Ah, yes, I see. These are the wrong jeans for your body shape. Your size? I'll bring you the correct jeans."

Thea glanced up at Conall whose eyes were currently glued to her ass in a way that left no doubt in her mind he was imagining her naked. When he dragged his gaze back up to her face, she raised her eyebrow at him. Instead of looking away, embarrassed for being caught like most guys would, he stared at her wolfishly.

Wolfishly.

Heat pooled in Thea's belly and she snapped the curtain shut on his face, pressing her hands to her burning cheeks.

The next few days were going to be the longest of her life.

After a few tries, they found a pair of jeans that worked. The assistant, a born saleswoman, brought more shirts for Thea to try that she had no intention of buying. Thea handed a few shirts and jeans to Conall to go purchase while she changed. "I'll meet you outside."

He walked away, seeming lost in his thoughts, and Thea was left with the shop assistant.

"You must try this shirt," the girl said, holding up a red silk blouse.

The shirt was gorgeous, but Thea would never wear such a bold color. It was like painting a target on her. But seeing the determination on the girl's face and realizing it would be quicker to indulge her, she nodded and closed the curtain.

Once it was on, she stared at the way the color brought out the warmer tones in her dark hair. Her brown eyes looked warmer too, like mahogany. It was the kind of shirt a woman would pair with nice jeans and heels, some jewelry maybe. Hair styled. Makeup on.

It was a shirt that belonged to a woman with a different life.

She pulled the shirt off.

"Is everything okay?" the store assistant asked.

Thea assumed she was talking to her and opened her mouth to reply when the curtain pulled back and Conall stepped in, crowding her in the tiny space.

"Sir, you can't go in there," the shop assistant reprimanded.

Conall ignored the girl, his whole body taut with tension as his attention zeroed in on Thea's breasts. They were hard to miss considering all she wore was a black bra and jeans.

"Conall," she snapped, refusing to cover herself like an outraged prudish miss but pissed at him for barging in.

He reached past her, brushing against her body in a way that made her flush. Whatever he was feeling he hid it as he pulled her own shirt down over her head. Thea pushed her arms through it, confused by his actions, and even more so when he deliberately drew his fingertips along her bare waist in a gentle caress, before releasing her.

"We've got company."

Understanding dawned.

Thea nodded and bent over to pull on her socks and boots. She quickly packed the bag with her new clothes into her rucksack and then Conall grabbed hold of her hand.

She was too stunned by the action to react.

He led her out of the changing room and Thea shot the frowning assistant a tight smile. "Thanks."

Conall's long legs ate up the floor as he hurried them across the store, his grip on Thea's hand unrelenting.

Despite their current danger and her lack of information on exactly who had found them, Thea stared at where her hand was wrapped in his, trying to remember the last time someone had held her like this because they cared.

She flexed her hand, an involuntary reaction and his squeezed hers like he was reassuring her.

Conall glanced over his shoulder as they reached the shop exit. "Wolves. Two of them. They're across the street, watching this shop. We need to lose them in the crowd."

She tugged on his hold. "How, Conall? How did they find us?"

He shook his head, scowling. "There's no way to track—" He bit out a curse and dropped her hand to pull the cell phone out of his back pocket. "The same man who brought the car, brought the phone. They werenae tracking the vehicle."

"They were tracking the phone," Thea surmised.

Shit.

Conall dropped the cell at his feet and crushed it into smithereens with a casual stomp of his boot. Then he grabbed Thea's hand again, his expression fierce. "These wolves arenae armed, which means they came to fight me. We're going to lead them somewhere no one can get hurt, and that includes you."

She frowned. "I can fight."

He smirked humorlessly. "I'm aware. But this is my kind of fight and I'm not letting them anywhere near you. I dinnae know if a wolf bite can harm you, but it can kill or turn a human. We're not taking the risk."

Thea wanted to argue but Conall was already pulling her out of the store.

And then they were running.

She tightened her hand in his as they ran as fast as they could without drawing even more unwanted attention. The burning tingle of warning fizzled uncomfortably down Thea's neck and she knew the wolves were giving chase.

Most shoppers jumped out of their way as they hurried down the tree-lined streets. Conall raced across intersection after intersection, causing car horns to beep and pedestrians to shout at them in aggravated German.

Finally, after a mile of running in a straight line, Conall turned left down a random street, his eyes on the doorways to their left. Around the midway point, he dove into an open doorway, pulling her through a windowless, empty lobby. They jumped a pile of filled trash bags and Conall burst through the door at the other end. Abruptly they found themselves in the shadowed courtyard of the commercial buildings surrounding them.

He pushed Thea into the farthest corner, and she looked up to note that anyone could witness what was about to happen from the windows above. But better here where no one else could get hurt, she supposed.

"I can fight," she insisted again as Conall dropped his pack and gave her his back, guarding her.

"I told you, Thea"—he shrugged out of his clothes—"this fight is mine. They touch you, they die."

Thea barely heard his words—she was too busy watching the

reveal of his naked body in awe. Somehow without clothes he seemed even bigger. His broad shoulders and back were powerful in muscle and width. He threw his shirt on top of his backpack, still facing the doorway, and then kicked off his boots and worked the belt on his jeans.

She braced herself, feeling a flush high on her cheeks as he pushed down his underwear and jeans, kicked them off, and straightened to his full height. She shouldn't look. Shouldn't ogle.

But Jesus Christ, he was magnificent.

His ass was round and taut with muscle, his thighs thick, his calves the same. He was like one of those Roman statues of male perfection. That feeling of primal female want and need that was becoming too familiar flooded deep in her belly.

Conall glanced over his shoulder at her, his nostrils flaring. She could only stare, stunned by her own reaction to him.

"Ceannsaichidh an Fhìrinn," his voice rumbled over the foreign words.

Before she could ask what they meant, he curled his hands into fists and Thea felt the energy around him amplify. All the hairs on her body rose as she witnessed Conall transform. First his claws sprang free, long and sharp and deadly, his jaw elongated, and sharp teeth filled his mouth. Thick black fur pushed through his skin at the same time she heard the first snap of bone.

She winced, thinking it sounded painful, but Conall's groan suggested otherwise. The grunts and moans he made were like ones of pleasure as he dropped to his fours. His limbs cracked and changed.

The appearance of their two hunters in the doorway drew her attention from the Scot and Thea braced to fight, to protect Conall while he was in the middle of shifting. But the wolves immediately tore off their own clothes.

Conall was right.

These two weren't armed.

They'd come to fight the honorable way.

But there was two against Conall.

Worry tightened her gut, a concern that gave way to awe as she watched Conall's transformation complete. Where once was a man was now a massive wolf, twice the size of an ordinary wolf.

He huffed through his snout and bared his teeth at the new arrivals, waiting for them to shift before he pounced.

Another wolf wouldn't have been so courteous, especially when it was two against one.

Thea stepped forward and the black wolf whipped his head toward her, Conall's pale gray eyes glaring at her. He snarled and she knew it was a warning to stay back.

Annoyed but daring to trust him, Thea retreated and he bobbed his head, which she took for appreciation. He turned his attention to the wolves, who had almost completed their transformation.

They were smaller than Conall, Thea realized. One pure gray, the other gray and brown.

She had to hope they were weaker too.

Her heart jumped in her throat as they suddenly flew at the Scot. His growl was deep and terrifying as he lunged, soaring over the two of them, landing on his front paws, only to twist in a blur of movement, his teeth coming down on the flank of the gray-brown wolf.

Tense with determination to jump in if he needed her, Thea watched, balanced on the tips of her toes, ready to join the fray, as Conall fought off the wolves. She winced when their teeth met his fur and inwardly whooped when he got in a hit.

They tried to circle him, but his size and reflexes made it impossible. Conall bit and clawed, getting in more hits to the two than they managed between them.

Then finally with one impatient swipe of a giant paw, he ripped open the gray wolf's belly. The wolf whimpered, crumpling to the ground, his whines hard to listen to without feeling an echo of sympathy despite his enemy status. Conall turned on the gray-brown wolf, pinning him to the courtyard floor with his huge clawed paw. He bared his teeth, his wolf lips vibrating as he communicated something to his challenger.

Whatever it was, slowly, the gray-brown wolf turned, showing Conall his belly.

Submitting.

Thea relaxed marginally.

Letting him go, Wolf Conall padded around the smaller wolf, his big, muscular body bristling as he pinned Thea in place with his eyes. It was hard to look away as he moved toward her, expression predatory, his huge body rippling with power. He was the most majestic thing Thea had ever seen.

But the flicker of movement behind him drew her attention. The gray-brown wolf rose, his sharp teeth bared.

"Conall!" she warned.

With a growl of animal outrage, Conall spun just as the wolf lunged, using his body weight to pin Conall to the ground. His dominance lasted a mere second before Conall reversed their positions, clamped his jaw around the wolf's throat and ripped it out.

The wounded wolf behind them whined even louder in obvious grief.

Thea's sympathy, however, died. Conall had been walking away, letting them both live, but the gray-brown wolf had acted dishonorably.

Wolf Conall made a guttural sound of annoyance and then padded toward Thea, his muzzle now wet with blood. She stood still with wonder, waiting for him to stop and shift, but he came right up to her.

A normal wolf, standing on all four paws, would have come to Thea's waist. Conall's head stopped at chest height. His black fur shimmered in the shadows, looking as soft as velvet, and Thea had the unstoppable urge to touch it. Tentatively reaching out, she waited for a sign that Wolf Conall was against being touched. He didn't give one and so Thea rested her palm gently against the top of his head.

He made a chuffing noise, like he was pleased, and Thea grinned. Growing bolder, she began to pet him. He *was* soft as velvet. And he liked to be petted. If he'd been a cat, he would be purring. "You're beautiful," she whispered.

She'd seen werewolves in their wolf state before. They'd guarded Ashforth's grounds in wolf form during the full moon. But none had been as magnificent as Conall. He really was king of the werewolves.

At her compliment, Wolf Conall turned the side of his face that didn't have blood on it into her breasts and nuzzled them lovingly. She laughed and pushed his face away. "Opportunist."

The sound he made was like a wolf version of laughter, and she knew without a doubt as he shot her an amused look far more human than animal that Conall never lost who he was when he shifted. She'd always wondered about that, whether a werewolf held onto their human consciousness when they turned.

So caught in the moment, she'd forgotten about the other wolves. But she realized as Conall padded away from her, the energy around him becoming static, that the gray wolf had stopped whimpering. His pelt still rose and fell with deep breaths—he was still alive.

Conall shifted. She knew it was wrong to watch but found herself unable to look anywhere else. First his fur began to shrink, disappearing into golden skin, and then the cracking of bone sounded as his forelegs became arms. He settled onto his hind legs as the transformation moved through his body, until Conall emerged, standing, his skin flushed. He faced her, chest heaving with exertion, and she got a second look at his ripped abdomen before her attention was inevitably drawn downward.

A blush crested high on her cheeks.

Conall was aroused.

Impressively, impressively so.

Her eyes flew to his, and he gave her an unembarrassed shrug. "Pay no attention. Just a side effect of adrenaline after a fight."

Thea nodded, trying to appear nonchalant. "Well, I learn something new every day."

He shot her a dry look and pulled on his clothes, turning to do so, giving her the backside view instead.

She wasn't disappointed by that at all.

The air across the courtyard changed, drawing their attention, and the gray wolf slowly transformed into a man. His groans were not ones of pleasure but of pain. He sat back, naked on his haunches, his belly wound raw and red but closed. Thea remembered Conall said werewolves healed faster in wolf form.

This was the proof.

The man glared his hatred at Conall but didn't move. Conall grabbed his backpack and strode over to the waiting werewolf.

"Who sent you?"

The attacker didn't speak.

"Do I need to kill you too?"

The werewolf looked at his dead companion.

"He acted dishonorably. He forfeited and then attacked when my back was turned."

Anguish darkened the werewolf's eyes, but he reluctantly nodded. His gaze moved to Thea. "Eirik wants you dead," the werewolf said in a German accent. "If he wants you dead, there is no escaping that." Out of nowhere, he pulled a silver blade and Thea went to lunge in front of Conall just as the wolf drew the blade across his own throat.

She grabbed Conall's arm, her grip probably bruising as she stared in shock at the dying wolf.

After a few seconds, Conall drew her hand from his arm and curled his own around it. He drew her into side. "Eirik?"

Thea shook her head. "I've no idea. The Blackwoods?"

Conall exhaled slowly, wearily. "I dinnae think so."

Realizing there might be more than one group after her, Thea stared up at Conall who was glaring at the dead wolf in thought. If he couldn't protect Thea, get her back to Scotland before someone else got to her, Callie would die. But somewhere deep down, Thea knew she'd begun to hope that Conall cared about protecting Thea because of *Thea*.

Something had changed between them, gradually, compelling them forward to a new state of understanding, one that finally sank its teeth into Thea as she watched Conall fight to the death to protect her.

Like he knew she had been fighting for too long.

Like he knew just once someone should care enough to fight for her.

Thea so wanted to believe that.

Only days ago, she would have told herself she was ridiculous to even contemplate trusting another being with her life. But she was so tired.

So tired of being alone.

Of being without faith.

The promise she made to Amanda floated across her mind.

"Iron," she blurted out.

Conall frowned down at her. "What, lass?"

She licked her dry lips and then unconsciously squeezed the hand holding tight to hers. "My weakness, Conall. The thing Ashforth lined the walls with, the metal of the cat-o'-nine-tails. Pure iron. I'm allergic to pure iron."

He was disturbingly silent for what felt like forever. And then he turned into her. "You trust me a little then, Thea?"

Although it was difficult, she nodded.

Something flared in his eyes. "I know someone who might be able to give us the answers we need. About you … about the Blackwoods and this Eirik person. Will you trust me to take you to this man?"

There was still a part of her that wanted to flee the truth, to flee trust, hope, but Thea accepted that everything had changed when Conall came into her life. There was no going back now.

"Okay …"

"He's a friend but he's also a vampire."

Surprised by this information, Thea could only nod. She'd been under the assumption that vamps and wolves tolerated each other but weren't exactly friendly.

Conall tugged on her hand and led her out of the courtyard of death. "Then we're taking a detour."

"To where?"

He flashed her a quick grin over his shoulder. "Ever been to Norway?"

17

"I still can't believe *you* have a fake ID," Thea said as Conall drove north.

He shot her a look, wondering at what point she stopped seeing him as most people did. Everyone else would take one look at him and immediately think "That is a man with a fake ID, a Harley, and a knife collection."

"Most supes I know have fake identification. Strange things happen around us. We need to be untraceable if the authorities poke around."

She nodded, seeming to accept this.

Conall had used said fake ID, an ID that Ashforth did not know about, to rent an SUV in Düsseldorf. They were traveling toward Neumünster in northern Germany. It was over a five-hour drive, so they'd stop at a hotel for the night before continuing in the morning through Denmark to Frederikshavn. That drive would be followed by an almost ten-hour ferry crossing to Oslo.

"Ashforth used to scare me with the threat of the government. That they were interested in me after the plane crash and it was only his protection that was keeping them at bay. Do *you* think the government knows about supes?"

Conall didn't like that Ashforth had held government exposure over her head like an axe, but he also wouldn't lie to the lass. "It would be naïve to think they arenae aware of our world. I've heard stories of certain governments … experimentation, captivity, recruitment, that kind of thing."

"Doesn't that concern you?"

"As long as they stay out of my way, I'll stay out of theirs." He wasn't looking for a war. His whole mission in life was to protect his pack from that very thing. Conall thought of Callie, whom he'd called from a pay phone before they'd left Düsseldorf. She hadn't answered, and it was Ashforth who rang the pay phone back.

"The Blackwoods attacked again," Conall had lied to Ashforth. "They were using the cell to track us."

"And yet you survived," Ashforth had murmured. "You're proving yourself to be quite impressive, Conall."

He'd almost choked on his bile as images of Thea's back flitted across his mind. This man had used a vampire to whip Thea with a cat-o'-bloody-nine tails. She'd been nineteen years old. Rage had welled inside Conall just thinking about it, and he'd pulled the phone away from his ear, taking deep breaths and ignoring Thea's questioning eyes.

Finally he'd pulled himself together. "I'm going to bring Thea back without your help. Your people cannae be trusted."

Ashforth had sounded affronted. "I assure you they can."

"Well, that *doesnae* assure me. I'm doing this my way, which means I'll be taking an out-of-the-way route back to Scotland to shake any tail we might have. I'll not lead a dangerous coven into my country and anywhere near my pack. It'll probably take us a few more days to get home."

"Frankly," Ashforth had spat, "that's not good enough. I'm a businessman, Conall. I have fucking responsibilities elsewhere. You get back here immediately."

The wolf had risen from inside easily after having been let loose earlier. The grizzle of the wolf made his voice coarse. "Dinnae ever dare speak to me that way. You're not alpha here. I call the shots."

"And I have your sister."

Conall had let rip a feral growl, not caring who around them heard it. "Aye, but I have Thea. And I think I might only now understand just how important she is to you, so we're even in that respect. Do you know where we're not even, Ashforth? I have your scent. There is no amount of money in the world that can protect you from me. Nowhere for you to hide. If you touch one hair on either Callie's or James' heads, I will hunt you to the ends of the earth and fucking skin you alive. And that's not a figure of speech."

Ashforth had gone silent, and Conall had flicked a look at Thea leaning against the wall beside the pay phone, staring at the ground. A small, darkly satisfied smile had curled her lips as she'd listened to Conall's threat. It'd made him feel about ten feet tall to give her that moment.

"Like I said, we'll be a few days yet. I'll call again when we're getting closer. Now I'd like to speak with my sister."

And so Conall had a few moments with Callie to hear her voice and assure himself she was okay. She sounded tired and bored, but beyond that, fine.

Afterward Conall made Thea move quickly, knowing Ashforth would no doubt trace the call and try to follow them.

They'd been on the road for more than an hour, mostly driving in silence. Over the last few days he'd learned that Thea, like him, wasn't particularly loquacious unless you asked her something that required detail. He liked that about her. Their silence was easy, like two friends who had known each other a long time. However, it left Conall to his own thoughts, and his own thoughts were not a good place to be.

Thea had told him her weakness was pure iron. That revelation opened his mind to the most absurd conclusions that couldn't possibly be true. Which was why he was taking her to his friend, Vik. Vik was a two-hundred and thirty-four-year-old vampire who split his time between Glasgow and Oslo. They'd met when he'd bought one of the oldest bottles of whisky in the GlenTorr collection. Conall had delivered it to him in Glasgow and been surprised to find the buyer was a vampire. They shared a similar sense of humor, and Vik's breadth of knowledge on many subjects fascinated Conall. He was a devout researcher, with a plethora of degrees from several of the world's best universities, and contacts all over the planet.

They'd kept in touch and Conall visited anytime they were both in Glasgow. He knew Vik was at his Oslo home because Conall had just sent a small crate of whisky over before he'd left to find Thea.

If anyone might know what Thea was, it would be Vik.

He knew everything about the supernatural world.

He'd be able to dispel the utter nonsense rolling around in Conall's mind.

Conall flicked a look at his companion. He enjoyed looking at her. Too much.

She'd trusted him.

Fuck but that pleased him.

He wanted to reach over and tuck her hair behind her ear so he could better see her face, but he resisted. Wanting to touch her all the time had crept up on him. And he knew Thea was attracted to him too. He'd scented it.

It was a complication they didn't need.

One Conall had to ignore.

For Callie's sake, for the packs'.

For his and for Thea's.

Conall needed to distract them both. "Did your parents know? About the iron?"

Her cognac eyes were almost black in the shadowed interior of the SUV. Her eyes appeared dark as jet in the photos Ashforth first showed Conall, and their rich warmth in real life had been unexpected. As was their soulfulness. How could he have thought this woman had any evil in her?

Arse, Conall. You're a total and utter arse sometimes.

Thea's voice pulled him from his self-derision. "There aren't a lot of objects made from pure iron. Well, there wasn't." She shot him a sardonic look. "Recently there's been a trend in using pure iron for decorative railings and such instead of wrought iron. That's been fun."

Conall thought about that. Pure iron was a silver-gray metal, a little more pliable than iron but it was still strong enough to do damage. Thea's back was evidence of that. Then again, if it was as poisonous to Thea as she said, it wouldn't matter how strong the iron was. Like silver to a wolf, one touch to the skin would burn.

He blanched, imagining what it would feel like to be whipped by a silver-tipped cat-o'-nine-tails. Fuck, but he was in awe of Thea's strength.

"So they never knew?"

"Honestly, possibly. But it never came up. Pure iron has less carbon in it, so it isn't as strong or frequently used as other iron materials. Now there's more of it. They use what they call commercial pure iron, but it still affects me. It's what blacksmiths use to make those goddamn decorative railings … but …" She exhaled shakily. "It's also used in aviation. Pure iron was one of the first things I googled when I got away from Ashforth. There was this page that said commercial pure iron is utilized in aviation."

Conall was silent as he let this sink in. Did she think … "Thea," he said, his tone gentle, "most planes are made of aluminium."

"Aluminum?" She pronounced the *u* like "ooh" and excluded the last *i*.

"Aye, that one. But the way I said. The right way," he teased, trying to coax the taut expression off her face. She couldn't possibly think she was to blame for her parents' deaths.

She didn't smile at his teasing. "But what about all the little parts a plane is made of? There could be commercial pure iron in there somewhere."

"Enough to make you bring down a plane?" He shook his head. "I dinnae think so, lass. Were you …" He hesitated to take her back to that place, but he felt it was important to assure her. "Did you feel pain or the flu-like symptoms you spoke of when you got on the plane with your parents that day?"

She swallowed so hard, he heard it. "No," she whispered. "I didn't know it at the time but what I felt was the feeling I get when I know something bad is going to happen. I get this tingling burn down my neck, my heart races, and a feeling of dread comes over me."

Conall raised an eyebrow. "And you feel this every time you sense danger?"

"Yeah."

"But you didn't feel pain that day?"

"No."

"Then it stands to reason, Thea, that your instincts knew there was something wrong with that plane. You didnae bring it down. Your instincts were just screaming at you it would go down."

"But what if my emotions made it worse? I fried Ashforth's plane, blew the windshield off it before that."

Conall wished he could pull over so he could look her in the eyes when he said this, so she could see his certainty and sincerity. "Thea, you did not kill your parents. You tried to save them … it's not your fault they didnae know to listen."

She was quiet so long he thought he'd upset her. Then, "Sometimes I blame them for that. Because they should have known. They knew me. They knew … I was different. That if I thought something was wrong, they should listen."

Glad he'd steered her away from self-flagellation, he asked, "When did they realize you were different?"

"As soon as I was born, they knew something was up because of the blood tests. My DNA isn't entirely human. In fact, it's no DNA that's ever been catalogued."

Conall nodded. "Werewolves too. We wolves use fellow were-wolves for doctors and midwives."

"Smart. But my parents were both human, which makes what I am an even greater mystery. The doctors ran the tests again, and they wanted to keep me at the hospital, but after months of tests that didn't prove my abnormal DNA equated to health problems, another doctor advised my parents to take me home. And they left town. Mom was making good money with Ashforth so they moved to Westchester to be close to the city. Mom and Dad told me it wasn't until around a year old they realized I might be special. I began talking in full sentences."

Conall huffed. "That's fast."

"Extremely. And I was strong. Stronger than my dad. And I … I could move things."

He furrowed his brows, not only at the information but at the trepi-dation in her voice. "Move things?"

"Without touching them."

Conall snapped his eyes to hers and she was staring at him warily.

Hell, he wished she wouldn't do that. Keeping his expression neutral, he said, "I wasnae aware you could do that."

"I can't." She shook her head. "I mean, not anymore. Ashforth doesn't know about it. It freaked my parents out so much and they were trying to protect me, so they asked me to stop. I did. It's like the years of disuse put a mental block on it or something. The only time I've come close to using it is when I'm emotional."

"Like when you turned the lights on in the hotel room yesterday?"

"Exactly. Obviously, my parents knew something was up, to put it mildly. Dad didn't even consider the idea I wasn't his. He trusted my mom completely. Plus, there's no denying I'm his child."

Conall looked at her again and she was smiling softly. His gaze dropped to her mouth before moving back to the road.

"I have his dark hair, his eyes, and his smile. My mom was a redhead."

"So was mine." Conall smiled in memory. "As is Callie."

"I, um … I've seen a picture."

"How?"

Her expression was sheepish. "When I stole money out of your wallet."

"Oh, aye." He grunted. "That time you broke my neck."

"It could have been worse."

His reply was dry. "I'm aware of that."

Thea smirked, but her smile fell. "My parents started researching and Dad soon began to realize that there was this whole other world around us. And like I said, as I got older my parents taught me to hide my strength, to control it. They absolutely forbade me to use any of the mind stuff. Moving things without touching them and manipulating what people saw."

"But you can still do the latter. Why that and not the telekinesis, for lack of a better word?"

Thea seemed to take a breath before she confessed, "Because I didn't stop using the mind trick." Shame colored her words. "My only excuse is that I was a stupid kid. I used it on classmates, on teachers. I even used it after my parents died. I used it to make the authorities who found the plane crash think I had *some* injuries. I can't remember waking up in the debris. Instead, one moment there was the dark of impact, the pain of fire, then the next I was outside the wreckage. Without a scratch on me. I was old enough to know that would raise more than eyebrows. So I made them see a cut forehead, a broken ankle, that kind of thing. I did the opposite with it too … like if I hurt myself and was healing too fast in front of a human, I'd make them see I was never hurt.

"It wasn't until after Ashforth kept me in that room I realized how wrong it was to use it. He took away my freedom, my free will. And I realized that using my ability was the same thing. I was taking away someone's control over their own mind." She exhaled slowly. "I've never told anyone that before."

Something inside Conall's chest seemed to expand at her confession.

Thea shifted in her seat like she was uncomfortable. "I've made it sound like my parents were ashamed of what I was, but they never meant to make me feel that way. They were just trying to protect me."

"If they researched you, do you think *they* knew what you are?"

"Yes," she admitted, drawing his surprised gaze. Her eyes were bright with regret and grief. "I think they did. When I was a kid, there were times I'd get upset about being different. I just wanted to be normal."

"Understandable." Conall couldn't imagine growing up without people like himself around. "Your parents were human. If you'd grown up in a pack, you would never have felt 'other.' You would have been accepted. Not that I'm saying your parents didnae accept you."

"No, I get you. And you're right. I wanted to be like my parents, to be human. Once when I was twelve, not too long before … before they died … I pushed a friend out of the way of a stray baseball. It would have knocked her out. It came at us with such a force, so I took the hit, knowing it would barely hurt. There were too many witnesses from the game to mess with their minds about it. And the school made a huge fuss and my dad got mad at me. He said that no matter what, I couldn't step in to save other people from bad things because it would only expose me, and people would come to take me away."

Her voice grew hollow, flat. "I cried so much because I hated that I couldn't even save my friend without being told not to be myself. They hated seeing me in pain and that night, my mom told me something I've thought a lot on over the years.

"She said that when I turned eighteen and I was old enough to make my own decisions, I'd have the opportunity to learn about who I really was, and when I had that information, it would be up to me how I used it. It would be up to me to make the right choice about my abilities. I didn't know what she meant then …"

"They knew," Conall answered decisively. "They discovered what you are, Thea."

He saw her nod out of the corner of his eye. "Yeah, I think so too. Now we'll never know for sure."

"One thing is for sure: Ashforth thinks he knows what you are." Conall remembered the drug that hurt Thea. "The drug? Does it contain pure iron?"

"No. But I heard something when I was his little lab rat. He thought I was unconscious because he'd taken a lot of blood from me. But my blood regenerates faster than a human's. Much faster." She turned in her seat, angling her body toward him. "So we all have iron in our blood, right?"

"Right."

"But it's got oxygen in it. Like iron ore. Which is possibly why iron ore doesn't affect me. There's iron in food too. That doesn't bother me. What I heard this lab guy that Ashforth had hired to run tests on me explain was that injecting me with an iron supplement overwhelmed my system while my blood tried to oxidize it. It isn't like pure iron, which would probably paralyze me indefinitely if I were injected with it. Instead, it was … well, it burns. Like fire running through my veins. And when I was weak from the room he'd lined with pure iron, my body struggled to heal as fast as it normally would."

"That's why it didnae work when I gave it to you." He flinched at the reminder he'd inflicted pain on her. "You're stronger outside the room. Your blood oxidized it within an hour."

"Exactly."

It was then it truly hit Conall just how powerful Thea was. She had one weakness. That was it. *One* weakness. There was something comforting about the fact that Thea Quinn was so incredibly difficult to kill.

A true immortal.

She'd been alone so long because of it, not trusting anyone. But she'd trusted *him*. With her story, with her weaknesses. Conall owed her the same.

"You should know the drug mutes my ability to track you."

She was quiet a moment and when he glanced at her, her expression was blank.

"I have no idea why. All I know is that my ability only works on sentient beings."

"Sentient beings?" Thea frowned. "It works on animals too?"

"Aye. When Callie was younger, she would guilt me into looking for people's lost pets whenever she saw a poster for a missing dog or cat. She once had me track down a bloody guinea pig."

Thea giggled. Conall grinned at the sound. "That's hilarious."

"Aye, well, that's Callie for you."

"Tell me more about her."

He grunted at having the conversation turned on him and his family.

"What? I want to know who it is I'm saving."

The reminder he'd hand Thea over to Ashforth in exchange for his sister caused a flare of anger he had to forcefully quell. "She's fierce," he said, deciding he owed her this too. "Much like our mum. Callie is also an alpha and was the pack's lead warrior before she got sick."

"She'll be strong again soon."

A flood of confusion hit Conall. He was desperate to see Callie well again, but he dreaded the sacrifice it would take. "Aye. Well, she's single-minded and opinionated enough. She's also the bloody nosiest wolf I've ever met." He smirked, remembering the many times she'd interfered in the love lives of their pack. Sometimes she triumphed, sometimes she just pissed people off. His smirk fell. "She cares too much."

"Too much? Is there such a thing?"

"Aye. Callie cares about everything. Not just our pack and our lands, but everyone in the entire universe. She jumps from one crusade to the next. Sometimes it's personal, an old university friend dying from cancer, or something bigger than us all. Like human trafficking, climate change, animal cruelty." He looked at Thea, who was frowning. "It hurts her. I see how caring that much about everything hurts her."

Thea gave him a sad smile. "You're in awe of her."

Conall nodded, grief clogging his throat as he turned back to the road. The world would be such a dark place without Caledonia MacLennan in it.

"It's brave to care that much, Conall. I'm glad I have the chance to save someone like her."

His fists tightened around the wheel as a sharp, knifelike pain slashed across his chest.

"Do you want her to be with James once she's healed?" Thea asked.

Uncomfortable talking about his sister's romantic life, he merely grunted again.

She chuckled, the sound throaty and far too appealing. "I'll take that as a no."

Conall sighed. "It's not a no. James is a good man. Their match is unusual—he's a beta, she an alpha. An alpha male often marries a lower-ranked female, but a female usually looks for her equal or stronger. Yet, for them it works. He'll … well … he'll love her the way she deserves."

"Good."

Conall could feel Thea eyeing him and when he glanced quickly at her, he saw speculation in her expression.

"You said you've never been in love. There was really no one you felt like … what do you guys call it? Mating with?"

Sienna Canid's face infiltrated Conall's thoughts, and he nearly swerved off the road with the jolt it gave him.

Jesus fuck.

Sienna.

He'd fucking forgotten.

Sienna.

The betrothal.

Everything.

What the bloody hell?

"Sorry. Too personal?"

A tight feeling crawled across Conall's chest at the realization he was supposed to be getting engaged upon his return home. Before he'd left Torridon, the idea of betrothal hadn't touched him apart from giving him satisfaction that the pack's future would be assured.

Now ... now he felt trapped.

Fuck.

"Conall?"

He threw Thea an impatient look. Bloody lass was ruining everything. "No," he bit out. "And a mating differs from marriage. Most wolves marry as finding your true mate is rare."

"Rare?"

Deciding that explaining pack life was as good a distraction as any, he replied, "Aye. My parents were true mates but they're the only true mates our pack has seen in a century. It's an inexplicable bond and as rare as it is, it's also rare to see a true mating ever dissolve. The love of true mates is said to be as passionate at the end as it is from day one. My parents' relationship attested to it. But most wolves, like humans, enjoy relationships and marriage. Some pack marriages are arranged for political or financial reasons, especially if a pack is wealthy." He should tell her about Sienna, but the words got caught in his throat. He cleared it. "But for most werewolves, marriage is, like it is for humans, practiced in love."

"Arranged marriages, huh? That sounds archaic."

His mind conjured Sienna again. Reserved, dutiful Sienna. From what he'd surmised of her so far, Conall had liked her, had even been attracted to her. Now the thought of her left him cold. "Aye, they seem to work. Sometimes they fall apart, especially if one finds their true mate."

"Arranged marriages sound like a disaster waiting to happen."

"So are many human arranged marriages."

"I don't disagree." He felt her eyes on his face. "So how does a wolf know when he's met his true mate? Do sparks literally fly?" she teased.

He snorted. "Not that I'm aware of. My father told me it's hard to explain. He said he just knew when he met my mum she was his mate. There was a certainty in his mind that no one on earth could persuade him otherwise. After two mates have sex for the first time, their scents become intertwined, and it signals to other wolves so they know not to trespass upon another wolf's territory." He flashed a grin at Thea's indignation. "That goes both ways. It's not just about a male marking his female. A female wolf is just as territorial of her mate. Sometimes more so."

Conall remembered the way his parents had been around one another. So much passion and love, he'd often been embarrassed by it growing up. Now he'd give anything to see them laughing and cuddling like smitten teenagers.

When a comfortable silence fell between them again, Conall glanced over at Thea. Suddenly he saw an image of Thea in a faceless man's arms, finding comfort after her escape from Ashforth, and the thought made Conall restless.

No, not restless.

It made him jealous as fuck.

There.

He'd admitted it to himself.

And now he needed to know. He shouldn't ask. It wasn't his business. "What about you?" he blurted out before he could stop himself. "You said you've never been in love but that doesnae mean you've never tried."

Thea shrugged and glanced out her window. "I tried once. Not love, just … connection, I guess. It was about a year after I got away. The guy was human, and we bartended together." She gave a snort of joyless laughter. "I was so worried about losing control, being too strong, hurting him that …"

Conall's gut tightened. "What?"

"Nothing. It just wasn't very good."

Don't ask, don't fucking ask. "And you never tried again?" *Prick. Moron. Masochist. Nosy fucking bastard.*

To his surprise, Thea answered. "I've never trusted anyone enough to try again."

Feeling her attention, he glanced at her and she was glaring at him, an attractive blush cresting high on her cheeks.

"Can we change the subject now?"

Conall grinned despite himself. "You asked first."

"I didn't ask *you* about sex."

The word hung heavily in the air between them, and Conall found he couldn't think of another subject to distract them with. Instead, they fell into a silence that wasn't as comfortable as it had been before.

———

THE HOTEL AT NEUMÜNSTER HAD TAKEN INSPIRATION FROM ITS Scandinavian neighbors. The reception was a huge, open-plan space with a quirky mix of industrial and natural materials. There were exposed pipes along the ceiling, but a beautiful fire on a partition wall. The fire was low to the ground, built between two pieces of marble, the top part of which had holes cut into it where the firewood was stored.

A massive corner sofa sat opposite the fire, with bean cushions and a large wooden coffee table. There was a reception desk near the fire, a bar, and a shop selling everything from wine to clothing.

Beyond the reception was another bar and restaurant and all the rooms were on the two floors above.

Conall watched Thea take in the surroundings with a quiet look of pleasure. Her expression made him book a suite. "With twin beds instead of a king," he requested.

"I'm sorry, sir." The blond receptionist was almost as well built as Conall. "Our suites only come with a king." He'd flicked an inquisitive look at Thea, obviously wondering why Conall wouldn't want to share a bed with her.

He buried an agitated snarl. "But the room has a pull-out sofa?"

"Yes, sir."

There was nothing technically to stop him booking two rooms. He trusted Thea not to run. But for her safety, she should stay with him.

"That's fine." He'd take the sofa.

Once they had their room sorted, Conall booked them a table at the restaurant and went one step further by insisting on buying Thea a pair of pajamas in the hotel gift shop.

"You don't have to do that." She waved away his offer.

"Do you want to sleep in your jeans?"

She wrinkled her adorable nose. "Well … okay, then." Thea grinned up at him, her eyes dancing. "Thanks."

Conall quickly looked away. His heart was beating too fast.

It was that fucking conversation in the car.

"Pick something." He was gruff.

Things only worsened when they strode into the room. The bed was luxurious and inviting and the sofa was absolutely not. His legs would dangle over the bloody thing.

"I'll take the sofa," Thea said, dropping her rucksack on it.

"Like hell." He grabbed the backpack and dumped it on the bed. "You'll take the bloody bed."

"I'm shorter. I'll take the sofa."

"You'll take the bed and be grateful for it," he snapped.

She scowled at him. "What crawled up your ass in the last twenty minutes, huh?"

"I'm sorry, I didnae realize offering you the bed was a bad thing." He was being deliberately obtuse, and they both knew it.

"It's not the bed, it's your tone."

"I dinnae have a tone."

"There." She gestured to him. "That is a tone."

Fuck, they sounded like his mum and dad when they argued. Like an old married couple.

Conall rubbed a hand over his face, feeling the thick bristle of a beard forming. He needed to shave, and eat, and he needed to sleep.

And he needed to not be a bastard to Thea just because he was totally and utterly fucked in the head. The big one and the little one. "Sorry," he sighed. "Just restless from driving so long."

"I told you I'd take a turn."

"It's fine, lass. I'm going to wash up before we head down to dinner."

The restaurant was busy with moody low lighting and a Scandinavian casualness in its simple furnishings. As they sat opposite each other at the small table Conall dwarfed, renewed tension fell between them.

Thea was the first to break the silence as they waited on their food. "Tell me more about Pack MacLennan."

So Conall spoke of his people and of Torridon, of life in the Scottish Highlands, and his role as alpha and CEO. "Sometimes I tire of all the paperwork but it's a small price to pay for our blessings."

"I can't exactly imagine you stuck in an office, signing contracts and going through accounts." She smiled wryly at the thought.

"You're not wrong. I visit the distillery as much as possible. I like to help there when I can. And my delta, Mhairi, runs our fishing company out of Loch Torridon. Sometimes I go out and help her crew. I also volunteer with Scottish Mountain Rescue. Anything to be out of doors."

"And to save lives." Her expression was searching, serious, and worse, admiring. "Don't sell yourself short, Conall. You do it to help people."

He shrugged. "I'm stronger. I can help where others cannae, I suppose."

"So you're not just about your pack," she teased.

"Dinnae be fooled, Thea. Callie was the one who talked me into volunteering."

She laughed, and Conall watched.

It was hard not to.

The tension lingered between them as they seemed unable to look anywhere but at each other. Yet conversation was easy as they ate, sharing childhood stories and more laughter than he thought possible after the violence of the last few days. Only days between them and yet it felt longer. Much longer.

"Without the memory of my parents and of Amanda, I think I might have become something different." Thea tried to hide the sudden bleakness in her eyes by lowering them to the table. "As it is, you know I don't always do the right thing."

Conall knew instinctively she was talking about her thievery. He'd judged her for it, inwardly and outwardly. What a wanker he was sometimes.

"I've never had to survive day to day with no money the way you have. In fact, I've been lucky enough to never worry about money at all. I've no right to judge you, Thea. I cannae say I wouldnae have done the same if our roles were reversed. And we both know you could have used your talent for mind trickery, to live a life of luxury, if you'd wanted."

Thea gave him a sexy little smirk. "Don't think too highly of me, Conall. Remember how this ends."

Like he could forget. "Aye. I remember."

"So your grandfather started the whisky company?" She abruptly changed the subject. "That's where all the money comes from?"

When he explained GlenTorr's history and spoke more of its unexpected success, Thea admitted she'd never tasted it. Upon hearing that, Conall led her to the bar after dinner.

Sure enough, they had a bottle of his whisky.

"You have to try it."

"I've never tried any whisky," she confessed.

"Well now, you definitely have to try it." Conall ordered one whisky with ice and the other straight.

"How come I get ice?" Thea frowned.

"Waters it down a wee bit. Trust me, you'll be glad for it."

"If you can drink it straight, I can drink it straight."

Conall grinned at her indignation. "Fine." He changed his order.

And then laughed when Thea took a gulp and spluttered when the burn hit her chest.

She shot him a filthy look. "You could have warned me."

"Now where would the fun be in that? Sip it, lass. A whisky is to be nursed, not downed."

Doing as instructed, Thea sipped at the drink.

"What do you think?"

"It's smoky. It's weirdly nice," she said.

"We dry our malted barley using peat smoke," he explained, and then his attention caught on a drop of whisky glistening on her lower lip. Conall reached out without thinking to catch the drop on his thumb. Thea tensed at the intimate action.

Their eyes locked and everything he'd been feeling all day pooled heavily in a visceral need in his groin. Conall wanted to touch Thea. Everywhere. And he wanted her to touch him. It was a haze that made his heart race, his breathing deepen, and *everything* else in his world fade out.

All he was left with was want.

For this woman.

It stayed with him as the mounting tension between them forced them to withdraw from the bar and head to their room. It remained with him as he showered, shaved, and changed back into his clothes since the hotel robe was too small for him.

And it became all-consuming as he sat on the sofa, staring at a blank television screen while he listened to Thea shower, control straining at the knowledge she was naked in the next room. His imagination was vivid.

He swelled uncomfortably against his jeans zipper.

His skin felt too tight, too hot.

The bathroom door opened, and Thea stepped out in the white hotel robe, her long, dark hair a wet spill down her left shoulder. Those big, shining, cognac eyes locked with his and whatever control Conall had been holding onto melted under the stress of the fire between them.

One second he was on the sofa, telling himself to stay put. The next he was a blur across the room, hauling Thea against him so he could crush her mouth beneath his.

She gasped, and he tasted her.

No one woman had ever tasted as perfect.

And Conall knew as he gripped her warm, soft body as close to his as he could get her that nothing would stop him from tasting every inch of her.

Nothing.

18

WHILE SHE'D SHOWERED, THEA'S HANDS SHOOK AS SHE USED THE HOTEL shampoo and conditioner to wash her hair. Her knees had trembled too, and her belly was a riot of nerves.

She was worried about what she should say to Conall when she came out of the bathroom and almost hoped he was already asleep. The tension between them was unbearable, and it was all his fault. He kept looking at her like he wanted to devour her, and it was making her desire things she never thought she'd want again.

When Thea stepped out, not only was Conall awake but the look in his eyes when he stared at her made her breathless. It was like he thought she was the most magnificent thing he'd ever seen. It was beyond mere sexual attraction.

No one had ever looked at her like that.

To know someone like Conall, so fierce and ruthless on the outside, so honorable and true on the inside, would look at her like that … Her heart was already racing when suddenly the guy was a blur across the room.

Her heart jumped into her throat as he hauled her into his arms and up onto her tiptoes so he could kiss her like she'd never been kissed before.

Thea gasped with excitement. A million reasons why they shouldn't do this flashed across her mind yet were easily silenced by the stroke of his tongue against hers. A shiver skated down her spine and she pressed closer against Conall's hard body.

Like the desperate grasp of his hands, his kisses were deep, ravenous, and intoxicating.

Thea never knew kissing could be like that.

Desire swirled between her legs and she dug her fingers into Conall's strong biceps, trying to get closer, closer.

At her eagerness, he made a low growling noise that vibrated in her mouth and caused a rush of instant arousal. She moaned and pushed her hips deeper into his, feeling his hardness buried against her belly.

Conall broke the kiss and Thea stared up into those gray wolf eyes, in awe that such a cold color could be so warm. His gaze was searching. Waiting.

They both knew they shouldn't give in to their attraction.

That it would make everything messy and complicated.

But the thought of walking away, of not knowing what it would feel like to be with him, made Thea want to cry. She was only twenty-five years old and yet she was weary and exhausted by life. There had been no moments of true happiness in her world since she was twelve.

No escape.

And no one had held her or made her feel *essential*.

As necessary as breathing.

Conall made her feel that way.

She wanted more of that. She wanted to be touched, to be loved, and to touch and love in return, and Thea knew just one night with Conall would be enough to last her a lifetime. He was worth risking those high impenetrable walls she'd built around herself.

Thea could go on surviving for however long time granted her.

Tonight, she would *live*.

She slid her hands up Conall's strong shoulders, wrapped them around his nape, and pulled his head back toward hers. He gave another animalistic growl of pleasure that caused a stir low in her belly. There was a tug on her robe and Thea tensed at the reminder he would see and feel her back.

Conall moved his lips along her cheek to her ear as the robe fell open. "I've never seen beauty like yours, lass," he promised, his voice a rumble of sexual need.

Thea believed him.

She relaxed, and he pulled away, his hungry eyes meeting hers before lowering down her naked body. Thea expected to feel exposed, to feel vulnerable, but she was hot and restless and aching in places she never realized could ache. She shrugged her shoulders and dropped her arms so the robe fell, pooling behind her feet on the floor.

Conall studied her so long, she was in great danger of melting into a puddle of want beside the robe.

When his eyes returned to hers, Thea gave a little moan at the awe in his expression. Then she was wrapped around his heat, the wind whispering across her skin, seconds before she found herself sprawled on the bed beneath him.

Thea chuckled. "Impatient?"

His answer was to kiss her, voracious, raw, and sexual until her thighs were climbing his hips, the rough texture of his jeans against the soft skin of her inner thigh surprisingly stimulating. At the agitated flexing of her hips, Conall gave her more of his body, rubbing his jeans-covered arousal between her legs.

She gasped, breaking the kiss as pleasure began to build, and Conall trailed his lips down her neck. As he fondled and caressed her sensitive breasts, his lips chased his hands, his hot mouth covering her in kisses, sucking and laving until Thea was a furnace of need.

He savored his exploration, slow, gentle, rough, devouring.

And when he moved lower and kissed her on the scar where Ashforth first stabbed her with iron, tears burned in her eyes. He was so loving, as though he was trying to kiss away the pain.

She ran her fingers through his hair as his kisses moved south to between her legs.

Then he licked her.

Thea let out a cry of hoarse pleasure. The bartender hadn't kissed her there, and she had no idea what she'd been missing. Conall grasped her hips in his hands, his hold almost deliciously bruising, and pleasured her until Thea no longer cared about anything else in the world but the coiling pressure building in the deepest part of her body. She felt the tension, this beautiful, all-encompassing tension, not able to give words to what made it the best goddamn tension she'd ever felt in her life, just that it was. And that it was leading somewhere spectacular.

Her heart raced faster than she thought possible, she couldn't catch her breath, and she suddenly understood why the French called climaxing a "little death." It felt like her heart would explode.

"Conall," she moaned, pushing against his mouth, the image of his dark head between her legs, his lips moving on her, the flash of his tongue, causing the tension to increase exponentially.

Then it snapped.

It broke apart and her cries of release echoed around the room as her lower body shuddered against Conall's mouth.

Thea shook against the bed, trying to catch her breath, wonder buzzing through her as Conall sat up, his face taut with need as he ripped off his shirt and threw it behind him. She watched him strip, revealing every inch of his powerful body, and she wanted more. Had to have more. She reached for him as he came back down over her, sliding her hands across the warm, smooth skin of his back. Her breath stuttered at the feel of him pressing between her legs. His rich scent of earth and spice surrounded her and as Thea ran her bare foot down the back of the hard muscle of his right calf, she had the urge to ravage this man until she was covered in his scent.

Conall kissed her, softly, sweetly, and then whispered against her lips, "Dinnae hold back with me, lass. I can take everything you've got."

She grinned, and he chuckled. The tenderness in his expression made her breath catch again. Whatever he saw on her face made him kiss her with a desperation that had her clinging to him.

Thea felt him nudge and then push and then thrust.

"Conall!" she cried out at the overwhelming feeling of fullness. Seeing his taut expression as he held himself above her, trying to give her time to adjust to him, Thea grasped his face in her hands. Her fingers lightly traced the scar on his face. It was a reflection of him, of the lengths he'd go to for the people he loved. A badge of honor. Thea couldn't imagine him without it, her fierce warrior wolf.

And he was hers.

For tonight, he was Thea's.

She launched off the bed, pulling him down to meet her lips, to wrap her arms around his shoulders. The movement drove him deeper, and they both groaned into each other's mouths, before Conall pushed them back to the bed, his hands on her thighs to open her wider. As they kissed, a breathless catch of mouth against mouth, he powered into her over and over.

Thea traced her hands down his back, wanting to learn every inch of him, and delighted at the feel of his hard ass flexing with every thrust. She dug her fingers into his cheeks, wanting him deeper, harder.

"Fuck, Thea," he grunted, his teeth clenched, his neck straining and his thrusts stuttering.

She understood when his hips jerked against hers and she felt him release inside her. Thea caressed his back as he pressed his forehead to her shoulder, trying to catch his breath.

It was wonderful. She was powerful. Needed. Wanted.

However, her own tension was unspent.

Conall began to press kisses along her shoulders, trailing his mouth up her neck to her lips. His kisses were slow, languorous … possessive. She wrapped her arms and legs around him and luxuriated in them. She didn't want the touching to stop, the closeness to end.

And neither apparently did Conall.

She felt it when he was ready again and this time Thea took over. She pushed him to his ass so she could straddle him but grew rigid when his hands slid over the scars on her back.

Conall felt the change in her. "Does my scar bother you, Thea?" he asked, his voice hoarse with passion.

She immediately trailed her fingers down his scar, her eyes locked with his. "No. It's part of what makes you, you."

Something she didn't understand darkened his expression, and he drew her closer. He trailed the tips of his fingers down the middle of her back, where the healed wounds made her skin uneven. She felt like she couldn't breathe.

"This doesnae make you less beautiful, Thea. It makes you more. More of everything. More than any man, especially me, deserves in his hands," he growled against her lips. "So fucking stunning wrapped around me. I couldnae care less if you were covered in scars. Your body is beautiful." He slid one hand around her rib to cup her right breast. "But that's not why I want you."

Disbelief clouded Thea's eyes. It was why men always wanted her.

He saw it and his gaze flashed in warning. "I'm not lying. We shouldnae be doing this. Both of us know that. And if you were just a beautiful woman, I wouldnae be here, doing what I know we shouldnae be doing. But you're not just a beautiful woman, are you? And I know I'm not just a warm body for you."

No, he wasn't.

But she didn't want to think about that. She didn't want to think, period.

Thea kissed him, wrapping her arms tight around his shoulders, flexing her hips as he tangled his fingers through her wet, dark hair and returned her kiss for desperate kiss. She began to ride him, hard, soaring toward another climax at the thick glide of him inside her and the pleasure suffusing his face.

They both knew this couldn't last, whatever madness this was between them, so they would take and take and take tonight until there was nothing left to give in the morning.

As Thea reveled in their passion, climbing upward to a bliss unlike anything she'd ever experienced, she wasn't cognizant of the static filling the air. She was aware only of Conall beneath her, the feel of his hard abs under her exploring fingertips, his teeth flashing with a hungry snarl, his fingers biting into her hips as he flexed his own upwards in impressive thrusts. She had no idea her eyes had bled gold. That her energy emanated out into the room. So when she reached orgasm, ecstasy more than she'd ever hoped to experience, it was any wonder every light in the room exploded, shrouding them in darkness.

Thea gasped and Conall wrapped his arms tight around her, rolling her onto her back. He didn't seem to care she'd caused a blackout as he continued to move inside her, murmuring how much he needed her, how much he wanted her as he chased his own release and came with a ragged shout in her ear.

19

THE MORNING CAME AND STILL THEY WANTED.

Thea wondered if human women felt sore after a full night of love-making. *She* didn't feel sore because, "Hello, magical healing powers," but she tingled between the legs with the knowledge that Conall had spent most of the night buried in her.

They'd woken up that morning with a silent understanding between them. There was no mention of a change of plans, that Thea wouldn't have to go to Ashforth. They both knew that was impossible if they wanted to save Callie.

However, they also both awoke still wanting each other, still wanting the connection, and seemed to come to the wordless agreement it was okay to indulge in that need until their time together was over.

They showered together, which was a new experience for Thea. It was wonderful to be petted and explored and washed clean by Conall. They shared wry looks at the broken bulbs in the room and Conall made a crack about the damage charge on his credit card. Thea thought he looked kind of smug that he'd managed to make her lose control like that.

And when they left the room, he reached for her hand. He held it as they went downstairs and while they looked over the breakfast buffet in the hotel restaurant, caressing her skin with a swipe of his thumb gently back and forth.

Every part of Thea was aware of every part of Conall.

Sitting at breakfast, they didn't say a word at first as they ate, but now and then their eyes would meet, and she'd know he was remembering something particularly delicious from the night before because he'd flash her a wicked smile that made her laugh.

She looked down at his plate, piled high with enough eggs and bacon to feed three men. "Hungry this morning?"

"Aye. Someone kept me awake most of the night with her insatiable appetite."

She snorted. "Insatiable, huh? Well, I'm sorry if I've got too much stamina for you."

Conall narrowed his eyes but she could see the humor dancing in them. "Dinnae you worry about my stamina, lass. I'm quite happy to prove I can keep you satisfied for however long you wish it."

Flushing at the thought of keeping Conall as her personal sex slave, Thea marveled at how she'd gone from being ambivalent about sex to feeling pretty goddamn turned on all the time.

She guessed that's what happened when you were attracted to a guy who was part animal.

Speaking of, Thea had a thought, remembering how she'd gently or maybe not so gently, bit Conall's shoulder last night as she came for the third time. He'd liked it. Very much. What he didn't do at any point was drag *his* teeth over *her* skin. She'd remembered what he'd said about a werewolf's bite either killing a human or changing them.

She lowered her voice. "How do you turn someone into a werewolf?"

Conall almost choked on a bite of scrambled egg. He coughed, took a swig of coffee, and stared incredulously at her. "Why do you ask?"

Thea shrugged. "Just curious. Why? Is it a secret?"

Shaking his head, he leaned across the table to tell her quietly,

"Werewolves are hard to make. Most wolves are born, not made. It takes a rare, strong human to survive a werewolf's bite."

"And does it have to be intentional? Or can an accidental nip cause the change?"

He nodded. "We have to be very careful. If our saliva or blood gets into the wounds, which, let's face it, our saliva most certainly will, the human becomes infected. It's like passing a mutation onto them and their body must be strong to take on that mutation. Most people arenae strong enough. A human dies of a werewolf's bite 98 percent of the time. In comparison, a human almost always survives the change to a vampire."

Wow. That was a low change rate. "But the TV shows got the vamp thing right? Vampires in comparison are made, not born. And a vampire has to drink a person to the brink of death for a human to turn?"

Conall scowled. "Aye. Then they make the victim drink their blood to complete the transition. Dirty bastards."

Thea burst out laughing. Sometimes he was hilarious without even trying. His scowl disappeared as he watched her laugh, his own eyes bright with mirth as Thea dabbed at the corner of her eyes.

"You're funny," she said, reaching for another slice of toast.

"So I see." His eyes watched her every movement. "Why the questions?"

She shrugged. "I don't know. I was thinking about last night and how it was nice we got to *be ourselves*." It was more than nice that she could let go with Conall without worrying she'd break him. "But I remembered what you said in Düsseldorf. And last night, you were careful with your teeth."

"Habit." He shrugged. "I doubt I can change you from whatever you are, but I'm used to being careful in bed with non-wolves."

The reminder he'd done with other women what he'd done with Thea made her instantly and irrationally upset. Maybe if she had more experience, it wouldn't bother her so much, but Thea somehow doubted it, and that worried her. She'd never imagined she'd feel so territorial or possessive of someone, and it did not sit well with her. Conall wasn't hers. A person couldn't belong to another person.

"Sorry." His gruff apology brought her eyes up from her plate. "I shouldnae have mentioned … that."

Thea gave him a half-hearted smile, wondering what the hell had possessed her to think she could handle this with Conall. But it was too late. The damage was done. No going back. "We should get going if we don't want to miss the ferry."

Once they'd cleared their table, he took her hand again, pulling her into his side, holding her close as he checked out of the hotel.

It was as if he knew she had the sudden urge to run as far and as fast from him as possible.

And he wasn't letting her go.

Conall led her out to their car, opened the passenger-side door for her, and just as she moved to get in, he pulled her against him.

He kissed her as if he were trying to steal the very essence of her into himself.

Thea was panting by the time he let her go, her body humming with renewed desire. Her hazy gaze lifted to his, and he slowly released her with a very smug, self-satisfied smirk on his face.

The haze instantly lifted. "Neanderthal," she said as she stepped into the vehicle.

Thea heard his chuckle as he rounded the SUV and she shook her head, bemoaning the fact she found everything he did this morning funny and charming. Not that she'd let him know that. Conall swung into the driver's side and grinned at her scowl.

"Werewolf," he said.

"What?"

"Werewolf, not Neanderthal."

Thea rolled her eyes. "I don't think there's a difference."

She tried very hard not to smile at his answering bark of laughter.

IT WAS A MISTAKE.

Rationally, Conall knew it was a mistake.

However, calling what he felt for Thea a mistake seemed like a betrayal.

As he drove them into Denmark, Thea sleeping soundly in the passenger seat beside him, Conall used the icy control he was known for to keep the fullness of his emotions buried deep.

Letting them out was dangerous.

Before her, he'd been a fairly simple wolf. The world was black and white, and although wolves felt deeply, his emotions had been pretty black and white too. There was right and there was wrong; there was loyalty and responsibility.

Everything he felt now was complicated and confusing.

His eyes kept moving from the road to her. Glancing off her cheek, her mouth, her lashes fluttering in her sleep. The urge to pull the car off the road somewhere so he could haul her into his arms was nearly overwhelming. He tried to squash it down deep too, but the animal in him made it difficult.

When they'd arrived in Frederikshavn at the ferry terminal, Conall had kissed Thea awake, and she'd pushed willingly into his kiss. It took a lot not to dwell on the feeling that rose swiftly in him. The same encompassing euphoria he'd felt as Thea came apart in his arms last night.

She'd trusted no one for years.

Until him.

It was a privilege and responsibility but more, it was a gift. A gift that made him want to howl from the tallest peak back home in Torridon. A gift that made him want to claim a woman he had no future with.

Now the ferry was on the move, cutting through dark waters to Norway, and Thea sat across from him in the busy restaurant. Conall's control was slipping. There was an invisible hourglass between them, the sand falling faster and faster with every second.

It made him feel powerless with despair, much like how he'd felt when Callie was diagnosed.

And from the way the tension thickened between them, Conall knew Thea felt it too.

They should never have touched each other.

But he couldn't regret it.

He'd never regret it.

In fact, he'd hold on to the memory of Thea in his arms until his dying fucking breath.

Thea pushed back from the table. "I'm not hungry."

Oh, aye, she was.

Conall's heart pounded hard in his chest as he nodded and stood, leaving cash for the meal on the table. His body brushed hers as he followed her through the wind of tables to the exit, all blood rushing south in anticipation.

As they turned the corner and into the narrow hallway that housed their small cabin, Thea suddenly slammed him into the wall, tugging his shirt front and him with it down to her so she could reach his mouth. The taste of her filled Conall, and he groaned, sliding his hands under her shirt to feel her hot skin.

Abruptly, he was flying.

Conall had never moved so fast in his life, and he was bloody speedy.

He heard the crash of a door seconds before he landed on his back on the small double bed in their tiny cabin.

Amusement and arousal flooded him as Thea was a blur of movement, undressing.

"Are you trying to get caught, lass?" He grinned, taking in her nakedness with much appreciation as she crawled over his body. She'd just used the full force of her speed to take them back to the room, and now Conall knew that when she ran with him, she was holding back.

Thea pushed his shirt up just enough to bare his stomach, and Conall's breath stuttered when she pressed kisses along his waistline. She stared up at him with those soulful eyes. "I've never kissed a man like you kissed me last night." She tugged on his belt and then his zipper, shrugging him free. "I want to."

Conall shuddered at the question in the words. Another gift from his Thea. He nodded, reaching out to caress her beautiful face. His heart almost exploded out of his chest watching her mouth bend toward him, and then he was in fucking heaven.

Hours passed.

Everything ceased to exist beyond Thea. She was everything. Every inch of her. It had never been this way for him. To want with this kind of madness. When he was inside her, he wanted the world to stop—to freeze them in that moment—with a desperation that fucking terrified him.

And yet he couldn't stop.

He couldn't stop touching and tasting and wanting her.

Needing her.

At one point their fucking was so primal, he cracked the small wooden headboard of the cabin bed right down the middle, he was holding onto it so hard. In fact, Conall was almost sure they were moving the entire bloody boat with their thrusts.

As the night wore on, they became less frenzied, less savage with fear that time was running out. They began to savor the moment instead. It became an exploration. Conall was certain no woman would ever know every inch of his body as well as Thea, and no man would ever know hers. The thought of any man touching her, knowing her like this, caused him pain he buried as quickly as he felt it.

He stared at Thea, her lush breasts cupped in his hands, as she rose slowly up and down his length, a tight sheath of heat slowly wrenching a climax from him. He held taut beneath her, wanting her to come first. Her low-lidded gaze locked with his and Conall mentally captured the image, to keep with him always.

Thea's panting grew faster, her rocking a little more frantic, until finally she tensed, her fingernails biting into his shoulders as she rippled in deep, throbbing tugs around him.

Conall let go, burying his hoarse shout of release in her breasts.

She trembled in his arms and he lifted his head to kiss her, but the shimmer of tears in her eyes made his heart stop.

He cupped her face in his hands. "What's this, Thea?"

In answer, she slid her arms around his back and buried her nose in his neck. Tremors moved through her, different from those brought on by their lovemaking.

Worry pierced him.

He should never have touched her.

He'd let this go too far ... and he was hurting the one person he didn't want to hurt.

Fuck.

"Thea?" he asked, voice gruff with an emotion he hadn't wanted to feel. He slipped his arms around her back, holding her tighter, closer.

She turned her face from his neck, just enough so he could hear her whisper, "It's been so long since anyone just held me."

His hold on her tightened, his throat thickening, burning. His eyes stung strangely too.

Who would hold her when he had to let go?

And why did the thought of Thea alone, without him, make him want to tear the world apart for its cruelty?

CONALL KNEW BEFORE HE EVEN OPENED HIS EYES THAT THEA WASN'T IN the room. He could smell her on the pillow beside him, but it was a lingering scent. Panic slammed through him and he bolted upright. Where was she?

He tapped into his connection with her, relaxing a little when he sensed her near. Of course she was close. They were on a bloody boat, for Christ's sake.

Still, he didn't like that she'd left the cabin without him.

The smell of sex was thick in the room as he got up to use the facilities he could barely squeeze into. He wished Thea were here. The scent of their time together was making him hard again.

Conall closed his eyes and hung his head as he stood over the tiny sink. Would this want of her never go away? Would it drive him fucking mad for the rest of his life?

Why her? He growled.

Why not Sienna, the dutiful werewolf he could have a future and family with? Even barring the fact that Thea was possibly immortal and would stay the same as he aged and died, there was also the fact they couldn't have children, and Conall was bound by duty to produce an heir to Clan MacLennan.

But more than any of that was the reality that Thea Quinn had a massive target on her back and keeping her indefinitely among the pack was putting his people at risk.

Sienna Canid was the right choice for his pack.

Conall ignored the pain in his chest that might as well have been a fucking silver bullet.

The Canids were still in Torridon, waiting for Conall to return so they could sign the betrothal agreement. Conall scowled at his reflection in the mirror. There was no way he could take Thea back to Torridon without telling her about Sienna.

How would he feel if Thea introduced *him* to the man she would spend the rest of her immortal life with?

The cold water tap head snapped off in Conall's hand. "Fuck."

Well, that answered that.

However, that didn't mean Thea would feel so strongly. It was possible her feelings were not his, and the better half of Conall hoped for it.

After he washed and dressed, a knot tightened in his gut as he strode out of the cabin to find her. He followed that tug on his mind and found her near the back of the ferry. She leaned against the railing, watching the boat push through the morning water toward Oslo. The low, mountainous coastline of the city grew steadily closer. Although it didn't bother him, Conall could feel how cold it was, and Thea wore only a shirt and jeans.

Her dark hair blew in the breeze and he greedily drank in the sight of her as his muscles tightened with the memory of her wrapped in his arms. Unable to resist the urge, he slid in behind her, pressing the length of his body to hers as he covered her hands on the railing and nuzzled her neck. That floral, sweet, exotic scent of hers flooded him and heaviness filled his groin.

It wasn't even about sex. Well, it was. But it was also just about wanting to be as close to her as he could get.

Thea rested against him, relaxing deeply into his body in a way that satisfied him beyond measure. "Morning."

"Good morning." He kissed her neck and rested his cheek against her temple.

"We're nearly there."

Aye. Soon they'd be at Vik's place. Then once he, hopefully, gave them the answers they needed, they would be on their way back to Scotland so Thea could face Ashforth. But first they'd stop in Torridon.

Where the Canids were waiting.

"Thea," he said, clearing his throat, "I need to tell you something."

He felt her grow rigid before she slipped her hands out from under his and turned in his embrace. Conall didn't move. He wanted to keep her there so she couldn't run from him when he told her about Sienna. He needed her to understand and to do that she had to stay put and listen.

She trailed her fingers down his chest, her brows pinched together. "What's wrong?"

"It's nothing, really." Then why was his heart pounding like fuck? "Just … you should know that before Ashforth approached me about you, I was just about to sign a betrothal agreement."

She stopped touching him. "What?"

"It's purely pack politics." He wanted to assure her. "The Canids are a large North American warrior pack. Peter Canid, the alpha, and I agreed an alliance between us would benefit both packs. We have money and Canid has wolves. Strong wolves. It was to secure the pack's safety. As our wealth grows, we become more susceptible to blackmail, fraud, challenges. Other packs, lone wolves, would be less likely to pick a fight with our pack knowing we had one of the largest North American packs as our ally."

Thea said nothing. She just stared up at him with those gorgeous eyes, wariness he thought he'd never see in them again when she looked at him creeping its way back in.

Fuck, he hated that.

"Thea"—he bent his head toward her, his tone almost pleading —"Peter's daughter, Sienna, has agreed to be my wife but we dinnae know each other. We'd barely just met, let alone anything else, when Ashforth arrived. But she and her father and brother are still in Torridon, awaiting my return so we can sign the betrothal agreement and move forward with the …" Conall's voice trailed off as he watched gold bleed into the cognac of Thea's eyes. The surrounding air stirred, growing static-like. "Thea?"

She shoved him with enough force to knock him back on his feet.

Panic made his breathing difficult.

"You son of a bitch," she whispered and even her voice sounded different.

Cold.

Unearthly.

Her hair moved around her head like it was floating in water and Conall shot a look down the boat at all the passengers who might witness the strangeness, or worse, get caught in the crossfire of Thea's anger.

"Thea, you need to calm down." He strode over to her and the boat lurched unnaturally beneath their feet, causing passengers to cry out in shock. "Thea!"

He watched her squeeze her eyes closed, her hands fisting at her sides as she took long, slow, deep breaths. Her hair abruptly dropped back into place, the static disappearing. When she opened her eyes, they were brown again.

Conall would have breathed a sigh of relief if she wasn't looking at him like he'd betrayed her. "Thea, I barely even remembered Sienna's existence until the other day."

If looks could kill, he'd be dead.

Thea brushed past him but Conall had to make her understand. He grabbed her arm, hauling her close. "Thea, please."

She jerked out of his hold and his panic intensified.

He was losing her.

He felt it.

Fuck.

"But you knew." She glared at him in disgust. "And you touched me anyway, knowing you're practically engaged."

"It's not like that," he spat out in angry desperation. "You're simplifying it. I barely know the woman and there are no promises between us. We never signed an agreement. I didnae betray her and I didnae betray you. This ..." He gestured between them. "You know neither of us meant for this to happen."

"Yeah, well," she said, her voice as flat as her expression, "it happened. Now it's over."

No! His mind vehemently denied it, taking him even by surprise. "Thea." He reached for her, but she flinched away.

"Don't touch me."

A burn scored across Conall's chest, turning fiery with pain as she continued. "You're just like everyone else." Her expression turned heartbreakingly bleak. "I can't trust anyone."

Something snapped in him. He hauled her into his arms, refusing to let go. "That's not true." His voice was rough with impatience. "You can always trust me."

"Conall, let go of me."

"I cannae." He pressed his forehead to hers, realizing the tragic truth in his words. "Fuck, Thea, I cannae let you go."

Her voice was small, a whisper of pain. "You have to. For Callie."

The impossibility of his choice had never been clearer or more agonizing. "Whatever I choose … I risk a woman I care about."

Thea tensed in his arms and then abruptly pushed out of his hold. Her eyes were hard, her countenance cool, unfeeling, her words even more so. "You know your choice. You save your sister, you marry a wolf who can give you a future and a family, and you forget about me. Just like I will forget about you."

Conall watched her walk away. He wanted to hate her for her words. But the only person he loathed right then was himself.

He'd damaged the trust between them.

It would be easier to let things lie. Let Thea build her walls against him. Going their separate ways wouldn't be so difficult with animosity and distrust between them instead of intimacy.

Yet as they drove off the ferry, the SUV's sat nav leading them toward Vik's apartment, Conall couldn't stand Thea's icy silence.

There was no way he'd last a day with such fucking awful distance between them.

Never mind a lifetime.

20

Perhaps it was childish to slight Conall but seeing the muscle flex in his jaw every time she ignored a question and looked right through him was too satisfying to stop.

She tried to concentrate on the fact that she was in Norway for the first time. Oslo was still cold in late April, so she'd changed in the cabin before they'd departed, putting a T-shirt on under her shirt for added warmth. She'd watched their approach to Oslo from the other side of the ferry, trying to ignore the ache in her chest.

Dark green, snow-dusted islands sat within the gray waters of Oslofjord. Homes of all sizes dotted the islands and the coastline, houses made of timber with wooden shingles exactly like the houses along the New England coastline. These homes were brightly colored in reds and oranges and blues and greens—like little birds of paradise in amongst all the gray.

Thea had shivered in the chilly, crisp, fresh morning and couldn't remember the last time she'd taken in a lungful of such clean air.

The city had morphed into a different personality than the one that greeted her on board the ferry. As she'd reluctantly reunited with

Conall and he'd driven the SUV into the city, Oslo had become surprisingly commercial as they drove through a system of concrete tunnels and convoluted traffic circles. They passed glass buildings, stores, and tall hotels, but it all soon changed again as they moved out of the central roadway.

The buildings aged, painted like the houses along the fjord in a variety of pretty colors. In the summer Oslo must be lush with green because they passed park after park, all the grass and trees still slightly brown and bare as they slowly woke up with the spring.

Thea wished she was in Oslo alone, not chasing answers, and instead enjoying being somewhere where the air was so beautifully crisp and the buildings a remnant of a history she'd love to discover.

"Are you ever going to speak to me again?" Conall asked.

Lost in watching the city pass by, she'd almost forgotten how much he'd hurt her.

Thea knew deep in her gut he hadn't meant to. That it wasn't a deliberate deception. But she was still angry at him for having never mentioned Sienna.

However, it was jealousy and hurt that was truly ripping her up inside.

Thea had never hated anyone but Ashforth, yet she was pretty sure she hated a woman she'd never met and who had done nothing wrong beyond agreeing to marry Conall.

His fiancée.

It made their inevitable separation so much more real.

And he expected her to walk into his hometown and probably meet the werewolf he would spend the rest of his life with.

Ah well, Thea told herself, it wasn't like she and the Scot had a future, anyway. They'd both known that.

Deciding churlishness was beneath her, she looked at Conall. "You trust this guy, right?"

If it surprised him she'd spoken, he didn't show it. "Aye, like I said, he's a friend."

They'd barely been in the car fifteen minutes when Conall pulled off a main road onto a quiet street facing a park. Behind a row of prickly hedges and large trees were several small blocks of apartments, all architecturally different. Thea followed Conall out of the SUV and past parked cars before coming to a gated driveway with a sign on it.

"This is it."

The driveway led to a large red-and-blond sandstone apartment building with a secure entrance. Conall reached for the door and then halted.

He turned to look at Thea.

Puzzled by the searching expression in his eyes, she shifted uncomfortably. "What?"

"You were right." His words were clipped, gruff even. "I shouldnae have kept Callie and James apart all this time." He bent his head toward her. "I didnae understand that until now."

Thea's breath caught.

What did that mean?

Was he trying to tell her he *more* than cared for her?

That the short moments they'd shared were worth experiencing, even if he never got to have more time with her? Or was she reading what she wanted to read into his words?

Her heart, even so used to pain, ached in a way it had never ached before. She broke his gaze. "Let's just get this over with."

Ignoring the feel of his eyes burning into her, Thea pushed open the door with enough force to break the lock. "Which floor?"

"The top. He owns the penthouse." Conall fell into step beside her, his arm brushing hers. Perhaps it was childish, but Thea couldn't withstand any closeness between them. She fell back. "Lead the way."

Conall sighed, taking the stairs first. "Will it be this way from now on, then?"

Why was he pushing this? Why couldn't he just let it go? "What way?"

"I touch you." He looked down at her as he took the next flight of stairs; his icy eyes burned with obvious anger. "And you pull away?"

"Well, I'm not yours to touch so, pretty much." It was a taunt, and they both knew it.

He glowered down at her as she followed him up the stairs. "Dinnae push me, Thea."

She pursed her lips. "A threat only works if there's something to fear. I could crush you, Conall, and we both know it."

"If that was supposed to deter me, it failed." He flicked her a hungry look. "It only reminds me how strong you are, how hard you fuck, and how hard you like to be fucked."

Thea flushed at his language and the reminder of the bed they broke on the boat. He was being deliberately crude to piss her off and get a reaction out of her. "Treasure the memories, Wolf Boy."

"Oh, I will, Thea, lass," he said, his tone softening with fondness and if she wasn't mistaken, despondency.

It killed her attitude, and she fell silent, brooding at his back.

They soon stepped up onto the top floor where only one door awaited them. When Conall knocked, there was absolute silence. He knocked again, louder.

"Maybe he's not home."

He flicked her a smirk. "It's daylight out and he's a vampire. He's bloody well at home." He knocked harder and called loudly, "Vik, it's Conall MacLennan."

A few seconds later they heard several locks being turned and then the door swung open. A tall, blond-haired vampire stood in the shadow of the doorway, his inquisitive, big blue eyes on Conall. He wore a Metallica T-shirt and a pair of gray jogging pants. Although skinny, Thea noted the wiry, muscular strength beneath his pale skin.

"Hei Venn."

"Hei Venn," Conall returned.

His blue gaze turned to Thea, catching in the light, flicking to mercury and then back to blue. "I knew it was you." Vik gestured between them, his accent a mix of Scottish and Norwegian. "I have security cameras."

"Can we come in?" Conall asked.

Vik frowned. "Of course. But I think I should be worried. It's not like you to turn up without warning."

Conall shook his head. "We need information." He reached for Thea's hand and she cursed him as she let him lead her into the apartment. He knew she was unlikely to make a scene in front of his friend by refusing to take his hand.

Bastard.

He brushed his thumb over her skin, almost absentmindedly, as he strode into the huge loft. "This place seems big for Oslo."

"It was two apartments. I bought them both and knocked them into one." Vik finished locking the door, and Thea noted the many, many locks. Paranoid much? Or just a protection from the sun? She noted the floor-to-ceiling windows on one side of the apartment fitted with thick blackout blinds. Not a crack of sunlight shone through.

Large overhead steel light fixtures kept the space as bright as possible.

The floorboards were stripped and bare, but there was a rug here and there to add some texture and perhaps coziness. They failed on the coziness part. A large black-leather corner sofa took up one area of the open-plan space. It faced the biggest flat-screen television Thea had ever seen. Behind the television was a large king-size bed tucked into the back corner of the room.

In the opposite corner of the space was a shiny white kitchen. Glossy cabinets, white quartz countertops, and white kitchen accessories made that area shine like an iceberg.

Thea wondered how the vampire kept it so clean.

Yet the most interesting area was directly before them. Floor-to-ceiling shelves filled with books lined the wall from where the kitchen ended to the windows on the opposite side. In front of the shelves sat what appeared to be a mini research center. A large desk hosted a computer with three screens. To the side, built up against one of the windows, was a display unit filled with different artifacts, what looked like an old Viking helmet, coins, goblets, a sword, a small shield, and an assortment of daggers.

An unpleasant tingle moved through Thea and she followed the feeling to a silver-gray dagger pinned to the wall of the display. She almost hissed.

Pure iron.

Wrenching her eyes away, Thea studied the vampire. Despite the Metallica shirt he was wearing, a female opera singer played from a sound system that seemed to encompass the entire apartment.

She steadfastly ignored the discomforting awareness of the iron blade in the corner.

"Who is your lovely friend, Conall?" Vik asked, flicking Thea a mercury look as he wandered into the kitchen. "Drink?"

"This is Thea. And I'll take a water if you have it."

"Me too," Thea said.

The vampire nodded and pulled two small bottles of water out of the fridge. Thea knew from her time with Ashforth that vampires ate and drank like humans, but they also needed blood to survive.

Thea thanked Vik as he gave her the water. She used it as an excuse to drop Conall's hand.

"So, what is this about?" Vik crossed his arms over his chest. "You know this is my nighttime hours, friend."

"And I apologize for the rudeness of our arrival. But this is important." He turned to Thea, his eyes questioning, and she knew he wanted her permission to tell the story. She reluctantly nodded.

It was difficult to stand through Conall's retelling. Thankfully, he left out the nitty-gritty of her captivity with Ashforth but told Vik enough for him to grasp the story. Conall explained to him about being chased by the Blackwood Coven and the new mystery enemy who went by the name Eirik.

When Conall was finished, Vik was unnaturally still, staring almost unseeingly at the floor.

"Vik?"

His blue eyes flashed to Thea. "Tell me about your abilities again."

Something about the intensity of his stare unnerved her, but Conall's encouraging nod prompted her to reply. "I'm fast, strong."

"Faster and stronger than any supernatural I've met," Conall added.

"I can … I can make people see things. Things I want them to see."

Vik's expression flickered but it was difficult to know what that meant.

"And … when I was younger—not now—I could move things without touching them."

He frowned. "Not now?"

"I stopped using the ability a long time ago. I haven't been able to do it since. Well, sometimes I make things happen when I'm upset. Moving things, messing with electricity, anything that emits energy, really. I can turn on a car without an ignition key. That's been handy in the past." She tried to be droll to ease her own nervousness.

Vik abruptly turned away, striding toward the bookshelves. He studied them, running his eyes up and down the books. "And you can heal. Instantly?"

"Yes."

He moved along the shelves as Thea and Conall shared a questioning look. Vik glanced over his shoulder at Thea. "Can you move from one space to another by merely thinking about it?"

She frowned but something flickered in the back of her mind.

The plane crash.

How she'd been in darkness, in pain, smelling the most horrific smells, and then the next, outside the plane.

"I … not that I know of." She avoided Conall's eyes, wondering if he was thinking about the plane crash too.

"And iron. Pure iron. Do you know if it can hurt you?" His gaze flicked to the iron blade on his display unit before turning back to Thea.

She felt Conall tense at the same time she did. They hadn't mentioned the iron yet. "Yes," she whispered, butterflies erupting to life as Vik nodded.

There was a light of disbelief and excitement in his eyes as he stared at her.

"Well?" Conall snapped.

Vik reached up and grasped a small volume from his shelves. He turned around and moved back toward them before dropping the book on the desk with a light *thwomp*. "You're right. Thea is immortal."

Something withered inside her at his declaration. She looked down at the book. "As in …"

"Never age, never die. A true immortal."

"That's what Ashforth called her." Conall scowled. "And he knows about the iron."

"Then he knows what she is."

"Which is?"

Vik gestured to the book, and they both edged closer.

Embossed in gold across the leather was the word *FAERIE*.

Thea's eyes flew to Vik's in consternation. His regard upon her was intense. "You're one of the fae. I thought that would be obvious."

"Fae?" Thea spluttered incredulously. "As in fucking fairies?" She shot a look at Conall, angry at him for bringing her to this lunatic.

But Conall was glaring at Vik. "Those are just myths. Legends."

Thea shook her head, taking a step back from the crazy guy. "You … are you telling me you think I have something to do with the were-wolf and vampire origin myth?"

"They're not myths." Vik shot a quelling look at Conall who had opened his mouth to protest. "I know you think only religious supes believe in this stuff, but it's not religion, Conall. I've been researching a long, long time and there is enough evidence to prove its truth. I'm talking about primary sources. Supes who were actually there during the time of the fae." He gestured to the book.

Confused, Thea sighed in exasperation and mounting panic. "I've only read a little about this stuff, so I'm lost here."

Vik nodded. "Then allow me to explain. To understand you must know that there exists more than this dimension. The existence of fae proves there is at least one more than ours. They belong to another world. It's similar to our own but different too. In our world, there are people connected to the earth. They use energy in a way that other humans could never hope to."

"You're talking about witches and warlocks," Conall said, impatience edging his words.

"Exactly. We call it magic. In the fae world, magic is different. For a start, everyone who belongs to the fae world belongs to magic. To an earth witch, the magic on Faerie would be unstable, unusable without causing great destruction. But the fae are stronger, more complex beings than our witches. And thousands of years ago they opened a gate into our world."

"You're telling me that all the legends and stories about fairies are based in truth? That the fae walk among us?"

"Thea." Vik grinned, shaking his head. "They didn't just *walk* among us. They *made* supernaturals."

"Religious bullshit," Conall scoffed.

"Not religious bullshit. Truth! How else did we get here, Conall? Evolution in our dimension doesn't work this way." He gestured between himself and Conall. "We're beings of a different kind of magic than what is found here on Earth, and deep down you know that too." Vik turned back to Thea. "The fae are ruled by one queen—"

"The Faerie Queen?" Thea guffawed.

Vik scowled. "She could turn you to dust with the snap of her fingers, so show some respect, please. The fae are immortal. Truly immortal. When they grow weary of their long lives, it is said they drink from the queen's cauldron and they're reborn anew. The queen, Aine—spelled *A-i-n-e*, pronounced 'awn-ya'—never grows weary, has never slept, and is the most powerful being in their world."

"Fairy tales supes tell themselves to explain our existence." Conall shook his head in disbelief.

Vik transformed from smirking young college student to cold-faced predator. He snarled, "Your ignorance is showing, Conall."

Conall bared his teeth but didn't comment.

The vampire rounded the desk to stare intensely at Thea. Some might say in awe, even. "Many stories have mixed up truths with myth over the years but here is the truth: For thousands of years, humans were taken to Faerie through the gate that Aine opened. They say the gate opened in Ireland, which is why the country is rife with folktales and the fae get their names from the Irish. It was said the queen had a particular fondness for humans who were like themselves but so fragile, so finite. The problem was that the fae are not actually like humans. They cannot be when they live forever. Boredom, eternity, it has a way of twisting a being who already has darkness in their soul. And we are all born with darkness and light. It doesn't mean they are entirely 'bad'. Like I said, the fae are complicated. And they amused themselves with court games and wickedness. They were in constant competition with one another.

"Queen Aine rules over Faerie, which is split into four countries ruled by royal houses. Whatever the fae call themselves, we'll never know because fae language is unintelligible to human ears. They picked up on our languages with ease and all my sources tell me they spoke in human tongue around humans. As such, the words I use relating to their world are human—Irish—in origin.

"We called their world Faerie and those within it the fae. They lived with a hierarchy much like our own. There was the queen and below that her royal subjects, below them the aristocracy, below that a middle class, and then below them the equivalent of peasantry. Aine, although ruler of all, lives in the Samhradh Palace among the fae courtiers of the Samhradh Royal House. As the centuries passed, storytellers nicknamed them the Day Lands because they lived in a part of Faerie with eternal sunshine. And among them lived princes, princesses, lords and ladies, and their servants.

"On the other side of Faerie, there is the Geimhreadh Palace, ruled over by a Geimhreadh prince of the Geimhreadh Royal House. It is known as the Night Lands—they live in a country of constant winter darkness.

"Between these two are the countries ruled by the Earrach and Fómhar Royal Houses, nicknamed the Dawn and Dusk Lands. The royals are powerful fae who rule over a slightly less powerful aristocracy, and even less powerful middle and peasant classes.

"When the fae first invited humans into Faerie, the royal houses began to play dangerous games with them. Some say it started with one human woman. A courtier of the Geimhreadh House was fighting over her with a member of the Samhradh House. In their fight, the woman was killed and the fae of Geimhreadh tried to heal her with his blood. This was forbidden. Now we know that fae blood heals us when done in *our* world"—he gestured pointedly to Thea—"but on Faerie, magic is unstable for humans. It *changed* the human instead. She was called Isis, and she was the first vampire.

"Despite the use of forbidden healing, this creation amused the queen, but her Day courtiers were furious. And being the twisty little buggers they are," he said, curling his upper lip, "they cast a spell over Isis so a wooden stake, a weapon of nature, could kill her. And the greatest weapon they spelled against her was the earth's sun. It was amusing to them to take a creature of the Night Lands and trap it in an eternal night. After all, it wasn't borne of Samhradh House, and sun was *their* purview. They sought to make Isis the antithesis of nature. So she was, and those she passed her gift onto are forever locked in night." He nodded to the blinds covering his windows. "Pure sunlight turns us to ash."

"And so began the ultimate distraction from boredom. They used humans in their twisted games and the queen allowed it. She was fond of humans, but they were still inferior. Playthings. Something to amuse her courtiers.

"When a shape-shifting fae, a rare species among the Day Lands, bit a human while wolf and accidentally transferred her gift to the human man, the werewolf was made. Those of the Day Lands were pleased to have made their own creation, but the courtiers of the Night Lands remembered what Day did to Isis, and they spelled the wolf. While their vampire 'children' were controlled by the earth's sun, they made sure the full moon would control the werewolves. Moreover, Night had a penchant for silver metal. Because Day fashioned a weapon for the vampires, they fashioned a weapon for the wolves. Silver."

Vik grew silent, studying Thea until she was scowling in increasing impatience. Her mind was whirling with the new information. Conall was right. It sounded ridiculous.

And yet, something was shifting inside her. The restlessness that had flowed through her for years, the restlessness of not knowing what she was, was settling. The hum, the itch of it, was relieved somehow. She needed to know more. She needed to know it all.

Because there was no other explanation for what she was.

"Pure iron doesn't exist on Faerie, which is why we call them true immortals. The beginnings of the Iron Age in Ireland was quite a shock for the fae. No one knows why it affects them, a secret they've guarded well, but once humans realized it was a weapon, they began to use it to hunt the fae whenever they crossed through the gate."

Conall's gaze drew Thea's, and she thought she saw a flicker of fear in his eyes. "In your theory, iron can *kill* fae?"

"Here on Earth, yes. Mostly it causes pain if a fae merely touches it. But if you stab a fae in the heart with a knife of pure iron, they cannot recover. It is a slow, painful death for the fae. Iron does not exist in their world. There they *are* true immortals. Here, they are merely immortal until someone sticks a piece of iron through their heart."

"And you really believe Thea is fae?"

"Yes." Vik smiled in boyish wonder. He strode toward Thea and stopped to study her. "To meet a real fae … I never thought it would happen. You're as beautiful as the stories." He flicked a glance at Conall. "All the fae are purported to be lovely. A beauty that cannot be explained. Their bodies made for sin—"

"Watch it," Conall growled.

Vik threw his friend a puzzled look but merely shrugged as he turned back to Thea. "There are so many things you're capable of and don't know it. Abilities trapped inside that extraordinary mind."

Thea didn't like the way he was looking at her.

It reminded her too much of Ashforth.

Which also reminded her. "So why is Ashforth obsessed with me? Why do I have witches and warlocks and some guy named Eirik hunting me?"

The intensity snapped out of Vik's eyes, replaced by a flatness he hid as he turned from her. He rounded the desk and slumped into his chair. "As Conall will tell you, our origin story has become legend to most supes. But those of us who know the truth know that the Fae Queen closed the gate between our realms two thousand years ago."

"Why?"

"Eirik, the vampire hunting you, is said to be the oldest living vampire in the world." Vik refused to look at her. "He's immensely powerful. A normal stake won't kill him because the bone around his rib cage has grown so strong. And he's too fast to catch or to outrun. He was there." Vik finally looked at her. "He and his brother Jerrik were there when the gate closed. My research suggests they were born in the late Bronze Age, early Iron Age in Denmark, and were warriors, leaders of their community. The brothers were twins, and they caught the eye of a vampire on her travels across the world. She took them back to Ireland, and they'd socialized with the fae on Faerie. Vampires loved Faerie because the sun there does not harm them. Jerrik wrote about it."

He tapped the leather book on his desk. "This is a rare copy of his firsthand accounts of life at the fae royal houses. He knew Aine. In his writings, he states that the queen, after thousands of years interfering with human life, had grown concerned that the scheming and competition between the houses would continue to spawn more supernatural beings. Possibly more powerful than the next.

"And as beings of human origin, she doubted the faes' ability to control them. These supes were originally human so their loyalty, ultimately, was still to humans, to Earth, not to the fae. Her houses had no intention of ceasing their meddling with humans or pulling them into their wicked, often violent games. What if the supes decided they'd had enough of watching humans be used? What if it led to war?

"When rumor grew among the supes that blood from a pure fae could heal people from the brink of death but only in *our* world, tension built between the races. There were power-hungry vampires and werewolves excited about keeping fae on Earth just to use their healing abilities. To extend werewolf life and to ensure vampire immortality. To keep humans they loved alive when disease and death came knocking.

"So Aine expelled humans and supernaturals back to Earth and closed the gate. It is thought amongst scholars in the know that the closure led to the Irish Dark Age, a period of economic and cultural stagnation that lasted to around AD 300. Jerrik wrote it relieved some humans to see the fae gone, while those starving to death cursed Aine for abandoning them.

"But that's not the interesting part nor the part relevant to you, Thea. Jerrik also wrote that before Aine turned the humans out of Faerie, she cast a spell. Unable to bear an ending without a game, she held a final feast for favored humans and supernaturals. Jerrik and his brother Eirik were among them. There Aine informed the supes and humans alike that fae children would be born in the human world to human parents. Seven of them. She said that many years from now, seven children would arise with gifts supernaturals would recognize as fae. If the children proved themselves worthy, the gate to Faerie would reopen and they and their chosen companions, human or supernatural, could live among the fae. She offered any human who crossed over with the children the gift of immortality."

Oh my God, Ashforth knew this. "Ashforth," Thea whispered.

Conall ran a hand over his face, incredulous. "I cannae believe this."

"It's the truth. And what you're describing, this businessman, the Blackwood Coven, and … Eirik … well, this is what the queen intended. No one knows what the children would have to do to even open the gate. We don't know if they'd all have to be together to do it or if just one is required to open it. Some believe the seven children need to be brought together at an exact point in Ireland where the gate opened. It's what Jerrik believed. But he knew that Aine didn't care about the endgame. She cared about the *game* and the carnage it would create over the centuries as supes and humans hunted for any sign of these children.

"The Blackwood Coven are like any powerful magical family—they believe their magic is a poor imitation of fae magic. They want to live among the faeries." He snorted with laughter.

Thea didn't find it particularly funny.

"And Eirik?" Conall practically growled.

Vik's laughter instantly died. "His brother Jerrik believed the children needed to be protected. He created a cult of sorts, a religion, devout in its belief that these children are the key to reopening communication with the old ones. The Blackwood Coven belong to that cult. Although they might have been trying to harm you, Conall, they would never have intended Thea to be hurt. She's too important to them. But Eirik … he has no desire to lose his place at the top of the food chain again. He doesn't *want* the fae meddling in our world.

"He killed his brother … that's how badly he doesn't want it. He's been hunting for signs of the children for centuries with one purpose—to kill them."

"Even if this isnae true, they believe it is." Conall turned to Thea, anger etched in every feature. "And they'll just keep coming for Thea."

Thea's stomach dropped. She would be hunted for the rest of her life, she realized.

"There's something else you should know," Vik continued. "The Fae Queen didn't just fear that humans and supernaturals would hunt fae for their blood. Jerrik wrote of a story he heard in the Day Lands, a story he believed was the real reason Aine closed the gate. A story that, if true, proves the fae are not true immortals on Faerie or Earth."

Thea's heart pounded at the thought. Not true immortals. Meaning they could die. *She* could die.

"A fae of Samhradh House fell in love with her werewolf consort. The tale goes she couldn't bear the idea of immortality without him and asked him to bite her."

Thea's ears perked. "You mean … change her into a werewolf?"

"Yes. Exactly. And it worked. She was no longer a true immortal. When a very weary prince of Earrach House discovered this, he asked to be bitten too. He didn't want to be immortal anymore, and the cauldron couldn't truly end his suffering. So the wolf did it but the fae *died*."

"From a wolf bite?" Thea's eyes flew to Conall, his jaw locked with tension.

Vik nodded. "The Fae Queen was so furious she killed the wolf and his mate, and the pack they belonged to, and forbade anyone to speak of it. But Jerrik was in love with a fae of the Day Lands and she confessed this story to him. This was a few weeks before the gate closed."

"You're saying a werewolf can kill the fae? That's why she really closed the gate." Conall flicked a concerned look at Thea. She knew he didn't know whether to believe Vik, but if it was true, just one slip-up and a bite of his teeth through her skin might have killed her. "I could kill Thea with one bite?"

"Or turn her into a werewolf." Vik shrugged. "Fifty-fifty chance."

"There's a fifty-fifty chance I'm going to throw up," Thea muttered, turning away from them.

Fae.

This guy believed she was an immortal fae.

She gave a snort of hysterical laughter.

But beneath the rising panic was a flare of hope.

If Vik was right, if this was true … then she wouldn't have to live forever. There were ways to die when she was ready. Not that there was a chance she might get to choose when that time would be with a two-thousand-year-old vampire on her tail.

"Uh, closer to two thousand five hundred years old. Give or take a few decades," Vik said, and Thea realized she'd said the last sentence out loud. "And you're right. I hate to be the bearer of bad news, but no one can escape Eirik. Not even you, Thea. Maybe if you were working at your full capacity as a fae but from what you've told me, you've only tapped into a small part of what you're capable of. And Eirik … if he knows you exist, he will never give up until you're dead, and he will kill everyone who stands in his way."

21

Vik promised to show them the firsthand account from Jerrik about the fae, but he needed to sleep first. Thea and Conall agreed to return to the apartment after nightfall and left Vik to his rest. The vampire recommended a restaurant that served "pulled pork sandwiches that will change your life" in the center of Oslo.

They located the restaurant near the Royal Palace on Slottsplassen, a square in the heart of the tourist area, a rustic, casual place with an energy that was too overwhelming for a stunned Thea.

Her mind was reeling. The food came and Conall sat silently across from her, eating the pulled pork sandwich as if they hadn't just been given the most incredible information. The wolf could eat through a natural disaster.

She stared at her plate, her stomach roiling.

After every impossible thing that had happened to her, that she might be a faerie just seemed a step too far.

"Thea, you need to eat." Conall nudged her plate impatiently toward her. "You need your strength."

At his implacable stare, she'd picked up the sandwich and forced it down. It was delicious but it also sat heavy in her nervous stomach. The noise of the lunch crowd was making her jittery. She needed to think. To work out what the hell it all meant.

Conall seemed to sense this and paid for their meal, ushering her quickly outside. Thea drew in cold lungfuls of air and tried to ignore how comforting Conall's hand was on her lower back.

"Talk to me, Thea."

She looked up into his face, wondering when it became so familiar to her. Thea realized she trusted him. Despite the whole Sienna prevarication. "Let's walk."

He fell into step beside her as they meandered up toward the Royal Palace. People didn't look at Conall so much here and she wondered if it was because they were in the home of the Vikings. Big tall guys were a thing here, right?

"Thea?"

She withdrew from her silly musings and sighed. "Do you believe him?"

"I think the better question is, do you?"

Thea exhaled slowly. "Conall … I know what he said sounds insane, but …"

"But?"

"It feels true. I don't know how to explain that … it just feels true." She gazed up at him. "My body is certain, while my mind is screaming that it's ludicrous. And … there's something else."

He nodded at her to continue.

"There was a young woman in Prague, around my age. The night those vamps attacked me, she pulled me out of the crowd in the club and she was strong, Conall. Very strong." Thea pictured the woman's lovely elfin face. "I sensed something from her. I think she was fae."

Conall's brows drew together. "How did she feel?"

"Feel?"

"Yes. Her energy should feel stronger than other supernaturals. It would draw you to her in a crowd. To me you feel like the moon just before the change. An ancient, compelling energy, integral to everything."

Thea gaped at him in awe. "I feel like that to you?"

"Aye. I imagine you feel somewhat different to vampires, but still powerful. They probably presume it has something to do with your blood."

She considered that a moment and shook her head. "Conall, that's not how this woman felt to me. It was more that she felt so familiar. I just … she touched me and I felt like I was home. That feeling I used to get when I'd finish my homework and come downstairs to sit at the dinner table with Mom and Dad as they listened to me talk about my day and made me laugh. Made me feel safe. I don't know how else to explain it. It was weird. So, so weird. And that wasn't even the strangest part."

She stopped in the middle of the street and he drew to a halt beside her. "She told me I could trust *you*. But she spoke to me in my head." Thea tapped her temple. "I heard her speak in my mind. How did she do that?"

"A telepath?"

"I guess. And a psychic. She said you weren't my enemy. How did she know me and how did she know you?"

"She could have been a witch or even a werewolf. Some wolves, like myself, are born with extra abilities."

Thea shook her head. "That doesn't explain that feeling of *family* I got from her."

Conall began to walk, his strides so long Thea had to hurry to catch up. "If you're saying what I think you're saying, then you and this woman are in terrible danger."

"She's like me. I know she's like me. I mean, I didn't at the time, but now I *know*. Like I know Vik is right, that I'm … fae. It sounds ridiculous, but I know." She lightly punched her fist against her gut. "I know it in here."

He was silent as they walked.

Her heart fell. "You don't believe me."

He cut her a bleak look. "Aye, I do. I just wish it wasnae true."

She recoiled. "You … are you disgusted by what I am? Afraid of me?"

"God, no." Conall scowled. "Not disgusted, Thea. Or afraid of you.

But I'm fucking afraid *for* you. How do I protect you from this? This is bigger than anything I could have imagined."

She understood. "Conall, as soon as we get to Scotland, we make the exchange and I'll get Ashforth out of there. Your pack won't get caught up in this mess."

"The pack." He stopped in the middle of the street, glaring down at her. She felt the air around him grow eerily still and glanced down at his hands to see he was curling them tightly, as if quelling the shift. Her gaze met his furious one. "It isnae about the pack," he bit out, the words ending in snarls from the wolf's awakening. "I care what happens to you, Thea, far fucking more than I should."

"Then stop."

Conall gave a bark of incredulous laughter. "I could sooner ask the sun to stop rising."

Her heart swelled in her chest, but his words only made everything that much harder. "Please don't."

"What? Speak the truth? That I have to choose between you and my duty to my pack?" He gritted his teeth and looked away, the muscle in his jaw flexing. "I'd give anything for them …" He turned to her, his expression making her breathless. "But how do I sacrifice *you* for *them*? Tell me, Thea. How do I do that, when the very thought of handing you over to Ashforth, leaving you alone to this mess, makes me want to rip the fucking moon to shreds?"

Tears filled Thea's eyes as she turned away, blinking back the burn, refusing to let them fall. Conall allowed her time to compose herself, waiting patiently at her back. Finally, she took a deep breath and turned around to do the bravest thing she'd done in her life.

She gave up Conall MacLennan so he wouldn't have to choose.

"I care about you. I *do* trust you. And I know you trust me and care about me. That's a gift to me, Conall. One I truly treasure despite what I might have said this morning. And I will not repay that gift by endangering your pack. So I'm taking the choice away from you. I'm going to Ashforth because I *need* to end this with him, and you need Callie back."

He was silent a moment and then he snapped, "And then what?"

She smiled, trying to ease the tension. "Maybe when you're old and gray, I'll come to Torridon and ask you to bite me so one way or another, I don't have to live forever." *So one way or another, I don't have to live forever without you.*

But Conall didn't think it was funny. His words were bitter with anger. "Is this what it is to truly be the alpha, then? To live an empty fucking life so my pack can live in safety."

Thea stepped into him, resting a palm on his chest where his heart was beating too fast. His hands automatically closed on her hips, pulling her closer. "Your life will never be empty, Conall. One day I'll be just a memory."

He bent his head, his words a snarl against her lips, "You'll be a ghost, Thea, haunting me for the rest of my goddamn life." He pushed her away from him. "And if you cannae see that, then you dinnae feel for me what I feel for you." He stalked away, striding through the crowds of tourists and into the park surrounding the palace.

Thea stayed put, wishing she could tell Conall how she truly felt, but knowing that to do so would only make things worse. And with him gone she finally let the tears she'd been holding back fall.

HE FOUND HER HOURS LATER, USING THAT ABILITY OF HIS, AN ABILITY THEA now realized he'd always have. No matter where she went in the world, he could always find her. She just had to convince him to let her go. Hard to do when she didn't want him to.

She'd wandered aimlessly down a street heading toward the harbor when Conall pulled up in the SUV.

"I shouldnae have left," Conall said, his voice was flat and emotionless as she got into the car. "Not while there's still danger."

There would always be danger for Thea. Even if she dealt with Ashforth, she'd never stop running.

She merely nodded in acknowledgment of his apology, their drive back to Vik's apartment chilly.

The sun was just setting when they walked into the vampire's loft. Vik flashed them a smile as he led them toward the sitting area but there was something off about the expression. It seemed nervous and false. Apparently Conall thought so too.

"You all right, Vik?"

A tingling sensation that was all too familiar scored down Thea's neck. Her heart raced. The dread washed over her. "Conall … something's wrong."

His head whipped toward her and then his eyes traveled over her shoulder and narrowed. Thea turned slowly and the sight that greeted her made her knees tremble.

Crowded into the back of the loft were fifteen men and women.

What the hell?

The tallest man stepped forward, and the air seemed to shimmer around him as he did, as if he was stepping through an invisible barrier. Suddenly his energy blasted into Thea.

A vampire. An extremely powerful one, if the way all the hairs on Thea's body rose in greeting were to go by.

He had an interesting face. Square and blunt. Not truly handsome but appealing nonetheless. His black eyes were hard to look away from. Thea felt Conall step closer to her as the vampire neared. He had broad shoulders like Conall and was almost as tall. Even dressed casual in a black sweater and dark jeans, Thea could see the money in the clothes and in the watch on his wrist.

Her eyes flicked behind him to his fourteen companions who all moved forward as one. The air shimmered in the same location in the loft and once they had all passed the spot, Thea felt their energy.

They were all vampires.

Pale and expressionless and all humming with the kind of cold dynamism that sizzled over Thea's skin. They were old and powerful. Every one.

Fear Thea tried to hide clawed at her and she took a step back toward Conall, trying to place her body in front of his.

"You are wondering how you did not feel us here." The tall vampire gestured to his companions at his back. "A little magic. To mask our energy. We knew you would feel us from outside if we did not enlist my favorite witch to cloak us."

Thea studied him as her whole body rang with internal warning.

He spoke with an accent, every word was precise and clipped, like he'd spoken a different language once upon a time and his English was just a little too formal to be natural.

"Vik," Conall growled. "What the fuck did you do?"

"Viktor has been extremely helpful," the tall vampire answered.

"I'm sorry, Conall." Vik walked into view, standing near the entrance hallway. He couldn't meet Thea's or Conall's eyes. "I don't want the gates to open either."

Realization flashed through them, their gazes locking in guarded horror before Thea turned to the vampire. "Eirik?"

He nodded, his dark eyes unreadable. "I was alerted to your existence, Miss Quinn, when word reached me at my home in Copenhagen that a human had enlisted the help of the strongest alpha of his generation." His intense regard shifted to Conall. "Your reputation precedes you. Few wolves have a gift such as yours. Jasper Ashforth's increasing desperation to find Miss Quinn, his dangerous bargain with someone as well known as you, led to my discovery of that which he coveted and attempted to hide from the world." Eirik turned his regard back to Thea. "I hear we are not the only ones that hunt you."

In that moment Thea wished she had telepathic abilities because she'd tell Conall to run. Instead, she tried to edge in front of him again without drawing Eirik's attention.

It didn't work. Eirik cocked his head at her movement and then frowned. He took a step toward them, which made Thea retreat into Conall and his hand came to rest on her back. Bizarrely, Eirik sniffed the air.

Surprise filled his expression and Thea got the sense he wasn't often taken off guard. He cut a look to Vik. "I am afraid I cannot hold up my end of the bargain, Viktor."

Vik swallowed hard. "You … you promised you'd spare the wolf. He's my friend, Eirik."

Thea felt Conall stiffen at the same time she did.

"And I am grateful for your loyalty, Viktor. I truly am." Eirik sounded almost weary. "However, you are too young, your senses cannot detect what mine do." He looked back at Thea and Conall, his black gaze moving between their faces. "Their scents have merged as one."

Conall's hand tightened on Thea's back and she heard his soft exhale of shock.

What?

She glanced over her shoulder at him, but he was staring at Eirik, stunned.

"I ..." She turned back to Eirik. "I don't understand."

"You would not. And your wolf was probably so focused on his tracking of you, he did not notice the change in your scent. Ironic."

"Scent?" Thea snapped.

Eirik's eyes narrowed. "You have mated with the werewolf, Miss Quinn."

Thea felt a flush crest her cheekbones. How did he know that?"

Eirik chuckled softly. "Not sex. Anyone can have sex with a were-wolf. *Mated.* As in true mates. Although I hear the mating scent only occurs after two mates first have sex." He looked at Vik as Thea almost staggered back into Conall at the realization. "Like Adélie fucking penguins, the fae mate for life. They passed the ludicrous bond down into our bloodlines. Thankfully—unlike my brother who wasted centuries trying to return to his mate on Faerie—in all my years, I have escaped the disease of love and a lifetime of imprisonment to another." Again, he said the words without venom. Just jaded fact. "I cannot allow the wolf to live. I am sorry. When I kill his mate, he will try to plague me until his inevitable death. It is better to kill him now and save him the pain."

Mate.

Mate?

Mate!

Thea turned to Conall, and he stared down at her, not in shock or horror, but with such realization, such feeling, she felt like her heart might explode.

Mate.

The breath whooshed out of her.

"I am sorry it has to be that way. You are one of a kind, Conall

MacLennan." Eirik's voice cut through Thea's moment of over-whelming emotion. "I do hate to snuff out those who are particularly special."

The threat was made with such casualness, it was almost like he was talking about what he would have for his dinner that evening.

The threat to Conall stirred a rage inside Thea, and she watched his eyes light with fierce pride as the air around her grew static.

"Now, now, Miss Quinn, we cannot have that."

She whipped around to Eirik, knowing her eyes were gold, that all the supernaturals in the room could feel the energy buzzing through her, looking for somewhere to unleash it. "Touch him and die."

Eirik flicked a casual finger behind his shoulder. "Now."

The vampires flew at them. A blur of black figures, shooting at them in overwhelming speed. These were no ordinary vampires. Six were on Conall while eight fought Thea. She ducked and spun, a punch sending a vampire soaring clear across the loft. Fists and legs glanced off her body, barely hurting, barely making an impact. But she broke necks, snapped wrists, punctured ribs through lungs until—

"Thea," Eirik's voice cut through the chaos and he didn't even have to raise it. There was something about the taunt that made her stop. The four vampires still left standing peeled back to reveal Conall on his knees. They had plunged a silver knife into his gut while five of the vampires who had attacked him held his arms spread wide so he couldn't remove it. The sixth was dust on the ground.

And Vik was no longer anywhere to be seen.

The traitorous bastard.

Thea squashed the panic that wanted to rise from her chest at seeing Conall captive and in pain.

She watched Eirik as he crossed the room to tower over her. His eyes swept down her body and back up again. "You are almost as lovely as the fae."

His wording confused her. "I thought I was fae."

"You are. However"—he studied her carefully—"it is almost like you are a fae trapped in a human body. Does that make sense? Viktor told me of your capabilities, and they are nowhere near the power of a fae."

"If you let Conall go, I won't fight you."

"No," Conall growled, low and deep. Fierce even while in agony.

"Unfortunately, that is not an option."

Thea narrowed her eyes, feeling the energy inside her shift. It felt different now that she knew what she was. Almost like that part of her, that energy, that magic, never fit until she was given the knowledge of its origin. Like a misplaced key finally slotting into place and opening a door to unimaginable power.

And it was there, in the depths of her.

A golden, sweet, heady, beautiful, terrifying eternity of power.

Suddenly, Thea wasn't afraid. "If you kill Conall, I'll end you."

Eirik smirked, the first real expression she'd seen on his face. "I am two and half thousand years old, Miss Quinn. I have killed my brother to stop the gate opening between realms and I have hunted many children whom I believed to be bearers of the fae queen's spell. In the last twenty-five years, I have snuffed out three of the lives of your fae siblings.

"And now I finally have you in my grasp. The fourth. I will not stop until all seven of you are dead. Now, you can make your death easy or difficult."

Thea's heart bled at the news three others had died already. Three beings like her, like the woman in Prague, killed by this bastard just because they'd been born. The rage churned in her gut. "I'll make it easy if Conall lives."

"Thea, no!" Conall roared in fury.

She couldn't look at him.

Eirik cocked his head. "I have heard it is an awful thing to force a man to live with the death of his mate. So, no. What I will do is spare him having to watch you die." He turned toward the vampires holding Conall, and Thea felt that door inside her blaze wide open.

"Kill him."

Her eyes widened in horror as a vampire, a blur of movement, ripped the silver knife out of Conall's gut and plunged it into his neck.

THE AGONY WAS MOMENTARY.

Conall stared across the room at Thea as the knife plunged into him, the pain so intense, he almost blacked out.

However, the sound of Thea's scream was so unearthly, so forceful, it blew like a gale into him with such an impact it kept him with her. The physical manifestation of her grief was the last thing he felt before his body went numb.

He seemed to float, weightless, except for the crushing pain of watching Thea's grief-stricken face. The heartbreaking horror in her expression made him feel desperate and powerless.

He'd never said he loved her.

Conall tried to feel his lips, to make the words come out, but before he could, blackness spilled into the edges of his vision as Eirik grasped Thea by the throat. Her eyes blazed bright gold.

There was a jeweled-handled knife of silver-gray metal in Eirik's hand. Pure iron.

Conall wanted to lunge forward, to save her, the howl of his wolf trapped and screaming inside.

But as Eirik moved to plunge the knife into Thea's heart, she swiped a hand over the incoming blade and it turned to liquid, splattering in thick mercury to the floor, the jewels from the handle rattling across the floorboards like marbles. Eirik snarled in outrage and tightened his grip on Thea's throat but …

Conall blinked in amazement, forcing the darkness back, as Thea began to shimmer. Eirik hissed, baring his fangs, as he dropped Thea and stared at his palm.

His burnt raw palm.

Thea's gaze moved back to Conall and tears slipped down her cheeks. He tried to say how he felt with his eyes and perhaps the message read loud and clear because Thea abruptly threw back her head and let out a piercing scream.

Light exploded out of her body, and Eirik and the vampires at his back screeched in agony as it tore through them.

Then they were gone.

Every one of them.

Piles of ash remained, dust dancing in the rays of pure sunlight beaming from every part of Thea's body.

Relief soothed Conall's pain.

She was safe.

His mate was safe.

And so he let the darkness come for him.

22

SHUDDERING THROUGH THE FIERY HEAT UNLIKE ANYTHING THEA HAD EVER experienced, she gasped for breath as the blinding white light disappeared, and she could see again.

Her clothes stuck to her skin, soaked with sweat as she took in the piles of ash where Eirik and his vampires had once stood.

She'd killed them.

All of them.

Her eyes flew to Conall, collapsed, surrounded by six piles of ash.

He was covered in blood.

So much blood.

Terror flooded Thea.

"Conall." She flew across the room and reached for his chest. Relief almost suffocated her when she felt the tiniest flutter from his heart. But there wasn't much time left, and Thea couldn't bring someone back from the dead.

Scoring a fingernail deep across her wrist, she forced open Conall's mouth and pressed her bleeding wrist into it. "Come on, come on, drink."

He didn't move and her wound sealed, instantly healing.

"Fuck!" *Think, Thea, think.*

She glanced around in panic and then it hit her. Her eyes flew to the back corner where the iron dagger was on display. Thea was a streak of energy crossing the room, yanking the dagger from the wall, ignoring the blazing agony ripping up her arm from her hand. Her reflexes wanted to drop the knife, but she forced her grip around it, pushing through the pain.

Weakening from the dagger, she fell to her knees at Conall's side. Fresh sweat glistened along her brow, and she bit her teeth against the scream that tore up from her throat as she dug the blade into her wrist.

It was pure fire.

Tears streamed down her face as she dropped the dagger and pressed her sliced wrist to his mouth. Her blood dripped, the iron-made wound taking longer to heal.

Conall didn't move.

"No, no, no, no," Thea panted. "Conall, you have to drink. You can't leave me." She bent over him, pressing desperate kisses down his scarred cheek, her tears splashing onto his skin. She rested her cheek against his, her body shuddering with panic. A sob burst out of her. "P-p-please ... p-please don't leave me."

A grunt, a choking sound, drew her head up.

He was choking on her blood.

Alive.

Healing.

Thea made a garbled sound of pure happiness and cradled his head so he could drink without choking. His eyes didn't open but he raised a hand to clasp her wrist to his mouth. "Sorry," she whispered, kissing his temple. "I'm so sorry."

Then she watched as the wound on his neck healed.

His grip on her wrist eased and when Thea pulled back, his eyes were open.

Thea laughed through her tears. "Hey, you."

Conall pushed up into a sitting position, tugging Thea into his lap. He buried his head in her neck and they shuddered in each other's arms for a second as they tried to get a hold on their emotions.

"You almost died," she whispered, her voice hoarse with grief.

His grip tightened. "But you didnae let me."

Thea drew back, cupping his face in her hands, wondering how it was possible to need a person so much. Her blood stained his lips, reminding her of how close he'd come to death. The idea was unbearable. Losing her parents left her with a gaping hole in her soul. Losing Conall would obliterate her. It was as beautiful as it was terrifying.

"I was so scared," she admitted.

Conall nodded slowly. "Aye, lass. Me too. That's what it is to be mated. It's a 'cannae live without each other' deal." Anger blazed in his icy eyes. "Which is why I dinnae appreciate you offering your life for mine."

He was lecturing her? Now? She hadn't even wrapped her head around the whole mating thing yet. "Seriously? You would have done the same thing."

He grumbled at that, but his gaze drifted over her shoulder. Awe crept into his expression. "You wiped out fourteen vampires, Thea. You became pure sunlight."

She nodded, more than a wee bit wary of the door she'd opened inside her soul. "I'm a little scared of myself."

"Don't be." He turned her face to his. "You can control this."

Thea studied him, hoping he was right. He had so much faith in her, it was humbling. "Did you really not know? About … our mating? How can it be true?" There was a part of her, the part that just wiped out fourteen vampires to save his life, that believed it to be true. She'd trusted Conall because she'd known deep down who he really was, and how could she have known that without some bond or connection pulling them together?

Yet, her logical side, belonging to that person who had been running on her own for years, found the whole idea a little too spectacular. After all, she and Conall had only met a few days ago, even if it did seem much longer.

Conall's brow furrowed in thought. "I smelled you on my skin the morning on the ferry. But I thought it was just from sex. Now"—he nuzzled her throat, drawing in her scent—"you smell of me too." His grip tightened, and she felt his body harden against her. "I cannae let you go now, lass."

Truthfully, Thea didn't want him to. She couldn't deny what she'd felt when she thought he was dying. Everything inside her had wanted to die too. But it wasn't that simple. "The pack, Conall. I'd put the pack in danger."

"You just killed the biggest threat." He nodded to Eirik's ashes. "Once word reaches the Blackwood Coven you fried the oldest vampire in the world, they might think better of coming after you. And if they dinnae, we'll go somewhere they cannae find us."

Shocked, Thea slumped against him. "You'd leave the pack?"

"To protect you, I would. But first we need to get Callie back." His expression hardened to granite. "There is no way on earth I'm letting you face Ashforth alone."

Sensing his resolve, Thea didn't see any point in arguing. Honestly, she wanted him by her side when she finally dealt with Ashforth. Still, the thought of him leaving his pack did not sit well with her at all. She knew how much they meant to him and how much Torridon meant to him.

However, it was a discussion for another time. "What now?"

"We go back to Torridon and we rally the pack. We'll need to come up with a plan to get Callie and James back without them coming to harm."

Nodding, Thea stood and reached for Conall, who got to his feet with ease. "I feel stronger," he said, staring at his hands.

"My blood." Her stomach flipped unpleasantly at the blood covering Conall's shirt. There was so much of it. It was all over her too from when they'd held each other. "We need to clean up."

Hearing the rasp of pain in her voice, Conall grasped her chin in his fingers and leaned down to brush a kiss across her lips. She could taste the coppery tang of her blood on his lips. "I'm fine, Thea." His eyes dropped to her wrist, and he frowned before pulling it toward him for study with more force than he probably intended. The wound from the iron blade had barely closed, the jagged cut swollen and painful.

Scowling, Conall's gaze fell to the floor where the iron dagger lay in a pile of vampire ashes. His eyes flew to her. "Thea," he whispered, realizing what she'd done.

Thea tugged on her wrist and he reluctantly let it go. "The wound wouldn't stay open long enough for you to drink. I had to."

"It'll scar permanently," he said, his voice hoarse.

"You're alive. That's all that matters."

Conall's eyes blazed. "You know I'd do the same for you."

She nodded, emotion thick in her throat. She had to clear it to speak. "I'll go out to the car for our backpacks. You use the traitor's shower." Thea squeezed Conall's arm as she felt the tension riot through him. "I'm sorry about Vik."

The muscle jumped in his jaw. "I'm sorry I trusted him and put you in danger."

"No." Thea stepped into him. "I won't let you blame yourself." She glanced around the apartment, noting all the research material and books Vik had left behind. "I wonder where the bastard took off to."

A growl rumbled up from Conall's throat. "I know where he is. I'll always know and when this is over, there's nowhere on earth he can hide from me."

Thea couldn't shake the image of that vampire stabbing Conall in the neck, especially not with Conall still covered in his own blood. Vik would pay for that. "*Us,*" she bit out, her eyes bleeding gold. "There's nowhere on earth he can hide from *us.*"

23

As Conall was out of cash and unable to use his credit card to buy Norwegian *krone*, Thea suggested they steal Vik's credit card. She laughed at the Scot's expression. "He betrayed us, Conall. A little financial aid is not a lot to ask."

"I shouldnae have to steal from anyone," he muttered, drying his hair with a towel as he slumped on Vik's sofa. His hair fell in damp curls around his forehead and at the nape of his neck. Thea had to resist the urge to stride across the room and bury her hands in it.

The need to feel him, real, alive, his body against hers, was almost unbearable.

Mate.

It explained these overwhelming feelings, yet it was still difficult for her to wrap her head around. So instead, she rummaged through Vik's drawers, and when that was unsuccessful, she moved to the next logical location. The jackets hanging by the door.

"Jackpot." She tugged the leather wallet out of a tailored wool coat. The vampire really had been in a rush to get the hell out of Dodge. Weaselly little coward. "Ah, even better." Thea pulled out a thick wad of *krone*. "No one can follow a cash trail. This should be enough for a hotel room." She frowned. "But not enough for the ferry."

While Conall had been showering, Thea had used Vik's computer to find a ferry crossing to the UK. Unbelievably, there wasn't a direct passenger ferry. There was only a freight ferry from Brevik, Norway, to Immingham, England.

It was a thirty-six-hour crossing with no cabin, but it would have to do. The plan was to get a hotel room in Oslo, sleep away the exhaustion of almost dying, and then drive to Brevik in the morning where they'd catch the ferry to England.

"We'll use my credit card," Conall said, standing up to pull on a fresh T-shirt. "We're on our way home. It doesnae matter if Ashforth tracks us."

"But a ticket from Norway to England will make him suspicious. He'll want to know why we detoured this way. We'll use Vik's." Thea gave him a look. "We do what we have to do to survive."

He deliberately looked around the apartment at the fifteen piles of ash they'd leave as a present for Vik. Conall's pale gray eyes returned to hers. "That we do, lass."

Deciding to shower at the hotel, Thea changed her clothes and scrubbed off the blood spatter on her face. Conall had used the first aid kit to bandage her wrist and as he did so, Thea admitted to herself she'd be glad for a night's rest. The iron had weakened her, and she felt slightly lethargic. The last thing she did before they left Vik's apartment was grab his copy of Jerrik's writings on Faerie. When she had time, Thea wanted to read about Eirik's brothers' accounts for herself.

They found a hotel in the center of Oslo and as soon as they walked into the room, Conall ordered room service. In the shower, Thea scrubbed her body clean and fought the urge to scream as images of Eirik clasping her by the throat while Conall lay dying beyond her grasp flashed over and over in her mind.

Conall had been right earlier. It didn't matter if she really was a member of a now-mythological race. There were people out there who *believed* she was. Even she believed she was. It was enough to put her in danger for the rest of her life, and thus anyone who came into contact with her. Nearly everyone she'd ever loved had died, and the thought of adding Conall to that list was soul destroying. She should leave him. After she helped him get his sister and beta back, Thea had to leave him to protect him. The thought trembled through her as she leaned her forehead against the hard tile and fought back an indignant sob.

Before Conall, being alone was a fact of life. One she bore.

Going out into the world, leaving him behind … it didn't bear thinking about.

And there was the fact she could never outrun him.

Somehow Thea didn't think Conall would let her go so easily.

That thrilled her more than it made her despair.

She was so selfish.

Yet something else Vik had told them that morning prodded at her, pricking to life a spark of hope she couldn't shake.

While drying her hair, Thea watched Conall dive into the food room service had delivered. In fact, they watched each other, as if afraid to look away in case one of them disappeared.

Exhausted, Thea had eaten some food, but her wrist still throbbed, and her head was messy and full and foggy. She just wanted the events of the day to disappear for a while.

She couldn't remember falling asleep, yet she awoke before dawn, on her left side facing the wall. She was naked, obviously having been disrobed before tucked under the covers. Thea could feel the warm length of Conall's body pressed along her back, his heavy arm draped over her waist, his hand resting between her breasts. His soft, even breathing on the pillow behind her told her he was asleep.

Everything that had happened came flooding back in a deluge. She tensed, biting back a whimper. Conall had nearly died.

She couldn't get the image of him dying, that silver knife in his neck, all the blood, out of her head.

There was a small, not very nice part of her that wanted to be angry at the wolf for becoming so integral, so important to her happiness. *A mating bond.* Jesus Christ! Why did he have to come along and wolf-bond with her?

Or was it her fault?

Eirik had said the mating bond had been passed down by the fae, so if she was fae, then actually the mating *was* her fault.

So lost in her thoughts, Thea didn't hear Conall's breathing change. She only realized he was awake when she felt a kiss upon a scar on her back. Thea went rigid for a millisecond, then his lips caressed another scar. And then another. Her body melted. His clasp on her breast became fingertips trailing down her stomach as he placed reverent kisses along her scarred spine.

Thea had never felt more cherished.

"Conall," she whispered, wondering if he could hear how much she loved him in that one word.

Because the truth was she *did* love him.

Thea realized that the moment she thought she'd lost him forever.

"One day, very soon," Conall said, his voice gruff with a strange mix of tenderness and rage, "I will help you eviscerate the bastard."

Knowing he meant Ashforth, Thea turned to face Conall. He immediately wrapped his arms around her, pulling her into his body. His equally naked body.

"You undressed me."

"You fell asleep, and you felt warm." He frowned, gently picking up her hand to press a kiss to her bandaged wrist. It still throbbed. "Too warm."

"I'm okay," she reassured him. "It just takes a little longer to heal. It should be good in a day or two." Tracing her fingers along his stubbled cheeks, Thea drew in a deep breath as she prepared herself to make her proposal. Even though she knew Conall seemed perfectly content with the idea they were mates, that they were permanent, she still feared he'd reject her idea. It would mean a different kind of permanency between them. "I've been thinking."

He reached for her fingertips and pressed a playful kiss to them. "About?"

"About bringing so much trouble to the pack." She ignored his frown and forged ahead. "The Canids will be pissed about the broken betrothal and let's not forget that I'm a constant source of danger for your people."

Conall pushed up, bracing his elbow against the pillow so he could rest his head in his palm. Thea tried not to get distracted at the way his biceps flexed. It reminded her of his muscles flexing during sex, and now was not the time.

"Thea, the Canids will understand. After all it's better I found you now than *after* a marriage arrangement with Sienna."

The mere thought of Conall marrying another woman made her stomach lurch unpleasantly. The possessive anger that heated her blood never failed to surprise her. She hadn't thought herself capable of territorialism. It was animalistic and primal and a little embarrassing.

She knew she'd failed to hide what she was feeling by the smug quirk to Conall's mouth. "Are you sure you're not part wolf?" He bent his head to nuzzle her face, his stubble scratching pleasantly against her cheek. "You're possessive enough."

What a helpful segue. "Speaking of …" Thea pulled back to look into his eyes. She wondered if he could hear her heart pounding. "Vik told us that story about the fae woman whose mate turned her into a wolf …"

He looked confused by the mention of the story and then understanding quickly dawned. Conall jerked away from her, his features taut with tension. "Aye, he also said another fae died from the werewolf's bite."

Thea could already feel her heart faltering with his coming rejection. Still, she persevered. "Shouldn't we consider it? If I'm not fae, if I become a werewolf instead, then I'll no longer be a target—and the pack, *you*, won't be in danger." Forcing herself not to run from his horrible silence, Thea instead snuggled into him, pressing her forehead to his throat. "I don't want to live forever." *Not without you.*

His hands tightened on her biceps.

Then he pushed her away.

Thea watched, angry and dejected, as Conall rolled across the bed and got out. His movements were jerky, agitated as he hauled up his underwear and jeans. "We dinnae even know if you are fae."

She swallowed past the lump of hurt in her throat and sat up. "But we know there are people out there who believe I am and that's what matters. If I was like you, we wouldn't have to worry. And I wouldn't have to watch you grow old and die while I stayed stuck like this for eternity."

If he heard the bitterness or heartbreak in her voice, he didn't show it.

"But if you don't want me to be one of your pack, I get it."

Conall had been mid-stride across the room, seemingly in pursuit of his T-shirt, when he halted and turned to look at her with such incredulous anger, she flinched. "You're my mate," he bit out. "You're *already* a member of my fucking pack. It isnae about that. It's about the fifty-fifty chance that my bite could kill you. So the answer is no."

Outrage swamped Thea at his high-handed dominance. She threw back the covers. "It's not up to you." She crossed the room, avoiding him as she reached for her own clothes. Pulling on her underwear, she couldn't even look at him. "It's my goddamn body, Conall. My life. My decision."

"You're my mate." The words sounded torn from him, drawing Thea's regard. His expression was haggard. "Life-altering decisions are made together." He moved to her, his eyes dragging down her half-naked body and back up again. "Your life is now my life. Your body is now my body."

Thea inwardly shuddered against the magnetic pull of their bond. She wanted to launch herself into his arms so they could take out their frustration on each other but ... she'd made her own decisions for years. No one, not even Conall, would take that independence away from her.

She turned away, pulling her shirt over her head. As she shrugged it down, her voice was ice. "Caveman bullshit." She glared at him over her shoulder. "Ashforth took away my choices for six years. I've been fighting for the right to own myself for another six. Whatever this is between us, I don't belong to you. I belong to myself."

He looked like she'd gutted him, and pain flared across Thea's chest at the thought of hurting him. Still she remained steadfast against the pull of their bond.

"I would never ..." He cleared his throat, furious reproach blazing in his eyes. "Do not compare me to him. There is a difference between thinking someone is a possession and belonging to someone, Thea.

Whether you like it or not, this mating bond means I do belong to you and you do belong to me. Because we're a part of each other." His gaze darkened. "At this very moment, I wish that wasnae true because I never imagined I'd end up with a mate that could even *think* about asking me to do something that might kill her. Aye, I could bite you and you could live a wolf's life, with a shorter life span, and no eternity to worry over. Or I could bite you and you could die." He took a measured step toward her. "And I would have to live with the fact I'd killed my mate for the rest of my miserable fucking life. You would ask that of me?"

Understanding dawned and remorse instantly wiped out Thea's anger. "You know I didn't mean..." He was right. She hadn't thought about that. She'd only been thinking of herself.

Not knowing what to say, Thea slumped into a chair and buried her head in her hands.

The silence between them was unbearable.

Finally, Conall moved around the room. When Thea got up the nerve to look, she saw he'd packed their stuff. Without looking at her, he shoved his car keys into his pocket and shrugged his rucksack onto one shoulder. "We need to go."

So they did.

They left the hotel without speaking a word and as Conall drove out of Oslo toward Brevik, the distance between them grew until it overwhelmed Thea with an entirely new kind of misery.

Upon reaching the ferry at Brevik, Thea and Conall were displeased to discover that the freight ferry only allowed commercial vehicles onto it. Conall had turned to her, expression pinched. "I need to get Callie back as soon as possible. You have to use your gift. I'm sorry."

She heard the genuine apology in his voice, and she understood. The truth was that if anything happened to Callie, it would destroy Conall, which in turn would destroy Thea. And that was why, even though it made her sick to her stomach, she manipulated the port authority who were checking vehicles driving onto the ferry. She made them see the SUV as a small commercial van with required papers and all.

"We do what we must to survive," she repeated softly as Conall drove them onto the ship.

Renewed silence descended upon them as they made their way to the main lounge where they'd have to sit for the long crossing. There were tradesmen and long-haul drivers already settling in, some heading directly to the cafeteria for lunch.

Thea couldn't even think about eating.

She followed Conall toward the back where there was a group of empty seats in the corner, but just before they reached them, he abruptly turned. Thea staggered to a halt as he towered over her. His expression was etched with harsh intensity.

"I love you," Conall said, the words rough as if they'd been grounded out. "But I willnae force you to stay with me and *endure* a mating bond. Not if it makes you feel like a prisoner. When we get to England, you can leave. I dinnae expect you to come to Scotland with me and I dinnae expect you to heal Callie either. God forbid you see me as anything like that bastard who tore your back to shreds." And on that, he strode away, fists at his sides, before pushing the door to the deck open with such force it slammed, drawing everyone's attention.

Thea felt a sob rise from her chest and wondered what had happened to the woman who could control her goddamn emotions. Hurrying out of the lounge, away from prying eyes and ears, she held the tears in until she could find a restroom. Finally, she found the ladies' toilets where she sat in a stall and did her best not to bawl her eyes out.

I love you.

I love you.

I love you.

He was choosing her over his sister. By setting her free, he was choosing her over Callie. He loved her so much he was letting her go.

Quiet tears slipped down Thea's cheeks as she tried to be strong.

Yet sometimes being strong wasn't about weathering storms alone. Sometimes being strong was admitting you needed someone.

Thea needed Conall.

More than she was comfortable with.

However, there was no changing the fact that her happiness depended upon his.

And she'd hurt him.

Pulling herself together, she drew in a shaky breath and moved back out through the lounge and onto the deck. He stood in the distance, braced against the railing as the ferry cut through the choppy waters. The wind battered him, but he was an immovable force. Conall MacLennan was the most steadfast, honorable man she'd ever met.

Thea swayed slightly as she approached him. Feeling her presence, he turned to look at her. Once upon a time his face, those wolf eyes, had been intimidating and fierce. Now they were beloved. And while others might see a menacing flatness to his expression, Thea saw the bleak. It broke her heart.

She held out a hand, praying he'd take it. "Please."

A muscle flexed in his jaw, but he reached out and enfolded her small hand in his. She squeezed it and then turned, leading him back down the deck. They were silent as Conall followed her through the ship and back into the empty ladies' restroom. Thea locked the door behind her and leaned against it. Conall stared around and turned to her with a questioning expression.

"I should never have compared our mating to what happened to me with Ashforth. I didn't mean it to come out like that and I hate that it did." Tears shimmered in her eyes and the intensity in Conall's was no longer icy. "For a … for a long time, I've been alone, and not just physically alone, running from Ashforth." She swiped impatiently at a tear. "I gave up on love years ago. I never thought I'd love anyone, and I never imagined that anyone would love me again."

He moved toward her. "Thea—"

She cut him off, holding up her hand to stop his advance. "You have to remember that the idea of finding a *mate* is new to me. There are still parts of my life that are very human. Finding out we're mates … you've just accepted it. And it's not that I don't believe that we are. I know"—she pressed a fist to her gut—"I know deep in here"—and then her chest—"and in here that's it true. It's just taking me a little longer to understand what it *means*. But I don't want to walk away from this. Yes, my fear wants me to because I've watched the people I love die around me, and moving on with my life has been impossible every time." She took a step toward him, her heart hammering so hard he had to hear it. "But when I saw that vampire plunge the silver into your neck, when I felt you dying in my arms …" Her tears fell freely now. "I wanted to die too. Running from Ashforth was just about surviving until you came along. You woke me up, Conall. You gave me a reason to fight instead of run. After everything I've lost, you terrify the shit out me"—she laughed through her tears and his gray eyes darkened with tenderness—"but the thought of losing you terrifies me more." She gasped when he moved, crowding her against the door.

He pressed a hand to her breast, right over her heart. "Say it," he demanded, guttural.

Thea nodded, trembling with the feeling that overwhelmed her entire being. "I love you, Conall. I love you."

His answering kiss was ferocious with need and Thea met him, searching lips against searching lips, hungry tongue against hungry tongue, as their hands roamed each other, devouring, loving.

"I need you." Thea broke the kiss, panting, as she fumbled for his belt buckle. "I need you."

"I need you. I *love* you," he breathed harshly against her mouth, unzipping her jeans as she worked on his.

Thea pushed them down with her underwear, kicking off her boots so she could free her legs. As soon as they were, Conall grabbed her by the ass and lifted her up against the door. She wrapped her legs around his waist, and she felt him hot against her. Then he thrust in deep with a battle cry that excited the hell out of her.

Thea held on tight, groaning against his mouth as pleasure zinged down her spine and legs. Their eyes locked as he drove into her in powerful, primal glides.

"Ceannsaichidh an Fhìrinn," he growled against her mouth.

He'd said that before, just before he shifted to wolf back in Germany. "What does that mean?" she gasped as he moved, faster, deeper, harder inside her.

"'Truth conquers,' Thea." His wolf eyes gleamed with satisfaction. "And this is our truth."

She loved that.

God, she loved him.

"Yes," she agreed, her fingers biting into his shoulders as his hips thrust faster, more desperately.

He kissed her, swallowing her gasps as she masked his groans, and the tension built and built and built—

Thea froze as it split apart inside her, and she couldn't contain her cry of release as she throbbed around Conall in delicious tugs. He came seconds later, his roar buried in her throat as he shuddered through his climax.

Surrounded by his scent, spice and earth, feeling his hot breath on her skin, her arms wrapped around his powerful shoulders while he was buried deep inside her, Thea never wanted to move. This was a kind of bliss, happiness, she hadn't expected from life.

She would fight for it until her dying breath.

"I love you," he murmured against her neck before lifting his head slowly to look deep into her eyes. That love was open and clear for the entire world to see. "There are no words for how much I love you, Thea Quinn."

Gratitude and exultation flooded her as she clasped his face in her hands and whispered, "I don't think there is a word for this much love. It's too big."

Pleased, he kissed her slowly, his grip on her almost bruising. When he finally pulled back, it was with obvious reluctance. His eyes turned molten when she let out a little gasp as he withdrew from her body.

"When we get home, we're spending an entire week in bed. No. A month."

Thea chuckled as they set themselves to right, unable to look away from each other as they dressed. She loved that to him, his home was already her home. Thea was excited to see the beautiful place he'd described to her so lovingly.

And then she remembered something else she had to apologize for.

"Conall, I shouldn't have asked you about changing me ... knowing the risks involved."

He clasped her face in his hands. "I would give you anything in the world, Thea love, I just ... I cannae lose you. And certainly not by my own hand."

"I know." She sought to reassure him. She reached out to touch the scar on his neck from the silver blade. "Believe me, I realize now what I was asking. And I'm sorry that I did. We never have to talk about it again."

At some point they would have to discuss Thea's immortality and their inability to have children, but it was a discussion for later. For now, they just needed each other. Their bond gave them strength, and Thea needed all the strength in the world to finally face the man who had brutalized her so many years ago.

THEY GRABBED A QUICK BITE TO EAT AND THEN AN EXHAUSTED CONALL slumped down on one of the lounge chairs, his legs sprawled, while Thea sat on the seat next to him. He pulled Thea's legs onto his lap, her feet dangling over the seat on his other side.

Her seat was next to the wall, so it meant she could recline.

"You should lie down," she said. The book she'd stolen from Vik rested on her knees. She'd gotten some sleep in the car while Conall had none.

He patted her knee. "I can sleep anywhere."

And true to his word, Conall closed his eyes, his head resting against the wall behind him. His breathing evened out quickly. Thea watched him sleep, her chest aching.

Hers.

He really was hers.

Wondering if she'd ever get used to the fierceness of her emotions, Thea reluctantly pulled her eyes from him and cracked open the book to a slightly yellowed page.

FAERIE
A Journal by Jerrik Mortensen
Oxford:
First Printed for Jerrik Mortensen
At Oxford University Press, Oxford
1963

Jesus, Thea mused. She wondered who Jerrik had in his thrall to get his book published at Oxford University press in the seventeenth century. Someone with a rare first edition had gone on to have it printed again and somehow, Vik, the obsessive researcher, had gotten his mitts on one.

Thea felt a little flutter of nerves as she turned to the page. According to Vik, Jerrik had been much older than when the journal first began, so he hadn't chronicled his time as a vampire until centuries later.

She read, falling into his descriptions of a fae world that was exquisite and brutal, and hours passed as Jerrik told his story to her from beyond the grave …

(Roman Calendar Year 132 BC)

Geimhreadh, Faerie

There is never a day here I do not wonder at Faerie. My brother and I move through this world without need of protection; the bright star in the sky here does not burn as it does in our world. Days of running free through the other lands to reach Geimhreadh. The journey on horseback would take weeks. Months. Our vampire speed holds us in good stead. Yet as soon as we cross into Geimhreadh, we feel peace. A world of eternal darkness, the moon here impossibly brighter than our own, a light upon our skin that soothes rather than burns. If I could, I would live here for all my days as the creature that was made of me. Eirik does not agree. Although he enjoys some pleasures afforded by Faerie, he takes more pleasure in the power he holds over humans back on Earth.

The eternal night is not my only sanctuary here. I fear that Eirik's growing distaste with Faerie has more to do with my mate than anything else. My mate. My slow, beating heart gallops faster at the mere thought of her.

Andraste.

A princess of the Night Lands.

Mine.

My mate.

As Eirik and I slow our speed upon entering Réalta, the royal city of the Night Lands, I cannot help but stare at the world so vastly different from ours and find joy in it. Eirik thinks me a fool. That I have not yet grown used to their superior living. But our world seems primitive in comparison. Our squat, brick dwellings with holes for windows. Here there are towering buildings carved into mountains, windows that stretch for miles, shielded from the outside by the opaque sheets called Gleamings. Some were transparent. From my lady's chamber, I can see every glittering star in the night sky.

Others, like those along the front facade of the Geimhreadh Palace, were stained with colors so exquisite the beauty was almost too much. The palace itself was built entirely of a material like the marble used in the city of Rome. Yet the Romans built with brick and merely covered facades with the expense of marble, a show of power and wealth. Once upon a time, I thought Rome the most superior place I had ever visited.

That was before Faerie. Where entire villages are built from marble.

The marble here was inset with the tiniest gemstones that sparkled like diamonds beneath the moon's glow. I had never seen its like.

We moved as ghosts over paving stones across the Royal Square where market dwellers sold their wares. There were stalls of meats, sweet pies, clothing, furs, jewelry, weapons, and even blood for their visiting vampire kin for sale.

A shriek drew my attention toward the center of the square where a large water fountain stood. It was a marble sculpture of my beloved and her two sisters, their hands raised as if to the heavens. Water fell from those hands by way of magic.

Another shriek tore my attention from the middle sculpture of Andraste. A human female was crying and begging as fae wearing royal guard uniform tore at her clothing, hell-bent on taking their pleasure from her. Another shriek rent the air but not from her.

Only feet from her another human woman was on the ground, her gown ripped open to reveal a back that was now bloody from a flogging. A tall fae I recognized stood over her, wielding a weapon much like the flagrum I'd seen in Rome.

It was Lir, the queen's captain, a brutish son of a bitch who found joy in human misery.

"The queen is here," I said to Eirik.

I turned to him. Eirik's eyes blazed at the scene playing out on the square.

"There is nothing we can do for them," I reminded him.

My brother had strange morals. He would drain a human dry without thinking about it, but he detested rape or any abuse of those he felt were weaker than him. It was dishonorable. I, myself, did not partake in any of the more abhorrent activities against the humans we sometimes witnessed during our visits to Faerie. Moreover, I rarely lost control when drinking from a human.

Yet I could see past the brutality against humans to the marvel and wonder of Faerie. To me this world was far more eminent and illustrious than ours and the fae within it. However, Eirik considered humans our people, to be treated as we saw fit, not as how the fae saw fit.

He curled his lip as his eyes connected with Lir's. The queen's captain sneered at my brother. I cursed under my breath as Eirik refused to look away.

"You will get yourself killed," I growled.

"Let him try."

"Eirik, he is thousands of years old and borne of pure magic. You would be dead in an instant."

"Queen Aine would never allow it." His answer wasn't smug. He did not enjoy Aine's attentions when others would. But his continued refusal of those attentions perversely made my brother one of the Fae Queen's favorites.

"Perhaps you should give her what she wants."

"And deny Fionn his time with her?" he joked, speaking of the queen's consort.

When we finally were led into the palace, we were directed to the throne room where Queen Aine held court. Andraste and her sisters sat near and my eyes connected with my mate's. Everything around me disappeared but her. The sparkling marble floors, walls, the magnificent paintings that graced those walls, the balls of lights that glowed around the room with no aid of fire. Just pure magic.

Nothing was as magical as Andraste.

I could almost feel her love warming through me.

My brother would be sick if he heard my thoughts. He thought love was a disease.

I disagreed.

Vehemently.

Fae, humans, werewolves, and vampires crowded into the throne room. It was here on Faerie I first heard the unusual music that often played in my mind whenever I returned to our world. We did not have such beauty of music. It reminded me of the sounds made by the lyre, but on a celestial level of bliss the lyre could never achieve.

Fae musicians played in the corner. We were forbidden from taking anything from the fae world back into ours, but I often contemplated ignoring the rule just to steal one of those instruments made of wood and string. The humans needed this music more than the fae did.

"Fionn looks as delighted as ever to be here." Eirik smirked.

My eyes moved to the queen's human consort who stood by her side. Six years ago, Fionn had been one of the youngest kings of Éireann. The fiercest warrior. He stood at a great height, taller than even many of the fae, and powerfully built. The male had the most startling green eyes. So vivid, he could almost pass for fae. His people thought him a god. And he and his tribes hunted fae, determined to wipe them out of existence. I had wanted to kill him.

Eirik applauded him.

My ungrateful brother.

Aine could not let the murders go unpunished and so she ventured into our world herself to mete out his punishment. It is said Aine was so taken with Fionn, she offered him a bargain. If he stayed with her on Faerie as his consort, she would spare his beautiful wife and two young children.

At the display of unearthly power Aine rained down about his village, Fionn accepted the bargain.

The mighty warrior had been her whore ever since.

"I fear he will try to kill her someday," I murmured.

Eirik's hungry eyes studied Fionn. My brother could not hide his desire for the warrior. I was inclined to think it was his obvious passion for the warrior that had Aine so taken with Eirik. She had something he wanted. Aine did so delight in bargains.

Yet I think my brother and I both knew she would only push Fionn so far, and the warrior was not interested in taking any male to his bed.

Much to Eirik's disappointment.

"He will never attempt to kill her," Eirik replied. "She will kill his wife, and if she is no longer alive, his children, and if they are no longer alive, then his grandchildren. He is stuck with her. Until his mortal life ends. Such a waste."

"I doubt Aine sees it as such."

My brother scowled. Aine had a penchant for men, human or supernatural, who were not under her thrall. She seemed to delight in the novelty of it.

Ignoring Eirik's foul mood, I moved through the crowds to bow at Aine's throne. My eyes flicked to Andraste who watched me with impatient hunger. Soon, my expression said.

Eirik reluctantly bowed beside me.

"The Mortensen brothers. You do add a rough sort of beauty to any room." Aine smiled down at us. Her own beauty was almost too much. The golden hair, the golden eyes, the golden skin. She was like a fallen sun. In comparison, my Andraste had silver-blond hair, pale moonlight skin, and silver eyes. Like a single fallen star.

The sun burned.

A star was something to place a wish upon.

All my wishes were bound up in my star.

I adamantly did not look at Andraste again. A mating between a fae and a vampire was unheard of, and Andraste was terrified of Aine's reaction. So far, we'd been lucky. No one had detected the mingling of our scents. Except for my brother and her sisters. But not one of them would put our lives in jeopardy by sharing our secret.

"No beauty could eclipse yours," I answered.

She gave me an amused smile and turned to Eirik.

He stared stonily up at her.

"What say you, Eirik Mortensen?"

"Your captain is torturing a human female out in the Royal Square while his men fuck another against her will. An interesting way to announce that the queen is in residence."

I could feel the disapproval of the queen's subjects at my brother's lack of deference.

Yet I was not surprised when Aine scowled. "How vulgar of him."

The queen of the fae was an odd, complex being. She could be benevolent and kind and then wicked and cruel within the space of a mere thought.

Suddenly, Captain Lir appeared at my side. Outside his shirt had been unbuttoned, sweat dotted his brow, and his hair had been askew. Blood had flecked his face. There was not a trace of that in his immaculate appearance. He bowed low. "My queen."

Aine dragged her eyes down his body and back up again. "We do not visit Réalta only to make a spectacle of ourselves in their marketplace, do we, Captain?"

He inclined his head, a flick of a dangerous look at Eirik.

"Do you have a reason for your attentions upon the human females?"

Lir shrugged. "They refused to pleasure me and my men. So we took our pleasure from them."

"They are not slaves to your every whim," Eirik bit out.

Lir raised an eyebrow. "Are they not?"

"No," Aine answered.

The room hushed.

Lir straightened, his expression flattening. "My queen?"

She stood. The golden dress she wore clung to her beautiful body, but the train flowed around her feet like golden water and as she moved down the dais, the sound of it was like a gentle stream.

Aine drew to a stop before Lir. "Humans are not slaves to your every whim, Captain. They are my guests in this world and therefore friends who bow to my every whim. I did not give you leave to take your pleasure from them."

He bowed his head deferentially. "My queen."

"You have embarrassed me, Lir. To be scolded by a vampire for your

behavior is not at all how I envisioned my visit to the lands of eternal night. What say you?"

"My apologies, My queen." His gaze flicked to Eirik again. "Do you wish me to cut down the vampire who would scold you?"

"No," she answered immediately. She smiled at Eirik, devious and wicked, beautiful and sparkling. "He amuses me greatly." She turned her golden eyes to the watching crowd and pouted prettily. "Pity he does not want me."

The room gasped at the idea, outraged on behalf of their queen.

"I know." Aine gave a dramatic little sigh. "I must take comfort in the fact that it is merely a case I am not equipped"—*her eyes dropped deliberately to Eirik's groin*—*"to satisfy him."*

The court laughed at her joke as she moved back up the dais. Instead of sitting on the throne, she halted beside Fionn, staring up at the large warrior king. He stared straight ahead, ignoring her. Aine placed her hand on his bare chest. Whatever she whispered to him, it caused the muscle in his jaw to tick before he turned to offer his hand.

The surrounding air shimmered, and then they were gone.

We all knew why and where.

Eirik stared at the space they had stood with envy tightening his features.

I finally looked at Andraste.

There were no words for how much I needed her. Sometimes I feared the extent of my feelings because they were infinite, never ending, like the stars themselves. Too much feeling. Too much love. It hurt as much as it pleasured. I feared I would die without her. The hunger, the need for her, did not seem to abate. It was stronger than my need for blood. No matter how many times I found bliss between her pale thighs, it was never enough.

I wanted more.

It felt like hours before I could be with her. Eirik disappeared as I spoke with friends we had made among the supernaturals and fae. The human guests were treated much better within the court than those who wandered outside of its protection, like the human girls Lir had tormented.

At last Andraste and I made it out of the room without detection, no words passing between us, so eager were we to be alone. She led us to a set of stairs used only by the servants. We hurried up the coruscate marble, the servants we passed turning a blind eye to our appearance. Andraste scolded me for watching a fair maid hurry past us, but I assured her, I was as ever merely caught up in my wonder. The fae, whether aristocrat or servant, were lustrous in their attractions.

"There is not a crow among you," I once teased Andraste.

"Oh, there are," she assured me. "However, they dwell in parts of our world that no one ventures. Nasty, horrible creatures."

"Are they kept separated because they lack beauty?" The thought had troubled me.

"No. Because they despise beauty and once upon a time sought to destroy it."

"There was a war?"

"Millennia ago. Yes. They wielded weapons that could kill us but Aine was too powerful for them. We won the war, Aine destroyed any trace of the weapons and was benevolent enough to let most of the challengers live. There is another continent on Faerie, across vast, dangerous waters. We have not seen or heard from them in centuries. Thank goodness."

My curiosity on the subject had grown, and Andraste had allowed me use of the royal library to read of the war. There I read that during the war, Aine discovered what she called the cauldron. It had the power to strip a fae of their memories so they could be reborn, something the fae required now that they were truly immortal. In their newly eternal evolution, fae children became rarer and rarer until only one or two fae children were born every century.

Now, however, was not the time to be thinking of such things when my glimmering mate was leading me toward her chamber.

It was as we moved from one floor to the next that we heard a harsh male grunt and a cry of pleasure. Both our gazes flew to an open doorway, a servant's bedroom, where I flinched to see my brother and Lir naked. Lir was on his hands and knees as my brother powered into him from behind. And I knew him well enough to know he'd deliberately left the door open.

I curled my lip in distaste.

It was a sight I'd have liked to have gone an eternity without ever seeing.

As Andraste and I hurried away, she giggled.

I glowered at her.

She shrugged. "Your brother is so contrary."

"He's a dominating bastard." He would just love that. Taking pleasure from Lir, making him vulnerable to him. It was his own way of punishing the fae for hurting the humans. To make him want him so much, to have power over him.

Eirik was good at that.

"I need you to spell the image from my head," I grunted, pulling Andraste into her bedchamber. "Love me until there is nothing but you."

And so she did.

The queen left the following day. Andraste and I stayed in bed for four nights to celebrate our privacy.

Thea glanced up from the entry to find Conall out for the count. If Jerrik's journal of his time in Faerie was a lie, then the guy had an amazing imagination.

Staring at Conall, however, Thea believed Jerrik had once had a mate. The way he described his love for Andraste was the way Thea felt about Conall. The mating. It was *intense.*

She fought the urge to lean over and kiss Conall's scarred cheek and instead turned the page to the next entry. Jerrik filled the pages with tales from the court, and as Vik had mentioned, he spoke of the queen's fury over the fae who turned to werewolf and the fae who died trying to do so. The revelation had worried Andraste as she feared the queen discovering their secret, but Jerrik had refused to leave her side.

Finally, Thea skimmed through his entries until she got to the one that interested her most: the closing of the gate and the supposed spell upon the human world that Thea was a consequence of.

(Roman Calendar Year 128 BC)

It cannot be. I sit here in my cold stone home, no windows to guard against the sun, and I cannot fathom that Andraste is lost to me. Hours ago, she'd been in my arms. Hours ago, another world had made my existence worthwhile.

It is now lost to me too.

"Are you going to mourn forever?" Eirik had asked upon our arrival home. "Because that will grow tedious."

"Do you not care she is forever lost to me?"

"No. She was beneath you. As they all are."

"They made us, you ungrateful heathen."

"Yes, but rather like a man whose mother pushed him out as a babe only to leave him to starve in the woods, I bear no loyalty to my creators."

I'd attacked him.

Viciously.

Both of us were bloodied and broken but healing physically.

I did not know if my heart would ever heal.

Listen to me. My mind is so overwhelmed by the happenings. I need to find order in the chaos. I've started at the end. I must go back to this morning. To explain.

The queen's seer had a vision.

I had been living on Faerie for months. Eirik would visit occasionally. "To make sure you are still alive."

For me, however, even separated from my twin who had once been my other half, my life was here. With Andraste.

The fae celebrated each country throughout the year and it was time to pay homage to Samhradh, the lands of eternal summer. Samhradh Palace stood in the heart of Solas, the royal city of the Day Lands. If I thought the palace at Réalta astounding, there were no words for the queen's home. It differed from the other palaces. Where they were long and rectangular, a building wrapped around a huge inner courtyard, the palace at Solas was tall and enchanting. A castle. Towering turrets of different sizes, spires, and a magnificent gated entrance created from gold. It appeared to be crafted entirely of shattered pieces of the opaque glimmering utilized for windows. Those shattered pieces, placed together, miniscule bit by miniscule bit, gave the castle the appearance of a building made entirely of diamonds.

It shimmered, flashing and winking in the blazing sun. It was a wonder to even walk beneath a sun that could not kill me, but to enjoy the beauty of Samhradh at the same time was a marvel. It was a joy to escort Andraste to the Solas Festival.

That morning, Andraste woke me, frantic. "The palace is abuzz," she said, hauling me out of bed. "The queen's seer has had a vision and now the queen has demanded we all attend the Reckoning."

I groaned, as I had already decided I did not want to attend the Reckoning. It was the fae version of a justice system. Any supernatural, human, or fae caught breaking the laws of Faerie were kept in confinement at a prison near the gate between worlds on the coast of Samhradh. They were brought out of confinement every quarter during a festival to be judged by Aine.

"Hurry, it has already begun."

"What has the seer prophesied?"

"No one knows. But rumor is rife that the queen found the news disturbing."

"The queen is never disturbed."

"Hence my current disquietude."

So we stood beside Eirik, who had to come to Faerie to enjoy the festival, as prisoner after prisoner was brought into the throne room to be judged by the queen.

As I neared almost unconsciousness with boredom, they brought the final prisoner forth.

She was human.

A beauty at that.

Since discovering Faerie, I'd found little attraction in humans so it was rare that one could catch my eye. The girl was dressed rather vulgar in leather leg coverings, as a man would wear. Leather strips, pieced together, made a vest that molded to her torso in a strangely becoming way. Her dark hair was held back from her face in long braids. There was an appealing boldness to her beauty. I soon noted I was not the only one to think so.

"We just caught this one, Your Highness." A fae guard threw the girl forward, and she glared at him. He ignored her, holding up a sword. "She came through the gates armed and we caught her stealing from our fruit trees."

The crowd gasped at the effrontery. It was common law among fae and human: you stole nothing from the fae to take back to our world. Unless it was freely given.

Aine eyed the young woman. "Name?"

The girl lifted her chin in defiance. "Catha."

A rumble of displeasure moved around the room. I heard Andraste hiss, along with a few other fae females.

The guard pushed Catha. "You will address the queen with the proper respect."

"She is not my queen," Catha said recklessly.

The hissing grew in sound, restless feet moving closer to the girl.

Aine lifted a hand to silence the crowd. Her golden eyes peered intently into Catha's. "Why did you venture into Faerie to steal from us?"

Catha shrugged off the guard's touch and faced the queen with apparently no fear. "My family is starving. I hunt but the prey is dwindling. I heard the food of the fae lasts longer than mortal food, and I had hoped the fruit would see us through winter."

"There are no men in your family to hunt?"

Catha shook her head. "My father died three winters ago. I am responsible for my mother and four sisters now."

"You are the eldest?"

"No. The youngest."

Aine dragged her gaze up and down the girl. "And a beauty. Are your sisters beautiful like you?"

"More so. But they are too poor to interest men with more wealth than our own."

The queen scowled at that. "Humans and their lack of fealty to women is tedious. In my world, young Catha, you would be a warrior for you have a warrior's heart." She lifted a graceful hand to point toward the girl's heart. "I sense it."

The girl lost some of her defiance and she bowed her head slightly in thanks.

Aine lifted her eyes to the room. "I have called you all here for a reason. Before I make my announcement, I grant one last token to a race that often consternates but always amuses." Her golden eyes drifted back to Catha. "You shall return to your world unharmed, young Catha, and when you do, you will find yourself the keeper of riches beyond your imagining. Your family will never suffer from poverty again. Your sisters shall marry well and you, if you wish it, will be a queen."

Catha's eyes darkened with intensity. "I wish it, Your Highness."

With the queen's nod, Catha was gone, presumably back to our world, to the astonishing gifts Aine had promised.

"Now," Aine stood from her throne, "I fear I have unwelcome news for our guests." A movement to my left drew my attention, and I noted a fae man sidling up to my brother. His face was … it was hazy, as though his features did not want to fall into place. And he seemed hunched. Eirik stiffened at the sight of him and the fae gave him a quick shake of his head to silence him. Whatever passed between them, my brother merely nodded and turned back to the queen.

As did I.

"It has come to my attention that humans have discovered the healing use of our blood."

A gasp rippled around the room.

Eirik had brought the rumors with him and had told me a few days ago of this discovery. Apparently, fae blood could heal a human or supernatural from any wound or disease, even from the brink of death. There were murmurings that war bands of humans were gathering to steal fae back into the human world as their own constant source of immortality.

I had thought it mere ridiculous human posturing.

But the queen's seer had declared it was beyond that.

"We are on the brink of war. Again. And I will not let beings we have so benevolently graced our gifts upon ruin our world. I am afraid the gate must close."

Good. I wished to stay here.

"*I am sending all non-fae back to their own world. Human, vampire, and werewolf alike. I am afraid you are no longer welcome on Faerie.*"

Horror rooted me in place. I felt Andraste clasp at my hand as she whimpered.

No.

"*Do you think*"—Aine's gaze drifted around the room and stopped upon certain individuals for a few deliberate seconds, before turning to Andraste and me—"*I am not aware of the inappropriate bonds that have been forged between fae and non-fae?*"

I stiffened.

She knew Andraste was my mate.

"*There are matings in this room that should never have come to pass. The stars, however, choose as they see fit and I have let it stand so long as it has not caused injury to our world. First, there was Abellio and her wolf. The grief they caused Earrach when they killed one of their princes ...*" Aine's eyes glistened with tears. "*Now, a royal subject of Fómhar has given her blood to her human mate to save his life after he was injured in a human war. This is a grave threat to our home. So I am sorry ... but for the sake of peace, you are all expelled from Faerie.*"

Outrage swelled out of the fae as I turned to stare at my love. "Andraste," I whispered, terrified of never seeing her face again.

She burrowed into me, silver tears falling down her pale cheeks. "*I cannot lose you.*"

I shook my head in denial. This could not be happening.

"*However, I am not so cruel ...*"

We whipped around to stare in hope at the queen. My heart thudded at the devious smirk on her face.

"*I am not so cruel as to deny our children a chance to live here forever. As I close the gates, I will cast a spell out into the human world. In time, that spell will come to fruition in the form of seven children, born to human parents, but fae-borne.*"

Everyone gasped at the idea.

Aine smiled. Smug. "*Yes. Seven children and with them the ability to open the gate. They and their companions will enter Faerie. If they succeed, I grant them leave to remain here with us forever.*"

Then the world shimmered, my head spun, and before I could kiss her one last time, Andraste was ripped from me.

I stumbled into the darkness of a familiar forest, the smell of pine and earth filling my nostrils.

No. I whirled to find my bearings and instead found Eirik standing with ... Fionn.

But ... I sniffed the surrounding air.

He was no longer human.

"Did we ..." I looked around, frantic.

"We are home," Eirik said flatly. "The bitch sent everyone back to Earth and closed the gate. Good riddance." His gaze drew up Fionn. "What the hell happened to you?"

Fionn glared at my brother. "Aine made me fae."

Eirik raised an eyebrow. "Immortal?"

"Yes." He sneered. "She intended to keep me on Faerie with her. But a princess of Samhradh owed me a favor. She cast an illusion spell over me so I could find my way to you in the crowds. The queen's seer, she told me if I held onto someone who would be glad to return to this world, I would be transported back with them. You are the only bastard I know who hates the fae almost as much as I do."

"Then it is true," I whispered, feeling like my heart might crumble within my chest. "The gate has really closed."

"Yes." Fionn nodded.

No, no, no.

"What now?" my brother said to the queen's consort.

"Now, I return to my home, to my family. Where are we?"

"Germania. You are some ways from Éireann. How do you know the queen will not open the gate to return you to her?"

"She will not risk it. Her seer saw much bloodshed between the fae and human world if the gate remained open."

My brother grinned. "She fears us?"

"No, you fool." Fionn glowered. "She is trying to protect us. A war with the fae would wipe out this world. Aine might be a selfish, self-indulgent bitch, but she would not see to the destruction of an entire world. Especially not one that bears fae children. And whether you like it or not, vampires and werewolves are fae children."

"This is not happening," I murmured.

"Well," Fionn said, clearing his throat, "thank you for the transportation. I will take my leave."

And then he was gone. A streak of movement through the forest, faster than even Eirik or I could move.

"The children," I whispered. "The children she spoke of. We must find the children." They were the key to opening the gate. They were the key to delivering me back to my mate.

"Yes," Eirik had muttered. "The children must be found."

I did not know then that it was the beginning of a war between my brother and me, as he sought to destroy my only hope of returning home.

"Interesting read?"

Thea blinked, coming up out of Jerrik's story to stare at Conall. He gave her a sleepy smile. Her heart beat a little faster. "It wasn't just about his love for the fae world." She tapped the book. "Jerrik was mated to a fae princess. He wanted to use the children—me—to get back to her."

"You believe then?" Conall's brows pulled together.

"I believe he was mated." She dropped her eyes to the pages. "He describes it so realistically."

"And the rest."

Thea shrugged. "It sounds like a fairy tale."

"Ironically."

Thea met Conall's gaze. "He describes the fae as contrary, often brutal. They thought themselves superior to other races. Why would the Blackwoods want to open a gate to that?"

"Magic," Conall replied. "It's purported to be a place of pure magic. Witches can only tap into a certain energy here. Faerie is something entirely different."

She nodded and sighed, closing the book. Their eyes locked. "We live in a very strange world, Chief MacLennan."

He grinned, shaking his head. "I hate to tell you this, lass, but you and I … we're two of the very beings that make it a strange world."

Chuckling, Thea lifted her legs off his lap and then scooted into his side so she could snuggle against his chest. Conall put his arm around her and drew her close. Stretching out her long legs—though nowhere near as long as his—she tried to quell the nervous fluttering in her stomach.

It wasn't just from reading Jerrik's accounts of a world she still wasn't sure she believed in.

The fluttering was about Scotland. Torridon.

Thea was about to meet the pack.

Conall's pack.

She watched as Conall slid one leg under one of hers, inviting her to curl it around him, which she did. Tangling them together.

Together, Thea reminded herself.

They were in this together.

25

To Conall's relief, he and Thea made it back to Scotland without incident. The Blackwoods had either lost their trail or word of Eirik's defeat was already making the rounds, and fear of Thea had taken root.

He still marveled at what he'd seen in Vik's apartment. What being on Earth was powerful enough to emit pure sunlight, killing only the vampires she'd been intent on destroying?

It was magic.

Pure and simple.

It was fae.

Conall couldn't think on it too long because he feared the danger it represented for her. Instead, he concentrated on watching her reaction as they drove toward Torridon. Upon arriving in Immingham, they'd taken the motorway all the way home past Yorkshire and the Lake District. They crossed the border into Scotland, driving past the pretty lowlands, none of which Thea could see because it was nighttime. However, the dawn broke just as they reached Inverness.

"It's beautiful," Thea whispered, staring out the passenger window as they crossed the Beauly Firth. The clouds hung low over the shallow mountains, turning the water of the firth gray.

"This is nothing," he promised.

Conall knew the moment the beauty hit her. The sun broke through the clouds; the skies cleared as they turned off the main road at Kinlochewe and toward the single track that would lead to Torridon. When they turned a corner a small loch appeared, surrounded by towering mountains, and Thea let out a little whoosh of breath. Keeping an eye on the road for oncoming traffic and watching Thea was difficult, but he caught the wonder on her face and pride bloomed in his chest.

Out here the rest of the world felt far away. It wasn't an isolating feeling. At least, Conall didn't think so. It was a piece of the planet that had been left untouched. Majestic and peaceful.

Thea didn't speak as they drove, her eyes wide, her head tilting back as she peered out the window. "The mountains are huge here," she whispered, craning to see the peak of the one they drove under. Sporadic clusters of forest interrupted her view.

"*Beinns*," Conall replied. "We call them *beinns*. This here is Beinn Eighe, two of which are classified as Munros."

"What's a Munro?"

"A mountain with a height over three thousand feet."

"Wow," she said. "Conall … it's majestic."

He smiled, nodding. "That's the exact word I always think of when I'm home."

"You never tire of it?"

"Never." He gave her a meaningful look. "There are special kinds of beauty that not even constancy can dull."

Her cognac eyes warmed as she realized he wasn't just speaking about his home. "Does your pack know how romantic you can be?"

Conall grinned. "No. And they'd never believe you."

Her laughter caused a pleasurable ache in his chest and he braced himself as they turned right past the entrance to Inveralligin, where his home was. "We're not heading to my place just yet. We're going to the Coach House. The Canids are staying there, and I'd like to get that confrontation over with so we can concentrate on bringing Callie and James home."

Her expression shut down, reminding him of the woman he'd met before he'd gotten to know her. If she was donning her mask, she didn't feel safe. That pissed Conall off. "No one will harm you here, Thea."

"I know that." She gave him a pained smile. "I'm just a little nervous. Wanting people to like me hasn't really been a priority in a while. But if your pack is to be my pack, I want them to accept me."

He took in her beautiful face, saw beneath to the tortured survivalist; to the woman who held within her a deep well of kindness and compassion, buried beneath a steel layer that had been necessary to endure what she had. "They'd have to try hard not to like *you*, lass."

She shot him a flirty smile. "You're a little biased."

Conall grinned but stopped when her smile fell as they pulled into the car park of the Coach House. There were more cars than usual, and Conall could only hope they belonged to the pack and not humans who'd dared to venture into Torridon.

The main door to the building flew open before Conall had even fully gotten out of the car. Grace hurried across the lot, her expression taut, and he didn't know if she would hug him or kill him.

He wasn't certain she knew either.

At the last second, however, she threw her arms around him and Conall bent down to embrace and comfort the woman who had been like a grandmother to him his whole life.

"Days," Grace said, pulling back, anger flashing in her eyes. "Days without word." Her attention caught on the scar on his neck. "What … how … There's a scar on your neck, young man, which can only mean silver was driven in there at some point." She paled.

Conall settled his hands on her shoulders. "I'm sorry, Grace. Things … have been complicated. I will explain all. But I need you to call the pack members who are closest for a meeting here in two hours."

"Some members are already here." She gestured to the cars. "When we heard no word, Mhairi and Brodie called out to the pack to regroup."

He nodded, pleased, because that was exactly what he expected of his delta and interim lead warrior in the absence of the alpha and his beta.

The sound of gravel underfoot brought Grace's head up toward Thea. She frowned. "Is this her?"

"Aye, but things arenae as they seem, Grace." Conall moved past her to take Thea's hand. "Grace, meet Thea. Thea, this is Grace. Grace is family, not just pack."

Thea's hand tightened on his and she held out her other to Grace. Conall almost grinned because his mate was not the type who could paste on a smile to reassure someone. Her inner anxiety made her scowl at Grace. "Nice to meet you."

Grace studied Conall's hand in Thea's. Confusion marred her brow as she slowly stepped forward to take Thea's hand and as she did so, a gentle wind blew up from the loch. Grace sniffed the air and her eyes grew wide.

Her head jerked toward his. "Conall."

Mating was rare. Conall's mother and father were the only mates the pack had known for a hundred years. Not even Grace and Angus, who were as good as. Yet, Conall knew Grace understood. She smelled their scents. Having been friends with the previous alpha couple, she knew what it meant.

"It was quite a surprise for us too," Conall told her dryly.

"Oh, Conall." Worry darkened Grace's eyes. "What does this mean?"

"We have quite a story to tell. That's why I'd like as many pack members here so I only have to tell it once. And so we can come up with a plan … to get Callie and James back."

Grace's eyes flew to Thea, wariness in them that Conall did not appreciate. The expression made Thea try to pull out of his grasp. He tightened his hold on her.

"She's my mate, Grace," Conall confirmed, his voice hard.

No one would mess with his mate, emotionally or otherwise.

Grace gave him a sharp nod. "That's all well and good, but we have to get my lass back."

Callie would be Grace's priority and Conall understood that. "We will." He gestured to the house. "While you call the pack, Thea and I need to meet with the Canids. I presume they're still here."

The older wolf's expression grew concerned. "Aye, they're still here. I doubt they'll find this news particularly welcome, Conall."

"It cannot be helped."

Thea tugged her hand again and unless Conall wanted to hurt her, he had to let her go. He scowled down at her as she refused to meet his gaze. Instead, she stared longingly out at the loch behind them.

"Grace, go inside, please. Ask the Canids to meet me in the dining room. Make sure it's empty. And then send out the call."

"Of course," she muttered before striding back to the house.

Conall turned into Thea and took hold of her hips to hold her against him. She frowned up at him as her hands came to rest tentatively on his chest.

What was going on here?

"Talk to me."

Thea lifted her chin in defiance. "She doesn't like me." She said it without betraying emotion of any kind, even though Conall knew she was trying to withdraw to protect her feelings.

In that moment, he wanted to lay her over the hood of his car and show her how much it didn't fucking matter what anyone thought beyond the two of them. Yet, he realized reluctantly that of course it mattered that his pack accepted Thea.

She may not be a werewolf, but she was an alpha of a sort in her own right.

The pack would have to *want* to follow her for this to work.

"She doesnae know you. And right now all she's thinking about is what she's been told by Ashforth, but mostly she's just thinking about Callie. Grace's husband Angus was my father's cousin. We never knew my mother's parents, and our paternal grandparents died before we were born. Grace and Angus are like our grandparents, and so Grace's first thought will be of Callie. However, once we explain everything, they'll come around. They have to." He bent his head toward her, his own expression hard. "I am the alpha and they will respect my choices."

"But you just said it wasn't a choice." Her eyes narrowed ever so slightly.

"What?"

"When Grace said the Canids wouldn't be happy about this"—she gestured between them—"you said 'It cannot be helped.'" Her smile was bitter and hard and cut Conall to the quick. "That's selling it a little differently to how you've been selling it to me."

Realizing his mistake, Conall cursed himself. "Thea," he said, gentling his tone, "I didnae mean it like that."

"Maybe you did." She attempted to pull away and he wouldn't let her. Her face flushed with exasperation. "It's not as if we both were looking for this and it has totally fucked everything up. Let me go."

His arms banded tight around her as he whispered against her mouth, "Never, lass." He gave her a little shake, his heart pounding at the mere thought of losing her. "I will never, ever let you go, unless you want me to. And I hope that day never comes."

She stopped struggling but was still stiff in his arms. Thea focused on his neck, specifically the scar. "I can't go in there if you're going to make me feel like you were trapped by this."

Guilt suffused him. "It was a poor choice of words, Thea. It willnae happen again. I will make it clear to the Canids and everyone else that I *want* this."

Finally, she met his eyes, and his arms automatically tightened around her when he glimpsed the sadness behind all her ferocious pride. One day, Conall vowed, one day he'd take away that pain in her eyes for good.

"I don't want to be the reason you lose them. I couldn't live with that." She shook her head and her voice dropped to a whisper. "We can put it off, but the inevitable truth is that I'm immortal and you're not. And I'm a danger to this pack."

Anger burned in his gut. "I dinnae care about your immortality. Maybe I should but I dinnae. Life is short anyway, Thea, and we should be grateful that we share something few people ever get to have in this life. And if I must leave the pack to protect them, I will. What I willnae do, ever, is choose them over my mate. End of fucking story. I willnae say it again."

"I don't know if I can live with that."

"Then you must, because I cannae live without you." He cradled her face in his hands. "Right now, we all need each other to get Callie and James back. So I need to know before we walk in there if you're willing to help me share your story about Ashforth. Not everything," he promised, "just enough so they understand the danger Callie is in."

Thea studied him a moment and then nodded. "I'm sorry. I don't mean to make this harder for you."

Love for her ached in his chest. "Thea, you've spent six years burying your feelings. No more. No matter what they are. You tell me. I dinnae want you to hide from me ever."

She relaxed into him and Conall felt much of his own tension drain away. "Okay," she whispered.

THE WAIT IN THE EMPTY DINING HALL FOR THE CANIDS SEEMED TO STRETCH forever but it was probably only a few minutes before Peter, Sienna, and Richard strode into the room.

Conall and Thea stood from the table where they were seated as Peter led his children. Before he even reached them, Peter's stoic expression faltered.

He drew to a halt, his son and daughter following suit with twin expressions of confusion.

Peter sniffed the air and his shoulders slumped ever so slightly. "Well, this is unexpected."

"What?" Richard scowled. "What's going on?"

Conall, realizing Peter knew, stepped forward. "We have much to discuss."

"Not really." Peter gave him a disappointed smile. "When you meet your true mate, you meet your true mate, Conall. Nothing anyone can do about that."

He flicked a look at Sienna, but her expression never wavered.

Richard, however, blew. "What the fuck? What the fuck are you talking about?"

Peter held up a hand to quiet his son. "Conall has found his true mate. Rare," Peter said to Conall, his eyes flickering to Thea, "but ours is a large pack. My beta and his mate are true mates and I recognize the mingle of scents." He took a step forward, his countenance hardening. "I must ask, however, if you knew about this before our agreement."

Conall reached for Thea's hand and she took it, drawing into his side, her eyes on Sienna Canid. He couldn't read his mate's expression. "This is Thea Quinn."

Sienna frowned. "The woman you were hired to find for that businessman?"

"Aye."

"She's not even a werewolf." Richard stared at Thea in disgust and Conall had to tamp down the urge to punch him. "How can she possibly be your mate?"

Ignoring him, Conall spoke to Sienna. "I am sorry to break the betrothal, but I hope you understand."

She shrugged, as if she didn't care. "I think it's better you meet your mate now than it happen after we were married, don't you?"

He felt Thea tense and gave her a reassuring squeeze. Nodding at Sienna, pleased by her pragmatism, Conall turned to her father. "I still think our packs could form a worthy alliance."

Peter nodded slowly. "Let's discuss."

"First, Thea and I have to speak with the pack. My sister and my beta are in trouble. I could come to Colorado, after everything is well here, to meet with you so we can discuss?"

The alpha studied Conall and Thea, then surprised Conall by replying, "If this is to be a worthy alliance, then it should be from the beginning. If your sister is in trouble, Conall, let us offer our services to you."

In that moment Conall knew it would not be a mistake to form an alliance with this wolf. "That's decent of you, Peter. Thank you. I've called my pack. They'll be here in a few hours and then I'll explain all. You're welcome to attend that meeting."

"This is bullshit," Richard snarled. "We've been waiting here for fucking days and now he's throwing my sister over for a fucking non-wolf." He bared his teeth at Thea. "But she's something. I can feel it."

The growl burrowed up from Conall's chest, but it was Thea who stepped forward, energy crackling from every part of her as her eyes bled gold. The air became almost suffocating with the pressure of the power emitting from his mate. "You'll show respect to Alpha MacLennan while you're in his territory or I'll *make* you show respect."

Conall sighed. They really needed to work on her temper when it came to him. She was worse than he was.

Despite the wary fear now scenting from the Canids, Conall couldn't help the smug affection he felt watching Thea's display of power.

Just like that the pressure in the room disappeared and Thea's eyes returned to cognac.

Richard was pale.

Sienna's eyes were wide, the first show of emotion she'd ever displayed.

And Peter was glowering at him.

Fuck.

Conall cleared his throat. "Like I said, we've got a lot to explain."

PACK MACLENNAN GATHERED IN THE DINING ROOM OF THE COACH House, while Conall stood before them with Thea.

Sitting nearest to him on his right was Grace, Angus, and his delta Mhairi Ferguson and her husband Brodie, who had taken over as lead warrior when Callie got sick. At the back of the room stood the Canids.

He'd just finished telling them as much of his and Thea's story as he could without getting too personal. He also didn't mention that Thea was fae. Instead he explained she was different, of unknown origin, and powerful. He loved his pack but the fewer people who knew what Thea was, the better. Conall watched the way his clan studied Thea, wary, almost hostile, despite the true mating bond between her and him.

The way she stared coldly back at them wasn't helping matters.

His mate had defenses a mile high and apparently, he was the only one she was willing to lower them for.

He couldn't blame her.

"So, you know enough now to understand that Callie and James are in the hands of a ruthless bastard. We need to get them back."

"What we dinnae know," Grace spoke up, her voice loud and clear, "is what this lass is. Why he so desperately wants her?"

There were murmurings around the pack.

Conall spoke out to the room. "We dinnae know what Thea is. It doesnae matter. What matters is that Ashforth wants to exploit her particular gifts. He held her captive for years. He hurt her"—the growl burrowed out of his chest—"and he will not do the same to Callie or James."

"Conall."

His eyes flew toward the voice. Hugh MacLennan rose behind a table in the middle of the room. He was an older wolf and first cousin to Grace. "I've seen the mating bond several times now. With your parents it was a wonder. But I've also seen how a true mating can blind a wolf to the faults of his mate." Hugh's gaze flicked to Thea and then back to Conall. "The bond can interfere with your rational thinking. Who is to say that this Mr. Ashforth is the one in the wrong here? Your mate may have lied to you, Conall, and you wouldnae know it for the bond confuses things. If her gifts are as dangerous as they sound, perhaps Ashforth is right. Perhaps you've been manipulated."

Fury flamed in his gut and swelled in his chest. The pack grew still as they felt the mounting energy building from their alpha. How dare they! How dare they question his rational thinking and mistrust his opinion. How dare they look at Thea as others had her whole life.

Bastards.

His own pack.

"Conall." He felt Thea's grip on his arm. "Conall."

Her touch soothed him enough to bring him out of the haze of rage. Discomfort pinched his gums as his canines shortened. His fingertips tingled as his claws slowly retracted.

The room was eerily still.

And then Thea's clear, melodic voice filled the room. "I know you're just trying to protect your alpha and your pack, but I'm not lying about Jasper Ashforth. Caledonia and James are in danger. He …

Ashforth experimented upon me until he finally found a way to hurt me." She turned back to Conall, anxiety in her eyes. "I need to show them."

No.

Shaking his head, Conall refused to let her. "You dinnae owe them that."

"But you do. And we're a team now." Her smile was weak. "They'll never believe us otherwise."

"I dinnae care." He stepped toward her. Conall remembered how she'd run from him when he saw the truth. This was too much to ask of her.

"I care. It's time to stop hiding. They have to know." She gestured to the pack. "They need to know what a monster Ashforth is. They have to understand the magnitude of trouble your sister and beta are in." She faced the waiting pack, whose eyes had never left her. "But first I need a sharp knife."

There were a few murmurings, but it was Hugh who stood up and walked around the tables toward her. He pulled a penknife out of his back pocket and held it out to her.

Thea reached out slowly for it. "Thank you."

The older wolf nodded cautiously and stepped back.

"First, I need to demonstrate my healing abilities. It's the reason Ashforth wants me. And it's the reason Conall came after me for my blood—to give to Callie." Thea flicked the knife and lifted her wrist that wasn't scarred from the iron blade. Conall flinched as she sliced it open, but Thea didn't move a facial muscle.

Gasps, disbelief, and curse words filled the room as Thea's wrist didn't even have time to drip blood before it healed over.

The noise level in the room grew and grew until Conall shouted, "Enough!"

His mate wiped the blood from the knife on her shirt and returned it to Hugh, his own expression slackened with shock.

"There's not much that can hurt me," Thea announced to the quieting room. "But Ashforth found a way."

Conall's stomach knotted as Thea turned her back to the gathering.

She looked at him and he wished like hell she didn't have to do this. Not for him. "Thea," he begged. "This is too much."

"Do you trust them?"

"Even then," he said, his voice gruff, "I dinnae … I dinnae want you to look back and resent me for this moment."

Her smile was sad, weary, far too weary. "Never, Chief MacLennan. Never."

Then she drew her shirt over her head, exposing her bare back.

There was an inhale of breath and then utter silence.

Conall knew what they were seeing.

The crisscross of raised scars that covered the entirety of her back was evidence of not just a lashing, but of a brutality that horrified. It was obvious that the whipping she'd taken had torn her apart.

Conall saw tears in some pack members' eyes, anger in others, horror in the rest.

Finally, Conall could take it no more and he covered Thea with his body and gently helped her pull her shirt back on.

"I'm okay," she whispered as he turned her in his arms and pulled her into his side to face the pack. Still, there was a brittleness to her expression as she looked around the room, and her fingers dug into his waist she was holding on so tight. "I was thirteen years old when Ashforth took me in after my parents died. Not long after he realized I was … different. By the time I was fifteen, he was holding me captive in the basement level of one of his properties, guarded around the clock by armed supernaturals. Every now and then he'd pull me out of that room to be examined by his lab rats, and some days he'd force me to fight supernaturals to see how much of a beating I could take and how much of a beating I could give.

"I tried to escape a few times, unsuccessfully, mostly because the property was on an island. But one night, a few months before I turned nineteen, while I was under the effects of a drug Ashforth used to weaken me, one of his men tried to violate me."

Conall pressed his fingers into Thea's hip. He felt his energy expand outside of himself at the mere idea of any man touching Thea against her will. Thea froze in his arms, bringing him out of himself, and he realized the whole room was crackling with the pack's collective energy.

They were unwittingly affected when their alpha projected.

Pulling himself together, he watched the pack relax marginally.

"I had to kill him." Thea was blunt. "And I knew that I had to escape. Unfortunately, I was caught and to break me, Ashforth had a vampire take a cat-o'-nine-tails to my back."

There were murmurings, gasps, horror as Conall saw the wariness on his pack's faces give way. It was hard not to believe Thea and not just because she was his mate.

No one could look into her eyes and not see the terror she'd experienced. Not one of them could look at her back and say she was lying.

"Ashforth's wife, Amanda, cared about me, but she had her son to protect and she feared her husband. But … the whipping was the last straw for her. She arranged my escape." Conall looked down at Thea's face and saw her eyes were bright with emotion. "One of his men shot her as I was getting away. There was nothing I could do. I didn't kill her. I loved her." Her gaze dropped to the floor and silence filled the room. Conall was about to speak when Thea continued, "I've killed humans and supernaturals he's sent to kill me. It was kill or be killed." She looked back up at them now, defiant. "I won't apologize for that.

"And I never usually explain myself. As Conall will attest to."

He gave her a grim smile.

"But I explained myself to him when I realized"—she looked up at him, the love in her expression making his heart pound—"what he meant to me." Thea reluctantly turned her head toward the room. "Normally I wouldn't care if you believed me. I know the truth. I know what a sick son of a bitch Ashforth is. I've been on the run from him for six years. He stole my life from me." The air thickened a little as her anger filled the room. "But I need you to believe for Callie's and James's sake. You have to understand you're dealing with a man who will do *anything* in his pursuit of power."

When she finished, Conall looked around the room, saw partners exchanging questioning looks, other pack members staring at Thea in concern.

"I'm sorry, lass." Hugh was the first to speak, his expression haggard. "For not believing and for what has been done to you."

"Thank you," Thea answered graciously. "I appreciate that."

The older man turned to Conall. "What do you need, Alpha?"

Conall responded to the entire room. "We need a plan. Ashforth is holding Callie and James in Castle Cara. I was supposed to take Thea there, Ashforth would use her blood to heal Callie, and then we'd leave … and Thea would be left with Ashforth." The thought chilled him to the bone. "Ashforth doesnae know we're in Scotland. As I explained, we had some trouble on the road back and we used it as an excuse to avoid checking in with the bastard. But we must act soon before he gets too suspicious. We must find out what defenses he has in place at Castle Cara. How many guards, their race, and the best strategy to get in. From there we plan our rescue."

"Alpha MacLennan," Peter Canid's voice rang across the room, drawing everyone's gaze, "can I offer my services?"

Conall was grateful but felt he needed to be clear with Canid. "You are under no obligation to do so."

Canid's expression darkened as he looked between Thea and Conall. "I would hope if our situation was reversed, you would offer a helping hand. We may come from different packs, but the world of wolves is one world. *Our* world. A human doesn't come into our world and brutalize our mates and kidnap our pack members."

"I like him," Thea murmured under her breath.

So did Conall. "Then I welcome your help. Thank you."

Peter nodded. "A few warrior wolves accompanied my family on this trip. They're staying in Inverness. I'll call them here."

Conall nodded his thanks.

"Or," Grace said, standing, "we go through with the switch. Give him Thea in exchange for Callie and James." Her eyes moved to Thea, her fear obvious. "The lass is powerful. We can all feel her energy, humming against our skin. And look what she did with that knife. She can handle Ashforth. Callie cannot."

The growl surged out of him before he could stop, long and low, rumbling and dangerous.

Everyone grew tense as the color drained from Grace's face.

He didn't care if she was like a grandmother to him. How fucking dare she. "Did you not see my mate's back?"

Sympathy brightened Grace's eyes. "Aye, I did. And I'm sorrier for it than I can say. But I cannae bear the thought of Callie in the hands of someone who could do that to a young lass."

Mhairi turned on Grace, outraged. "This is Conall's *mate* we're talking about. How can you possibly look at what that bastard did to Thea's back and ask her to return to him? If she was so fucking powerful, do you think she would have allowed that to happen to herself? Those scars …" Mhairi looked at Thea in horror. "That was no ordinary lashing."

Conall tightened his grip on Thea as he felt her grow rigid.

"I'm sorry." Grace had the decency to look ashamed. "I'm just … I'm scared for Callie. I'm sorry."

Thea stepped out of Conall's protective hold. "Maybe we should go through with the switch."

It was his turn to tense. "What?"

"If you hand me over, then Callie and James don't get hurt. Then you can rescue me instead." She gave him a firm nod.

Denial flooded him. "We've already discussed this, and my answer is no. I willnae send you to face that monstrous bastard alone. We'll do it together, once Callie and James are safe."

She lifted her chin, and he knew she was getting ready to dig in her heels. "Maybe we should put it to a vote."

Conall ignored the pack's sniggers.

He took a step toward his mate, towering over her. "This isnae a fucking democracy. I'm alpha here and unless you want to go toe-to-toe with me, my decision is law."

Thea bristled, her own energy building, matching his and then overwhelming it. Her indignation overpowered his, and her feelings now impacted every one of his pack. And that never happened to an alpha and his pack unless someone more powerful came along. But usually it had to be an alpha *wolf*.

Thea didn't even realize her affect. "If your sister weren't in trouble, I would so take up that challenge."

The pack murmured but Conall could feel the excitement humming from them. Thea might not be a werewolf, but they knew they were in the presence of an exceptionally strong being. If she was a wolf, she'd be the alpha of all alphas.

Conall leaned down to whisper in her ear, "You'll just need to take that anger out on me once we're alone, Thea love."

She shivered, and he pulled back to find desire mingled with anger flashing through her eyes. "Oh, I intend to."

26

THE PACK DISPERSED. THEY SENT WARRIOR MEMBERS ON A RECONNAISSANCE to see what they could learn about the defenses Ashforth had set up at Castle Cara.

Everyone else had been sent home to await orders.

Thea waited near the main exit of the Coach House while Conall had a private word with the Canids. She felt off, not herself. For many reasons.

One was the unreasonable jealousy clawing at her insides at the thought of Conall speaking with Sienna Canid. From Thea's impression of the werewolf, she could see Sienna was potentially a good match for Conall.

A little hiss escaped her at the idea, and she turned away to lean against the wall, wishing Conall would hurry. Being left alone to her own thoughts was not a good thing.

But she couldn't help it.

It wasn't the fact that Sienna was a tall, athletic, gorgeous blond. It was her manner. She was cool, calm, and Thea could see the intelligence behind her lovely blue eyes as she listened and observed patiently. She was exactly the kind of woman she imagined Conall would have been happy to end up with.

The thought made Thea want to punch something.

Or jump Conall to remind herself that he wanted no one but her.

The utter vulnerability that settled over her since baring so much of her past to the pack probably heightened her feelings of jealousy. For years Ashforth's torment had been a secret she'd guarded. Now these people knew what had been done to her. She did it for Conall, for his sister and best friend, but it didn't mean it wasn't one of the most difficult things she'd ever had to do.

It was like she'd been walking around with metal armor covering her whole body for years and within the space of fifteen minutes, she'd shed plate after plate, until there was hardly anything shielding her. And her skin felt sensitive.

Raw.

All Thea wanted was to hide somewhere and instead she was stuck waiting in the Coach House while Conall talked with Peter Canid.

Thea liked Peter. He had honor, like Conall. Hopefully, her existence hadn't ruined that alliance. It would be a worthy one. Even if it meant Sienna Canid would still be around. And Richard Canid. Thea didn't get a great feeling from him. He bristled with impulse control issues.

"Conall will be along soon."

Thea started at the voice and turned to watch Grace MacLennan approach. She braced, not comfortable in this woman's presence despite her relationship with Conall. It wasn't just that she'd been willing to throw Thea back to Ashforth in exchange for Callie. There was distrust in Grace's eyes, and the feeling was mutual.

Thea nodded. Wary.

Grace glanced behind her, as if to check she was alone. Then her expression hardened. "What was the cat-o'-nine-tails made of?"

"Excuse me?"

"Dinnae be coy, lass." Grace took a step toward her. "It was iron."

Thea's heart began to pound. Grace had guessed. How had she guessed?

The older wolf nodded slowly. "My mother was a very religious woman. I grew up on her stories of the fae and how they birthed our species. She told me of their remarkable gifts and their one weakness. I never knew if I believed as she did until today ... because there is nothing else in the world that explains your existence."

Thea didn't speak, refusing to answer in the affirmative without first discussing it with Conall. They both needed to agree to tell the pack the truth about her.

Grace cocked her head. "If you're fae, then the danger you ran up against on your journey here ... it's still out there. You need to tell Conall what you are ... and then you must leave for the sake of our pack's safety."

Thea didn't speak. Hurt, stupid hurt, burrowed its way inside her, but that wasn't why she stayed silent. She was silent because she'd felt Conall's almost imperceptible approach as Grace issued her demand. Her eyes moved over Grace's head to where the alpha stood, his pale gray eyes blazing with disbelief as he stared at the back of Grace's head.

The woman tensed and turned slowly to face him. "Conall," she whispered.

Thea sensed Conall was attempting to control his emotions. Finally, when he seemed to have gotten a hold on himself, he bit out, "There is only so much lenience I will give you, Grace."

"You dinnae know what she—"

"I do." The wolf rumbled up from his gut, vibrating in his chest. "I know exactly what she is. It's not your concern. It is mine, and it is Thea's." He took a step toward Grace. "I dinnae care you're hurting for Callie ... I care that a woman who is supposed to be my family would try to send my mate away from me. That she would do that, knowing what it would cost me."

"Conall—"

"When this is over, when we have Callie and James back, you'll have many amends to make to my mate." He moved to stride past her to Thea when Grace reached out to touch him. Conall jerked his arm away and glared down at her. "You have no idea how close my temper is to the surface, so I wouldnae if I were you. And if you breathe a word of this to anyone, there will be consequences. You keep this to yourself, Grace. That's an order from your alpha, and I wouldnae dare defy me. You speak of this and you're as good as banished from the pack."

Hurt suffused Grace's face.

Dread filled Thea's gut as Conall took her hand and led her out of the Coach House. His grip on her was bruising, and she had to hurry to keep up with his angry strides.

She was already infecting his pack, damaging one of his closest relationships.

He led her to a Range Rover Defender, rather than the SUV they'd arrived in, and opened the passenger door for her with a yank. Trembling a little, Thea got in.

The inside of the Defender was utilitarian, a four-by-four built solely for traversing rough terrain. Conall got in and started the engine.

"Seat belt," he grunted.

She pulled it on and waited for him to drive.

Instead, he turned to her, the muscle in his jaw ticking. "Dinnae even think about using this as an excuse to leave me."

Thea was silent a minute, her stomach churning. "You're choosing me over a woman you've known your whole life."

The four-by-four jerked as Conall drove away. The silence was thick and heavy and horrible as they drove along the single-track road toward Inveralligin. There was the Coach House, a grocery store, and a camping site in Torridon, but beyond that nothing much else but little white cottages dotted along the coastline.

When they reached a fork in the road, Conall took the left, the one that spiraled down toward the water, and the trees gave way to reveal a modern-looking home that sat back from the rocky beach of the loch.

It was all gray and clean lines, at complete odds with the traditional white crofters' cottages she'd seen.

Conall parked in the empty driveway.

The entrance to the house was a wide white door set in between gray brick. There were two long shallow windows on either side. It was masculine and a little cold for Thea's liking.

"I cannae keep doing this."

Thea's heart stuttered as she turned to look at Conall.

He glared at her. "I cannae keep reassuring you I need you above all else."

She sighed and shook her head. "It's not that I don't believe that, Conall. I believe it because it's what I feel for you. Do you think I would have bared myself to a room full of strangers for just anyone? No. So I believe you feel what I feel. But I have nothing but you. You have a family and a pack that depend upon you ... and you can tell me until you're blue in the face you'd choose me over them, but you cannot tell me that choice wouldn't chip away at the core of who you are. That abandoning your pack wouldn't fester inside you."

The muscle in his jaw flexed, and he looked away, glowering.

They both knew what she said was true.

"We need to sleep," he bit out. "We have a big day tomorrow."

Weary beyond weary, Thea got out of the car and followed Conall into the house. Surprise rocked her back on her feet when she stepped inside. In front of her was a staircase that led upstairs to a mezzanine. Downstairs was wide-open space, light flowing in from the other side of the house, which was just wall-to-wall glass.

To Thea's left was a small wood-burning stove set between two large bookshelves filled with books. There was a massive leather armchair and stool, big enough for someone of Conall's dimensions, and opposite it a sofa with a chaise longue. In between was a coffee table. It was a snug little area, despite the lack of walls.

Beyond it, Thea could see the modern gray and white kitchen. It seemed to wrap around the entire back of the house, moving into the space to her right. At the top of the long length of the room sat the dining table with a bench fitted into the wall. Directly to Thea's right was a humongous seven-seater corner sofa; opposite that was a huge flat-screen television mounted to the wall.

His place was clutter-free.

Conall gestured for her to follow him.

He led her through the TV room. In the corner where the wall jutted out slightly as a partition between the TV room and the dining room, there was a much larger wood-burning stove with baskets of logs stacked beside it.

However, what really made the house special was the rolling glass doors that took up the entire back wall of the kitchen. They led out onto a deck where Conall had a table and chairs set up for alfresco dining. From there, a small garden led onto the rocky beach and the loch beyond.

Views of tranquil Loch Torridon surrounded them.

Despite the turmoil between them, Thea felt soothed by the sight.

"Conall," she whispered, staring out at the glass-like water and surrounding mountains. She could see little white dots of the houses that sat along the opposite coastline.

"You like it?"

She felt strangely emotional. "How could I not?"

He led her upstairs and pointed to their left. "There's a guest bedroom down there. I use it as my office."

The bedroom he took her into was on the right, and even more awe-inspiring than downstairs. It too had a sliding glass door that led out onto a balcony overlooking the loch.

Thea gazed out, unable to tear her eyes away when the view gave her so much peace. She couldn't explain it. It just ... it felt like they were at the end of the world, a place that had been left untouched, unspoiled. And in living there they too would be safe from harm.

Finally.

"Let's get some sleep, lass," Conall murmured.

She nodded, bemused as he began to undress her. Not wanting to argue with him about anything else, she let him remove her shirt and pants and raised her arms to help him slip his giant T-shirt over her head.

It hung off one shoulder, the hem brushing her mid-thigh. Conall's eyes glinted with pleasure to see her in it, and more than a little desire. She thought for a minute he'd make a move on her, but he pulled back the white duvet on the super king-size bed and nudged her in.

Thea sank into it, smelling Conall on the sheets, and nuzzled into the pillow. The mattress was like a cloud.

Tiredness weighed her to the bed and her eyes fluttered closed. Sleep was good. Sleep would take away all her worries for a little while. Aware of the whisper of Conall's movements, Thea only fully relaxed when the bed dipped as her mate got in beside her.

Then his heat hit the length of her back as he snuggled into her, wrapping his arm around her waist. He nuzzled her neck like she'd nuzzled the pillow, and he breathed in deeply.

Thea melted against him.

Why couldn't it be like this always?

Just him and her, a bed, a view, and no one else to bother them.

Fear filled her, quick and unexpected, as she realized she was going to lose Conall. It wasn't a worry. It was a *knowing*. She knew deep in her soul that her grip on Conall was tenuous. He was slipping through her fingers.

Her mate grew rigid at her back. "Thea?" He pressed down on her shoulder, forcing her to turn and open her eyes.

Concern marred his brow. "I can smell your fear."

Damn him and his wolf senses.

"It's just everything," she whispered, trying to assure. "It's been a long few days."

His expression was determined. "You have nothing to fear from my pack or from Ashforth. You know I willnae let anything happen to you."

Thea reached up to smooth her fingers across his bristly cheek. "And you know I won't let anything happen to you."

He grasped her hand as if he understood more than she was saying. "Thea?"

"Get some sleep." She pressed a soft kiss to his mouth. "Like you said, we have a long day ahead of us tomorrow."

How she'd slept through Conall waking and showering, Thea didn't know, but she had. She'd rolled over in bed to an empty place where her mate should have been and found a note scrawled in his handwriting.

I didn't want to wake you. I'm at the Coach House but I'll be back soon. There's food in the kitchen. Eat. Rest. Then we take this fight to Ashforth.

— CONALL

The thought of facing Jasper Ashforth sort of killed Thea's appetite but she got up and used Conall's impressive shower room with its two rainfall showerheads. She realized that everything in his house was a little oversized to accommodate her mate.

Downstairs she puttered around in the modern kitchen with its matte-gray cupboard doors and glossy white-tiled walls and floor, and ended up forcing herself to eat a banana, yogurt, and some granola. It was raining so she couldn't dine on the deck, but she could sit at the kitchen island gazing out at the water bouncing off the loch. The gray clouds had turned the loch gray and the greenish-brown mountains looked darker, more formidable.

Even then the place was stunning.

An hour passed and Conall still hadn't returned. Thea pored over his book collection, discovering he was a man of varied tastes. There were classics by Charles Dickens and Jonathan Swift, mainstream thrillers, cult classics, and quite a bit of sci-fi.

No surprise there, she'd thought, amused.

Thea flicked through his TV to see his recordings filled mostly with sports, history channel stuff, and comedy.

Good to know.

Realizing it had stopped raining, Thea ducked outside, hoping the fresh air would temper her impatience. If Conall didn't return soon, she would run to the Coach House to see what was happening. He was not leaving her out of the battle plans.

Thea didn't know how long she stood on the rocky beach, staring out at the water, listening to the gentle, relaxing lap of the loch against the shore. She talked herself out of thinking too hard about what awaited her and Conall beyond their fight with Ashforth.

So lost in trying not to think, she took a moment to hear the rocks move behind her. She whirled, alert, and relaxed only marginally when she found herself face-to-face with a familiar wolf.

Thea frowned. Had something happened to Conall?

"What—"

She felt the prickle of warning on her neck.

But it was too late.

The warning came too late.

The wolf had already closed the distance between them and plunged the needle into her neck.

Fire burned through her veins and Thea crumpled, in too much agony to think of anything beyond hoping for the darkness to claim her.

27

CALLIE STARED ACROSS THE DINING TABLE AT JAMES, HER WORRY AND impatience obvious. He felt it too. She could tell.

The great hall of Castle Cara was small, but they were in a medieval castle. Proportions were different back then. This size of room would have been more than adequate. There was a large reconstructed gothic window with wrought iron tracery and stained glass built into its original two-meter recess, highlighting the thickness of the castle walls. It allowed in only marginal light, so the room was lit artificially. Electricity had been installed years ago, and candle bulbs illuminated the great hall perched upon two large wrought iron chandeliers above the table.

Paintings of previous owners and beautifully woven tapestries covered the brick walls. Rugs were placed carefully around the hall to break up the uneven wooden flooring.

At one end of the room the large fireplace had been reinstated, and it crackled to life, the smell of burning logs filling the hall. Callie usually enjoyed the smell and was sure the human guards were grateful for a fire on a dreary spring day such as this.

But everything about Castle Cara chafed.

Although she'd never say so to Conall, she'd felt like a prisoner from the moment she'd entered Jasper Ashforth's domain. Guards, werewolves, and humans during the day, vampires at night, followed her and James everywhere.

It hadn't been so difficult to endure when they were in contact with Conall but they'd heard nothing from her brother, and Ashforth wasn't telling.

He'd stationed guards at each end of the hall, eyes and ears every bloody where. Callie knew from a visit to Eilean Donan that these medieval castles usually had little spy holes in the great hall, so the owner could listen in on his or her guests.

She wouldn't put it past Ashforth to use them.

For the millionth time since her disease had taken root, Callie cursed the uselessness of her body. Once incredibly strong, it was torture to be locked inside her own limbs. To rely on a wheelchair when once she'd been faster than the wind.

To depend on James, a man she'd once hoped would be her husband, to push her around the bloody castle in her bloody wheelchair! There was a scream of frustration trapped inside Callie, one she'd smothered with her easy, breezy attitude to keep her brother and pack happy. She never wanted them to know how much she despaired.

If Conall was in danger, there was nothing she could do, and Callie's bitterness over her powerlessness was growing by the hour. She'd tried so hard to stay positive, to be thankful for the time she'd had on Earth. To be grateful that she'd been born into an extraordinary world and blessed with a comfortable life and a loving family.

Yet as every hour crept by with no word from her brother, Callie finally lost her hold on the last of her optimism.

"He'll be okay," James said. "This is Conall we're talking about."

Callie wasn't so sure. Her brother would find a way to get in contact with her if he could.

She opened her mouth to argue, no longer caring about the guards listening in, when a ruckus from outside stopped her. Both she and James turned to watch the entrance to the hall as the heavy wooden door pushed open.

Two guards led by Ashforth entered and Callie's eyes widened when she saw they were carrying a young woman in their arms.

"Put her down," Ashforth said, staring at Callie.

Callie didn't trust the bastard. There was something oily and creepy about the fucker. She wondered how she and her brother hadn't sensed it from the very first.

Perhaps desperation?

No. There was no perhaps about it.

They'd seen what they wanted to see because they were eager for her cure.

Dragging her eyes from her captor (because she was sure that's what he was), Callie watched as the two guards dropped the woman as if she were of little importance.

Callie winced as the young woman's head hit the hardwood floor, her dark hair falling away to reveal a beautiful face. She remained unconscious. Callie felt the air around the stranger. Her energy was dulled but it seemed to swell against Callie, like a force against her chest. That swelling sensation increased by the second. It almost reminded her of the pull of a full moon.

She wasn't human.

Of that Callie was certain.

But she also wasn't wolf or vampire.

Witch?

"This is Thea," Ashforth announced.

Shock moved through her as she drank in the murderer Conall had been sent to hunt. This … this lovely creature was Thea Quinn?

Her eyes flew to James who was scowling at Ashforth. "Then where's Conall?"

His mere name brought her brother's scent to mind.

Callie's head whipped back to Thea, and she pushed her wheelchair out from the table to roll a little closer. Her brother's scent was on Thea.

No.

Not just on Thea, it was—

Surprise locked Callie in place.

Conall's scent was a part of Thea's scent. A mix of spice, earth, and something heady and sweet.

Thea's scent mingled with her brother's. Just like Callie's mum's and dad's scents had become one.

No. Fucking. Way.

Her eyes flew to James but from his expression, he hadn't picked up what she had.

"Your brother is alive." Ashforth drew her attention and she tried to wipe the shock of the latest revelation off her face. "He attempted to betray me, but he's still alive."

"Betray you?" James asked.

Yes! Callie wanted to shout, her eyes darting to Thea in wonder. Because Ashforth was trying to take her brother's true mate! *Holy bloody Nora on a shit chute.* Obviously, Callie's feelings about Ashforth were true. The fucker had lied to them. And this was Conall's mate.

Her brother had found his true mate.

Happiness and anger overwhelmed her as she realized … they were all now trapped with the enemy.

Bugger.

"He had no intention of handing over the woman who killed my wife. He was going to keep her to himself, use her abilities for his own purposes."

"Bullshit," Callie snapped.

"I echo that sentiment." James pushed back from the table and rounded it to place a protective hand on Callie's shoulder. "What the hell is going on here?"

"None of your concern."

James continued to argue with the businessman, but Callie's attention drew back to Thea. Her energy had stabilized, no longer a suffocating sensation against Callie's chest, but there was a musky, coppery scent drifting toward them from the young woman.

Fear.

And that could only mean one thing.

Thea was awake. She knew Ashforth had her, and it terrified her.

Callie's protective instincts flared. She couldn't leave Conall's mate to this arsehole.

"You're free to leave," Jasper said, stepping aside. "You're no longer required to remain here."

"Not without the cure for Callie," James insisted. "You promised."

"Conall didn't live up to the bargain. Why should I?"

"Because we've sat in this castle like fucking prisoners for days and done everything you've asked. Give Callie the cure or face a war with Pack MacLennan."

"Give her my blood." A whisper from Thea.

Ashforth whipped around to stare at her, a kind of madness glazing his eyes. "Thea, you're awake."

Eyes the color of warm liquor stared at Callie, almost like she was afraid to look at Ashforth. Empathy echoed in Callie's chest.

"Give her my blood," Thea repeated softly as she slowly sat up.

"How—" Jasper nodded at two guards who stood over Thea. "The drug—"

"Doesn't last so long anymore." Thea held up her hands in a surrender gesture as she got to her feet. The guards instantly bound her wrists with metal handcuffs and agony flared across Thea's face, her legs giving way.

She didn't scream but dropped to the floor, teeth gritted as tears streamed down her cheeks.

"What are you doing to her?" Callie demanded, horrified.

"Iron," Ashforth said. "Pure iron."

Callie didn't understand.

He smiled, a wicked, mad smile. "I'd leave if I were you."

"No!" Thea bit out through the pain, her eyes blazing as she finally glared at Ashforth. "Give her my blood and I'll play nice."

Ashforth considered this and then nodded to a guard who disappeared out of the room. He strode slowly over to Thea and reached out to touch her cheek. She strained away from him with a snarl. "It's true, then," he whispered.

"What is going on?" James cut Callie a look.

She didn't want to tell him if Ashforth didn't know, but Thea was obviously determined to hold up to the bargain for Conall's sake.

They couldn't leave her.

Conall would never forgive her if she left his mate to this … brute.

And what was with the iron? Why did it hurt Thea so badly?

"Take the handcuffs off her," Callie demanded. "It's unnecessary."

"Do I have your promise, Thea? I give the wolf your blood and you will submit to me."

Thea jutted her chin out, her defiance in the face of her agony impressive. She was a warrior.

This pleased Callie beyond measure.

"I swear on Amanda's grave I'll play nice."

Ashforth slapped her. Hard.

"Hey!" James shouted.

Callie's nails bit into the arms of her wheelchair.

Thea merely smirked at Ashforth. "You can tell the entire world I killed her but we both know you got her killed. You put the bullet in her head. And you'll never be able to lie to yourself about that."

Another smack.

"Stop it!" Callie cried.

Thea laughed softly and then bared her teeth like a wolf at the billionaire. "You can't hurt me anymore."

Ashforth narrowed his eyes. "We'll see about that, darling girl." He nodded at the guards behind Thea and they bent to remove the handcuffs.

She hissed and slumped, bringing her arms forward. Her wrists were red, raw, and blistered like they'd been burnt.

"New scars to add to the collection," Ashforth mused. "You'll never be free of the marks I've made on your life."

Thea didn't answer this time, just stared at the wounds. Callie scowled. The woman was supposed to heal remarkably fast. That's why her blood was a cure. But iron must be to Thea like silver was to a wolf.

"You bastard," Callie sneered.

Ashforth cut her a dark look. "You have no idea what she's capable of."

"Shut up and give her my blood," Thea ordered wearily.

The words were barely out of her mouth when the guard from earlier returned with a large needle. Thea sat back on her heels and rolled up her sleeve. She held out her hand. "I'll do it."

Ashforth decided not to argue and handed over the needle.

Thea turned her gaze to Callie as she plunged the needle into her arm and pulled on the plunger. The syringe filled quickly with her blood and when she pulled out the needle, there was no mark at all on her skin. The small prick healed over in an instant.

Callie's eyes widened as Thea handed over the syringe to Ashforth. "Playing nice only continues if you give it to her now. I want to see for myself."

With a curt nod, Ashforth turned and moved to the table. He emptied the blood into a glass and handed it to Callie.

Callie felt a little nauseated as the coppery smell filled her nostrils.

"Drink it," James urged.

Ugh, really?

"Callie," Thea spoke.

Her eyes flew to her.

"Drink it."

With a nod, Callie closed her eyes and threw back the blood. It was disgusting, and she felt like retching it back up. Instead, she forced herself to swallow.

"Well?" James asked, his expression bright with hope.

Not feeling anything but the yucky, sludgy blood sitting in her gut, Callie shook her head.

James's face clouded over and he opened his mouth to speak, to rage, probably, when Callie felt the sharp twinge in her spine. She held up a hand to stop James. The twinge turned to a flood of heat, like a course of hot water flowing down her back and settling at the base.

And then everywhere began to tingle. Energy sparked through her being, the fatigue melted from her mind, her limbs, and with a gasp of disbelief, Callie pushed up on the arms of the chair and her body moved.

It moved with ease, with a strength she never thought she'd feel again.

Tears flooded her eyes.

There was no more pain.

No more weakness.

In fact, she felt stronger than ever before.

Her blurry eyes caught on James's.

Her love.

They could be together now.

"James …" She laughed, tears spilling down her cheeks.

He gave a bark of disbelief, his eyes shining, and then she was in his arms as he held her so tight. "You're okay?" he whispered, his voice hoarse with emotion. "Jesus fuck, you're okay."

Callie squeezed him tight and over his shoulder, she met Thea Quinn's gaze.

The woman was staring at her, a sad smile softening her lips.

They couldn't leave her.

She pulled back from James and moved to take a step toward Thea when the guards moved forward in warning. Callie drew to a stop, threw Ashforth a dirty look, and then faced Thea.

"Thank you," she said solemnly. "Those words seem inadequate, but thank you."

Thea nodded.

Callie looked to James, who still seemed confused by the whole situation. "We cannae leave her."

The room went tense.

Callie couldn't give a shit.

She'd take them all on.

"You have to," Thea spoke, surprising her.

Callie looked back at her. "But—"

She shook her head. "He can't lose you too. Please. You have to go."

The thought of leaving Conall's mate, who was willing to sacrifice herself for her brother's family, made Callie want to howl the roof off the fucking castle. Indecision warred inside her.

Thea seemed to sense it. "Callie, you must go. You have to warn Conall. Tell him it was Richard Canid."

"Shut up," Ashforth demanded. "That's not playing nice, Thea."

Conall's mate clamped her lips closed but her fierce eyes pleaded with Callie to go.

James took hold of Callie's hand, his silent support telling her he'd follow her lead. Reluctantly, Callie realized if one of the Canids had betrayed her brother, he needed to know. She gave Thea a nod, but she hoped the woman could read the message in her eyes.

They would come back for her.

After the gift she'd given, there was no way Callie MacLennan would leave Thea here to rot in Jasper Ashforth's hands.

And she understood her brother well enough to realize Conall would burn the world to the ground to get his mate back.

Leaving the building, Callie's mind reeled as she got to grips with moving again. Her strides were easy and long-legged, and she knew if she wanted to, she could run and dive off a parapet of the castle straight into the loch with ease. Her whole life stretched before her again. A future. Options. Love.

She marveled, even as dread followed in her wake.

Taking the speedboat back to shore from its island in the middle of Loch Isla, Callie hated leaving Thea alone; and yet at the same time, she was selfishly glad to be free of the place.

Once she and James were on shore and alone, she turned to him.

"You're walking, Callie," James stared at her in awe. "I cannae believe you're walking. You're saved."

"Aye." She flashed him a quick grin that didn't quite reach her eyes. "And after this is over, you will marry me, James Cairn."

His lips trembled with laughter. "What a romantic proposal, Caledonia MacLennan."

"I'd jump you," she said, taking a step toward him to cup his handsome face in her hand. "But we need to move."

His gaze turned questioning. "What did I miss back there?"

"She's his mate, James. Thea is Conall's true mate. His scent is her scent now. Like Mum and Dad. Why do you think she insisted on saving me before we were released?"

James staggered back a step, his expression slackening. Then understanding quickly slipped into place, hardening his features. "Her scent." He nodded, realizing. "Of course." His eyes flew to the castle in the distance where a large boat waited at the castle dock. A boat probably intended for Thea. Their time was running out.

James bared his teeth. "Well … this definitely means war."

28

WANTING THEA TO GET AS MUCH REST AS POSSIBLE BEFORE THEY RESCUED Callie and James and faced Ashforth, Conall decided to go ahead with strategizing with his pack at the Coach House without her. He would fill Thea in on the way to Castle Cara.

That had been the plan.

More hours had passed than he'd intended, but Conall had assumed if Thea had awoken and was restless, she would find her way easily to Torridon Coach House. Since she hadn't shown up, he believed she was sleeping, and he was glad for it. Neither of them had much rest lately, and she'd need every ounce of energy and strength within her to face Ashforth and all the demons he represented.

However, something knotted in Conall's gut as he approached his house, a feeling of unease he didn't quite understand until he walked inside and felt the emptiness.

That was when he realized he couldn't *feel* Thea. He was unable to track her. Fear slammed through him as he tore through the house looking for her. Then out into the garden, to the rocky loch shore.

She was nowhere.

Absolutely nowhere.

And he couldn't feel her to track her.

It could only mean one thing: someone had drugged her with Ashforth's concoction.

Conall got into the Defender and sped back to the Coach House, kicking up dirt and stones in his wake, the vehicle bouncing over terrain that was meant to be traversed carefully.

It was impossible to be careful.

He had no time for fucking careful.

His heart was thumping so hard, he was nauseated. His legs and hands trembled as he dove out of the car, just stopping himself from howling right there to draw his pack to him. Yet Conall knew he needed to stay focused and clearheaded. He couldn't let himself think about Thea in Ashforth's hands.

He'd lose control entirely.

Instead Conall hurried across the car park where he knew his warrior wolves, along with three of Peter Canid's, were waiting to set their plan in motion.

Before he could reach it, the Coach House door blew open and Sienna Canid ran toward him, yanking a gag from her mouth, stumbling as if she were weak. Her eyes flared when she saw him, and concern had Conall hurrying toward her.

He caught her as she fell against him, panting, her eyes wild. Dried blood marred a cut near her temple. "Sienna?"

"Conall," she gasped, "I'm sorry. I'm so sorry. I tried to stop him, but he knocked me out and when I came to, he'd tied me up. I'm so sorry—"

"Who? What?" Conall cut off her rambling.

But before she could answer, they both spun at the sound of squealing tires as an old Honda blew into the car park and skidded across the concrete to a halt. The doors flew open and Conall's heart lurched at the sight of James and Callie.

Callie!

She ran toward him.

Ran.

Glowing with strength.

"Conall!" She threw herself into his arms, knocking him back on his feet. Disbelief and joy, along with mounting fear, overwhelmed him. If Callie was cured—

"Conall." Callie pulled back to grab his shirt, her gray eyes bright with anxiety. "He has her, Conall. Ashforth has Thea at Castle Cara. We have to save her. I know she's your mate. I recognized the scent. Ashforth was going to throw James and me out but Thea wouldn't let him until she'd cured me. She *cured* me, Conall."

Thea was with Ashforth.

She'd cured Callie ... and she'd done it because ...

Conall stumbled back, remembering her expression as she turned to him in bed last night.

"And you know I won't let anything happen to you."

She was sacrificing herself for him, for the pack.

Well, fuck that!

His claws shot out, his gums aching as his canines slid down. He bared his teeth as Callie gave him a dark grin and released her claws in support. His next words were guttural but clear. "Let's end this bastard."

"As your reinstated lead warrior"—Callie tipped her chin back—"I hope you know I'm coming with you."

He wouldn't dare deny her. His sister was one of the fiercest wolves in his pack. And she was saved—*alive*. Thea had done that. Thea gave him that gift. Emotion threatened to overwhelm him, but he pushed it down.

"Thea told me to tell you who betrayed you." Callie glowered at Sienna.

Conall turned to the American.

Sienna flinched. "It was Richard, Conall. I tried to stop him."

Richard Canid. Fuck.

"Why?"

"Richard gambled away a significant amount of the pack's assets, which is a catastrophe on top of the pharmaceuticals fiasco. He hoped he could play hardball with you for our betrothal. That he could get enough money for my dowry that would cover the debts so that my father would spare him. But with the betrothal broken, Dad told Richard that when we returned home, he was to be demoted to enforced omega status. Early this morning, I awoke and found Richard sneaking back into the Coach House. He had a package with him, and he told me he'd gone to Castle Cara to make a deal with Ashforth. Ashforth would give him the money we needed in exchange for Thea." Her gaze turned pleading. "I tried to stop him. But he attacked me. I just came to … I'm so sorry."

"No."

The word was harsh with grief and torn out of the mouth of another American.

They all whipped around to see Peter Canid at the entrance to the Coach House, his pallor ashen from overhearing his daughter's tale.

"Dad." Sienna's face crumpled. "I'm so sorry."

Peter's expression hardened as he turned to Conall. He seemed lost for words.

"Where is he now?" James demanded.

Sienna shook her head.

Peter said, "I can't find him anywhere."

Conall respected Peter … but his rage was too great. "You find him, you tell him he comes back here. I have his scent so I can find him, but it would be in his best interests *not* to make me hunt him down. Get him back here, Peter. When I have Thea back, when this business with Ashforth is dealt with, your son will meet me in Challenge."

Canid suddenly looked haggard as Sienna whimpered. But he nodded his consent.

"I'll understand if that means you want to withdraw your warriors."

The older alpha shook his head. "The least my pack can do now is offer you aid."

Conall looked to Callie and James. "We had a plan to rescue you— now we use it for Thea. Get familiar with it, and quickly. We leave in ten minutes. Even that is too long."

Ashforth would die today. Conall knew he'd promised Thea she'd be the one to drop the killing blow but Conall was a six-foot-six mountain of wrath, and Jasper Ashforth would never survive the avalanche about to be set loose upon him.

That's what happened when you kidnapped an alpha's mate.

Thea … Conall wished she could hear him through the bond. *Thea, I'm coming for you.*

29

THE DRUG WORE OFF COMPLETELY AND HER WRISTS NO LONGER BURNED from where the iron shackles had been.

She was at full strength.

Thea had thought that very unwise of Ashforth, even if she'd said she'd play nice (a lie), until her captor pushed her into a chair at the dining table and said, "If you try to escape, I'll destroy your mate's pack. Every single one. I'm not bluffing, Thea. And you know I have the means to tear their world apart. There are certain people that would be happy to receive information that the owner of GlenTorr Whisky turns into a *dog* every full moon."

She bared her teeth at him.

"God, he's turning you into one of them." Rage flashed in Ashforth's eyes. "How dare he try to take what belongs to me."

Thea shuddered. "No matter what you do to me, I will never belong to you."

He harrumphed. "I assume you will not cause me trouble?"

If it meant protecting the pack, she'd let him think so. Just long enough to kill him. "No, I won't cause any trouble." She sneered at him. "All this because you want to open a fucking gate."

Ashforth raised an eyebrow. "It appears you've learned some things in the six years we've been apart."

"I know what you think I can do."

He pulled out a chair and sat beside her, casual, as if they were sitting down to dine.

She wanted to rip off his head.

"As a child," Ashforth said, his expression hard, "I was powerless. I had to watch as my father beat my mother daily. When I was ten years old, he accused her of sleeping with our neighbor, and then he raped her for it on the kitchen table, in front of me."

Despite herself, horror filled Thea.

Ashforth studied her carefully. "As I got older, I started to fight him, but he was a big man, my father, and I never won. Not even having youth on my side. So, I decided that I would have to take him down another way. Find a different kind of strength and power. I studied hard, got a scholarship, and from there I used every opportunity put in front of me. None of it went to waste. My plan was to become wealthy and influential, give my mother a house of her own, give her freedom, and do everything I could to squash my father beneath my thousand-dollar shoes.

"But he killed her." Ashforth's eyes filled with tears. "He killed her before I could save her." He blinked rapidly, that granite expression returning. "I made sure he died in prison. Yet I'd lost, hadn't I? I'd never won that battle. I vowed to myself that it would never happen again. If I could become as invincible as any man could hope to be, nothing would ever make me feel weak or helpless like that again."

He glared at her, his eyes filled with hate. "I admire you almost as much as I despise you for being born with gifts you're not even grateful for. You're almost impossible to kill and you'll never die of old age, Thea.

"Immortality. I didn't know it then, but it is everything I have ever wanted. And until I have it, this emptiness inside me will never abate. I don't expect you to forgive me, but I hope that you can understand why I'm doing what I'm doing. Maybe if I'd explained all this years ago, things would have turned out differently."

Thea sighed, her heart pounding at his confession. "It's not going to work," she told him, the words echoing around the great hall. "Instead of a hundred years of emptiness … it'll be a goddamn eternity of it."

"No." He pushed back from the table. "You don't understand. You don't know enough about the world of the fae. They live forever there. They … wouldn't live forever if their lives weren't everything it could never be in this world."

He was crazy.

Thea knew that.

But listening to him … talking about a place he had no concrete evidence even existed, Thea realized the utter depths of his insanity. And she feared that it had started long, long before she even knew him.

"Eirik killed three of the kids, you know that, right? You can't open the gate."

"One is not enough." Ashforth shook his head. "My research is sure on that. But two will suffice. You're not the only one I've been hunting for six years."

Her heart lurched again. "Have you found one of them?"

He smirked. "I'm getting close."

"And how does the gate open?"

"Well, that would be telling, wouldn't it?"

Thea let her hatred for him show. "Is it worth it? Is this worth all the death … Amanda's death?"

"Don't you speak her name," he spat, a rare moment of discomposure.

"She was afraid of you. The only reason she didn't come with me was because of Devon."

Ashforth abruptly nodded to someone behind her and two seconds later, she felt the hands around her neck, a quick burn, followed by the sound of a loud crack before the world went dark.

———◦———

IT COULDN'T HAVE BEEN THAT MUCH LATER WHEN THEA WOKE UP. SHE healed fast, even from someone breaking her goddamn neck.

As she sat up in the unfamiliar bedchamber, she rubbed at her nape even though it didn't hurt. Still, she winced. A neck break was unpleasant. She'd forgotten just *how* unpleasant.

Suddenly she had the urge to apologize to Conall for that time she'd broken his.

Conall.

Thea moved her hand from her throat to rub at the ache in her chest. Her eyes caught on the new scars around her wrists.

"You'll never be free of the marks I've made on your life."

Until the moment Ashforth said that, Thea had begun to bear her scars like a warrior would. Because of Conall. He made her feel proud of them. They were evidence of everything she'd endured. She'd especially been proud of the scar across her wrist where she'd cut it with the iron blade to save Conall's life.

Now it was concealed by the much wider scar caused by Ashforth's shackles.

Marks from Ashforth to match those on her back and the one on her lower gut.

He'd stolen their meaning from Thea as soon as he'd turned them into brands. And now, if she lived, she was stuck with the fucking things, always remembering it was him who had done this to her.

"You're awake."

She startled, whipping around to look behind her.

The bedchamber was small, the exposed brick covered with paintings and tapestries, much like it was in the great hall.

Standing in the gothic doorway was Devon Ashforth.

Thea drank him in, nostalgia hitting her in wave after wave.

She could see them running around the Ashforths' Hampton estate, playing in the ocean, laughing together at school.

Devon was older now, of course. His jawline no longer soft with boyishness but angular and covered with a little designer stubble. There was an unkemptness to his blond hair that matched his style, which wasn't preppy like it had been six years ago. He wore faded blue jeans and a fitted sweater that showed enough of his physique to tell Thea he worked out. The hardness of his body matched the pitiless expression in his eyes.

This was not the Devon she'd left behind.

Thea slowly stood to face him. "I didn't kill her."

The muscle in his jaw flexed but to her relief, he nodded. "I know. My father thinks I'm an idiot. But I bribed the guards who were there … I know she died helping you escape, and that it was one of *his* men who put the bullet in her head."

Despite her gratitude that Devon knew the truth, Thea couldn't understand why he was here. And why he was looking at her as if she meant nothing to him when once upon a time, he'd loved her like a sister. "Then why are you here?"

"I told him I wanted to be here to watch him make you suffer for her death."

Thea took a wary step back.

Devon shook his head and pushed the door open wider. "I just wanted to be here to finish what she started."

"Devon," Thea whispered.

"End this, Thea, or he'll never stop." He lifted his hand and in it was a gun. It had a silencer on it. "I've taken care of the guards in this part of the castle. They're gearing up to get out of here before your pack arrives to attempt rescue, so they're distracted. I said I'd watch over you while they organize our departure. Instead, I'll lead you to the great hall and then I'll trick my father into coming to you. Alone."

Sickness roiled in Thea's gut.

This was it.

This was the moment.

"Are you sure you want to be a part of this, Devon? You don't know how this will affect you."

Rage flashed across his face. "My mother was murdered, and it's his fault. His obsession led to this. Let's go."

There were two dead guards outside her room, bullet holes in their heads. Devon must have been quick with the gun. Thea glanced away, despair washing over her. What had Ashforth done to his family?

Tortured his adoptive daughter, inadvertently murdered his wife, and turned his son into a cold-blooded killer. It was horrifyingly tragic.

They hurried down the narrow, dark, windowless hallway and when they reached a tight, turreted staircase at the end of the hall, Devon raised a finger to his lips. Thea sent out her shadow energy that cloaked them both in silence. Being human, Devon didn't feel it, but neither of them could be heard as they slowly took the uneven spiral stairway down to the first floor.

To their left was an archway that led to what looked like the kitchens. Thankfully, they were empty. To the right they crept past two small rooms that served as pantries, stocked to the brim with food. The dark hall was empty as they moved silently along it, coming to a small set of stairs that went up, leveled out, and then went downstairs.

Devon stopped her where a light shone on their left from a doorway. A chill wind swept over her and he turned to mouth "Exit" as he pointed to the opening. Then he gestured ahead and mouthed, "Hall."

Thea nodded, and they made to move off when voices from outside caused them to halt. It sounded like the two voices were getting nearer.

"I'll be glad to be out of this place," a deep male, American voice said.

"Yeah, me too. I'm sick of being this close to vamps."

A snort. "Yeah, lucky bastards, get to sleep in the fucking wine cellar while we do all the grunt work."

"Let's just get Rick and Drew and get this bitch on the boat."

Their footsteps came closer.

Thea gently pulled Devon toward her and then urged him behind her. He scowled but acquiesced as she pressed her back to the entrance wall and waited. Twin earthy scents hit her nostrils. They were werewolves.

As soon as the first booted foot appeared, Thea attacked. She grabbed the large wolves by the scruff of the neck and yanked them deeper into the castle hallway so no one outside would see. Before they could get their heads around what was happening, Thea smacked them together. They snarled, staggering apart, and she threw a punch at the bigger out of the two, hard enough to knock him on his ass.

Once he was down and dazed, Thea spun as the other swiped out, claws protracted. She ducked, narrowly missing a hit, balanced her hands on the cold castle floor and swung a leg out, catching his with enough force to put him on his ass too.

Thea whirled to her feet as the big guy recovered, fists guarding his face, ready to fight.

So she opted to hit him in the place he wasn't protecting. His balls.

He dropped with a muffled yell; Thea cut him off with a quick twist of his neck and the sickening crack echoed around the entrance hall. She hoped he was the one who'd broken her neck earlier.

Tit for tat and all that.

A popping sound startled her, and Thea jerked around to find Devon pointing a gun at her.

The color drained from her face.

But then a loud thump behind her drew her attention.

The second wolf was laid out on the floor with a bullet hole in his head.

Thea swallowed the bile in her throat. She'd been determined not to kill anyone. Glancing warily back at Devon, she saw nothing.

There was nothing in his eyes as he lowered the gun.

"You were taking too long," he whispered. "Help me hide them."

Thea brushed Devon's assistance aside. It was quicker for her to move the bodies. She hid them in the pantries they'd passed, closed the doors, and tried not to worry about the emptiness in her adoptive brother's eyes.

Hurrying down the hallway, she followed Devon past the entrance and up another small flight of stairs. They turned left at an open landing and up two more steps where he shoved open a large, gothic wooden door.

They were back in the great hall.

He led her across the room to another door near the fireplace. Beyond it was a small drawing room with no windows. It was lit by wrought iron sconces on three walls. "Stay here. Hide. I'll be back with my father and then you can come out and do what needs to be done."

Distrust niggled at Thea as Devon disappeared. She stared up at the massive tapestry covering most of the wall opposite the door. It depicted a battle scene. Probably a famous Scottish battle but Thea didn't know enough about Scottish history to figure out which one. Conall would know.

She immediately threw her mate out of her head.

She needed to focus, and she couldn't do that if she worried about how Conall was dealing with her disappearance.

Thea focused on Devon and why he'd brought her to this room. She had to consider if this was a trap to hurt her further, why kill the guards and bring her here? He could have easily tried to dispatch her in that bedchamber.

The thought made her stomach turn.

The last person Thea wanted to hurt was Devon, but if he betrayed her, she would.

It felt like an age as she waited with her ear to the drawing-room door. Despite her vow not to think about him, Thea wondered if Conall was already on his way to the castle with the pack. She knew he would come for her, there was no question of that. But Thea feared how many of the pack would lose their lives trying to rescue her.

Gut churning, sweat gathering under her arms, Thea waited impatiently.

Then finally she heard the murmur of voices.

Ashforth's and Devon's voices became clear as they entered the hall.

A door slammed.

That was Thea's cue.

"What is going on that is so urgent?" Ashforth snapped.

Thea stepped out of the drawing room, the creak of the door announcing her presence.

Ashforth whirled from glaring at his son to wiping his expression off his face when Thea stepped into the room. Ever the master bluffer. "What is she doing here?"

"She's here to make you pay for what you did to my mother," Devon said, the words robotic.

His father turned to him, incredulous as he gestured to Thea. "You believe her lies?"

"I believe the guards who witnessed the escape. I've known for years what you did to Mom."

Shaking his head, Ashforth took a step back. "It was an accident."

A *BOOM* buffeted against Castle Cara, followed milliseconds later by the shattering of the stained glass window. Shards sliced through the air and Thea ducked, covering her face, feeling tiny little stings all over her arms that healed as quickly as they'd opened. Her shirt sleeves were covered in tiny little tears.

Heart pounding and disoriented, she stood, hearing a roar of sound through the hole in the wall where the window had been. There was popping and crackling amongst the roar ... like a blaze.

There had been an explosion, Thea realized.

Ashforth staggered to his feet as Devon pushed out of the doorway of the great hall, a satisfied smile on his face.

"What did you do?"

Devon shrugged. "I blew up the boat. All the guards in the castle are dead; everyone on the boat and dock are most likely dead. And your vamps are locked in the wine cellar. You're on your own, old man."

"Why?" Ashforth looked grief stricken.

"You made me stand by while you tortured Thea. You hit me when I disobeyed you. You intimidated Mom, and all the time with this sob story about how your father was such an abusive bastard," Devon spat this time, no longer calm, no longer in control. "You're so far fucking gone, you don't even realize you became the monster you were trying to fight."

"I love you," Ashforth whispered. "That is the difference between me and my father. I love you. I'm doing this for both of us."

"You're doing this for yourself." Devon looked to Thea, defeated. "Whoever this is, it's not the man I remember as my dad." He stepped back, giving her space. "End it now."

She was a blur of speed and light across the room toward Ashforth, channeling the little girl terrified of this man, so she could give *her* the closure she needed. Thea was so focused, so sure it would be an easy battle, she never saw it coming.

One minute she was on Ashforth, her hands on his neck, about to snap it—make it clean, make it quick, more than he deserved—when the fire blazed through her ribs just below her heart.

The breath left her, and she felt the energy around her flicker as her legs gave way with the agony. Glancing down, she saw the iron dagger stuck between her ribs.

Even as the pain made her want to die, Thea felt relief. He'd missed her heart. She glared up at him from her knees as he shrugged his suit jacket back into place like she hadn't just tried to kill him.

"Well, this is unfortunate." Ashforth shook his head.

Thea yanked out the blade, gasping. "You missed. You fucking maniac."

"Yes, but you'll be weak enough for now until I can deal with you."

"Wrong." Devon stepped up behind his dad, the muzzle of the silencer against his temple. "That's not how this ends."

No! Thea shook her head. No, she couldn't let Devon do this. And not because it would deny her right for revenge. She didn't need revenge. She just needed this to be over and Ashforth would never let her go. There was no other way. He had to die.

But Devon would not live with his father's blood on his hands.

Pushing through the weakness caused by the iron blade, Thea shot up, pushed Devon out of the way, her super strength sending him flying across the room, and she turned on Ashforth.

Wary, obviously out of weapons, he took a step back, hands in the air. "You can't do it. You won't let Devon do it, so how do you expect to?"

"I won't let him live with your death on his conscience." Thea shook her head. "He will be better than you, and he can't do that with that kind of legacy."

Melancholy filled Ashforth's eyes. "Thea—"

Three moves.

That's all it took.

A step toward him. A punch through flesh, muscle, and bone. And he gaped in shock, like he hadn't expected it. Thea fisted his heart, not surprised to find it small. "You never had any use for it anyway," she whispered.

Then the third and final move.

She tore Ashforth's useless heart from his body.

The light dimmed from his eyes and he dropped with a juddering thud. Thea let go of the warm, bloody muscle and wiped her hand against her jeans a little desperately. She shuddered, feeling cold.

"You did it."

Turning, Thea watched as Devon limped toward her.

"I'm sorry." She gestured to his leg. She hadn't meant to push him so hard.

He waved off her apology, his eyes on his father. "I heard what you said." His voice was soft, his eyes glazed over with shock. "Thank you."

"Devon, we need to get out of here. If we're found—"

"Don't worry." He shook his head. "I set this place to blow in ten minutes."

Thea's eyes rounded. "What?"

He didn't look at her but fell to the ground beside his father's body. His shoulders shook. "I wanted it all gone. All evidence of what he's done. The vamps who helped him … they'll die too."

"But the castle …" Thea gestured to the hall. Maybe it shouldn't be her first thought, but this was a medieval castle. It seemed like sacrilege to destroy hundreds of years of history because some asshole took up residence in it.

"Fuck the castle. Fuck Scotland." Devon sniffled. "I'll meet you outside. Just give me a minute to say goodbye."

Thea wasn't particularly happy about leaving bombs to detonate, killing vampires and destroying a piece of important Scottish heritage. But she also didn't know how to defuse a bomb and she only had ten minutes to get whoever was left in the castle out.

Thea looked down at Ashforth's body. There was no time to process his death. It would have to wait. Hurrying from the hall, she searched the castle. The vamps couldn't leave but any werewolves could.

Sadly, the ones she found, Devon had already killed. Including the guard whose neck she'd broken. Devon had returned to the pantry to put a bullet in him before he searched out his father.

Rushing out of the entrance, down the uneven concrete steps, Thea felt the heat from the large boat ablaze down at the dock. She dashed across the courtyard and took the steps down onto the dock, wary of how close the flames were getting to the wooden structure. She found a man and a woman, but they were already gone. Bodies floated in the loch beyond the boat. Thea damned Devon to hell. Why did he have to kill everyone? Wasn't Ashforth enough?

A shout carried across the water and Thea turned from the blazing boat to shore.

"Thea!"

"Conall," she breathed, hurrying toward the opposite end of the dock. People gathered on the shore.

The Pack.

And Conall was getting into a speedboat with James and Callie.

Relief flooded her. She waved and Callie waved back. She could feel Conall's intensity from here.

Footsteps from behind drew her around. Devon limped down the planks toward her, his expression grim, his cheeks tearstained.

"Help is coming. Unless you want to tell me how to defuse those bombs, we need to get everyone as far away from here as possible."

Devon stared out at the approaching speedboat and then turned back to Thea. He stumbled and Thea reached out to steady him.

He grabbed onto her, and she pulled him upright. "Devon, are you okay?"

He shook his head, his eyes meeting hers. "I needed you to do it. I couldn't do it."

"I know," she reassured him. "I know."

More tears slipped down his cheeks. "But that doesn't mean I don't blame you. You saved me ... but you also ruined me, Thea. Just existing ... you ruin lives."

Hurt shattered through her. "Devon ..."

His expression hardened. "It has to end."

Pain exploded through her heart seconds before Devon stumbled back, sobbing.

Agony ripped through her chest, taking her to her knees again.

Thea glanced down, her hands wavering uselessly over the iron dagger Ashforth had slammed into her ribs, missing her heart.

Devon hadn't missed.

"THEA!" she heard Conall's roar in the distance.

Tears spilled down her cheeks.

It really was the end.

30

"THAT'S DEVON!" CALLIE SHOUTED OVER THE SPEEDBOAT'S ENGINE. "Ashforth's son. Creepy as fuck too, just so you know!"

Conall narrowed his eyes on the man as they approached Thea. "Thea spoke affectionately of him. He's like a brother!"

His sister grunted at his side.

When they'd arrived at Loch Isla, they heard the explosion before they saw it. Upon skidding to a halt at the dock across the loch from Castle Cara, they'd all jumped out of their vehicles to see the boat on fire.

Confused as to the goings-on, his wolves advised they hold back but Conall got into the speedboat James was happy to commandeer. He hot-wired the boat just as Conall saw Thea appear on the castle's dock.

Alive.

She was alive.

He couldn't wait to get to her, and Conall hoped for Ashforth's sake, he was already dead.

"Conall, Devon's hand." Callie gripped her brother's arm, fingers biting into his skin. His gaze narrowed on Devon.

Even from this distance, he could make out the silver-gray blade.

Pure iron.

Panic slammed into him with the force of a cannonball. "THEA!" he roared in warning.

She couldn't hear him.

She couldn't fucking hear him.

He lunged forward, rocking the boat. "THEA!"

Devon plunged the blade right into her heart.

"THEA!" His bellow echoed around Loch Isla, his rage almost like a sentient being, echoing and swelling over Castle Cara.

Vik's voice came to him like a fist through his chest. *"If you stab a fae in the heart with a knife of pure iron, they cannot recover. It is a slow, painful death for the fae."*

Thea's legs gave out on the dock, her body slumping forward as she stared at the knife in her heart.

Thea.

No.

"No," he exhaled, trying to catch a breath beneath the crushing pressure in his chest. "No."

Conall's eyes flew to Devon, who staggered back from his mate.

He was going to kill him.

His claws protracted, his muzzle lengthened, his jaw cracked with the partial change, and his wolf teeth grew, filling his mouth with razor-sharp weapons.

James turned the boat as it neared the dock, kicking up water, and Conall leapt across the distance between the boat and dock. It was a jump no human could have made. His feet hit the wood with such force, a plank cracked. But Conall didn't care. He couldn't see anything but Thea dying and Devon ...

The man, Ashforth's son, stared at him wide-eyed.

That's the only movement he had the chance to make.

Conall was on him before he could speak. A slice of his claws up Devon's belly to disable him and then he clamped his teeth down on his neck and tore his throat out with animalistic satisfaction. Dead instantly, the traitor fell off the dock and into the water below.

"Conall!"

He whirled, muzzle covered in blood and gore, and saw Callie bent over Thea as James docked the speedboat.

Conall could feel the fire from the boat behind him, hear its crackling blaze, still going, ready to light up the dock at any moment.

What he couldn't bear to feel was the grief desperate to take hold.

Because that was admitting there was nothing he could do.

That meant admitting Thea would really die.

He staggered toward her, changing back from half-man, half-wolf, and wiped the blood from his face as he fell over his mate.

"Thea …" He reached for her, caressing her cheek.

She was so pale.

Too pale.

Looking down at the dagger in her heart, he didn't know if it was best to keep it in there or take it out.

"Thea."

Her lashes fluttered and with a groan of what sounded like deep-seated agony, she forced her eyes open.

"Thea." He braced over her, pressing his lips to hers, gently, so gently. "What do I do? I dinnae know what to do." Conall was not a man who cried. The only time he'd shed a tear had been when his parents died, and even then, it had been in private. Yet he could not stop the wet that blurred his vision. "You cannae leave me, lass, so tell me what to do," he choked out.

She parted her lips, straining to speak. "C-Conall," she began to choke, and he raised her head up gently, despair filling him as she spat out a thick glob of blood. "G-Get off. Bomb. Castle. G-Go."

What?

His eyes flew to Callie's.

"Conall." Callie reached under Thea. "I think that means bomb in castle. We need to go. Now!"

Together they lifted Thea onto the boat, his heart wrenching at every moan of pain she emitted.

"Should we not take the dagger out?" Callie shouted over the noise of the speedboat as they sped across the water. "She cannae heal while it's in."

If he took it out … if he took it out, that meant …

Callie seemed to understand. "I'll do it."

Conall nodded, grabbing Thea's hand. He bent to whisper in his mate's ear as Callie wrapped her hand around the blade's hilt. "My love for you is infinite, Thea Quinn."

Thea jerked with a guttural groan as Callie wrenched out the dagger, her eyes flickering open again. She gazed up at him, her love visible through her pain. "B-Bite," she gasped. "C-Conall … b-bite …" Her eyes closed, and she went so still, Conall's heart dropped. He reached for her, his fingers at the pulse in her neck. It was faint but still there.

"James, warn everyone to get back!" Callie called to him.

His beta yelled "bomb" to those on shore but Conall was too focused on Thea to see if his pack heeded the warning. "Bite?" he muttered to himself.

"A fae of Samhradh House fell in love with her werewolf consort. The tale goes she couldn't bear the thought of immortality without him and asked him to bite her."

"You mean … change her into a werewolf?"

"Yes. Exactly. And it worked. She was no longer a true immortal."

Conall ran a shaking hand through his hair as he stared down at his mate.

He wouldn't do it before because …

"When a very weary prince of Earrach House discovered this, he asked to be bitten too. He didn't want to be immortal anymore, and the cauldron couldn't truly end his suffering. So the wolf did it but the fae died."

Thea was dying anyway.

"Conall, let's move!" Callie shouted.

With hope flaring, he slid his arms under Thea's limp, cooling body and cradled her as they leapt off the boat onto the dock. The car park at the dock was clear, his pack at least three hundred yards away on the other side of the road that ran along the base of the hills.

He ran, cradling Thea, using his full speed as he, Callie, and James tore across the car park to safety. They'd almost made it when the sound of the world ending filled his ears.

At least that's what it felt like as he stumbled to the ground, turning at the last second to protect Thea as he landed on his back.

The sky filled with black clouds and flickers of fire and debris. Conall sat up, checking Thea for injury. She was so still, he frantically searched for a pulse.

It was fading.

There was no time.

People called his name, cried out, shocked by the explosion, but Conall only had eyes for his mate. He laid her gently on the ground and forced his jaw to lengthen, for his muzzle to grow again, his wolf teeth to fill his mouth.

"Conall, what are you doing?" he heard Callie ask.

He didn't answer. Instead, he pulled down the neckline of Thea's torn sweater to bare her collarbone. He then gently settled his mouth over the arc between her neck and shoulder and bit down into her sweet flesh. She shuddered underneath him as he made sure his teeth sank deep into her.

Pulling back, he forced the shift again, wiping Thea's blood from his mouth.

He stared at the brutal, bleeding, swelling puncture wounds he'd made.

His bite wasn't healing.

Was it too late?

"Conall?"

He looked up at his sister, who was eyeing him like he might have lost his mind.

"She's fae, Callie. Thea is fae. And an iron blade through the heart kills a fae slowly. There is no coming back from it."

Her eyes darkened in sorrow.

"But there's a story that a werewolf once bit his fae mate and she turned. She was no longer fae. She was …" He looked down at Thea. "She became a werewolf. No longer immortal."

"Conall, we need to go." James kneeled beside him. "We have to get the pack out of here. We cannae be implicated in this."

Nodding, Conall lifted Thea into his arms. "Get everyone back to Torridon. Call Brianna, see how fast she can get there."

Brianna MacRae was their pack doctor; she lived and worked in Inverness.

Most of their cars were undamaged by exploding debris; those that weren't, they tore the license plates from and left them. Conall carefully laid Thea across the back seats of his Defender. Her body bowed slightly between the seat gap but there was nothing for it, much to his distress.

"She's fine," Callie assured him. "I'll drive."

He shook his head. "I need something to focus on or I'll go mad."

His sister nodded and got into the passenger seat instead.

The desire to keep glancing back at Thea was great, but he forced his eyes on the road and followed the conspicuous cavalcade of cars leaving Loch Isla. Thankfully, Castle Cara had been built on a low-level loch, far from towns and amenities. There wasn't anything but tight, single-track roads leading downward to Loch Isla until your ears popped from the drop in altitude. No witnesses.

"James will anonymously call the emergency services once we're clear," Callie told him.

He nodded.

"Fae, Conall?" she asked tentatively.

"I know it sounds insane ... but there's no other explanation for what she can do." He refused to say *could*. Thea was still alive.

There was a chance.

But if not ...

His hands clenched around the steering wheel.

Silence fell over them.

The bite would work.

It had to.

He did not want to prepare himself for a lifetime of fucking emptiness without Thea Quinn.

The drive northward was just over an hour but he and the others who were heading back to Torridon sped where they could, as long as it didn't endanger any humans. Still, Conall was grateful to see the turnoff at Kinlochewe, signaling they were near home.

Callie glanced into the back seat, something Conall hadn't dared to do during the awful silent drive.

He felt his sister go rigid and fear swamped his lungs. He looked at Callie.

Her eyes had widened.

She's gone, he prepared himself. *She's going to tell you Thea's gone.*

Callie slowly turned to him, shock glittering in her pale gray gaze. "Conall," she breathed.

"What?" he bit out.

"Her … her cheeks are flushed."

He blinked. "What?" He pulled the rearview mirror down, angling it to take in Thea across the back seats.

Sure enough, every inch of her skin on display was flushed, feverish and dewy with sweat.

Conall felt that buried hope take hold again as he looked at his sister.

Slowly, a smile kicked up the corners of Callie's mouth. "Fever: the first sign of the change."

31

S o   i t   h a d   c o m e   t o   t h i s .

There *was* an afterlife for Thea, and it was hell. Or some kind of hell dimension where her skin was constantly on fire, slick with sweat, her mouth dry, burning, desperate for relief. In the darkness of the fever world, a black figure, a demon, waited. It was mammoth, long, crooked limbs, massive claws, and every inch black as tar. Yellow eyes blinked from its face to match the sharp yellow teeth.

Thea kept running, tangled in walls of arms that reached out to her, every touch burning as they tore at her scalding flesh. Every step seemed to take centuries, and the demon was always there, following, taking its sadistic time to catch her.

The worst part of the hell wasn't the sweltering heat or the demon or the walls of arms, but the soft murmur she could hear out somewhere beyond the fiery darkness. A beloved voice, deep and soothing, whispered words of love and reassurance. Memories. They couldn't be anything more because he couldn't be here with her. He was too good. Too decent.

She'd tear the roasting pits of hell to shreds if they dared to keep him here.

The wall of arms pulled on Thea's wrist so hard it broke. A scream wrenched out of her as the arms tore at every inch of her being.

Still she heard the murmurings of reassurance beyond the torrid hell.

It didn't stop her from screaming bloody murder as she felt every bone in her body break.

32

Conall's heart thudded hard and fast, every beat for Thea.

He stared, not quite believing what he was seeing.

Lying panting amongst his sweat-soaked and torn bedsheets was a werewolf, smaller than him, only somewhat larger than your average wolf. Her fur was dark brown with flecks of caramel, to match the unusual gold of her eyes.

She pulled her muzzle back and growled at the people standing around the edge of the bed.

Conall, Callie, and Brianna.

"Thea," he said her name softly, taking a tentative step toward her.

Her ears twitched as she cocked her head, watching his approach.

Her muzzle wrinkled again with another little growl.

"Thea, it's me. It's Conall."

The last seventy-two hours had been the worst of Conall's life as he'd watched over Thea through the feverish and painful transformation. Until Brianna arrived, he'd been afraid to even hope that his bite was taking effect, but the doctor had assured him that every sign Thea showed was that of the change.

Conall had never witnessed someone transform from a wolf bite. Almost every hour, he thought his mate was fucking dying from it. He'd never imagined anyone's body could reach the temperatures Thea's had without expiring. Instead, she'd writhed, coated in sweat, her face scrunched in pain and fear—Jesus fuck, the room had reeked from the stench of her terror, tearing Conall's gut.

"It's one of the most prolonged changes I've witnessed," Brianna had said the previous night, concern marring her brow. "I can only assume it's because she wasn't human ... and because she was dying."

"But she will make it?" Conall demanded.

His doctor had placed her hand on his arm. "I hope so."

Conall had almost fallen into despair until the early hours of the morning when Thea woke him from his bedside vigil with her moaning. There were tears on her cheeks as she writhed on the bed, and then he heard the ugly noise as her shoulder visibly popped.

From there ... fuck, from there Callie and Brianna had come flying into the room and Brianna held Conall back as Thea's body began to break before his very eyes.

"It's normal," the doc assured him. "It's the first change."

Thea's screams tore through his heart, powerlessness crushing his ribs as she went through three hours of agony. Just when he thought he couldn't take it anymore, a bright golden sunlight flared from her body, blinding them all.

When the light finally diminished, Thea was a wolf, lying on his bed, panting.

Alive.

But did she recognize him?

She growled, low and deep from her belly, and he faltered. "Thea," he whispered. "Thea love, it's me. Conall."

Her ears twitched again and her snout lifted into the air, her nostrils flaring as she sniffed.

Her intelligent gold eyes lit with recognition and she whined, shuffling along the bed toward him.

Emotion overwhelmed Conall as he crossed the distance between them and held out his hand to her. Wolf Thea sniffed and then licked it ... and then nuzzled into him. Conall laughed, blinking back the sting of wet in his eyes, as he slid his hands into her velvet fur and kissed the top of her head. She made a little chuffing sound and buried deeper into his hold.

33

At first all Thea could feel was terror and discombobulation. She recognized the room she was in and the people were familiar, but she didn't recognize herself.

Her vision was sharper, her peripheral vision wider, and there was a film of color over it. Not to mention she could see a snout where her nose should be, see fur-covered forelegs where arms should be.

When the tall man with the scar said her name, a wash of familiarity flooded over her and she wanted to go to him, but a much bigger part of her was scared out of her fucking mind.

He kept saying her name over and over.

And she kept growling at him in warning like a beast.

But then … something started to niggle at her as she looked up at him. Memories. A castle. A fire. A man stabbing her in the heart. Then this man's face. Tears in his eyes.

The words "bite" falling from her lips.

"Thea."

Conall!

His name came to her in a burst of realization.

Conall was a werewolf, and he'd bitten her to save her.

She moved toward him and he reached out a hand. His scent was the final piece of the puzzle. It wasn't just his scent. It was hers.

Her mate.

It was like rushing through a tunnel of memories and Thea was herself again. But she was something else too. After Devon had stabbed her in the heart, all she could think about through the pain was the story Vik had told her of the fae who was bitten by her werewolf consort. She'd conveyed enough to Conall that he'd understood. Thea remembered thinking she was in hell, but it had obviously been the change.

Fuck, it had been awful.

But now … she laughed inside her head as Conall hugged her in her wolf form. Burying into him, she smiled to herself. She was alive. And she was a wolf! How weird! How wonderful.

Conall pulled away and turned to his sister Callie. She stood with a woman Thea didn't recognize. "I'm going to shift. Take her for a run. Is that all right?"

The stranger nodded. "She needs to get used to her new body, so take your time with her."

The two women left and Conall grinned down at Thea as he began to strip naked. She made a moaning sound, which came out like a throaty growl. Her mate laughed. "There's enough time for that later. In fact, we have a perfectly extraordinary but mortal life ahead of us."

Understanding what he meant, Thea would have wept if she'd been in her human form. She no longer had to worry about an eternity of loneliness. Nor about running from Ashforth, who was finally dead and gone.

But mostly she didn't have to concern herself with the heartbreaking reality of staying forever young while Conall aged and died. They would age together. They would have a family. Hopefully.

She laughed to herself. She was perhaps the only person on the planet who wanted to grow old.

Thea watched with fascination as Conall's body morphed into his wolf. He didn't seem to feel the pain she remembered feeling, and a little uneasiness shifted in her gut. Would it always be painful for her because she wasn't born to it?

And then she became aware of a new feeling, one that emanated from Conall. His energy, one that tasted of his spice, earthiness, and her mingled scent, one that felt like a solid wall of power moving toward her, made contact. It surrounded Thea, pressing in around her. It was his alpha energy, much more magnified now that she was wolf.

It eased a little as Wolf Conall padded across the room toward her and licked at her face. Thea laughed and it came out as a hoarse bark. Conall gestured with a jerk of his head for her to come off the bed.

Shakily, Thea flexed her muscles and stood on her four trembling limbs.

It was the weirdest feeling in the world.

"Dinnae think."

They both turned to see Callie standing in the doorway, her gaze on Thea. "Dinnae think about it, Thea. Just trust your instincts."

Taking that advice, Thea relaxed and let the wolf take over. With a graceful, swift movement, she jumped off the bed on all fours, laughing at the feeling.

The wheezing, joyful sound made Callie chuckle as she pushed the bedroom door wide open. "Happy running."

Conall padded over to Thea. He was much bigger than she was, powerfully built. He nuzzled his face against hers and her heart squeezed inside her wolf's chest. With a low, excited growl, he gave her one last nudge and ran ahead.

Instinct completely took over and Thea ran after him, leaping down his staircase with ease and out the front door James was holding open.

Conall waited in the driveway for her and then took off again.

She ran.

And she was lightning fast.

Thea kept up with Conall and he made a sound of approval in his throat as they tore across the road and up into the tree-covered hills. Then Thea pushed her new limbs to their limits, charging ahead of her mate, delighting in the sounds and smells of the surrounding land. Everything was just ... *more*.

Thea didn't know how long they ran.

Sometimes Conall would catch up, sometimes he'd fall behind. There weren't trees everywhere, and Thea felt a little warier out in the open of the Torridon hills, but the view beyond them overpowered that wariness.

She drew to a halt. From here she could see where Loch Torridon fed into the Atlantic Ocean. It was breathtaking.

Soon Conall herded her back toward the trees. Running like this, it differed from when she'd been fae.

She wasn't as fast.

But this was better.

It felt like soaring.

When they reached the trees, the breath was knocked out of her suddenly. She rolled among the brush and bracken of the woodlands to find her mate had just wrestled her to the ground. A primitive feeling replaced shock.

He wanted to play.

Delighted, Thea lunged at him.

They wrestled in the woods, rolling, pinning, nipping playfully at each other.

Much to her bemusement, she discovered that although she was faster, Conall was now stronger. He seemed to take far too much pleasure in that discovery. She snarled at him as he pinned her beneath his oversized paws, and the bastard gave her a wolfy grin, his tongue hanging out comically.

It was hard to stay mad at him.

When he let her up, Thea sniffed around the woods, taking her time learning her new senses. She could smell the different plants and trees that grew there, smelled the different soils, the insects, the animals hiding from them. She could smell her mate stronger than any other scent.

And she could hear his heart as well as her own.

Moreover, she could hear the little beating hearts of the animals who waited for the large predators to leave. In the distance, Thea heard music playing from a house.

It was a marvel.

Eventually, however, weariness set in. Sensing it, Conall nudged her and began to lead her back toward his home.

Once they'd returned, Thea stepped over the threshold and halted at the sight of the people gathered in his sitting room. She recognized faces from the pack meeting. Uncertainty filled her as they peered at her in shock and curiosity.

Conall brushed against her, drawing her attention to him, and she watched as he lunged upstairs. Glad to be away from the scrutiny of the others, Thea followed him into his bedroom.

Watching from the doorway, she felt the air crackle as he shifted. In less than a minute, he was human again. And naked. He watched her, affection warm in his eyes as he pulled on his clothes and then came to kneel, their faces level. Conall caressed her fur. It was a lovely feeling, a tingle that sparked all the way down her spine. No wonder Wolf Conall had liked it when she'd petted him.

"It's time to shift, Thea love."

Worry tightened her gut.

What if she couldn't?

What if she was stuck as a wolf forever?

A musky scent filled the air, and she realized it was coming from her. What on earth?

His nostrils flared. "Dinnae be frightened, lass."

Oh.

So that's how he always knew when she was afraid.

Jesus H. Christ.

"Imagine yourself shifting, push that feeling into your limbs. Your body will take care of the rest."

Thea padded back from him and glanced down at her forelegs. This was still so weird. She wondered if it would ever stop being strange.

Doing as Conall instructed, she imagined the change, and she strained to force it into her limbs. Nothing happened. She let out an exasperated whimper.

"You're trying too hard. Gentle. Easy."

Nodding to herself, Thea attempted it again, this time nudging the thought toward her wolf's body.

A sharp pleasure-pain burned through her as her back cracked, the same feeling popping around her body as it transformed. Relief flooded her as she realized it wasn't agonizing. Not like the original shift had been.

Her head juddered as her muzzle disappeared, her canines and extra wolf teeth disappearing like magic into her gums. Like they'd never been there. She pushed her human fingers against her gums, prodding, but nope.

Her mouth was as it always had been.

As Thea drew back her hand, something that was missing made her heart pause.

Thea lifted her hands to her face, turning her wrists inward.

No scars.

Her skin was perfectly smooth.

"Thea," Conall's voice was hoarse.

Looking over her shoulder at him, she saw his shocked gaze on her back.

"Thea." His pale eyes flew to hers. "They're gone."

Her attention dropped to her naked belly.

The scar there was gone too.

Her fingers brushed over the smooth skin.

What the …

Launching to her feet, she nearly fell over, her limbs still weak from shifting. Conall rushed to haul her against him and she melted into his chest. Her fingers curled into his shirt as she stared up at him in confusion.

Then she went rigid when she felt his hands coast down her back.

There were no bumps or ridges.

No scars.

Thea pushed away from him, stumbling toward his bathroom where she knew there was a mirror. And sure enough, as she twisted to look, her back was smooth and scar-free.

Conall appeared behind her and Thea turned to him. "I don't understand."

He cupped her face in his hands. "You're werewolf now, Thea. Our bodies wouldnae scar from injuries caused by iron. As the change wiped out the poison created by the iron in your heart, I can only assume that same magic wiped away all traces of iron from your body. Including the scars made by it."

Ashforth was gone.

He was really gone.

"I get to start over," she whispered, scared to believe it. It seemed too good to be true.

Conall gave her a slow, sexy grin. "Aye, lass. And if you didnae guess it while we were out there"—he jerked his head toward the woods beyond the house—"you're an alpha."

Her eyes widened. "I am?"

"Fast too." His grin was smug, pleased.

Thea laughed at his boyishness. "Faster than you."

"Aye, but not stronger." He drew her into his body.

She rolled her eyes. "I could still take you."

"Maybe," he murmured against her mouth. "But for sure you could take anyone else in the pack. That's why they were staring at you downstairs. You could lead a pack with the amount of alpha energy pouring off you. I should have known it."

Thea couldn't contemplate that. It was still bizarre to her she was now something completely different. What she *could* think about in relation to it, however, was … "The pack is safe?"

Understanding, Conall nodded. "The Castle Cara explosion has been on national news. It's been divulged to the media that Ashforth and his son were renting the castle and they and their guests were killed in the explosion. The cause hasn't been made public but is under investigation. A member of our pack lives in Glasgow and is a policewoman with the criminal investigations department. The pack is not under suspicion. In fact, we're not even on the radar. They think it might have something to do with one of Ashforth's business deals. We're in the clear."

Exhaling in relief, Thea nodded. "That's great. But what about the danger I present?"

"James was in contact with the Blackwood Coven while you were going through the transition. They are going to pay us a visit."

Thea tensed. "That doesn't sound *safe*."

"They're only sending representatives. And they just want proof you're a wolf. That people were mistaken about your identity."

"James lied?"

"He informed them you were a lone wolf. I recognized you as my mate and I was trying to bring you back to the pack when we were accosted by Blackwood and Eirik who was misinformed about you. He told them that Eirik's demise had nothing to do with us."

"They believe him?"

"They willnae believe him until they see you shift into a wolf, and we need to give them that for us all to be safe."

Although Thea nodded, she couldn't just let that be the end. "I want to find the woman. The psychic from Prague who tried to help me."

Conall tightened his hold on her. "It could be dangerous if anyone found out we're poking around in fae business."

"I know. But I … I don't know if I can leave her out there, knowing she's in danger."

"And what do you plan to do when you find her?"

"Offer her the same chance that's been given to me."

Conall frowned. "The bite could kill her."

Thea understood that. "She deserves the option. It should be her risk to take or not."

Her mate let out a shuddering exhale. "Fine. But can I ask for at least one month of peace and quiet before you look for her?"

Snuggling into him, resting her head against his warm, hard chest, Thea sighed. "Yes, considering I could sleep for a month."

He smoothed a hand down her back to cup her ass as he whispered roughly in her ears, "Oh, I intend to keep you far too busy for sleep. *Mate.*"

Despite her exhaustion, Thea felt a deep ripple of need in her belly as she looked up at him, lips parted.

Conall's eyes darkened with desire. "I'll tell everyone to leave, then you can sleep. In the morning, I'll hold you to that promise in your eyes."

She was almost a little disappointed at the idea of delaying sex because it had felt like an age since he'd been inside her, but as he led

Thea back to the bedroom, the weariness flooded her limbs again, like sand in an hourglass.

Someone had made the bed. The sweat-soaked and torn sheets were gone.

"Callie," Conall explained. "While we were running."

"Did I mention I like your sister?" Thea asked as Conall pulled one of his T-shirts down over her.

"Good." He smiled. "She likes you too."

That was something at least. Thea still had to convince the rest of the pack she was one of them now. But that was a worry for another day.

Conall helped her into bed, and Thea was out as soon as her head hit the pillow.

SHE FELT THE WET HEAT BETWEEN HER LEGS, THE DELICIOUS PRESSURE, drawing her up from sleep. Thea writhed against the feeling, her eyes fluttering open as it intensified. Morning light flooded Conall's bedroom, spilling over his broad back and his muscular ass.

Thea gasped at finding his head between her thighs, his tongue doing fantastic things to her.

"Conall," she breathed, pushing against his mouth.

He clamped his hands down on her hips and devoured her, voracious.

The tension built quickly and soon Thea was shuddering against his tongue.

His gray eyes flashed with dark need as he crawled up her body, his fingertips sliding under the T-shirt to remove it. Thea lifted her arms to help him, her heart pounding with anticipation.

It occurred to her as Conall spread her legs to wrap them around his waist, that she was no longer as strong as she had been. As he braced his hands on the pillow at either side of her head and his eyes locked with hers, Thea wondered if it would make a difference.

If she'd be able to keep up with him now.

Conall throbbed between her legs but he didn't push inside.

Instead, he frowned. "What was that?"

Thea frowned back. "What was what?"

"That little pucker of worry." He smoothed a finger between her brows. "You had a thought I think I'm not going to like."

Deciding honesty was the best policy, Thea sighed. "I just realized I'm not as strong anymore."

"And that applies to what we're doing how?"

She narrowed her eyes at his obtuseness and flushed. She couldn't believe he was making her say this out loud. "What if ... what if it's not the same because I'm not as strong?"

Conall seemed stunned by the question. And silent.

Very silent.

Thea's cheeks burned with embarrassment.

He finally answered, but not with words. He thrust inside her, pleasure shooting down her spine, tightening in her belly, tingling down her legs. Conall wrapped his hands around her wrists, his expression taut with desire as he rocked against her in slow, deep glides that pushed her toward climax.

"Heaven," he grunted against her lips, "fucking heaven, Thea. That's all I ever feel when I'm inside you."

"My love for you is infinite, Thea Quinn."

Thea gasped, remembering. He'd whispered that in her ear when she was dying.

She pushed against his hold on one of her wrists and he immediately released her, sliding a hand down her chest to caress her breast. Thea reached up to cup his face, smoothing her thumb over the scar on his cheek. "Your love for me is infinite."

His eyes flashed. "You remember?"

Thea nodded. "I remember. I remember your voice in the dark."

Conall groaned and kissed her, his thrusts quickening until they were moaning and panting into each other's mouths. They came together, Thea's legs tightening around his waist as he relaxed into her, his head buried in her neck.

"Thank you for saving my life, Chief MacLennan." She smoothed her hands over his wide shoulders.

Conall lifted his head, his expression serious, his gaze making her breath catch. So much love. No one had ever looked at her with such love and adoration. "I would go to the ends of any world to keep you with me ... Thea Quinn MacLennan."

Her heart fluttered. "MacLennan?"

"It's your name now, if you'll have it."

Thea's answer was to tighten her legs around him, and push up and over, forcing him onto his back so she could straddle him.

She grasped his warm length in her hand, watching his nostrils flare. "I'll take that as a yes," he groaned, hardening in her grip.

Oh, but it was good to be mated to a supernatural.

"It's a hell yes." She braced her hands on his shoulders, feeling him pulse where she wanted him most. Thea pushed down on his length to ride him. She rode him with a fierceness that made it feel like their hearts might explode in unison, proving that it wasn't the strength of her body that made their lovemaking so passionate, but the strength of her love for Conall.

Thea was sure her cry of release and his roar resonated around the entirety of Loch Torridon, announcing her official arrival as the alpha's mate.

And Thea wasn't entirely wrong, much to the dismay of Callie MacLennan, in bed with James a few houses away.

"That was something I really didnae need to know about my brother."

James pulled her into his arms, laughing hard in a complete lack of sympathy.

Callie grumbled, snuggled deeper into his warmth, and covered her ears.

"What are you doing?"

"Preparing for round three."

The beta shook with renewed laughter. Despite not wanting to hear anymore of her brother's lovemaking, Callie couldn't help but smile. Her brother may have tainted her ears but she was alive because of his bonnie mate, and tangled naked in the arms of her soon-to-be husband.

She supposed she couldn't complain.

However, when the third round of alpha-on-alpha lovemaking

could be heard in the distance, complain Callie did, muttering under her breath about her brother's indecent appetites until James rolled her onto her back and promised he'd make her moan loud enough to drown out the alpha couple.

It was a promise he kept.

34

Butterflies fluttered in Thea's belly, but it wasn't fear. It was nervousness and anticipation.

To say Conall was not happy about the recent turn of events was an understatement, but as she met his gaze in the crowd encircling her, he gave her a stoic nod of support.

Inside she knew he was probably desperate to tear Richard Canid's head off and be done with it.

The murmurings of the gathered Pack MacLennan grew an octave, and they parted as Peter Canid led his son and daughter and three of their warrior wolves through the crowd.

On the opposite bank of Loch Torridon there was a little cove of beach that for some inexplicable reason was host to pure golden sands. This was where Pack MacLennan had congregated to watch their new alpha female challenge Richard Canid.

Thea had only been a werewolf for three days, which was kind of the reason Conall was pissed. But when she'd woken in his arms after a vigorous night of lovemaking in her new existence and her mate had told her he would face Richard Canid in a Challenge, Thea was not happy.

For starters, a Challenge could be anything two dueling wolves wanted it to be. Conall had declared it a fight to the submission or death in wolf form. It wasn't that she didn't think her mate could take Richard. It was because she thought he could, and that Richard would be too stubborn to submit. Thea believed Peter Canid a worthy ally for Pack MacLennan, and she didn't want to ruin that. Mostly, however, *she* was the one who'd been kidnapped, so why the hell was Conall requesting the Challenge?

"It should be me," Thea had argued as she followed Conall out of the shower the previous morning. He'd just told her Peter had found his son and returned him to Torridon to face Conall.

Her mate threw her an incredulous look as he pulled on his jeans. "Forget it."

Indignation had stolen her tongue for a few seconds, long enough for him to stride out of the room with a casual, "Coffee?" over his shoulder.

Coffee?

She hauled one of Conall's shirts over her head and hurried after him. He was in the kitchen and as soon as she walked into the room, he said without looking up, "I'm not arguing about this, so forget it."

"Conall, Richard kidnapped *me*. Not you. *Me*."

His eyes flashed with anger. "You're *my* mate and my pack member. The offense was against me."

Okay, no way. Thea's hands flew to her hips. "Oh, I'm sorry, was it you who felt the agony of Ashforth's iron concoction being injected into you or the despair of being handed over to your tormentor, all for cash?"

Conall slammed the fridge door shut and whirled to glare at her. "No, but it was me left behind panicking about your whereabouts." He strode toward her, his furious expression probably menacing to anyone but her. Still it was intimidating enough she had to force herself to stay put as he bristled and towered over her. A bleakness entered his eyes. "It was me who watched Devon Ashforth plunge a fucking iron dagger into your heart. It was me who had to bite you all the while not knowing if it would save you. It was me sitting in a car with my sister, you dying on my back seat, contemplating if I'd be able to fucking go on if the change didn't work and I lost you. And all of that, Thea love," he bent his head to whisper angrily against her lips, "happened because Richard Canid kidnapped you."

Thea stared up at Conall's anguished expression and knew how it felt to watch that vamp back in Oslo stick the silver blade in his neck. She remembered what it was like to feel her mate's pulse fade and the terror at the idea of a life without him.

She reached for his face, her fingers caressing his scarred cheek. "You're right. He did do that to you."

Thinking that was it, Conall relaxed into her touch, lifted her hand from his cheek, pressed his lips to her wrist, and then turned back to the kitchen to finish making the coffee.

Thea took a deep breath and then exhaled. "But I still think I should be the one to Challenge him."

Conall's back was to her but she watched his shoulders tense as he stared at the kitchen cabinet in front of him. "Fucking save me from alpha females," he muttered.

"I heard that."

Turning around, it was his turn to sigh as he crossed his arms over his chest and leaned against the counter. "Fine. Explain."

She smiled because this was one of the reasons she loved Conall. He might be an alpha, but he was fair-minded, and he didn't bulldoze people with his opinions or feelings. "Okay, my first reason is pretty basic. I hate the little shit and I want to put him in his place."

Her mate conceded that with a nod.

"My second reason is that I think the clan needs to know that I'm a worthy addition to your pack. I know you're alpha and it's *your* pack. I don't expect you to consult me on pack business. I'm new," she shrugged, "and I get there's a hierarchy here. But I'm also your mate and I want to share your burdens. I want you to value my opinion."

"You know I do," he said, his voice gruff.

She smiled. "Then the pack needs to know that too. They need to know that I'm not your wife. I'm your mate. There's a difference. I'm here to stay forever. And they need to understand what that means. If I take on Canid in a Challenge, I think that will help pave my way to finding my place among the pack."

He was silent a second and then he seemed to begrudgingly agree. "You have a natural understanding of pack mentality already, Thea."

Confident she was making headway, she moved around the island toward him. "My third reason is that if you challenge Richard, you know he won't back down and you'll end up killing him, Conall. You'll want to because I know if he'd done to you what he did to me, I'd want to kill him. The alliance with Peter is too important to jeopardize, and killing Richard will create a barrier between you and his father."

Pushing off the counter, Conall came to her, encircling her waist to pull her against him. Thea tilted her head back to meet his eyes. "Everything you say is true," he admitted, "but what you failed to add is that you've been a wolf for two days, Thea. Yes, you're a natural. Brianna said she's never seen anyone make the change and adjust to it not only physically but mentally as well as you have." His eyes smiled. "I'm not surprised. You are and will always be the strongest person I've ever known."

She melted against him at the compliment.

"But you're still new. Too new to jump into a fight as a wolf."

Understanding his reasoning, even if chafed, Thea agreed but added, "That's why I'll fight him as me. In this body. And I won't kill him, but I'll put him on his ass and that'll be it, dealt with."

His hands flexed on her waist. "Thea love ... you're still fast but you're not as strong as you were as fae. You havenae fought in *this* body before."

"Yeah, but I still remember how to fight."

"I cannae risk it."

Her expression turned mulish. "You're going to let me kick Richard Canid's ass, Conall. If you don't, I'm going to think you don't have much faith in me anymore."

He released her. "Dinnae. Dinnae try to manipulate me into this."

Her eyes narrowed. "It's not a manipulation. It's truth. How can you possibly expect your pack to accept me as your alpha mate if you don't even believe I can kick the ass of a weasel like Richard Canid?

He's a beta, for Christ's sake, and soon to be demoted to enforced omega. Now, I'm not sure what that means, but it definitely sounds like he'll be pretty low on the totem pole. Are you saying I can't kick an omega's ass?"

Conall strode over to the coffee machine and made his coffee. "Were you this bloody cocky as a fae?"

"I didn't need to be cocky. I was awesome."

She thought she saw a hint of a smile curling the corner of his mouth. "Well, be that as it may"—he turned to hand her a cup of coffee as he took a sip of his own—"enforced omega means that's the official status Richard will have in his pack. It doesnae mean he loses the strength of a beta."

"But I'm an alpha."

"Aye, but many beta males have beaten alpha females in Challenges. It's just a scientific fact, Thea, that many men are stronger than women. It's not a deliberate attempt to keep females down in the ranks."

Thea curbed the urge to growl. "Did I outrun you yesterday?"

"Aye."

"Did I keep up when we were tussling?"

"Aye, but I was going easy on you."

"Ugh, you just love the fact that you're more powerful than me now."

Conall gave her a chiding look. "A wolf is only as strong as his heart, and my heart belongs completely to you. So who really has the power here?"

She melted a little. "Okay, not fair sweet-talking me right now. Here's the deal. You're one of the strongest, fastest alphas I've ever encountered, Conall. And I'm faster than you. Not stronger, but faster. That's what a woman needs in a fight against a stronger male. She needs to be fast and strategic and since I've been running for six years, fighting for my life, I'm both those things." Feeling hurt twinge in her chest, she glared at him. "Becoming a wolf doesn't wipe that out, and suddenly this isn't just about making a statement to the pack, it's about you. If you don't think I can do this, we've got bigger problems."

"Jesus fuck," he snapped. "It's not that I dinnae think you can do it,

Thea, it's that I just got you back after days of thinking I might have to bury you. And no matter how strong or fast you are, anything could go wrong in a Challenge. I dinnae want to lose you!"

It was like being bellowed at by your loving, pet bear.

A little intimidating, even though you knew he'd never hurt you.

Thea stared at him in silence, all her love for him in her eyes, but she refused to stand down. "You can't swaddle me in bubble wrap, Conall. That's not what the pack expects from us as the new alpha couple."

"They'll expect what I tell them to expect," he grumbled.

Smirking at his adorable grumpiness, Thea set her coffee down and closed the distance between them, resting her hands on his chest as she leaned into him. He stubbornly didn't touch her, which made her smile widen. "I'm a fighter. I didn't start out that way and I didn't want it … but it's who I am now. And yes, I am looking forward to starting a life with you where I don't have to run and where I don't have to fight all the time. But I faced a man I spent six years running from and no matter the consequences of that, facing him changed me. I took back my power. I realized the importance of facing my fears. I'm a fighter. *You* made me believe that. Now Richard Canid did do all those things to you, but he took away my choices, Conall, when he attacked me. I deserve retribution for that.

"I deserve to make the choice to fight him."

Her mate studied her for so long, she worried this argument would end badly. However, he put his coffee cup on the counter to free his hands. His arms slid around her waist and he sighed, long and deep. Bending his head, he rested his forehead against hers. "That was a pretty good speech."

Hope bloomed. "Meaning?"

He raised his head to look into her eyes. "I willnae stand in your way if you want to take the Challenge to Richard, but he may not agree. He might choose to fight me instead. But if he does agree, you must promise to make it fast. Dinnae make me endure watching a long battle."

She agreed.

And so did Richard.

The smug, cowardly, son of a bitch was obviously terrified of facing Conall because when they met at the Coach House to put Thea's Challenge to the Canids, Richard had jumped all over it. Even if it was out of the ordinary for them to fight in human form.

He thought he would kick Thea's ass.

Watching him stride onto the beach while Peter and Sienna Canid and their wolves took their spot next to Conall, Callie, and James, Thea sneered. Richard was looking at her like he was about to gobble her up. He strutted with arrogance as he walked back and forth in front of her, kicking up sand.

There was a niggle in the back of Thea's head that had her wondering if she was overconfident in her abilities, considering this would be her first time fighting without her fae strength.

Yet, she knew she couldn't let those doubts cloud her mind.

She had to believe she would put Richard on his ass.

After all, the pack had come out in force to see what she was capable of.

Last night in bed, after another torrid few hours of lovemaking, Conall had talked to her about her alpha aura. It was the energy she felt from Conall, and she had it too. He'd coached her through connecting to it and pushing it out into the room so it encapsulated everything around her.

Thea did it now, channeling it toward Richard and the pack. She felt it, like extended hands, pushing against all their shoulders, as if to force them to their knees. The pack trembled against her, but their excitement levels rose. Whereas Richard … well, Thea watched the smugness flicker out of his expression as he strained against her energy.

She smirked at him as if to say, "Yeah, I'm kind of a badass."

He snarled.

As lead warrior, Callie strode forward. "Alpha and Pack MacLennan, Alpha and Pack Canid, we're here to witness the Challenge between Thea, Alpha Female of Pack MacLennan, and Richard, Son of Alpha Canid. Richard Canid," Callie spoke, keeping her expression impressively neutral, "Thea MacLennan charges you with assault, kidnap, and causing danger to Pack MacLennan's safety. Do you answer the charge?"

"I do," he bit out, glowering at Thea.

"Thea MacLennan"—Callie turned to her, her eyes now burning with pride—"you challenge Richard Canid to a fight of submission only, is this correct?"

"Yes." Thea nodded at her.

Callie's eyes said, "Then kick his arse," but her mouth addressed the crowd. "Let the Challenge begin."

She stepped out of the way just as Richard shot toward Thea.

He was not fast. Okay, he was faster than a human, but lumbering for a wolf.

Thea easily sidestepped his running punch.

Richard made a feral sound, whirling to face her, and then he did what all dishonorable bastards would do. He grabbed a handful of sand and flung it at her eyes. Blinking against the sting of the salt, Thea heard the crowd hiss seconds before she felt the blinding punch. Pain shot up her cheekbone as she landed on her back, and she had seconds to realize Conall had been right. She felt pain like she hadn't felt it before. Her face was goddamn throbbing, and she was discombobulated.

Suddenly Richard was straddling her, his hands around her throat, his face dark with intention.

Fight to submission, my ass.

Rage flooded Thea as she grabbed one of his wrists and although it took a lot more from her than before, she still snapped that fucker. He bellowed in pain and fell off her into the sand, clutching his broken wrist to his chest. Thea kicked out with her legs and flipped up onto her feet with ease.

Yeah, she wasn't fae but she was still epic. She had to believe that if she wanted to win this fight.

"That's one of my favorite moves. I do enjoy a good wrist snap," she said casually as Richard struggled to his feet, hatred blazing in his eyes. "Do you submit?"

He lowered his useless left hand. "I will make you pay for that, you mongrel bitch."

Thea heard Conall make a primitive noise of warning behind her. "Sticks and stones, Canid."

He came at her again and swung a punch with his good arm, but Thea ducked and spun so she was behind him. With agility and speed, she slammed her foot into the back of his knees. Richard hit the sand on his bad wrist and growled before rolling up onto his feet.

Enjoying his frustration, Thea danced on her toes.

"Stop playing, Thea," Conall demanded from the crowd. "And end it."

She turned to smirk at her mate over her shoulder and sensed the shift in the air as Richard attacked while she wasn't looking.

Thea may not be fae anymore, but her awareness of her surroundings was still otherworldly. It was the reason she knew exactly the moment Richard was within reach without even looking. Eyes on Conall, she shot out a hand, making purchase with Richard's throat. She squeezed and turned to him. He'd momentarily frozen in shock at being caught when he thought she wasn't paying attention.

"Do you submit?" she demanded.

Feeling the tension in his body, it took Thea less than a second to compute he was readying to attack again, so she twisted fully toward him, grabbed his head in her hands, and felt the burn in her muscles as she jerked his neck.

Everyone hushed at the resounding crack and watched the life flicker out of Richard's eyes before his body hit the sand with a thump.

Inside, she was trembling, but when she spun to face the crowd, she kept her expression blank.

Until Conall stepped forward, his look chiding. "Now that was just showing off."

Thea's lips twitched. "I'm new at this, so does that"—she gestured to Richard's temporary deadness—"count as submission?"

Her mate crossed his arms over his chest. "It does for me."

Everyone looked at Peter, frowning at his son's body. He lifted his eyes to Thea and nodded. "It counts."

Callie stepped forward. "Then I declare this Challenge over and Thea MacLennan the winner. Are you satisfied, Thea?"

"I'm satisfied." She strode over to Conall, who grasped her hand in his. Gazing beyond his look of pride, she felt the pack's collective energy press in on her. And they seemed pleased, if those beaming grins were anything to go by.

"We'll leave you to look after your son," Callie said to Peter. "The rest of us will celebrate."

Conall, still holding onto Thea, approached Peter. "I'm sorry it even came to this."

"As am I." He glanced between them. "Most alphas would have made this a challenge to the death. I'm grateful for your mercy."

"I am too." Sienna gave them both a tight smile. "Thank you."

Thea wasn't comfortable around Sienna Canid. It was irrational—she knew it—but it was hard to want to spend time with a woman who had been weeks away from marrying Conall.

"We'll talk?" Conall asked Peter.

"Definitely."

Conall led Thea through the congregated pack, and she smiled as they offered her congratulations and compliments. Many reached out to touch her in awe, as if she were a holy relic of some sort. It was a little disconcerting.

They climbed out of the sand dunes and up onto the single-track road where Conall had left his car. Everyone but the Canids and Callie and James had traveled on foot so as not to block the road.

Thea waved to Callie who was grinning wolfishly at her as she got in her Jeep with James, Grace, and Angus. Hopping into Conall's Defender, Thea waited impatiently for her mate's words of congratulations.

Instead, he was silent as he drove toward the Coach House where it was tradition to celebrate after a Challenge win. She wasn't worried because he didn't seem angry, but he was certainly something.

Then, as they blew past the Coach House entrance, Thea began to understand what she was sensing from her mate and a deep tug of need pulled low in her belly.

"Conall," she whispered.

"We'll join them later." His voice was hoarse.

"But—"

"I need inside you." He threw her a dark look of desire. "I'm not doing that in front of my pack."

Thea's heart raced, her smile smug. "Got you hot watching me fight, did it?"

"Got me hard watching you squash that wee arse like a bug." Conall's lusty expression now mingled with pride. "You are something to watch, lass. Now take off your jeans."

That tingle of want between her legs intensified. "Now?"

"Right now."

His tone brooked no argument, and Thea didn't feel like arguing. She felt like burning her unspent energy with her mate whatever way he wanted to. Fingers shaking with excitement, she kicked off her shoes and unzipped her jeans. She felt Conall watching her as she pulled them off.

"Underwear too," he grunted.

Excitement rippled through her and she knew when he scented her arousal because a rumbling, sexy growl vibrated up from his chest. Thea slipped off her underwear, her skin hot against the cool leather. She shot a look at Conall's lap.

He was ready for her too.

The Defender swung left and raced down the drive to the house. It skidded to a halt with a squeal of tires and Conall cut the engine, pushed back his seat, and unzipped his jeans in one smooth move. Thea jumped him, kissing him hungrily as he fumbled to free himself from his jeans. She heard the crinkle of a condom wrapper, something Conall had started to use now that they could get pregnant.

And then she felt him throbbing between her legs.

Thea pushed down as Conall thrust up, their eyes locked, their gasps sounding against each other's lips.

All control fled and soon the Defender, a vehicle used by the goddamn army, began to rock hard as Thea and Conall celebrated the Challenge by screwing each other within an inch of their lives.

When they eventually tumbled out of the car, it reeked of sex; they were both covered in scratch marks, and Thea's legs were a little unsteady.

Conall solved that by swinging her up into his arms and carrying her into the house like a bride. He took them directly upstairs to his shower room where they undressed again. Washing each other soon turned to lovemaking and as Conall held her against the tiled wall, gliding in and out of her in slow, deep thrusts, Thea panted, "Do you think …ah!"

"Do I think what?" His grip on her tightened, his movements deliberately teasing.

"Will it stop?" She clutched his shoulders, her fingers biting into his skin. "Will this need ever stop?"

"Fuck, I hope not," Conall admitted before crushing her mouth beneath his in a voracious kiss.

When Thea climaxed around him, her moan swallowed in his mouth, she heartily agreed.

If this mad passion lasted their entire lifetime together, she'd die a very satisfied werewolf.

35

STEAM COVERED THE MIRROR ABOVE THE BATHROOM SINK AND THEA reached to wipe it clear. Compelled to look, she glanced over her shoulder at her naked back, taking in the complete lack of scars.

The thing was, the memories of how she got the scars were still there. Perhaps the memories would fade as time wore on, now that the scars were no longer there as a daily reminder. There was a small part of Thea that missed the scars. She never thought she'd ever miss them, but at some point, they had become part of her. They'd helped to carve her, quite literally, into who she was.

And maybe who she was, was someone pretty impressive after all.

Thea began to towel dry her body, getting used to the slight difference in her limbs. They didn't feel as light anymore, as if she were carrying more weight in them. She hadn't put on weight … it was just that ethereal strength of the fae was gone. All of her fae gifts were gone.

When Conall had taken her shopping in Inverness for a new wardrobe, she'd experimented by trying to manipulate a shop assistant and nada. Nothing. Her dastardly ability to manipulate human minds was no more.

Truthfully, Thea was glad to be rid of the gifts. They had made her feel like the bad guy, so much so that even after all she'd done for Conall and Callie, she still thought she was in hell. She hadn't told Conall about believing the fever dreams of the transformation had been her afterlife. One, he didn't need to know how much pain she'd been in; and two, he would be mad at her for thinking she deserved to end up in hell.

It was only now Thea realized how foolish that was.

Yes, she had killed people in self-defense.

She'd stolen from people.

But she'd also tried to do good where she could.

Her gifts never made her the bad guy. It was the choices she made with those gifts that determined that. Now that she was finally at peace, Thea could see she'd done her best in a terrible situation. She was learning to forgive herself for the moments she'd failed.

And if she could win the love and trust of Pack MacLennan, Thea guessed she couldn't be all bad.

After the Challenge with Richard Canid, the pack seemed to revere her. Not only for her strength as a wolf but as the woman who made their alpha very happy. The only person she shared any awkwardness with was Grace. The older wolf had apologized profusely since Thea's transformation and Challenge. Thea had accepted that apology. It didn't mean she fully trusted Grace, but Callie, aware of the distance between them, was doing her best to forge a bridge there.

As for Callie MacLennan, Thea had formed an instant bond with her. She didn't know if it resulted from the true mating—that the qualities she loved in Conall she saw in Callie too—or if the act of saving Callie's life had created a special friendship between them.

They had different natures. Callie was loud and had no filter, whereas turning wolf hadn't changed Thea's personality. She was still somewhat reserved, dry-witted, and stubborn.

Moving through the bedroom she shared with Conall, Thea stood by the window as she dressed, staring out across the loch to the mountains beyond. It was a beautiful day and the clear skies had turned

Loch Torridon a vibrant blue. Green from the hills danced into the water, turning it aquamarine. The placid loch wouldn't have looked out of place in the Mediterranean.

Thea was still getting used to the many changing faces of the Highlands. Depending on the season, on the weather, Torridon could be chilly and atmospheric one day and then a peaceful paradise the next.

A boat cut through the water in the distance. It would be one of Mhairi and Brodie Fergusons'. They ran a fishing company from Loch Torridon that brought in quite a bit of revenue for the pack.

Once dressed, Thea shot a look at her reflection, smiling softly at the red tank top she'd matched with jeans. She hadn't worn a tank in years because of her scars, and red had been a forbidden color because it made her easy to spot in a crowd.

Life had changed in huge ways.

And in little ways too.

Thea walked quietly downstairs. Usually she'd pop her head around Conall's office door to ask him if he wanted a coffee. Although her mate kept her up through the night with his insatiable lovemaking (okay, to be fair, sometimes she initiated it), Conall was up at the crack of dawn to work. Thea would tumble out of bed hours later and he'd already be four hours into his to do list for the day.

This morning, however, he'd left the house early to greet three representatives from the Blackwood Coven. They were staying the night at the Coach House. It had been agreed that they would visit on the first night of the full moon to witness Thea shifting. Not only did witches draw power from the full moon, but members of Pack MacLennan were coming out in force tonight for their first run with their new alpha couple.

It meant the witches had power on their side while the pack had numbers on theirs. An even playing field seemed the fairest way to ensure everyone's cooperation and safety.

Thea felt the fluttering of butterflies as she moved around the kitchen, making coffee and heating the oatmeal Conall had left her. Porridge, he called it. He ate it plain.

Blech.

Thea drizzled a generous amount of honey over the top of hers as she slid onto a stool at the island.

Once the Blackwood Coven had evidence she wasn't fae, Thea could only hope that would be the end of her story as one of the fae children being hunted. That finally she would be free to live her life as a werewolf in Pack MacLennan. She would lay low for a while until they felt the coast was clear, but then she would have to think about what she wanted to do with her life.

"Would it be crazy if I went back to school?" Thea had asked Conall the night before as they laid together on his sofa, listening to the rain beat against the roof.

"Why would it be crazy?"

"Because I'm twenty-five years old and I don't even have a GED."

"If you want to go back to school, go back to school."

"I like architecture," she'd admitted a little shyly. "Traveling around so much, I was always fascinated by the way architecture told a story about the history of a place. I don't know."

Conall had tilted her chin up so he could look into her eyes. "You can do anything you put your mind to, Thea. And you have options now. If you want to go back to school so you can go to university to study architecture, then that's what you'll do."

"I'll get a job too," she'd assured him. "I don't want you to think I'm just going to live off you."

He'd scowled at that. Fiercely. "Every member of this pack gets a stipend from the proceeds of the pack businesses. If you think that doesnae include my mate, you're wrong. And if I want to spoil the fuck out of you for merely being grateful that you fucking exist, I will. No arguments."

Thea snorted, outwardly, while inwardly she squirmed with pleasure at his words. "You got it, Chief."

She smiled around a mouthful of oatmeal.

Had they only known each other a month?

That was kind of crazy.

It might have only been a month, but Thea didn't care. Not only had Conall brought love and friendship into her life, he didn't make her feel like she'd come to their relationship with less than he had. He gave her his trust, which few people had done in her life. It was strange how a person didn't realize the impact being trusted and respected had on the psyche. In fact, Conall trusted her enough to leave her behind in charge of the pack when he traveled to Colorado with James next month to meet with Peter Canid.

They were planning on working out a new alliance between them. Callie was going too as Conall's lead warrior. Conall asked Thea if she wanted to come—in fact, he would have preferred it because he was still a little cagey about letting her out of his sight after Castle Cara—but Thea was still afraid of flying, even if she couldn't blow up a plane anymore. Moreover, she was ready to just be in one place for a while and was interested to see how the pack reacted to her when she didn't have Conall at her side.

Upon her mate's return from the States, he'd promised they'd begin their search for the woman from Prague whom Thea was convinced was fae. She needed to be protected, and she needed options, like Thea had been given. Conall had warned her not to get her hopes up regarding finding the young woman. At this point, she was a needle in a very large haystack. Still, Thea couldn't help but hope.

A knock at the door brought Thea's head up but before she could make a move, it opened and Callie strolled inside, carrying a shoulder bag.

"Morning," she announced with a pretty smile.

Pleased to see her, Thea responded in kind. "Did your brother send you to distract me from the fact that there are three powerful witches waiting at the Coach House for me to make my wolfy appearance tonight?"

"Pretty much." Callie slammed the shoulder bag down on the island and flicked open the flap. "And what better way to do that than force you to help me plan my wedding."

As she removed the piles of wedding magazines from the bag, her diamond-and-moonstone engagement ring flashed on her finger. James had given it to Callie in front of everyone in the Coach House pub a few nights ago.

It had amazed Thea that she was there to witness and celebrate it when only a mere few weeks before, she'd had no family to speak of.

"Does it bother you?" Thea asked as Callie slid onto the stool beside her.

"Does what bother me?"

"That you and James aren't mates per se?"

Callie wrinkled her nose. "Not really." She grinned at Thea. "Do you know how rare it is to find your true mate? I mean, the fact that Conall has found his after our mum and dad found theirs is practically unheard of. Not finding your true mate doesnae mean we cannae find deep, abiding love. I know it for a fact because that's what I have with James. Even if I did miraculously find my true mate, I'd tell him to bugger off. I only want James ... but dinnae tell him that."

Thea chuckled. "He's a lucky man."

"Yup." Callie didn't disagree. "So, I was thinking for bridesmaids' dresses ... emerald green." She looked Thea up and down. "Yes, emerald green would work lovely with your hair and as a nice accent to mine."

Wait?

What?

"You mean ... am I ...?"

Callie raised an eyebrow. "One of my bridesmaids? Of course."

Stunned, Thea lapsed into silence as her soon-to-be sister-in-law waffled on about venues and invitations and other things Thea was clueless about.

"You should pay more attention," Callie mused. "You'll be doing this with Conall soon."

Thea didn't think so. "Conall doesn't seem like the wedding kind of guy."

"Oh, but he'll marry you. Even if you're true mates, he'll legally want to make sure that everything that belongs to him belongs to you. I know my brother."

The thought of Conall putting a ring on Thea's finger was more appealing than she'd imagined. She had never really pictured herself getting married, but she'd even put up with a huge meringue dress if it meant getting to shackle herself to him forever.

Okay, maybe not a meringue dress.

But wedding plans. She'd put up with wedding plans for Conall. It was only fair since she was putting up with it for Callie. Not that she was "putting up" with anything. Especially not for Callie who wanted her to be a bridesmaid.

Gratitude swept through the nervousness the Blackwoods arrival had caused. With this pack, this gracious and loyal pack at her side, she had nothing to worry about it. Moreover, she wouldn't allow anyone to hurt her new family.

Thea may not be a fae anymore, but she was the biggest, baddest female alpha around and if she had to, she would set her wolf loose to see just exactly what that meant.

"YOU READY?" CONALL ASKED, SQUEEZING THEA'S HAND AS THEY WALKED toward the backyard of the Coach House. It was an impressive building. The entrance door sat within a tall tower with a conical roof. Wings expanded on either side of the tower, built from brick and topped with a gray slate tiled roof. It had a gothic vibe to it, like it might have been built in the Victorian era.

Thea could feel the collective energy of the pack. They made the air thick and caused all the hair on the back of her neck to stand up.

"It won't hurt?"

"No. The last few times you've changed, you've been in absolute control. When the moon hits its crest, it will command control of your body. It's unsettling at first but you get used to it. More than that, you'll revel in it. There's something …" he flashed her a wicked grin, "pagan about it."

She knew what that wicked grin meant. "Hey, no funny business in front of the pack."

"I make no promises."

Shaking her head at his playfulness, Thea let Conall lead her around the back of the house. He released her hand but stayed close to her side as she witnessed the awe-inspiring sight of over a hundred werewolves gathered in the yard.

Thea did as she had at the Challenge and projected her alpha aura.

It was like a humming, sparking, golden spirit she could taste on her tongue as she imagined it propelling toward the pack.

Conall said it fed the pack, it bonded them together, and they reveled in the power they felt from their alphas. Their response to it at the Challenge confirmed it.

Despite Thea not knowing most of the pack members that well, they gave her respectful nods of their heads, murmuring her name in greeting as she passed along their lines with Conall. Callie and James stood off to the side, separated from the pack to highlight their rank. Beside them were three strangers.

Feeling out the air around them, Thea detected a little bite of energy from their collective magic. A warlock stood between two witches. He had a shock of white-blond hair and pale skin, in complete contrast to the dark-haired, golden-skinned witches at his side. The women, according to Conall, were sisters, and the man, a high-ranking warlock within the coven.

Her mate stopped in the center of the gathering and Thea stood by his side, her expression carefully neutral. The strangers studied her in surprise, like they hadn't expected her to really be a werewolf. But they could sense the alpha in her. She could tell by their expressions.

They were not amused.

"Are you satisfied?" Conall asked without preamble.

The man lifted his chin. His arrogance was palpable. "We'll witness the shift before we are satisfied."

Conall emitted a little snarl but turned away from them to face the pack. Thea followed suit. Her eyes danced over the gathering. Grace and Angus eyed the strangers with distrust, as did some other members. But most were watching her, some wearing smiles, others vibrating with the call of the moon.

And Thea could feel it. She could feel the pull toward the celestial being in the sky. Her eyes rose to it as the sun dipped out of sight and moonbeams cut through the dark landscape. It glistened across the loch in the distance.

A burning, tingling sensation rippled down Thea's spine and her gums began to throb.

Conall was right.

It was unsettling to feel the beginnings of the shift when she had not initiated it.

Her mate undressed and the pack immediately followed his lead.

Shit, she'd forgotten about this part.

Public nudity.

Thea cut Conall a look for not warning her and he threw her that boyish grin. "It isnae anything they havenae seen before, Thea love."

She heard chuckles from some pack members and gave her mate a dirty look before hauling her shirt over her head. His eyes darkened as he watched her shimmy out of her pants, and he didn't look so cocky about his pack members seeing her naked.

"It isnae anything they have havenae seen before," she mocked.

Conall's expression promised delicious retribution for her cheekiness.

She was about to respond in kind when the pleasure-pain of the transformation began. At the same time as Conall, her claws grew. Feeling Conall's power swell out of him, flooding the pack and her, her knees trembled.

He threw back his head and bellowed, "Ceannsaichidh an Fhìrinn!" and goosebumps covered Thea's entire body. Jesus, he was magnificent.

"Ceannsaichidh an Fhìrinn!" she yelled in unison with the pack. Her mate turned to look at her with pride bright in his gray eyes seconds before they both fell to their knees and let the change take them.

Conall had been right. It was odd to not be in control of shifting, a little alarming at first, but once she let herself relax, it was easy. Natural. The transformation didn't take long and soon Thea was closer to the ground, padding along the dewy grass to nuzzle against Conall in wolf greeting. He nipped playfully at her ear and she side-stepped him to make her way over to the members of the Blackwood Coven.

She stared up at them, communicating silently. "Well? Satisfied?"

The warlock appeared dismayed, but he nodded slowly. "Our business here is over."

He ushered the two women away. Remembering the casualties

they'd caused in their search for her, Thea pulled back her muzzle and let out a low, deep, menacing growl.

The witches jumped, throwing her startled, frightened looks over their shoulders before scurrying out of view around the Coach House.

Thea laughed, and it came out like a hoarse snarl. She turned to find Wolf Conall and Wolf Callie wearing their versions of wolfish grins, whilst Wolf James's expression clearly said, "Was that necessary?"

Yes. But more than that, it had been fun.

Seeing most of the pack had already taken off for the run, Thea lunged past her mate, his sister, and beta, and hurried up the embankment toward the road that would lead them into the forest that covered the hills.

Everywhere she could hear the pack as Conall fell into stride beside her.

They were all around her, their hearts beating in tandem.

And Thea realized as they gloried in the call of the full moon that she had never, not once in her life, felt more herself than she did right then, running with Conall and his pack.

Strike that.

Their pack.

EPILOGUE

PARIS, FIVE MONTHS LATER

Belly sloshing, Vik winced and slowed his lunging strides up the stairwell toward his apartment. Perhaps he'd overindulged tonight, taking more blood from the Parisian burlesque dancers than he should have.

They'd been twins. Redheaded, curvy twins.

Vik was weak before redheads and twins.

He also felt a little light-headed, which meant he'd definitely taken too much. A vamp on too much blood was like a man who had over-imbibed on alcohol.

Still, he couldn't bring himself to regret it. The dancers had offered more than their blood and Vik needed the release. He'd been too stressed lately, but after months of no word, he was finally starting to relax.

When he'd returned to his home in Oslo to find fifteen piles of ash instead of a dead Conall MacLennan and Thea Quinn, Vik had known he'd chosen the wrong side. He thought by choosing Eirik he was choosing to side with the most powerful being, the one who mattered. Yet he'd underestimated Thea.

Horrified, knowing Conall well enough to realize the werewolf would want what he considered justice for the betrayal, Vik left his Oslo home with a heavy heart. He'd taken his research with him, all but the rare edition of Jerrik's journal, which had been missing from his apartment. Guessing Thea had taken it, Vik had to just deal with the loss. If that woman could kill the oldest vampire in the world, then he certainly would not mess with her over a book. No matter how special that book was. Or how expensive it had been.

However, Vik's contacts had told him Thea was no longer fae. Apparently, Conall had bitten her, and she'd turned into a werewolf. They were happily mated, living in Conall's home in Loch Torridon. It had been six months since the incident in Vik's apartment and no word that the MacLennans were coming for him.

If he wasn't enjoying his time in Paris so much, Vik would head back to Oslo. Soon. But there were still plenty of burlesque dancers to meet.

Whistling to himself, the vampire slowly made his way to the penthouse at the top of the prewar building. What it lacked in Nordic simplicity, it made up for in style and views. Plus, he'd put impressive floor-to-ceiling bookshelves in the high-ceilinged property. He required a ladder to reach the top shelves. It was wonderful.

Letting himself into his temporary home, Vik swayed against the wall and cursed under his breath. "Definitely too much blood," he muttered. "Greedy, greedy."

Stumbling down the hallway, he threw his keys in the bowl on the sideboard and wandered into the dark sitting room. The pressure in the air hit him as he fumbled for the light switch, but he was too drunk on blood to process its meaning.

The bulbs from the chandelier illuminated the room—and the two alphas sitting casually on his couch.

Fear ripped through him.

Oh fuck!

"Hello, Vik."

He whirled around, diving toward the hallway when agonizing

pain ripped through his right calf and he sprawled to the hardwood floor on a cry. Whipping his head around, he hissed at the sight of the wooden stake lodged through his lower leg. A feeling akin to flames licking his leg swam up his limb, and he fumbled to pull the damn thing out.

As he did, the hallway light came on and a shadow fell over him.

Vik looked up in horror.

Beautiful Thea MacLennan stood over him, Conall at her back. Her mate crossed his arms over his chest and his expression veered between boredom and menace.

Fuck.

Oh well. Two hundred plus years was more than most people got to live.

Thea stepped over him, so he laid trapped beneath her. She rested her hands on her lovely hips as she cocked her head, studying him. Vik's heart raced sickeningly fast.

Her lips spread into a wolfish, predatory grin. "Did you miss us?"

The survivor in him shot toward the exit using his vampire speed but as he reached it, he felt a hand curl around the back of his neck, jerking him out of vamp speed. The owner of that hand slammed his face into the door. Befuddled, Vik blinked against the sting in his nose, feeling blood trickle down to his lip. He turned to look at Thea.

She was a werewolf now so how could she move that fast?

As if she'd read the thought in his eyes, Thea narrowed her eyes. "I'm faster than the average wolf. There's no point running."

Defeated, Vik glanced over Thea's shoulder and watched Conall stroll down the hallway toward them. The sight of the six foot six werewolf caused Vik's to almost piss himself. When he'd first met the alpha, Vik had been eager to make friends. Vik liked to have powerful people in his pocket, and Conall was the most powerful alpha he'd ever met.

Vik studied Thea, somewhat astonished.

He guessed now Conall was *one* of the most powerful alphas he'd ever met.

"Just make my death quick. Please."

Thea released his neck and stood back. "Here's the deal, Vik. Some information you provided saved my life, and Conall and I—"

Conall growled.

"Okay, *I am*"—Thea shot Conall a smirk before turning back to face Vik—"feeling a little benevolent toward you. Do what I want, and Conall won't kill you."

"Yet," her mate grunted.

Wide-eyed Vik nodded. He'd do anything. Anything to stay alive a little longer. There was still so much to learn.

"Good." Thea took a step toward him, her expression determined. "Because I'm looking for someone, Vik, and you're going to help me find her."

ABOUT THE AUTHOR

S. Young is the pen name for Samantha Young, a *New York Times*, *USA Today* and *Wall Street Journal* bestselling author from Stirlingshire, Scotland. She's been nominated for the Goodreads Choice Award for Best Author and Best Romance for her international bestseller *On Dublin Street*. *On Dublin Street* is Samantha's first adult contemporary romance series and has sold in thirty countries. *War of Hearts* is Samantha's first adult paranormal romance novel written under the name S. Young.

Visit Samantha Young online at
www.authorsamanthayoung.com
Twitter @AuthorSamYoung
Instagram @AuthorSamanthaYoung
Facebook @AuthorSamanthaYoung
Goodreads - Samantha_Young